NEWS FROM NOWHERE

JANE AUSTIN

CinnamonPress

INDEPENDENT INNOVATIVE INTERNATIONAL

Published by Cinnamon Press
Meirion House, Tanygrisiau, Blaenau Ffestiniog
Gwynedd LL41 3SU
www.cinnamonpress.com

Designed and typeset in Garamond by Cinnamon Press. Cover design by Adam Craig © Adam Craig.
Cinnamon Press is represented by Inpress and by the Welsh Books Council in Wales. Printed in Poland.
The publisher gratefully acknowledges the support of the Welsh Books Council.

Acknowledgements

I would like to thank those who gave me access to: Oxford Brookes University Wesleyan archives; The Queen Mary's Hospital Sidcup Archives; University of Bangor Library and Archives.

Thanks for permission to quote from *Up to Mametz...And Beyond* by Llewelyn Wyn Griffith and edited and annotated by Jonathon Riley, published by Pen and Sword Books.

Thanks to my aunt Siriol Chatwin, and cousin Gwen Harbottle, who gave me much encouragement.

Thanks to Rowan Fortune, Sue Orgill and Chris Bridge for their careful reading of the manuscript. And special thanks to York Novelists, who have piloted me through this project.

News from Nowhere is a debut novel inspired by a collection of letters from three of her family as they served on the Western Front. Jane first read this remarkable collection in 1983, when her grandmother, Elizabeth Dewi Roberts, published them in a slim volume, entitled *Witness These Letters*. Written to the family in Bangor, North Wales from 1915 to 1918, the letters vividly describe the torments of the trenches and the battlefield, and life as a prisoner-of-war.

I have drawn from the following sources in creating a fiction:

1. *Witness These Letters, Letters from the Western Front 1915 – 1918*, G.D. Roberts
2. *Unpublished war poetry*, G.D. Roberts
3. *The University College of North Wales, Foundations 1884 – 1927*, J. Gwynn Williams
4. *Up to Mametz and Beyond, Llewelyn Wyn Griffith*, Pen and Sword
5. *1915 The Death of Innocence* and *The Roses of No Man's Land*, Lyn Macdonald, Penguin
6. *The Virago Book of Women and the Great War*, Edited by Joyce Marlow, Virago
7. *Anglesey At War*, Geraint Jones, The History Press
8. *Goodbye to All That*, Robert Graves, Penguin
9. *Women at The Hague*, Jane Addams, Emily G. Balch, Alice Hamilton, University of Illinois Press
10. *Not so Quiet*, Helen Zenna Smith, Virago Modern Classics
11. *Evelyn Sharp, Rebel Woman, 1869 – 1955*, Angela V. John, Manchester University Press
12. *Of Arms and the Heroes, The Story of the 'Birtley Belgians'*, John G. Bygate, The History of Education Project
13. *Refugees and Forced Migrants during the First World War*, Immigrants and Minorities, 26: 1, 82 – 110, 2008, Peter Gatrell
14. *'A Wave on to Our Shores': The Exile and Resettlement of Refugees from the Western Front, 1914 – 1918*, Contemporary European History, 16, 4 (2007), pp427 – 444, Pierre Purseigle
15. *Belgian Women Refugees in Britain in the Great War*, Women's History Magazine, issue 49, Spring 2005, Katherine Storr
16. *Out of The Fire of Hell, The Welsh experience of the Great War 1914 – 1918 in prose and verse*, Edited by Alan Llwyd, Gomer
17. *Across the Blockade; A Record of Travels in Enemy Europe*, Henry Noel Brailsford, General Books.net
18. *The Battle of the Somme*, Imperial War Museum original 1916 film
19. *Comrades in Captivity: A Record of Life in Seven German Prison Camps*. F.W. Harvey, Sidgwick and Jackson
20. *My Story of St Dunstan's*, Lord Fraser of Lonsdale, Harrap
21. *Vogue Magazine*, July 1916
22. *The Women's Hospital Corps: forgotten surgeons of the First World War*. J. F. Geddes, J. Med Biogr. 2006 May; 14(2): 109 – 17
23. *David Lloyd George 1915 Bangor Speech quotations:* Project Gutenberg
24. Women as Army Surgeons, by Flora Murray, London, Hodder and Stoughton, 1920
25. YR EURGRAWN, June 1923 pp215 - 218, The Rev. Peter Jones Roberts, By the Rev. John Felix

For Trevor and Naomi

NEWS FROM NOWHERE

'Go back and be happier for having seen us, for having added a little hope to your struggle. Go on living while you may, striving, with whatsoever pain and labour needs must be, to build up little by little the new day of fellowship, and rest, and happiness.'

News from Nowhere, 1891
William Morris

CHAPTER 1

August 1914
Bangor, North Wales

It was Bank Holiday Monday and the air was jagged with heat. The family was gathered in the dining room, where the window frames, jammed shut in summer, leaked winter. The atmosphere was close and sticky with the scent of lamb.

Bronwyn looked up as Tada prayed, still miles away from the *amen;* Glyn's eyes were closed tight, frowning in concentration; Aubrey looked as though he might be asleep and Huw was inscrutable behind the reflection of his glasses.

A fly buzzed against the window and tried to escape in a rising frenzy, and Bronwyn thought she would die of boredom unless *something* happened. Almost anything would do, to shake off the torpid air that held them in suspense like shrimps set in aspic. Tada reached the end of his prayer and opened his eyes. He looked mildly surprised at seeing them all round the table.

Mam was already on her feet swatting the fly with her napkin. Her hair was still dark with widening grey streaks at her temples, like bands of silver. Tada said it made her look as distinguished as a Grecian queen, though he generally called her his own dear badger.

'Would you carve, Aubrey dear? You're so good at it,' Mam said, as she liked to make a fuss of him on the rare occasions he came home from Manchester.

'Of course, Mother, always glad to be useful,' he said, standing and rolling his sleeves to the elbow. How strong and stocky he looked with his rugby-forward forearms, thought Bronwyn, this big brother who'd been grown up for as long as she could remember.

'How's business at the bank, Aubrey?' Tada's tone was serious. 'They must be concerned about all this war talk.'

Aubrey looked from his task for a moment. 'We have contingency plans, if anything comes of it.'

A bubble of chatter went round the table about Germany, France, Belgium, men joining up, and she felt a jolt at the thought of one of her brothers becoming a soldier.

'The Kaiser can't be left to trample all over Belgium,' Glyn spoke with passion, 'and if it comes to it, I'd be ready to sign up, we all would, I mean the boys in my year.' He looked at Tada for approval.

Tada shook his head, 'Lloyd George won't support a war, I'm sure of it. There's a lot of posturing on both sides, it will all blow over in a few weeks.'

She saw a look pass between Glyn and Aubrey and for the first time, doubted Tada's words. When there was a tragic death or catastrophe he would say that God's unseen hand was at work, but this didn't square easily with the idea of war.

Huw's glasses glinted as he looked up from his plate. 'But if England *does* go to war, would you go too, Tada?'

Surely Tada was too old to go, Bronwyn thought, and felt her cheeks go hot. 'Tada?' she prompted.

Mam intervened. 'Enough of this nonsense,' she rounded on Glyn: 'and there'll be no running off to war, you're going straight to College.'

'Mam's right,' said Aubrey, looking up from his carving, 'if anyone volunteers it should be me, as the eldest. I imagine the bank would let me go and I'd get a commission soon enough. It might even do my career some good, showing willing, serving one's country, that sort of thing.'

'Well, I hope it never comes to that for all our sakes,' said Mam with a familiar finality.

Bronwyn watched her brothers settle to the serious business of eating as she picked at her plate. Talk bounced: who had scored at this or that rugby match at Kingswood; Tada's visit to the Llewellyn family after their son drowned; Chapel news and Lizzie had asked to be a daily help instead of living in, because she was needed at home.

'You're very quiet today, Bron,' said Tada, 'what have you been up to?'

'I've been swimming with Maddy at Siliwen baths and we met a few girls from school there. It's quite the thing these days.'

'I remember when I first took you into the sea, just a little tiddler you were. I held your hand and you pulled me into the waves, you couldn't wait to swim like your brothers. You were quite fearless.'

'You could be one of those lady Olympic swimmers!' Huw chimed in.

'Thanks, Huw, but I think not.' She got up to fetch dessert. When she came back they were laughing at Huw doing an impression of Kaiser Bill. He had them in stitches so that, briefly, the war was a joke.

As she cleared dishes onto the trolley Bronwyn felt oversized next to Mam's slight frame, standing at the head of the table and lavishing out servings of gooseberry pie and cream to her boys. The hubbub of male voices rumbled and Bronwyn longed to prise Glyn away for one of their summer walks, or a stone-skimming match on the shore, but she could see he was too taken up with putting the world to rights with Tada and Aubrey.

Instead, she excused herself and walked barefoot across the grass in search of a cool patch to sit and read. Her bedroom was stifling in the sun and she'd felt drawn to the shade of the old sycamore in the corner of the garden. She plumped herself down out of view of the house and fanned out her skirt, enjoying the slightest sensation of air. In one swoop, she coiled her thick hair into a bun, and felt a delicious cool round her neck. Too old for plaits, she longed to have it cut short and wear it in a bob like Madame Duchamp, who'd lent her the novel she opened now. It looked so exotic in its cream paper jacket, utterly French, the mysterious *Isabelle*, by André Gide. One day she would go to France, she knew that. Just riffling through the rough-cut pages gave her a surge of joy.

She looked up at the rambling house with its sloping garden fringed with trees. The house was one of the better ones they'd lived in on the Welsh Methodist circuit, and she realised how bleak it would feel if they all went away; well, not Huw, he was still too young, but Aubrey, Glyn and even Tada. She sighed with impatience at the unfairness. At the very moment her life was taking off, a wretched war loomed.

How worldly Aubrey had seemed, talking about his work at the bank and hopes for a posting abroad. She smiled thinking of Huw, a dreamer by comparison; then there was Glyn, her childhood champion, who always made sure she wasn't left out of the boys' games. All too often Mam was harsh with him, as if to hide what they all knew: he was her favourite.

But for now, she would lose herself in somebody else's world. She opened the book at the first chapter and *Isabelle* beckoned her in.

The storm of war broke the following evening. It was after midnight when the paperboys came rushing past the house shouting, *England declares war on Germany!* Her room was at the back of the house so she didn't hear them at first, but she heard a commotion in Aubrey's room and padded across the landing in her nightdress to see what was going on. The three brothers were hanging out of the window as cries of war penetrated the air. They turned around and seeing her dismay, looked sheepish.

'It's official,' said Aubrey, 'England has gone in; there's no turning back now. At least we know where we stand.'

Glyn wouldn't meet her eye, but turned to pull down the sash window to muffle the din. 'It can't be helped, Bron,' he said, and added half-apologetically, 'it'll be over in no time.'

She stood in the doorway, not trusting herself to speak. She wanted to take Glyn by his dressing-gown lapels and shake sense into him, but she knew he wouldn't hear her. She felt like an outsider, the little sister who couldn't be expected to understand. If she tried to dampen their enthusiasm they'd call her a wet blanket. Better by far to wait until the morning.

On the way back to her room, she passed the top of the stairs, saw a light under the study door and heard raised voices. She had never heard Mam and Tada disagree before and her fear bloomed into panic.

When she came down the following morning newspapers littered the kitchen table; it was written in black and white: *Britain is in a state of war with Germany.* She sat and turned over the pages: *Germany tried to bribe us with peace to desert our friends and duty, but Great Britain has preferred the path of honour.* It became inevitable that Britain should stand by a small country facing an invader. Countries need allies as people need friends.

Tada came in looking his usual untidy weekday self, in his reading slippers and old brown cardigan with patched elbows. He hovered, pipe in hand, looking at her over half-moon glasses, and came over to put an arm round her shoulders.

'It's a dreadful thing we're facing, Bron. I really didn't believe it would happen. I'm afraid it will be a terrible war, and the first time we've seen anything so close to home.'

She knew he was trying to help her understand, but her spirit fought against it. 'But why must they fight? Why don't they just talk?'

He walked around the table, breathing life into his pipe, as if brewing a sermon. That was what he was doing, working out what he would say to the congregation, to the families facing this calamity. He watched her stack the newspapers into a neat pile and said, 'God only knows, Bronwyn. I have no easy answers. I just know we must do what is right.'

*Do all the good you can…to all the people you can…as long as ever you can…*This was his credo, the Wesleyan creed he lived by to a fault where his congregation was concerned. More than once he'd taken in waifs and strays at Christmas against Mam's better judgement. *Such an impractical man, your father, a true Christian.*

He was anxious to get back to his study and she felt tender towards him, remembering times he'd comforted her when she'd had nightmares as a child. How much more comforting he would have to do now.

Bronwyn sat reading by the window and looked up at Mam, who was mending sheets and fighting against the dying light, delaying the moment she'd put on the lamps and draw the curtains. Her dark head lifted from her work to address Glyn as he propped himself against the mantelpiece.

'We've been over this a dozen times, Glyn. Aubrey will go first, so there's absolutely no need for you to volunteer. Your father and I don't want you to sacrifice your studies, and the war may well be over by Christmas. You're far too impetuous for your own good.' She pushed her spectacles back up her nose and carried on with her needle. 'Now pop, some more coal on the fire, would you dear, or there'll be no hot water in the back boiler?'

Glyn reached for the coalscuttle, shovelled on too much, and jabbed the smoking embers with the poker in a vain attempt to bring the fire back to life. Watching from the shadows, Bronwyn felt Glyn's anger and frustration radiate across the room.

'Mam, nearly all the boys in my year have signed up. Those who haven't have good reason, like Cunningham who wears leg-irons. I can't sit and twiddle my thumbs while they go and risk their lives. It would be dishonourable, surely you understand that?'

This time Mam didn't look up. 'Reading Classics is hardly idling, Glyn.'

Bronwyn squirmed as she heard her mother's temper rise and braced herself for the salvo to follow.

'If you were to sign up, we would insist you get a commission. Anything less would be a complete waste of your talents. I still think you're far too young, and you should go to College first.'

'I'm truly sorry to upset you, Mam.' He searched her face and stood, almost to attention, the poker held stiffly in his hand. 'You know it would break my heart to go without your blessing, but I have to do the right thing.' He turned his back for a moment and tended the fire purposefully, looked again at Mam, then withdrew from the room leaving a deathly quiet behind.

Bronwyn had never seen him in this mood. She skirted the room lighting the lamps, casting about for something to say.

'Don't be too harsh, Mam,' was what came out.

'Speak only of what you know, child,' her mother replied in Welsh, 'which is not a great deal at your age, for all your learning.'

Bronwyn knew she'd drawn blood when she'd meant to calm. Mam was diminished in the gloomy room, laden with over-stuffed furniture from another era, worn out by Wesleyan ministers' families over the years. Bronwyn sat next to her on a footstool and looked at the glass cabinet filled with Mam's fine china, wedding gifts mostly, which had remained a constant throughout her childhood. On the bottom shelf sat Barbara. She remembered the moment on her thirteenth birthday, when she'd announced she wanted to keep Barbara in the cabinet because she was too old for dolls. Now Barbara stared back at her wide-eyed and vacant from her bland china face.

'I'm almost sixteen Mam, and I want to help.' She'd overheard conversations about the work at the Wesleyan Book Room, how difficult it would be if Tada went away. 'I could do Tada's accounts and post out the Magazine.' She even liked the idea of helping with the editing.

'Now *Del*, let's not run ahead of ourselves. Tada may well only be accepted for Home Service, so won't be going too far away. We'll manage, whatever happens, don't you worry.'

Bronwyn knew Tada had applied for a commission abroad and had been refused because he was over age. He was still in London doing his best to change the decision, bending the ear of everyone from Lloyd George to the Chaplain-General, according to Aubrey. She hugged her knees and hoped Mam was right, but knew Tada was quite determined to work amongst the men at the front. *There is a call for fathers as well as sons,* he'd said, *and if there must be soldiers there must be chaplains too.*

She stood up to draw the curtains, but stopped for a moment to drop a kiss on her mother's head.

She looked for Glyn and found him in his room, cleaning up his school army kit.

'Glyn, please don't go,' she pleaded, 'not yet.'

'Bron, I have to sooner or later, I must. Please don't make it harder than it already is. We'll write to each other as we always do, I promise.'

She held his gaze and felt he'd changed in some indefinable way. It was as if he'd stepped over a threshold into the world of men and left her exiled in girlhood.

'We'll go out on our bikes sometime, just us.'

She saw in his eyes his mind was made up.

*

'He's put us all in a tight spot, with this talk of Christ versus country!' Tada was rarely animated.

'But sometimes war is the lesser evil,' replied Aubrey.

They were standing by Tada's desk, Aubrey a head taller. The desk was covered in a plethora of books, bookmarked with a system of coloured ribbons known only to Tada. It was Wednesday, when composing the Sunday sermon reached its peak.

'Who are you talking about?' Bronwyn asked.

They both turned, as she stood in the study doorway.

'Hello, Bron, I didn't see you. How's my favourite daughter this morning?'

It was Tada's way of disarming her, but she wouldn't be distracted.

'Well?'

'It's Professor Rees, at the Theological College. He's against the war on religious grounds.'

'Is he a pacifist?' She'd heard the term, but wasn't sure what it meant.

Aubrey raised an eyebrow, 'Yes. What's more he's undermining recruitment and giving Nonconformists a bad name.'

'It's a matter of conscience,' said Tada. 'The man's entitled to his views.'

Aubrey frowned. 'Anyone against the war is a shirker in my book.'

'Does that mean cousin Alwyn's a pacifist?' she asked, entering the room.

There'd been rumblings about him not signing up. She was fond of Alwyn; he'd always taken her side against her brothers' teasing when they were small.

'He's a good sort, but an idealist. If we let the Germans run riot over Belgian borders there will be no stopping them,' said Aubrey, reddening.

'And for the best of motives, to defend a small country in its hour of need,' Tada said, as if to modify Aubrey's tone.

'There must be a better way.' However hard she tried, she couldn't reconcile the fate of a faraway country with Glyn leaving. 'If I were a boy, I'd be against violence.'

'Well, lucky you don't have to worry your little head over it, Bron. The boys will do the fighting for you,' said Aubrey.

'Oh, so the opinion of a mere girl doesn't count?' She felt like boxing his ears.

'Now now,' said Tada, 'we all need to pull together. I'd be glad if you'd help out in the Book Room, Bron. Would you give Mam a hand when I'm called away?'

'Yes, of course, if Mam's happy about that.'

'I'll have a word.' He adjusted his clerical collar. 'She mustn't take everything on herself.'

'Sorry, if I upset you, Bron, I sometimes forget how grown up you are.' Aubrey glanced at Tada and down at the threadbare carpet.

'I'd like to know more about Professor Rees,' she said, refusing to cave.

CHAPTER 2

September 1914

The air was delicious, warm with a light breeze and perfect for a day's cycling. She thought of the bike the boys had clubbed together to buy for her last birthday, and kept a secret until the last minute.

They'd told her to close her eyes and led her to the shed, and after she was allowed to open them it was a few moments before her eyes got used to the dim light. She'd guessed it was something too large to hide in the house, but had no idea what it could be. There it was, shining amongst the old spades and watering cans. Glyn had painted it navy and Huw had found a basket for the handlebars, decked out with roses and sweet peas, which was Mam's touch. It had made her happier than she could remember, this gift of freedom on wheels.

'You ready yet, Bron?' Glyn called out from the hall, as she was loading up the basket with sandwiches and a flask of tea.

'I will be, when I've got this lot stowed away. It weighs a ton.'

He appeared in the kitchen, and laughed. 'Are you feeding a battalion? Come on, let's put the flask in my rucksack and leave the cake-tin behind.' He started rearranging things and tweaked her cheek, so she wouldn't mind.

'I can see you've done this before,' she said, admiring his tidy packing, 'must be what they teach you in the Officers' Training Corps.'

'Less lip young lady, on your bike with you.'

They were soon on the road and she watched Glyn speed ahead, shorts flapping, going helter-skelter down the hill and through town. By the time she caught up he was waiting for her at the Menai Bridge.

'Steady on,' she complained, breathless. 'You've got long legs and I'm lugging the picnic.'

'You're quite strong enough to keep up with me,' he grinned from under his tweed cap. 'I'll carry the picnic on the way back.'

'Thanks for nothing!' she retorted, and got back into the saddle, determined to out-distance him. The salt wind blew through her hair and filled her lungs as she swept across the bridge, overtaking a horse and trap and even a slow moving car.

This time he had to catch up with her, on the Anglesey side of the Straits. Skidding to a halt, he chanted playfully:

'...for I had just
completed my design,
to keep the Menai bridge from rust
by boiling it in wine.
What's that from?'

'*Through the Looking Glass*, but I can't remember who said it.'

'The White Knight!' he said in mock triumph. 'Can you guess how Telford actually did protect the chains from rust?'

'No, but I feel sure you're going to tell me.'

'He soaked them in linseed oil, though boiling them in wine is more picturesque.'

Without warning he took off ahead, and she just about kept up, feeling her calves working the pedals. Beaumaris was soon in view and they slowed along the streets filled with people and traffic.

They arrived at the ancient fortress and stopped to admire its squat grey turrets, repeated in a broken reflection in the moat as the breeze rippled the surface. There was gaiety in the air, families enjoying a day out and courting couples making the best of summer's final fling.

'Quite a few men are in uniform,' said Bronwyn. 'They must be in training.'

'Could be, unless they're back on leave. Do you remember my friend Gethin? He goes out next month.'

'Yes, I liked him; he was always nice to me. How about you? Will you be going soon?'

'It depends. I have to wait for my commission, then I'll go to Litherland for training. It could be months before I'm sent abroad, and it could be all over by then.

'Shall we go and sit on the beach? I love the view of Snowdon from this side.'

'Good idea,' she said, glad of an excuse to rest her legs.

They leant the bikes against an upturned fishing boat and sat on warm stones next to a stack of lobster pots. Bronwyn looked out to sea, closed her eyes for a minute and cast her mind back a couple of months to when life was normal.

As if reading her thoughts, Glyn said, 'It must be hard, Bron, being left behind.' He ran his fingers through dark wiry hair, a shorter version of hers.

She turned and smiled. 'Not as hard as it must be for you. Shall we stop talking about it? I don't want to be sad, at least not yet.'

A young couple appeared, holding hands with a fat toddler who was lunging towards the lapping waves. The woman was clearly expecting her next child.

'Will that be you in a few years' time?' Glyn asked, nodding towards the small family.

She felt herself blush. 'Well, I'm certainly in no hurry. I want to see the world, Glyn; I don't see myself staying in Bangor after College. And you? Do you still want to teach?'

'Perhaps. I try not to look too far ahead. I just want to do my bit, without making a fool of myself if possible. Brothers in arms and all that.' He shaded his eyes to look at a distant trawler, framed by the range of mountains.

'Joining up means a lot to you, doesn't it?'

He was lost in thought and they both sat watching the child as he teetered on the wet stones, free of his socks and shoes.

'I need to know what I'm made of,' he said eventually.

'Because fighting for your country is the right thing to do?'

'Is this an inquisition?' he said, laughing. 'If I'm honest, it's more about proving myself. I'm not as hotly patriotic as Aubrey.'

'What about Alwyn, is he unpatriotic?'

Glyn looked into the distance. 'No. And he's not a coward. I think he's genuinely against violence. But there are people who are against the war for other reasons, such as the socialists. They say it's a battle of the Titans, the great powers carving up the world to increase their influence.'

She began to see that the truth was many-layered, not a single nut to be cracked open.

'I wonder if you want to prove yourself to Tada. I know you've had your differences.'

They used to clash about free will and God, and when Mam intervened Tada would insist they were only sparring.

'I don't think God has anything to do with it, do you?' he said with an ironic smile.

Only then did it dawn on her that one of them might not come back; Glyn, Aubrey, even Tada, and she welled up. 'I'm scared for you,' she said turning to Glyn. 'I couldn't bear it if anything happened.'

He wouldn't meet her eye. 'Chances are I'll come out without a scratch, so let's not be gloomy. My commission could take months; you haven't got rid of me yet.'

She looked up as he uncurled his long limbs and sprang upright in one bound. It took her longer to get up. She felt sluggish, half-formed questions preying on her mind.

'Nice skirt, Bron, I don't think I've seen it before. Is it shorter than your usual?'

She smoothed out the folds of blue and white gingham. 'Do you like it? I took it up an inch for cycling. Mam says I'm showing too much calf.'

'She may have a point.'

'What do you mean?'

'You don't want people having a pop at you over trivia.'

'Well, skirts are a nightmare on a bike, they get caught up.' She felt mildly irritated.

'I'll take your word for it, Bron. Now let's get to Llanddona in time for lunch. Ladies first.' He beckoned her forward.

It was hard going in the heat and a good few miles before they saw the sign to the village. When they arrived, she came to a halt and Glyn pulled up alongside, looking collected.

They propped their bikes against a tree and Bronwyn stood, hands on hips, enjoying the rush of blood to every part of her body. Her blouse had come untucked and she flapped it in an attempt to cool off.

'It's a steep descent to the beach,' said Glyn. 'We could walk it if you prefer.'

'I don't mind riding down, if you go first. We can use our brakes.'

'Right you are,' he said and took off, progressing fitfully, brakes squeaking.

She set off slowly, eyes fixed ahead, seduced by the notion of letting go. Easing off the brakes, the bike gathered speed and she was soon swerving past Glyn, who shouted something from behind. Now she was whizzing down the narrow track, left with a choice of braking and flying over the handlebars or steering into a hedgerow.

The next thing she knew, the bike went from under her and she landed heavily. When she opened her eyes, everything looked blurred.

'Bron, are you alright? Talk to me.' Glyn was leaning over her.

'My head hurts and I feel a bit sick,' she said, as the horizon wavered. 'What happened?'

'You landed in a bush, thank God, and not on the road. That would have been curtains. Let's get you onto your feet.'

He helped her stand, and she brushed herself, with only a couple of scratches to show for it; even her skirt was intact. She reached for the bike. 'Ouch! That's my knee. I must have banged it.' She lifted her skirt.

'That's a nasty bruise, Bron. Let's get down to the sea and you can bathe it. I don't know, what are we going to do with you?'

She smiled weakly. 'Sorry, Glyn, I didn't mean to frighten you. I don't know what got into me.'

Leaning on Glyn's bike, she limped to the shore, while he took charge of her bike and the picnic.

They found a flattish spot amongst the stones and Glyn spread out the cloth and started to unpack lunch. He handed her a napkin, 'off you go. It won't do any harm to walk on it.'

Bronwyn gingerly touched her knee and saw a purple bruise spreading down her shin. Hobbling to the water's edge, she dipped the napkin into the sea, making a cooling salt-water bandage, which she tied on. She walked back unsteadily and eased herself down on the red-check cloth.

'Better?' Glyn asked, handing her a packet of sandwiches and a beaker of sweet tea.

'I'll be fine. Thanks for the tea, it's bliss.'

'That wasn't a very clever thing to do, was it? A pretty pointless risk, if I may say so.' He was definitely ticking her off.

'I know, it was childish. I said I was sorry. It was the speed, it was so exciting, like leaping into the unknown. By then it was too late to brake.'

'Mmm...you sound like someone looking for a challenge, but you don't have to break your neck in the process.'

She decided to ignore the dig. 'I certainly want to do something interesting with my life, something different. Do you think that's possible?'

'Yes, Bron, I do.' He moved closer, hunkering next to her, nursing his beaker.

She leaned into him. 'I remember last year when those Suffrage women marched from Bangor to London. Two came to speak to us in school, Charlotte and Mildred. We were on first name terms. They were so happy, laughing as they remembered it all. They wore hats with cockle shell badges, and showed us their battered haversacks, red with white and green straps, the Women's Suffrage Societies' colours.'

'I didn't know Bangor County Girls held such advanced views.' He looked amused.

'Maddy and I said we'd love to do something like that. They marched for weeks, stopping to speak along the way. Quarrymen stopped to cheer, but others threw stones and stopped the meeting. More terrifying were the vile things people shouted.'

It was the first time she'd realised standing up for your rights could attract abuse. Mam had said women like that were asking for trouble. Charlotte and Mildred were different; they were against violence and said their pilgrimage spoke for itself.

'I like to think of you taking on the world, Sis.'

They settled into a companionable silence allowing the heat of the sun and the emptiness of the beach to bleach their minds of thought. A pair of scavenging seagulls landed nearby and foraged in the pebbles, then soared skyward with disconsolate wails.

'Little beggars,' said Glyn, 'they'll always remind me of home. By the way, there was something I wanted to ask you,' and he started fumbling through his pockets until he found a letter. 'Would you read this, Bron? You'll see why.'

She unfolded the single sheet written in elegant German script.

August 1914
Dear Glyn,

Thank-you kindly for your letter. Today I write to you as our two countries declare war, something I deeply regret. I will serve my country, as I am sure you will. I truly hope that this will not tarnish our friendship. I look forward to visiting you in Wales and walk in your beautiful mountains of Snowdonia next year, when surely this war is over. One day we will ride together in the Harz.

As a veterinary student I will care for the horses in the war. We will need hospitals for animals as well as for people. I think I will have to leave soon. Do you remember I spoke of my elder sister Gisela? I will give her your address so she can write to you if anything happens to me. Please would you ask your dear sister to do the same, heaven forbid? I will write no more of this and speak of pleasant things.

Today I went for a ride in the forest with my old school friend and we saw deer and foxes and the weather was very fine. Afterwards we stopped at a bier-garten and drank a toast to peace.

I will leave you now and thank you for your friendship.
Yours truly,
Dietrich

'Your pen-friend?'

He nodded.

'Of course I would write to him,' she said handing back the letter. 'I just pray I won't have to. This war is seeping into everything.' She thought of Mam, who dressed with a frown each morning because Tada was doing his utmost to get posted to France, and because Aubrey had decided to join up even though he hadn't finished his accounting exams. Huw was least smitten by war fever; in fact Aubrey said he wondered if Huw was a pacifist at heart.

The letter made her think of Claudia at school, whose father wanted to fight for Britain even though he was German.

'I agree with Dietrich,' Glyn cut into her thoughts, 'if we lose sight of each other as people and friends, we lose ourselves. Our integrity.'

'You make it sound as if the war could steal your soul.'

'It's true. Whenever governments decide a thing is good for the nation, it will be harmful to the individual.' He was packing away the picnic as he spoke.

She got to her feet and moved stiffly towards her bike. 'So, why *do* you feel you have to go?'

'As I said, I have to test myself. To know my worth as a man. Sorry if that sounds pompous.'

'Growing up as a girl is bad enough, but it seems harder for you boys.'

He laughed. 'I doubt it. It's much harder for a girl if she's got anything about her, though I'm sure that won't hold you back, Bron.'

Wincing, she got onto her bike.

'Knee still complaining? We can go straight home if you want.'

'No, let's keep going, I want to see the dovecote,' she said, putting on a brave face.

They pushed the bikes up the hill, and set off for the ride to Penmon. It was well into the afternoon by the time they arrived.

'There it is,' said Glyn. 'Let's leave the bikes by the fence and go inside. You'll be amazed.'

It was a square windowless stone building with a domed roof. They had to duck to get through the doorway. Bronwyn felt the crunch of ancient bird droppings under her shoe. As her eyes got used to the gloom, she saw an outlet at the top that let in a shaft of light. There were countless nesting holes set into the walls, round a central pillar.

'It was built in Elizabethan times by Sir Richard Bulkeley; he bred doves for the table.'

Bronwyn smiled. Glyn loved to parade facts and figures.

'There are a thousand nesting holes,' he continued. 'That's a lot of eggs.'

'What's the pillar for?' she asked.

'There used to be a revolving ladder. They must have leant it against the pillar to reach the eggs. I'm not sure how they caught the birds.'

'Shall we press on?' Glyn said, bending double to step outside. 'I'd like to drop in at St Tysilio's on the way back. To pay my respects. Is that alright?'

'I'd be glad to,' said Bronwyn.

Glyn rarely mentioned his infant twin and she was touched he did so now.

They cycled steadily on the home run to the Straits; they slowed on the approach to the causeway that took them to St Tysilio's church, set on an islet.

'It's a long time since I've been inside,' said Glyn, opening the low wooden door.

They stepped onto the stone floor, transfixed by the light; vivid reds and greens lit by the low-lying sun streamed in through the stained-glass windows. Slowly the light drained, revealing rustic pews and a plain table that served as an altar.

Outside, they walked among the carved cherubs and angels and Celtic crosses.

Bronwyn noticed a stone book displaying a tender inscription to a wife and mother.

'Where is his grave, Glyn? I haven't been here for so long.'

'Look, it's right here.' He pointed to a simple plaque:

Here lies Tomos Peter Roberts, twin brother of Glyn, died aged 6 months on September 19th 1895, dearly beloved son of Peter and Sarah Jones Roberts.

'Goodness, it's today, Glyn; it's his anniversary. I'm sorry, I should have known.'

He looked embarrassed. 'Actually, it's only in the last few weeks that I've been thinking about him. I've been wondering how things might have been different if he'd survived. I sometimes feel as if part of me is missing, but then it's probably just an excuse for my own inadequacies.' He gave a lopsided smile. 'As I said, I'll write to you when I'm away, Bron, maybe let off steam a bit. Could you put up with that?'

She wanted desperately to mother him, as he stood bare-kneed and vulnerable, looking at her with hazel eyes. 'Of course, Glyn dear,' she said, and flung her arms round him, gulping back tears.

'Thanks, Bron old girl,' he said holding her stiffly, 'I'm glad that's alright.'

They cycled back along the Straits, turning at the sound of a train rumbling across the Britannia Bridge and looking up as the harsh-voiced terns swooped above the treacherous Swellies.

The light and warmth of the day had passed and they remarked on a chill in the evening air.

CHAPTER 3

Winter 1915

After a bleak Christmas Bronwyn found it a relief to return to school. Just the two of them now, Mam and herself left in the sprawling house that echoed with absences.

Tada had got his way, serving amongst new recruits in Manchester, and still hoped to be posted to France. He'd come home in November once Glyn had received his commission and the two of them walked to the station in uniform like any father and son.

Everyone was sucked into this national upheaval, she had to remind herself, but it still left her hollow, the way she always felt when her brothers went back to Kingswood after the holidays. Huw was in his last year there, too young for war, thankfully, and would be home at Easter. She even missed Aubrey, who'd left home a long time ago, now waiting for a posting in Intelligence.

It was freezing cold on the morning that the school boiler broke, as Bronwyn stood next to Maddy in morning assembly. Her heart lifted as Miss Hobson announced that the girls should go home.

Bronwyn felt a nudge in her ribs and knew instantly they would spend the day together. She nudged Maddy back, but daren't catch her eye or they'd get the giggles. A free day to do whatever they pleased felt as magical as sudden snowfall. Miss Hobson was on the hall platform gesticulating with her glasses, saying, 'Use the time wisely, girls. School dismissed.'

'Your house or mine?' Maddy asked from behind, as they filed out. It was then that Bronwyn remembered the backlog of Methodist Magazines to be dispatched.

She took Maddy's arm and asked, 'would you come to the Book Room to help me pack up the magazines? On the promise of tea and scones afterwards?'

Maddy made a shuddering sound, 'I don't know, Bron, it'll be even colder than it is here.'

'Look on the bright side, we're missing hockey! There's a paraffin heater and I'll have it warmed up in a jiffy, you'll see.'

'You're twisting my arm.' She mimicked extreme pain. 'Oh, alright, you win, but only for you!'

A consignment of the Methodist Magazine came directly from the printers each month and each one had to be rolled, labelled and posted to the large subscription list. It was something that Glyn and Huw used to do for pocket money, which Bronwyn had taken upon herself—as well as editing the *Handy Hints* page.

They arrived at the side-door of the plain redbrick building and Bronwyn produced the key from her coat pocket. The door gave way after a firm twist and push of the handle, and they stepped inside into the musty air.

While Bronwyn tackled the heater, Maddy stood huffing on her fingers then sat with her coat pulled round her. She started to roll magazines in brown paper, slowly, because her fingers were cold, having trouble making them a uniform size before sticking on a label.

'Does it matter if they're not all exactly the same?' She liked to be precise.

'Not as long as they're tight enough to go through a letterbox. Then pop them into the sack, the one next to you. Just don't fill it up, or it won't fit into the basket on my bike. I have to take them to the Post Office.

'That's it, I think I've done it.' Bronwyn looked up from the heater. 'There should be some warmth coming out of this thing soon, if we haven't already been overcome by fumes.' She went to join Maddy at the table.

'It could be worse,' said Maddy.

Bronwyn looked at her. 'How much worse?'

'We could be sitting in a trench up to our knees in mud. If we were boys, I mean.' She flicked her auburn hair back over her shoulders and allowed the magazine in her hand to unfurl.

'You're right; what a ghastly thought,' Bronwyn said, rolling and labelling a magazine, which by now she could do almost blindfold.

'I'm sure I couldn't face it,' Maddy continued. 'Imagine, just because you're a boy, you're expected to fight. Particularly for the quieter types, like Rhys.'

'Have you heard from him lately?' Bronwyn asked.

Maddy's brother was a gentle soul, who used to come round to play when they were children.

'We've had a postcard,' said Maddy, 'but he never gives much away. The trouble is Da expects him to come back a hero. He keeps harping on about Rhys showing those bullyboys at school what he's really made of. Poor lamb, it's the last thing he needs. How's Glyn surviving?'

'He seems glad to be out there after all the waiting around in Litherland. Said the boredom might actually kill him before the Germans got a chance. His last letter was more like a shopping list. They don't seem to give them the basics out there. He needs a Sam Browne belt as well as endless groceries and toiletries.'

She stood up to tie the neck of the already bulging sack, then brought over another pile of magazines to work on. They sat and continued rolling and labelling companionably, stopping only to rub life into their hands.

'I used to envy boys,' said Bronwyn, 'the way they could josh and push each other around and move freely in the world; now I'm not so sure. Maybe all that schoolboy rough and tumble is meant to prepare them for actual killing.'

'So, we're left to keep the home fires burning and put Humpty together again.'

'Don't, Maddy, that's terrible!'

They burst into irreverent laughter, lapsing into silence as the paraffin heater coughed and spluttered and gave off a noxious pale-blue smoke.

'I don't know about you,' said Bronwyn, 'but I find myself avoiding writing to Glyn about certain things. Petty things, like when a pipe bursts, or the extra housework since Lizzie stopped living in.'

'I'm the same. You're afraid to say anything in case they worry, but then you wonder what to write about.'

'I look at some of the men who've come back, and I think how grey and battle-worn they look, and I wonder if Glyn and Aubrey will look changed.'

Maddy nodded. 'Well, our job is to keep them cheerful, isn't it? We have to carry on as normal or at least keep up appearances. Otherwise the whole pack of cards will come tumbling.' Into the swing of it now, she looked up and said, 'Did you know there's talk of opening a hospital at the University?'

'No, really?'

'That's what I heard at the Post Office. It must mean the war's going to carry on for a lot longer than we thought.'

'Or longer than they care to tell us. Some newspapers say they've seen this war coming for years. You'd think they'd have found a way of stopping it, if it was so obvious. But that doesn't seem to be the way of things.' And she hurled a rolled up magazine into the second sack, already half-full. 'Enough of this, Mads, it's freezing in here and I can finish off tomorrow. Let's go home for tea.'

'I won't argue,' Maddy said, stamping her feet as Bronwyn went to turn off the heater and pick up the key.

It wasn't noticeably colder as they stepped out into the street, setting off at a brisk pace up the hill and laughing, colour high in their cheeks.

'It's all Greek to me,' said Bronwyn, to a groan of sympathy.

They'd just been released from a Physics lesson and were noisily letting off steam.

'I thought you were good at languages,' quipped Edith, and they groaned again.

Claudia arched her perfect eyebrows and said, 'My father's an engineer, he'd be able to explain it.'

There was a hush. Claudia had a habit of boasting, but the silent treatment today was because they knew her father was interned.

'What's the matter?' she said, jutting out her chin. 'Is it because he's *German*?'

'Of course not,' said Maddy, 'it must be horrid for you.'

'I suppose they're worried about spies,' Edith blundered on, 'that's why they put them in prison.'

Bronwyn knew she should say something, but last week's incident in the changing rooms still stung. She'd made a clumsy pass during hockey and they'd missed the winning goal. Claudia had said she was worse than useless and the team would be better off without her.

'That's absurd,' Claudia shot back at Edith, nostrils flaring. 'My father has done nothing but good for this country.'

Pippa, thin lipped and waspish snorted, 'that's as may be, but where has your daddy ended up? I'd keep quiet about him if I were you.'

Firm footsteps approached as Miss Hobson appeared round the corner, gown flapping. They fell into single file and chorused, *Good morning Miss Hobson,* as she swept past, a sheaf of papers clutched to her bosom.

They regrouped round Claudia and Pippa, waiting for feathers to fly.

'You can talk,' Claudia hissed, 'why are your brothers still at home?'

'They're farmers,' Pippa flung back, 'no farmers, no bread, *Dummkopf.*'

'Watch out,' Maddy warned.

Madame Duchamp came out of her room and stopped, skirts swirling round her ankles. *'Et bien mes enfants, qu'est ce qui se passe?'*

Claudia's eyes were glassy with tears and Pippa went the colour of beetroot.

'So, what's happened?' She stood holding them in her gaze. 'Claudia doesn't cry for nothing.'

When nobody answered she looked directly at Bronwyn and said, 'I expect you to tell me the truth.'

'Edith and Pippa were picking on Claudia and none of us tried to stop it,' said Bronwyn.

Edith and Pippa looked shamefaced.

'Girls, girls, what sort of nonsense is this at your age? The two of you, come with me to the Head's office and we'll get to the bottom of it. No doubt Miss Hobson will speak to the rest of you later.'

Claudia sniffed and allowed the other girls to coo round her, but Bronwyn needed fresh air.

'Come for a walk round the block?' she said to Maddy. 'We could have lunch at second sitting.'

'Suits me. Anyway, I'm not hungry now.'

'At least you showed her some sympathy.'

They picked up their coats from the cloakroom that smelt of rotting gym shoes and boiled fish. The ventilation shaft from the kitchen went via the basement and you always knew what was being dished up for lunch.

The morning air was sharp and Bronwyn looked up for signs of a snow flurry; grey clouds scudded a pale sky. It was cold enough for it.

'What they did was horrible and we should have said something, I should have.'

Maddy nodded. 'It got out of hand so fast, I don't know how it happened.'

Bronwyn hugged herself against a biting gust and said, 'People are saying things they'd have kept to themselves six months ago.'

'You can understand why. I know it was uncalled for, but you'd think Claudia would have the sense to keep her head down.'

This wasn't the response she'd expected and it wasn't the first time. 'It's not her fault her father happens to be German.'

Maddy tossed back her curly mop. 'Excuse me for expressing an opinion. I sometimes wonder whose side you're on, Bron.'

Bronwyn gave a harsh laugh. 'Our side, naturally. I certainly don't want Germany to win. Surely the politicians should be able to find some sort of solution? The *Chronicle* is spinning a story that German spies are going under cover as Belgians, so the Admiralty has stopped Belgians being housed in Holyhead. Demonising won't help.'

'Agreed, we need an end to the war,' Maddy conceded.

'Politics is complicated, it's not like Maths where there's a proof and that's that,' Bronwyn teased.

'All right, I do tend to see life in black and white, but you can't solve the world's problems single handed.'

'I want to understand what's going on, that's all. Lloyd George is speaking at the County Theatre on Sunday; would you come?'

They were almost back at the school gates.

Maddy grinned, 'Entertainment on a Sunday, well I never. Count me in.'

The unappetising smell of overcooked food wafted down the corridor as they slipped through the side door.

'I'd better eat after all,' said Maddy, 'Mam only cooks for my Da in the evenings.'

In the dining hall, Bronwyn said, 'Let's sit next to Claudia, she's alone.'

By the time they arrived the theatre was packed.

'We can squeeze in at the back,' said Bronwyn, hoping they'd see over the Sunday best hats in the row in front.

The Cleo brass band was playing *Cwm Rhondda* with gusto, one of Tada's favourites and often sung in Chapel. The mood of the audience quickened, waiting for the great man to appear.

'The Chancellor of the whole land and one of our own, it makes you proud,' said one of the hatted ladies.

The bandsmen came to a close and a lectern was positioned centre stage. A hush fell as Mr Lloyd George briskly walked on from the wings. Tall, broad shouldered with silvering hair, he cut a fine figure.

Bronwyn took out pencil and paper to make jottings, determined to follow his reasoning. Increasingly, the papers were at odds with the realities Glyn wrote about, and she hoped today she might glean more truth.

He spoke softly at first, like any good preacher, drawing them in. He said Sunday was the only day open to him and so important were the things he had to say, he felt obliged to break the Sabbath. 'I am not the hypocrite to say, I will save my own soul by not talking to them on Sunday.'

There was a murmur of acknowledgement.

'I have come to lay bare the task before us. I do not believe in withholding from our own public information they ought to possess.'

Speaks directly, as an equal, Bronwyn noted.

'We are conducting a war as if there was no war.'

There was a collective intake of breath, an audible bristling.

Hasn't he noticed how few men there are? Bronwyn thought. We're closer to the action than he thinks. Only last week the *Cambank* was torpedoed off Anglesey and the lifeboat men hauled the crew out. Everyone here must know someone connected with the disaster.

'I have never been doubtful about the result of the war, nor have I been doubtful, I am sorry to say, about the length of the war and its seriousness. I've been accounted a pessimist, for thinking the war would not be over by Christmas.'

Bronwyn saw Maddy cover her mouth in disbelief. The women in front tutted and men whistled through their teeth.

He had the demeanour of a stern headmaster teaching a hard lesson. After praising the strengths of the allied forces and their potential to subdue German might, he said, 'Beyond all this is the moral strength of our cause. The task before us is a work of urgent necessity in the cause of human freedom, nothing less.

'Nobody, except Germany, wanted war, not Belgium, not France, and certainly not Britain. We never meant to invade any continental country. If we had, we would have raised an army adequate to such sinister purposes.'

Persuasive, she noted.

He changed tack. 'This is an engineers' war. We need more arms than men. We are not a timid race who cannot face unpleasant facts. John Bull doesn't want to be mollycoddled.'

She scribbled, *more privation, potato-bread spirit. Employers, workmen and public must pull together.*

He threw back his shoulders and launched in: 'It is intolerable that the life of Britain should be imperilled for the matter of a farthing an hour.'

There was a rumble of dissent. This must be about threats of a strike for fair pay.

'Some may say, "Employers are making their fortunes, so why are we not to have a share of the plunder"?'

A man heckled loudly from the back, 'Pay us a decent wage!'

'There is one gentleman here who holds that view. I hope he is not an engineer.'

Laughter broke out and dissolved the tension. Lloyd George smiled. Then he was deadly serious. 'In a period of war output is everything. The war will be won or lost in the workshops of France and Great Britain.'

There followed a tirade against *the lure of the drink*, France and Russia being the worst offenders. 'We are essentially moderate men,' he said, gathering them into his confidence, 'and I trust drastic measures will not be needed. But mark my words, the government will use its considerable powers if required.' He pounded the lectern to make the point.

Bronwyn listened, transfixed, as he depicted a Wagnerian struggle between good and evil for the possession of Man's soul, against a Germany that would quench every spark of freedom in rivers of blood.

'And I make no apology on a day consecrated to the greatest sacrifice for coming here to preach a holy war against that!

'War is a time of sacrifice and of service,' he said softly. 'Some can render one service, some another. Like ants in the old Welsh legend who banded together to gather the seed before sunset, we can all take some share of our country's burden in this terrible hour.'

The hall rose to its feet in an uproar of applause, and the ladies in wide old-fashioned hats blotted out any view of the stage.

Bronwyn stood up alongside Maddy, who wept, borne along by the tide of emotion as Lloyd George basked in the warmth of a homecoming. Each time he stepped back another wave of clapping pinned him to the podium, until they let him go.

It was at least ten minutes before they got outside; people dawdled and chatted as though they didn't want the mood of exhilaration to pass.

'Magnificent, isn't he?' Maddy said.

Bronwyn raised an eyebrow. 'If you don't mind being cast as an ant.'

'You're so cynical, Bron. What about saving humanity, surely that's what it's all about?'

'He makes a strong appeal to the emotions, but we shouldn't allow that to blunt our critical faculties. You're the scientist, you should know that.'

Maddy gave her a curious look. 'That doesn't mean I'm bloodless. Can't you see, it's an emergency and our chance to do something?'

'Such as work in munitions so more men are killed? He didn't once mention negotiating peace.' She was surprised how angry she felt.

A large shiny black car rolled by, carrying a distinctive silhouette in the back seat. Bronwyn's heart flipped. At least this was something to write about to Glyn, though she'd have to temper her views.

CHAPTER 4

Summer 1915

Bronwyn was sitting in the garden and should have been revising, but instead was writing a letter to Glyn.

She ran her eye over what she'd written so far, and felt the letter lopsided, distorted by omission, with a false brightness.

Dearest Brother,
You find me in the garden under the old sycamore with Tiger on my lap. He often sleeps on your bed; you'll have to oust him when you come home, he's made quite a nest there!

Aunt Hannah has just arrived from Holyhead and I am reminded of happier times. I should of course be revising, but that can wait.

Do you remember the antics you and Aubrey got up to when we stayed at Hannah's in Turkey Shore Road? We ran quite wild in those days. There was the time when you unwound the rope from the mail boat and trapped it between the buffers of the mail train. We watched as the mail boat huffed and puffed but couldn't budge. When Hannah read the headlines next morning, 'Prank Holds Up Mail Boat, Perpetrators Must Pay,' you both went chalk white. I'm sure Hannah knew, but nothing was said.

I'm impressed by your darning skills, by the way, I would never have guessed. Mam has already sent a new supply of socks and she hopes you won't have to march the next lot to shreds.

You'll be pleased to know I hope to do well enough in the exams for a College scholarship next year. You should be back by then, and the three of us will be studying at the same time! Mam would be in seventh heaven to have us all home again, and Tada too, of course.

It seems amazing to me that you and Tada managed to meet up for lunch. How is he? I mean really? Mam is convinced that he doesn't take leave when it is due, and we worry about him overdoing it.

Bangor is much the same, except for the arrival of Belgian refugees, poor things, mostly trades people. They speak Flemish to each other but can also speak French. Beautiful lace collars can be found in the better haberdasheries, as the women are lace makers.

What else can I tell you? Well, there's talk of women being drafted into all sorts of war work and in London there are already women replacing policemen. 'Copperettes' the papers call them. Mrs Pankhurst is working on a war-scheme so that women can become useful in lots of ways, not just as nurses. I wonder what I would do if I were old enough? I think I'd quite like to drive a tram!

It was a long time since she'd regaled him with details of the Lloyd George meeting, and he'd told her to be more guarded in her opinions. If he were at home, they would talk about the *Lusitania* being torpedoed, but it was probably sensitive information and anyway, she didn't want to burden him with her feelings when he was facing danger.

It had felt like other people's tragedy, until yesterday, when an old fisherman friend of Tada's had called in to speak to Mam. He'd found the body of a little girl that he'd managed to lift aboard. He wouldn't profit from grief by taking a reward from Mr Cunard; it was enough to know she would have a decent burial.

It would have taken eighteen minutes for the ship to go under, according to the papers, and this preyed on her imagination. It wasn't a topic to share with someone at the Front.

She was bursting to tell him about the Women's International Peace Congress in The Hague, and the government's shenanigans preventing most of the British women attending. The North Sea was closed to shipping so delegates couldn't reach Holland, Madame Duchamp had told them. Bronwyn had wanted to know more, but Madame changed the subject. After the lesson she said, 'I'll bring you the Congress report next term, Bronwyn, I see you care about such things. We need more young women like you.'

A search through newspapers at the library turned up the gleeful headline, 'Peacettes stranded at Dover,' then some weeks later a small piece in the *Chronicle* conceded that three British women had attended, having travelled earlier to The Hague. Who were they? She'd give her eyeteeth to have been there. One day, maybe.

She picked up her pen to continue the letter to Glyn, but Hannah was already beside her, draped in a long apron.

'Time to take a break, my dear, your mother needs you to taste the fruit cake mixture.'

Bronwyn smiled, putting away her books and papers and tipping Tiger off her knee. 'I don't really deserve it, I've been writing to Glyn, but don't tell Mam.'

Hannah chucked her under the chin, and she giggled like a ten year-old.

The house was quiet as summer dragged. Huw couldn't wait to start College and spent days in the library. He was in agonies about signing up, but Glyn told him he should delay as long as possible.

Bronwyn wrote in what she called her reporter's journal; *The air crackles with events that don't quite touch me.* She filled a scrapbook with cuttings and notes on the war, for *Snapshots at the Home Front,* an idea she'd had for the Methodist Magazine.

There was no shortage of material. An old friend of Tada's had talked about Welsh soldiers training in camps near Liverpool, banned from speaking Welsh. 'They mock anyone who isn't Church of England, you'd think we were foreigners,' he'd said.

She'd noted British losses on the anniversary of the war: seventy-six thousand killed, two-hundred-and-fifty-two thousand wounded and fifty-five thousand missing. This last figure was troubling. How could so many go unaccounted for? It was more than the population of the whole of Anglesey. Looked at another way it meant fifty-five thousand families caught between unreasoning hope and likely despair.

The Defence of the Realm Act created absurdities in its attempts to regulate visible lighting, and it amused her to collect these snippets. A Mr Williams, cycling late one evening was told to light up, arriving at Talybont was instructed to extinguish, and when he got to Bangor was told to light up again. The hapless man was fined five shillings, whereas David Lloyd George, stopped because his car lights were too bright, drove away unscathed.

CHAPTER 5

Autumn 1915

Today was the first day of the last year in school and she couldn't wait to join the hubbub. The first lesson was French and Bronwyn wondered if Madame would bring the Congress report.

'*Bonjour, mes filles*,' she said, sweeping in.

They stood, waiting for her to sit gracefully. Her dark skin glowed against a simple black dress, cinched with a bold white belt.

'*Asseyez-vous*,' Madame said smiling, 'I'm delighted to see you again.' She had on her desk a small pile of booklets in brown-paper jackets.

Nobody dared ask how she'd spent the summer, but they had pet theories. In the arms of her lover, Edith suggested, or shunning company as she waited for news of a husband, missing in action.

Bronwyn had other ideas. She'd be with like-minded women fighting in the cause of peace.

'Today, ladies, we'll study a text in three languages, yes, that's right. English, French and German. We're fortunate to have Claudia with us to read in German.

'Who knows, one of you may work as an interpreter one day. I met such a woman this summer, Miss Kathleen Courtney, official interpreter to the Congress we are about to discuss.' She handed out the booklets.

So, thought Bronwyn, Madame has decided to show us all the report. She examined her disappointment. It had been flattering to be singled out and now the whole class was involved. Which was right, as the more of us who know the better. And how clever to discuss the ideas under cover of a translation exercise.

'We'll start on page 4, Women and War. Bronwyn, please read the English.'

Bronwyn read, *We women, in International Congress assembled, protest against the madness and the horror of war, involving as it does a reckless sacrifice of human life and the destruction of so much that humanity through centuries has laboured to build up.* A lump in her throat made it impossible to continue.

'Thank you,' said Madame, rescuing her. 'Now Edith, please read the same passage in French. It's on the next page.'

Edith obliged, then asked, 'Madame, was the Congress held by pacifists?'

Madame leaned on the desk and looked hard at Edith. 'Yes, dear, in order to shorten the war. It may surprise you to know that envoys have already visited twelve countries, from London to Petrograd. I was fortunate to hear Miss Courtney speak at a study group in Oxford, where I obtained copies of the report.

'Claudia, perhaps would read us the same thing in German? There were twenty-eight women from Germany who braved officialdom to attend.'

Claudia read the text in her high-pitched voice, the first time they'd heard her speak her father's tongue.

A fly buzzed against the window as they listened. It was almost subversion, thought Bronwyn, to allow German to be read aloud. Particularly after Miss Hobson had decreed singing Brahms' German Requiem would be in bad taste.

A hand went up. 'Were there no arguments amongst the women?' Pippa asked.

'No, only healthy debate on how to bring warring nations to the table. American women played an important part in this, as did those from other neutral countries.'

She stood and walked up and down in front of the blackboard. 'You are of an age to consider these matters, which affects the lives of young men and women everywhere. You will go into the world and have a chance to make your mark. As a journalist perhaps,' she glanced at Bronwyn, 'or a teacher, who knows? There is great talent amongst you.'

'Or a farmer's wife,' Pippa said under her breath, causing a titter on the back row.

Bronwyn stared at a square of blue sky in the high window and felt her world expand.

Madame ignored Pippa and picked up a piece of chalk. 'People worldwide sent greetings, from Bulgaria, Iceland,

Portugal, Poland and Turkey. Can you call these countries out in French?'

Claudia suggested, *Islande*, and Bronwyn knew *Pologne*, birthplace of Chopin. Madame wrote them up in her neat curly handwriting, listing the others below.

I know nothing of these places, thought Bronwyn. I must research. 'Did the envoys have any success?'

'They had a surprisingly warm reception. One minister said the most important thing was to educate children about militarism; another was surprised women had remained silent for so long. However, some objected that talking of peace smacked of weakness, that war must be judged on the original causes. The envoys reasoned that we are getting further away from the causes every day. War has its own momentum.'

Claudia raised her wide pale eyes. 'How can anyone know the truth, Madame?'

'Use your intelligence to decide between right and wrong. Test your views by speaking out, you have more power than you imagine. Over a thousand women from a dozen countries gathered in The Hague to change the course of the war. An inspiration, is it not?'

Not to everyone: Pippa yawned noisily from behind the report. She'd been friendlier since the incident with Claudia, until one day, walking home from school; they'd passed a gang of German prisoners mending the road. Pippa said, 'They should go with Bron, she likes Germans,' and glanced slyly, to see the effect.

Bronwyn chose to ignore the double insult.

Curled up on her bed to read Glyn's latest letter, she unfolded the sheets of fine-lined paper and something fell out. It was a French five-franc note. She read on.

*

9th *Royal Welsh Fusiliers,*
British Expeditionary Force,
France,
1st *September 1915*

My Dear Bron,
Thank you so much for the parcel, which arrived on Saturday. The honey
had a quarrel with the cake but nobody minded. Picture us as we sat
round our impromptu table, a door balanced across two beer barrels.
There, we feasted by candlelight with two whisky bottles serving as
candlesticks. This is our 'Officers' Mess', in an old farmhouse kitchen,
now gaping with holes. We've done what we can with sandbags and our
engineers have patched up the roof a treat.

This morning we're sheltering from a barrage of shells, crouched in
the corner of a field. It's a lot safer in the open than being holed up in
billets. All hell let loose at 4am, when we had to run outside, and now it's
8.30am and still going. My head's thumping from the raucous bark of
the eighteen pounder in concert with the booming Lizzie and Annie guns.
We're several hundred yards behind the firing line in Brigade Reserve, so
not in any real danger.

I'm propped up on my elbows and can see a few stray green peas on
the hardened ground; perhaps this was a kitchen garden. I'll pop them in
the envelope and you can boast about my souvenirs. Yesterday I was
censoring letters, usually pretty tedious, when I came across a jolly account
of banter with the enemy: 'The Germans shouted, Hoch der Kaiser, and
we shouted back, B...r the Kaiser, and they answered, You are no
gentlemen.' A few months ago we'd have quelled this sort of caper, but
these days we let it go.

So, you're editing 'Handy Hints' for the Methodist Magazine,
congrats! I pen the occasional poem and would welcome your comments
one day. Writing, I find, stills the mind. I often think of you and Mam,
standing at the kitchen table, surrounded by swathes of brown paper
parcelling up the litany of requests from Aubrey and me. A propos, I'd
be glad of new shaving tackle (my razor's so blunt, the padre offered to
shave me with his cut-throat!), handkerchiefs (any colour), a lighter and
cigs. I'm down to Gold Flake, and stoking up a pipe takes an age.

I haven't forgotten your birthday, little Sis. Please buy yourself some
pretty thing with this five-franc note, perhaps flowers to trim your hat.
Remember the straw bonnets I used to concoct for your dolls? And

suddenly you're nearly seventeen. By the way, you can exchange the money at the bank.

Well, it's gone quiet at last, Fritz preparing breakfast, I expect. Time to scuttle back to billets and eat. Just to let you know, my company, regarded as the smartest in the Brigade, has a very special job to do soon. So don't be alarmed if you don't hear from me for a while. Some of the men are still green, but with my sturdy Sergeant W from Tregarth at my side, I know we'll come through with flying colours.
My love to you and Mam,
Glyn

A sigh escaped her, as she realised he'd be on the front line again.

It was hard to summon up the girl she was a year ago when flowers for her hat would have been fun. She gazed out of the window at the sycamore tree where she'd dreamt of Paris and realised that girl had gone. She'd become dull and earnest, swotting for exams.

Since the war there was so much to do: keeping the Book Room going, helping Mam send off parcels, as well as everyday chores. At least Huw was home now he'd started College and could give a hand with heavier tasks.

The five-franc note lay invitingly on the desk and she had a yearning for a box of fine notepaper. The thick and creamy variety, as luxurious to the touch as a pillowcase of Egyptian cotton. She'd have to treat herself right away or end up buying something more sensible.

Picking up the money she rushed downstairs. Mam was in the kitchen rolling pastry and looked up expectantly.

'How's Glyn? Does he need anything?'

'Cigarettes and a razor, oh yes, handkerchiefs, he doesn't mind what colour.'

'He's well?'

'Yes, he's fine; I'll show you the letter. Apparently they're expecting to be on a special job, so he won't be able to write for a while. He sounded quite chirpy about it.' She spoke casually, so Mam wouldn't worry unduly.

'He sent me five francs for my birthday. I'm off to the bank. I'll buy what he needs in town.'

Mam put the rolling pin to one side. 'We'd better send the parcel off today so he gets it in time,' she said quietly.

A jolt of anxiety passed between them, like lightning before a storm.

How selfish to be thinking about birthday presents when Glyn was back in the trenches. It was clear there could be no birthday celebrations, not until they knew he was safe.

When three letters arrived together, Bronwyn's heart soared.

Mam opened hers first; he said he was safe and well. The other two were addressed to herself, dated in quick succession. She took them to the Book Room, in case there was anything she wouldn't want Mam to read.

9th R.W.F.
B.E.F. France,
14th September 1915

Dear Bron,
Thank you so much for the pink cowry shell you saved from Llanddona beach. It reminds me of our day together and I promise to keep it with me at all times.

I'm writing from a village quite close to the firing line. We take our place in the trenches in a couple of days. At present we're bivouacking in a wet ditch and haven't had a change of clothing for ages. You know how I love camping!

I say village, but it's more like a ghost town. There's not a house standing and the people have long since fled. Imagine a town like Beaumaris razed to the ground, the streets littered with pots and pans, beds, sewing machines, bicycles, papers and books as well as household furniture of every description. The roads are pitted with shell-holes like small craters. And the church! It's just four tumbledown walls amongst a wreckage of tombstones. Every single tombstone is smashed. The worst thing is seeing bodies raised from the dead, scattered about the churchyard like poor abandoned scarecrows. Yesterday, I passed a lidless coffin that was a crock of bones. Shame overwhelmed me, how have we come to this? A life-size figure of Christ on a cross is the only thing that remains untouched. Sorry to be so graphic, but the reality is grim.

The guns rumble sporadically, saving themselves for the show to come. By tonight we should be out of this ditch and bedded down in the church vaults where the men are preparing a dugout. I'll be keeping company with an entombed medieval bishop, fitting for a son of the manse, don't you think? I'm sure Tada would approve.

The light is fading fast, dear Bron, and I must get some rest before things start to pop. Keep writing!
Your loving brother,
Glyn

9th R.W.F.
B.E.F. France,
16th September 1915

My Dear Sister,
I believe the above date is correct, but the last few days have been so chaotic, I really can't remember. Anyhow, it's Thursday and we've moved forward into the support trenches. I've got a rotten dugout. We share it with hundreds of frogs, peeping out of the sandbags from every nook and cranny. It's also unpleasantly close to the Officers' latrines, a pet target of German snipers, they put an 18 pounder plumb in the centre of it the other day.

Only breakfast will cure my mood. I can smell the bacon, we get three rashers, a fried egg, half a loaf of bread and a tin of jam, all piled up on a tin plate and washed down by a mug of tea. Splendid! Finer fodder than we get at home, say the lads from the valleys. Small wonder they are fattening up.

Today's task is to prowl around the sapheads, which are trenches we use for picking up enemy intelligence. Sometimes we get fed up in these shallow, narrow windings and run around on top, which isn't too bad as this part of the line is comparatively free of corpses. I've learned to control my stomach, but will never overcome my horror of the stench. Dodging bombs is surprisingly easy, when you can see them coming. One of the sentries shouts, coming over Right, or Left, and we clear into dugouts. At first you see a heavy puff of smoke, then the bomb, which looks like a champagne bottle, turning over and over as it flies.

Early this morning, men from another platoon got blocked at a corner of the trench when a bomb exploded under one of them. The poor fellow's foot was blown off at the ankle and his leg broken in several

places. We heard he died twenty minutes later. After that, we were more
on the alert.

You asked me if I'm afraid. After a few months you get used to the
drip, drip of danger, though under sustained attack, fear brings a terrible
thirst.

Grub's up, must fly. Will write again after we've taken our turn in
the line. We haven't had yesterday's mail yet, so can't reply to your latest.
Sleep tight, dear Bron.
Best love to you both,
Glyn

She put the letters aside and felt icy, and got up for her coat.

The door opened. It was Huw. 'Just popped in to see to
the accounts.' He peered at her. 'Are you alright, Bron? You
look terrible.'

'No, not really. It's Glyn, what he's going through, it's too
awful.'

'There, there old girl,' he led her back to the chair. 'Sit
down, I'll get you a glass of water, you've had a nasty turn.'

He was so grown up about it she didn't feel embarrassed,
and allowed him to fuss over her while she blew her nose into
his handkerchief.

'So what's this all about then? Has he been having a rough
do out there?'

She handed him the letters. 'You can read them. I just don't
want Mam to know.'

He sat beside her and read with deliberation, placing each
sheet on the table. 'Poor old Glyn,' he said looking up. 'And
poor you.' He reached over and gave her hand a squeeze.

'Before he left, he asked me if he could write and get
things off his chest. I don't know if I can face much more. It's
all happening so far away and there's nothing I can do. I don't
want to let him down.'

'I wish he'd felt able to confide in me,' Huw said, looking
crestfallen. 'Or else Aubrey or his friend Gethin. They're all in
it together.'

'He does write to Gethin, he told me so, and I'm sure he
talks to Aubrey when they see each other. He probably doesn't
want to frighten you in case you end up there.'

46

'Well, you can talk to me anytime; you know that? And for what it's worth, I'd say he's holding up quite well. Doesn't sound too bad at all. I'll be glad to know that he's clear of it, I must admit,' he said, pushing his glasses back up his nose.

'Thanks, Huw,' she said, with a wan smile. 'It makes all the difference, being able to talk. You're so sensible.'

There was barely a year between them, and as children Huw wasn't like an older brother; she was seeing him in a new light.

Huw gathered the pages of the letter into a neat pile and handed them back. 'You can put this away and stop worrying because Doctor Huw says you need cheering up. They're showing Charlie Chaplin at the Picturedrome at the moment. Do you fancy going?'

'The perfect tonic. And I still haven't bought a box of notepaper with the money Glyn sent me. Maybe you could help me choose?'

He smiled. 'Shopping as well? Now you're taking advantage!'

It was almost three weeks before they heard from him again. As usual he wrote to Mam, to say he'd come through and was resting behind the lines. The following day a letter for Bronwyn arrived; she took it upstairs and schooled herself not to think the worst. He'd come out alive, and however awful it was, she could share it with Huw.

She opened the letter at her desk; it was longer than usual, and judging from his handwriting, written in haste. She breathed deeply and heard his voice as she read.

9th R.W.F.
B.E.F. France,
11th October 1915

Dearest Bron,
This is the first moment I've had to put pen to paper since the battle. We are now out of range of shellfire for the first time in 40 days. What a blessed relief. The going's been tough and we've lost countless men. I hardly know where to start. Remember our outing in Anglesey, over a

year ago now, when I promised to tell you the truth about everything? I hope you'll forgive me if I do.

On September 24th, we received orders to move up the fire trench by 3am next day. At 1.30 I woke up my servant to sew a button onto my breeches. In the hurry and scurry he made a poor job of it and it popped off as soon as I bent over, so I went into battle in great danger of my breeches falling to my knees! I soon heard my Sergeant bellowing, What are we lads, the Quick or the Dead? The Quick Sarge! Came the reply, followed by a stream of invective, which translates loosely as, get your skates on or else.

We arrived at 3am on the dot and the men were very cheery. The firing bays were already choc-a-bloc so we had to stay in the communication trench. The attack was supposed to come at 4am. Nothing happened, and we were getting ready to go home again, when a sheaf of rockets went up at 5.50. This is the Brigade signal for the attack.

We were sitting ducks in the communication trench, unable to return fire. Three minutes after the attack was launched the Germans turned their heavy guns onto our parapet and rained down 8 inch shells. We could move neither forwards nor backwards.

We heard the hiss and whirr of every missile going, and saw columns of seething dust and smoke. The terrific noise and spray of it all was like a ferocious sea hurling itself against a rocky shore. Vindictive bursts of shrapnel tore through the air and all but finished me off. My mackintosh, which I wore rolled on my back, was riddled with the stuff.

Then the wounded began to push their way back, stumbling in the half-light. Sergeant W had his arm blown off and two of my lance corporals caught it badly. One from Bangor came down the trench holding the fragments of his left hand, shouting, Stick it the Welsh! Stick it, boys bach! And refused to have his wounds dressed, giving way to other men. He was one of the heroes that day. Heroes were legion.

My job was to lead the men to the firing line to replace the fallen. The men were retiring rather too far and my remaining Sergeant was a great help in rallying them. As we moved forward, I saw a man lying facedown in the trench. You could see half his back had been torn away and there was flesh and blood everywhere. Somehow I was able to step over him and the men followed behind me. I know how gruesome this is, but I need to put on record the hideousness of it all.

When we finally got to the fire-trench, I put my men into bays and went to see if there were any further orders. When I returned, I found that a heavy shell had landed on our parapet and buried about a dozen men of my two platoons. One little lad had half his leg blown off and a huge piece of shrapnel lodged in the ankle of his other foot. I eased his pain with morphine, but he died an hour later. Some were unrecognizable. An identity disc was all that remained of one, and the pay-book of another. The sight was terrible. Hands and feet lay amidst the debris, the parapet and parados were spattered with blood and fragments of flesh, and here and there a bone dripped with blood. But for the hands and feet it was like a slaughterhouse.

They shelled us for about six and a half hours, and then all was quiet. At three that afternoon another regiment relieved us. As we filed down the communication trenches there were dead everywhere, for the most part covered with blankets, but not all.

In another part of the trench we found the remains of what that morning, had been a platoon of the 9th Welsh. Headless and armless they lay, their skin turned a sickly grey-white. I could not step over them and had to go round, though it meant showing myself to the enemy.

At last I reached the reserve trenches and called the roll of my platoon, the hardest task of all. No. 9 Platoon was there too. There were only ten of them left and twenty of mine—well over half were dead.

As I finished the roll call I heard an explosion. Not ten yards away, I saw a young boy drop. A bomb he was carrying in his waistcoat somehow burst and he was killed.

All that night wounded men kept crawling back in a jagged line of despair. There was a moment of hope, when an Officer appeared. He was a terrible sight, dripping wet and covered with mud, hatless, coatless, and with wide staring eyes. He said he'd hidden all day with two men and an Officer, all wounded, in a shell-hole so shallow they'd had to dig themselves in with an entrenching tool, as the slightest movement attracted machine-gun fire. They survived four grenades and that night he'd brought them all in.

On September 30th we moved back four miles and thought we were going to get a jolly good rest. It was not to be. The next day we were moved again to another part of the line where the Welsh and ourselves held a supporting position. We left there on October 7th and are now in rest billets out of the range of guns, but not out of sound. There is still a vigorous bombardment going on.

Captain E's nerves were completely shattered by the explosion of a shell and I am now second in command of the company.

This letter has been rather an effort I'm afraid, so that's enough for today.
Love as always,
Glyn

She forced herself to read the letter twice, before putting it away in the tin box where she kept his letters in order, and put the box inside the desk drawer.

Huw was visiting a friend, so she couldn't speak to him yet. Meanwhile, the letter's contents roiled around in her stomach like a badly digested meal. She could feel a sick headache starting at her temples and knew she had to get out.

It was quiet downstairs as she pulled on her coat and remembered that Mam must be at the quilting circle. She left a scribbled note on the kitchen table to say she was visiting Maddy.

It started raining and she hadn't thought to bring an umbrella. Too bad if I turn up like a drowned rat, she thought, and pulled up her collar. She let her guard slip for a moment and her mind drifted back to Glyn's letter, bringing on another wave of nausea. Enough, she told herself. Tada would have said: *Sufficient unto the day is the evil thereof.* She clung to the words like a lifebelt, until she reached Maddy's door.

Thankfully, it was Maddy who let her in.

Maddy took one look and said, 'My God, Bron, you look deathly. What's the matter?'

'It's Glyn.'

'Wounded?'

'No, no, it's what he's been through, his letter, it's appalling. So many dead. Most of his platoon.'

'Well, thank heavens he's all right. Now come through into the kitchen and let's sort you out. You're in a terrible state.'

Maddy took away her sodden coat and brought out a blanket. 'Wrap yourself in this while I warm some milk. We'll have you right in no time.'

'Thanks, Maddy, you're the best pal ever.'

It was Saturday morning and Huw came in with the *North Wales Chronicle*.

'Look at this, Bron. Isn't this your French teacher?' He spread the paper on the table.

Bronwyn pushed aside a plate of buttered toast and read, *Teacher accused of subversion, furore in local school*.

'That can't be,' she said, heart pounding, trying to piece together the facts. 'Miss Hobson said Madame was away attending to private business.'

'Boiled eggs, Huw?' Mam asked from across the kitchen.

'Please, and a slice of your loaf if it's not too fresh to cut.'

'Yes, dear, when I've made Bron's toast.' She held a slice on the end of a toasting fork at the roaring stove.

'This is ridiculous, I was there and it's complete rubbish,' said Bronwyn, reading aloud: *French teacher Madame Duchamp at Bangor County School for Girls, stands accused of promoting the discredited Women's Peace Congress, to subvert young minds in the schoolroom. An extraordinary meeting to investigate the complaint will be held by governors next week. A spokesman said teachers should exemplify the highest moral standards and keep to the curriculum.*

Mam brought over the toast and said, 'She seemed such a pleasant young woman when we bumped into her at the market. You didn't tell me she was a pacifist.'

Huw said, 'A refreshing change from the tub thumping we got at Kingswood.'

Mam frowned, 'A teacher shouldn't go preaching against the war.'

'Mam, it wasn't like that. She brought in the Congress report and we read it in English, French and German, that's all.'

'Why's she teaching German in a French class?' Mam looked confused.

'She wasn't. We compared texts, looked at the translations and discussed.' Mam would get the wrong end of the stick.

'I see, dear. The governors will deal with whatever the lady has done, I'm sure.'

'One of the girls must have reported her,' said Huw, 'what happened, exactly?'

'I think I know who it is.' It could only be Pippa, out to punish Madame after the incident with Claudia. Edith was thoughtless, but not devious, it wouldn't be her. 'Claudia, the German girl, asked how can we know the truth, and Madame said we must use our intelligence to make up our minds. I hate the half-truths peddled by the papers.'

Huw and Mam exchanged a look.

'You shouldn't get mixed up, I don't want you getting into trouble,' Mam said, patting her shoulder.

'What do you mean, Mam?' her voice rose.

'Think of your reputation, you can be very impulsive.'

'If it was Huw or Glyn, you wouldn't say that, it's because I'm a girl!'

Filled with indignation, she flicked through the newspaper. Writing to the Magazine was pointless, as it wouldn't get past the editor. Then it came to her; she must write to the *North Wales Chronicle*. She reached for the jam and loaded her toast with strawberries.

'You've gone quiet,' said Huw.

'I'm going to write to the *Chronicle* and put matters straight.'

'Not if you want to go to College, young lady,' said Mam, looking daggers across the kitchen with piercing black eyes. 'You'll ruin your chances of a scholarship.'

'If they deny me the scholarship for speaking out, I'll be a volunteer like most girls of my age.' She was fed up with Mam reining her in.

Huw scratched his head and said, 'Shall I get the egg-cups?'

'They're not ready yet. You tell her, Huw.'

'Madame told us to think for ourselves, which is exactly what I'll be doing at College,' Bronwyn said through a mouthful of toast.

Huw smiled, 'If you're going to rock the boat, you'll have to come top in exams to be sure of a scholarship.'

Mam shook her head and lifted boiled eggs onto a plate with a spoon. 'I wish your father were here.'

If she wrote to the *Chronicle* using a false name it would keep her out of the limelight, but that would also be wrong, as she was prepared to accept the consequences of her actions.

'I wish he were here too,' said Bronwyn. 'Tada would know what to say.'

CHAPTER 6

1916

When Tada arrived at the beginning of January, Bronwyn and Mam had been expecting him for days. They were in the sitting room, wading through the mending pile, and he walked straight into the hall calling out, 'I'm home dearest.'

Mam threw her darning aside, leapt to her feet and almost ran out of the room to greet him.

Bronwyn was left sitting on the edge of her seat, and held back from running after them. She could hear the murmur of their voices blend like threads, the warp and weft of the seamless cloth that was their lifetime together, and knew the moment was theirs.

When at last her parents came in, Tada with hands aloft to embrace her, she allowed herself to be enveloped by the familiar male scent of tobacco, comforted by the rough surface of his greatcoat under her cheek.

It was a brief visit, Tada said, but like a bright star on a dark night, he filled the house with joy.

Tada was in good spirits and gave them news of Glyn and Aubrey over tea.

'We met up after Christmas in the Officers' Mess when the boys were resting behind the lines. We dined on a hotchpotch menu of gravy soup, jugged hare, sardines on toast and jam-roll pudding.' He winked at Mam, 'Not up to your standards, my dear.'

'Are they safe, at least for the time being?' Bronwyn asked.

A shadow passed over Tada's face. 'Nowhere is safe, but it's a lot quieter behind the lines. They're in God's hands, Bron, and we should pray for them.'

Over the next few days, Bronwyn tried to catch Tada alone, when he wasn't doing Book Room business or household accounts. One morning, she found him reading war reports, and decided this was the moment. 'How much truth is there in the papers, Tada? Is it a different story out there?'

He looked at her over his glasses. 'If they printed half of what actually goes on, there'd be riots at home. The country lacks leadership, and in my view, we've lost our way. It's high time the war was ended.'

She'd never heard Tada speak so frankly. 'Do you mean a truce? What about Belgium?'

'Belgium would have to be restored, of course. At present, all we're doing is pushing the line forward a few hundred yards, and a year later we're back where we started. And at what cost? One young man told me that it isn't death he fears, so much as the long drawn out expectation of it; and the sight of other fine fellows being killed, though his exact words are unrepeatable. You get the point.'

She nodded. 'You don't surprise me. I've had a glimpse in Glyn's letters.'

'Quite so. He did well to come through Loos unscathed.'

'Tada, if I were a few years older I'd write articles about real people's lives and show how the war affects us here, even in far flung Bangor.' She'd been cherishing the idea for a while and hoped Tada might encourage her.

Tada took off his glasses and smiled. 'I think you'd make a fine job of it, young lady. Why not write something for the Methodist Magazine and I'll have a word with the editor? Vignettes from the Home Front, that sort of thing.'

She kissed his forehead. 'Thank you, Tada, I will. I've already got some ideas.'

'So I gather. Thanks for sending me your letter to the *Chronicle*, I was impressed.'

'I'm glad you approve. Mam was worried I'd get into trouble.'

He winked, 'And did you?'

She drew her feet up under her skirt and hugged her knees. 'Nobody mentioned it, except Madame. She was back at school by the time it was published and thanked me in front of the class.' Pippa, she remembered, was unusually quiet.

Tada nodded. 'You have the makings of a fine writer, my dear, and getting into a spot of bother for your beliefs is no bad thing.'

His visit was all too brief, and Bronwyn woke to heavy rain on the morning he was due to leave; she missed him already and dreaded the dark evenings that stretched ahead.

As Tada stepped into the cab, he said, 'Post me your articles, Bron, I'll send corrections.'

He'd insisted on going to the station alone to cause the least fuss.

As the cab pulled away, Bronwyn stood shivering under the umbrella with Mam, and they waved him off with their handkerchiefs, waving higher and faster as the cab got smaller, dry-eyed until it turned the corner.

One bright Sunday afternoon, Bronwyn walked with Mam down to the pier, and passed a line of invalid carriages in the charge of nurses, perambulating in the salt air.

'I've never seen so many wounded men,' said Mam. 'They're having to open an overflow ward at College, in the Pritchard Jones Hall.'

Bronwyn nodded. 'They'll be putting up tents next, if the war drags. Do you think those girls are volunteers?' she said, looking at the nurses in a variety of self-styled uniforms. 'I sometimes think of it.'

'You've enough on your plate with school and the Magazine.'

'You're right,' she said, reserving judgement.

As they leant on the rail and looked onto the Straits, Bronwyn asked, 'Remember our shrimping trips when we were little?'

'Ah, yes, when Huw and Glyn would vie over the best rock pools.'

'And we'd bring home the catch in the white enamel bucket, I wonder where that went?'

'I gave it to the rag and bone man when he came collecting scrap for the war effort,' Mam said, holding onto her little black hat in the breeze.

They walked back arm in arm, and Bronwyn mulled over the changes she'd seen in the town. Horse-drawn vehicles had all but disappeared as horses had been pressed into war service; the singing in Chapel was high and thin now the pews were denuded of men.

She looked up to see two boys playing in the street, one crouching behind a lamppost and pointing a piece of driftwood in the shape of a gun at his playmate.

'How's school?' Mam asked. 'I expect some of the girls are wondering what to do next year.'

'One or two are going to be volunteers and Claudia wants to train as a nurse. Pippa's lot will stay at home and help until the war's over. Waiting in the wings of marriage, as Maddy puts it.'

At school Bron was known as the brain-box, which she didn't mind, but was hurt at sniggering in the changing rooms when they'd called her 'the spinster'. Maddy, however, was an enigma as they considered her far too pretty to be brainy.

'You could fall in love sooner than you think, Bron. I'd like to see you get a good education first. Girls in my day didn't have the same opportunities.'

'I know, Mam. I'm not likely to run off with a boy, most of them are too short for me anyway.'

The idea made them laugh as they briskly walked home up the hill.

As Bronwyn stepped into the porch to pick up the post, she felt an arctic blast under the front door. Holding onto her cardigan, she stooped to pick up the letters, hoping against hope to find one from Glyn. Her heart leapt when she saw his writing on an envelope addressed to her. She took the letters into the kitchen, placed them on the table and put on the kettle. This way she could eke out the anticipation or postpone the disappointment, whichever it was to be.

Unable to contain herself any longer, she tore open Glyn's letter and thought, please God, let it be the one where he says he's coming home.

*

57

9th R.W.F.
B.E.F. France
April 10th 1916

Dearest Bron,
I've been granted leave! I depart next week and transport permitting, I will be home for Easter.

My servant Evans spent all afternoon boiling vats of water for the deepest hottest bath. I lay soaking up to my neck in Madame's kitchen while he ironed my uniform and reported on fleas popping as he pressed the seams. By the time he'd finished it was like new, buttons gleaming, hanging on the clotheshorse by the fire. I took one look in the mirror, it had been a while, and decided it was time to give up on the moustache.

When I appeared in the Officers' Mess, a cheer went up and there was much taunting about Madame scrubbing my back, you get the gist! I brazened it out and felt myself blushing to the roots, until I was rescued by an older man, a visiting Major, who handed me a whisky and raised his glass and said, iechyd da.

He started telling me about his son.

About my age, he said, a gunner in the Lancashires. He'd only been out for a few months when gunners killed him from his own side while out on patrol with a grenadier. His lad was blown away, while the grenadier escaped scot-free.

As he spoke about his son in clipped English tones, I saw grief etched into the crag-lines of his face and felt the pain of a father losing a child. Listening to him was harder than writing a letter to a bereaved family. I thought of Herodotus when he wrote: 'Instead of sons burying fathers, fathers bury their sons.'

I went to bed early feeling rather sombre, and you find me now, under the 'rough male kiss of blankets' as the poet said, reviewing the day. The last thing I heard was the men singing a lullaby:

> *'Sing me to sleep where bullets fall,*
> *Let me forget this war and all.*
> *Damp is my dug-out, cold my feet,*
> *Nothing but bully and biscuits to eat.*
> *Sing me to sleep where bombs explode*
> *And shrapnel shells are à la mode.*
> *Over the sandbags helmets you find,*

Corpses in front of you, corpses behind.
Far, far from Loos I long to be,
Where German snipers can't pot at me.
Think of me crouching where the worms creep,
Waiting for someone to sing me to sleep.'

Which pretty well sums it up.

Thank you dear Bron, for helping me to keep my spirit alive over the past months.

Not long now. Tell Mam she only needs to bake for me, not for England!
Love,
Glyn

The kettle was whistling its head off by the time she lifted it from the hob. She was in a daze, with no thought of tea. Reading the song had left her hollow; she read it again and heard the men's mocking tones, wringing from it the last drop of dark humour. As Tada had said, the trenches were a living hell, and death, when it came, was sweet as a lullaby. She shuddered, and came to herself.

Only a week to Easter, and Glyn would already be on his way, heavens, she must tell Mam. She rushed upstairs to find Mam changing Glyn's bed.

'Glyn's coming home,' she said waving the letter.

Mam stood arms akimbo, surrounded by pillows, blankets and an eiderdown. She liked to keep the boys' mattresses aired and the beds made up in case they came home unexpectedly.

'When's he coming?' she asked, securing a mesh of silvering hair.

'Easter! That's all he says. He'll be home by Easter.'

Mam consulted her watch, and laughed at her own confusion. 'Goodness, we haven't got long. I'll put the warming pan in his bed. He could be back any time.'

'I think that could wait a day or two. Let me finish off the bed, and then I'll help with the cooking. Glyn sends his love and says don't bake for a battalion, or words to that effect.'

Bronwyn saw girlish pleasure in Mam's smile.

Glyn had sent a telegram announcing his arrival in the evening, so Bronwyn and Mam weren't expecting him when he appeared, and stood larger than life in the kitchen doorway. Bronwyn looked up from the table where they stood, both up to their elbows in flour. Her first thought was that he must have slipped in through the front door.

'I caught an earlier train,' he said half apologetically, 'thought I'd surprise you.'

'Goodness, what a fright I must look,' said Mam, laughing and flapping her powdery hands. 'Come here, young man and let me look at you!'

Bronwyn tore off her apron and ran towards him. 'Glyn!' she threw her arms round him and he held her in a brotherly hug. 'You've filled out,' she said, preventing herself from crying. She felt his frame, square and sturdy under his khakis.

His arms slackened and he stood back. 'Good to see you, Sis,' he said in his soft-spoken way.

He turned to Mam. Bending to kiss her, he said, 'I've missed your baking, Mam. It's the sweetest in Christendom.'

Bronwyn looked on as Mam stroked Glyn's face leaving traces of flour on his stubbled chin. She loosened his tie. 'Let's get you out of this and Bron will run you a bath.'

'There's no rush, Mam. I'm not going anywhere. At least not for a few days.'

He looks different, thought Bronwyn. He'd lost the boyish contours of his face and grown manly.

There were exclamations from the hall and they all turned to the door.

'Glyn, it's you,' said Huw, rushing in.

Glyn clapped Huw on the shoulder and they shook lengthily, the way men do when they want to embrace.

'Good to see you, old man,' said Glyn.

'I saw your rucksack in the hall, I could hardly believe it.'

'Any news from Kingswood? Are you in touch?' Glyn asked.

'After a fashion, you must have heard.'

'The Williams brothers, I know. Wretched business. Must have knocked you for six. I was sorry to hear it.'

Bronwyn remembered Huw leaving the table in a hurry after reading about the deaths in the paper. The boys were the first in his year at school to be killed.

'College life suiting you?'

Huw looked bashful. 'Yes, though not for much longer. I'm signing up before they actually march me to barracks.'

'At least you should get a backroom job with your poor eyesight,' said Glyn, with concern. He was interrupted when the door burst open. It was Lizzie looking windswept, a basketful of sheets under one arm. She looked up, saw Glyn, then promptly dropped the basket with a scream of delight and blushed crimson as Glyn stepped towards her.

'Good to see you, Lizzie,' he said, lightly kissing her cheek.

Lizzie stood back to look him up and down. 'You don't look a bit like yourself, Mr Glyn. You look like a real soldier.'

They all laughed, including Lizzie, as Glyn helped her pick up the sheets from the upturned basket.

Tiger had followed Lizzie in, and now curled himself round Glyn's trouser leg. Glyn lifted the cat into his arms and rubbed his cheek against the marmalade fur. 'Bron tells me you've taken up residence on my bed, you old rascal.'

'He's missed you,' said Bronwyn, as the cat purred like a steam engine.

Glyn grinned. 'Cupboard love. We had a kitten as our mascot, once. She ate half our rations.'

'In the trenches?' Huw asked.

'That's right,' said Glyn, fondling Tiger's ears. 'We rescued her from a crater, a tiny black ball of fluff. We called her Fortuna.'

'What became of her?' Bronwyn asked.

'One day she just disappeared. I'd like to think she grew up to be a fine ratter.' He bent and with infinite gentleness, lowered the cat to the floor.

Bronwyn felt a surge of love for Glyn and longed to take him to the beach where they would talk and skim stones. But that was selfish. Mam and Huw needed him too, in their different ways. Poor Glyn, they all wanted a piece of him.

The following morning Bronwyn stood in front of the bathroom mirror, dragging a brush through her tangled mane.

She twisted it into a French pleat and clamped the whole thing under a tortoiseshell clasp. The effect was pleasing, making her look more like a young woman than a schoolgirl.

She went down to breakfast in the morning room, which was filled with sunlight and the smells of bacon, eggs and buttered toast.

'Morning, Bron,' said Glyn. 'You look splendid. I like the chignon.'

'Thanks,' she said, catching his eye.

It was good to see him looking more like his old self, in baggy corduroys and an open-necked shirt.

Mam stood up to pour the tea in a timeless ritual.

'Fine breakfast, Mam,' Glyn said, as she filled his cup. The rift caused when Glyn first enlisted had long since healed.

'It does me good to see you enjoying home-cooking, *Del*. Remember to try Hannah's strawberry jam, she sent it specially.'

'I will, don't worry, and I'll take a jar back. Do thank her for me.'

Huw looked over at Glyn and cleared his throat. 'What sort of breakfast do you get out there?' There was an edge to his question.

Glyn smiled. 'A fry-up, on a good day.'

'A bit like camping, I suppose.'

'It's pretty organised. We eat at the same time as Jerry. It's like clockwork. There's a dawn lull and a sort of breakfast truce, and you can see the smoke rise and curl above the trenches.'

As he spoke, Bronwyn was able to identify the changes in him: the dark circles round his eyes and the drum-tight skin across his cheekbones.

'To be honest, I'm dreading it,' said Huw, pushing his spectacles up his nose. 'I'm not cut out for soldiering.'

'It's a shame about conscription. I'd hoped at least one of us would stay at home,' said Glyn.

'Cousin Alwyn is objecting, you know. He's serving with the Field Ambulances.'

'A conchie? I'm sorry to hear that. I don't blame him in principle; it's a brave decision. They'll make him a stretcher bearer, heaven help him, and they don't last long.'

Huw looked taken aback.

Glyn put down his toast. 'Remember, no heroics. Just get by and get out as best you can.'

'Thanks, Glyn, that's exactly what I needed to hear.' His shoulders appeared less rounded and he gave a shy smile.

Mam sighed. 'This war has gone on far too long. My dearest wish is to have you all back.'

Glyn took her hand. 'I know, Mam. Sometimes we forget just how hard it is for you at home.'

Mam dabbed her eyes. 'How's Tada? You haven't told me.'

'He's well, I saw him a few weeks ago. I lorry-hopped over to Aubrey's billet and we had lunch. Tada seemed full of beans. You should hear the men talk, they think the world of him.'

She nodded. 'It's still too much for a man of his age.'

'It's what he does, Mam. You told us so when we were little, remember? Tada's away caring for his flock, you'd say, when he didn't come home.'

'So I did. You'd wait up for him to read you a story and nobody else would do.' Her eyes were still moist as she looked round the table at them all.

'What will you do this morning, my dears? It's a fine day for a brisk walk.'

Bronwyn tried to blot out thoughts of having Glyn to herself, as Huw would want to talk to him too—man to man.

'There's an essay I need to polish off,' Huw said. 'You two could go for a walk, and I'll take Glyn into College later, when I hand it in.'

Bless him; he must have seen the look on my face, thought Bronwyn.

'Aubrey wrote asking for spurs and leggings and two dozen kippers,' said Bronwyn, as they walked along the stony strand of the Straits.

'The kippers would be for the Officers' Mess table,' said Glyn. 'They share all the food parcels from home. And the riding gear is purely for pleasure. Aubrey says it's the perfect antidote to compiling reports for the Brigade.'

'It all sounds rather incongruous, under the circumstances.'

'Aubrey always has landed on his feet. He's in magnificent diggings, I can tell you. The army doesn't often come up with a chateau.'

'A chateau? With turrets and towers and four-poster beds? You're pulling my leg.'

'It's the genuine article, complete with moat. Tada was mightily amused. Aubrey showed us his room. He shares with the Adjutant. It used to be the Count's bedroom and there's even a billiards table.'

'Astonishing. How did you all arrange to meet? By carrier pigeon, I suppose.'

Glyn took off his cap and scratched his head. 'Not exactly, but there are ways and means. Aubrey had a telegraph sent to Tada, and Tada sent me a message via the padre. Simple really.'

They were heading towards Britannia Bridge and the gulls keened on the crystal air. 'It's another world out there,' Bronwyn said. 'Could you ever have imagined it?'

'No, never.'

She took his arm as they fell into step and the shale scrunched rhythmically underfoot. Across the water was Anglesey like a faraway dream, where they'd cycled a year and a half ago. She looked up at Glyn as a stranger might; a tweed cap shaded his fine profile, he was a tall attractive man. There was a toughness about him, as though he'd never quite taken off his uniform.

'About my letters,' Glyn said without preamble. 'Huw had a word with me. I'm sorry that I upset you. I just had to get it down on paper. I posted the letters without thinking about you reading the stuff.'

Bronwyn caught his sleeve. 'It's my fault. I've let you down.'

He slowed his pace and she felt his arm round her shoulder. 'Far from it, Bron. You're a trooper.'

'Thanks, Glyn, I wish it were true. I've thought of coming out and doing something practical, like dishing out tea with the YMCA. Maddy and I have talked about it.'

'You mean coming to France?'

'Yes. At least I speak French.'

He gave a wry smile. 'So you do. Why not serve tea here in Bangor, at the station? There are troops coming and going all the time.'

For a moment she felt he was humouring her.

'I think you underestimate how much you're already doing, Bron. Helping Mam in the Book Room, for one thing. Tada said it's taken a great weight off his mind. And being here with Mam, especially now Huw's going. I think we've all rather taken you for granted.'

Bronwyn gave a wide smile. Rolling the Methodist Magazine and queuing with parcels at the Post Office, wasn't so bad after all.

'How's the Handy Hints page, by the way? I'm intrigued.'

'Oh, it's just a bit of nonsense. I invented a Girl Friday character and she fixes things round the house. Readers write in with novel ideas; mattress ticking made into curtains, that sort of thing. The column more or less writes itself.'

He was chuckling. 'That's ingenious, Bron, do you know that? Take a word of advice from your big brother, and concentrate on your writing. You've got a great turn of phrase and your letters always transport me home.'

'I'm glad you think so, because I've been scribbling something about life on the home front. Tada encouraged me, and it should come out in the next issue.'

'Excellent. It will stand you in good stead. Don't forget to send me a copy. I liked your letter to the *Chronicle* defending your French teacher. Ever nail the culprit?'

'Everyone knows it was Pippa. She split on Madame who reported her for being nasty to Claudia. I should have told Pippa to shut up at the time, but I was still sore at Claudia for twitting me over my rotten hockey. All rather petty.'

Glyn kicked a stone and said, 'Sounds familiar actually. People living in close quarters, it's what happens.'

Glyn stopped and turned to her, his hands deep in his pockets. 'There's no easy way to say this, Bron, but here goes. I'm an old man in war years and I've been ridiculously lucky so far, but I know the odds are against me.'

'Glyn!' she protested, 'why are you talking this way?'

'Because it's important. I want you to be prepared. Just one more thing. Trust in yourself. Whatever you choose in life, you will do well, I'm sure of it. Here endeth the lesson.'

She couldn't bear the distance between them and stepped forward to grab his lapels. 'Glyn, don't think like that, please, I can't stand it!'

He took her hands and kissed them, looking at her fondly for a moment, and without a word, turned away and started picking over stones. He was making a small pile to skim over the water.

Bronwyn followed suit, choosing the flattest that bounced best, and tried to forget what he'd just said.

Glyn opened the contest, sending a stone that skimmed the surface several times before sinking into oblivion. 'That's a sixer,' he said, squinting into the sunlight. 'Your turn.'

Bronwyn felt the stone's heft in her palm and with one swift movement, sent it spinning. She counted as it kissed the surface eight times in rapid succession.

'Beat that!' she cried out.

'Not a chance!' he said, grinning. 'You win. Until next time!'

He has to come back, she thought in the heat of the moment. Glyn never could resist a challenge.

CHAPTER 7

July 1916

Carefree and hatless, Bronwyn and Maddy walked arm in arm, their faces turned to the sun like houseplants craning towards the light. It was such a glorious release after long weeks spent revising, then sitting exams in a stifling hall. Bronwyn had suggested they get out and shake off the cobwebs, now falling away with each sinuous stretch of muscle and limb as they strode across the bridge.

They turned off towards Menai woods and skirted a group of women wearing pretty scarves, brightly coloured frocks and chatting in Flemish. The women looked easy with one another, each carrying a covered basket on one arm.

'That must be lunch they're taking to their men,' said Bronwyn. 'The promenade they're building will make a fine walk, don't you think? It's such a boon for the town.

'I'd like to do something public spirited too. We once talked about serving tea to the troops, remember? When I told Glyn, he said I should get a College education under my belt and not be distracted.'

'My Da says the scholarship isn't enough to make ends meet, I may have to find a job.' Maddy was despondent.

'That would be tough, Mads, on top of the lab work.'

'I know. He doesn't understand. Rhys sends what he can from his wages, but now he's wounded, who knows what will happen.'

'Poor Rhys. Any news of when he'll be sent home?'

'Quite soon, they say. It's worrying they haven't said what's wrong with him.'

'You'll soon nurse him back to health, I'm sure. We can take him out for walks.'

'I do hope so. Then I worry he'll be sent back to the war. It's cruel, the way they do that. How's Huw getting on in Ireland?'

'He likes Limerick, though things are still unsettled after the ruckus with the Republicans at Easter. He doesn't know when his regiment will be sent out, but says he'll send a postcard as soon as he gets to France.'

By now they were at the edge of the wood, which they entered by a well-trodden path and walked companionably under the fresh canopy.

'Look at the lushness and shiny newness of it all, as if nature were discovering green for the first time,' said Bronwyn.

'You're such a romantic. All I see is chlorophyll. It's a wonder we get on at all,' said Maddy.

Bronwyn laughed. 'What wonderful plans we concocted.'

'I still dream of Paris, especially after reading about Madame Curie. Will you keep in touch with Madame Duchamp? She could introduce us to people there.'

'Oh yes, she wants to know how I get on at College. She kissed me on both cheeks the way the French do, and said my letter to the paper meant a lot to her. It's been a year since the Congress.' It was depressing how little had changed.

Maddy stopped to pick a fallen horse chestnut leaf and fanned herself. 'D'you think there was any point in what they did, the peace women?'

'There's no doubt! They laid down principles, such as giving women the vote, general disarmament and setting up an International Court of Justice.' She saw herself there already, reporting on its deliberations.

Maddy stroked each finger of the leaf. 'It's very idealistic. Women need to help win the war and agree conditions later. Now's not the time to talk about disarmament.' She fanned herself again as if to take the heat out of the discussion.

'It's time for tough argument not more violence,' Bron replied. 'Yes, women should be nurses and bus drivers and so on, but we can still campaign for peace. We need to raise our sights beyond narrow national interests. We're the experts at finding common ground.'

Maddy smiled, 'That's true in our house, Mam always keeps the peace between Da and Rhys.'

Bronwyn took Maddy's arm and said, 'Let's pray it'll be over soon and we can get on with our lives. We're almost students, Mads, aren't you excited?'

Maddy raised an eyebrow. 'Sort of, as long as I'm not the only girl in class.'

'That would be odd. Especially if the men are anything like old Fumes.'

They both giggled at the thought of their chemistry teacher who had a nervous sniff and singed eyebrows, and wasn't in fact very old.

The path became narrow and winding as the foliage thickened and the air was perceptibly cooler. They continued through the woods until they found a track half-remembered from childhood that once led to a patch of wild strawberries.

'I think it's here,' said Bronwyn, stumbling through brambles, 'I can smell them.'

'Perfectly ripe,' said Maddy, as they stopped to pick the glossy red fruit. 'We'll have to eat all we can as we haven't anything to carry them in.'

And they ate their fill until their palms were stained bright pink. Finally, they emerged from the wood at Church Island and into the stark heat. The men were still at work, backs leathery under the sun and sweat rags tied round their foreheads. There wasn't a young man among them. The baskets that the women had brought sat empty on the side of the freshly paved path.

One of the men looked up and set his shovel aside when he saw them approach. The others must have sensed a change in the rhythm of sound and they all stopped work and stood awkwardly, waiting for the girls to pass.

A stocky man with grey-blonde hair straightened, nodded, and said, '*Goedendag.*' Bronwyn and Maddy said, 'Good day' in reply and 'Thank-you,' pointing to the new promenade. This prompted the men to step forward, and they were soon smiling and making friendly sounding remarks in Flemish, which Bronwyn and Maddy returned in nods and gestures.

The two walked on as the men returned to work.

'What must it be like, to be invaded and have to run for your life, not knowing if you'd ever go back?' Maddy said.

'It's true,' said Bronwyn. 'We don't know how lucky we are.'

*

When Bronwyn walked into the house she was seized by an animal fear. The first hint that something was wrong was the gardening glove lying next to the clock on the hall table, covered in soil and still holding the shape of Mam's hand. The clock marked time with its steady tick, amplifying the silence.

'Mam?' she called out. There was no reply. She ran straight to the kitchen and saw Mam sitting in the rocking chair quite still, as if on a ship becalmed.

'Glyn's missing,' Mam said, in a low voice.

The telegram was lying on the bare table and looked as though it had been torn open in haste.

Bronwyn sat and forced herself to read slowly.

O.H.M.S. War Office, London
Regret to inform you that Lieutenant and Adjutant C. Glyn Roberts, 9th Bn. Royal Welsh Fusiliers was posted missing on 3-7-18. This does not necessarily mean he has been killed, as he may be a prisoner of war or temporarily separated from his regiment. Will report any further news immediately on receipt.
Secretary War Office

She reached over to take Mam's hand and said, 'They don't know yet.'

'I'm going to ask Aunt Hannah to come and stay for a few days to help out. And we must get word to Huw. Will you help me do that?' Her tone was brisk.

'Yes of course, but how long will it be before they tell us?'

'I don't know, *Del*, we must be patient. I believe Tada and Aubrey will be told as they're already out there, and Huw could come back if needs be.'

'Oh, Mam, could he be wounded?' Images came flooding in: Glyn lying in a shell hole and unable to move, Glyn dragged roughly away as a prisoner of war, or stumbling his way back alone.

'We'll know soon enough,' said Mam, gently rocking.

Bronwyn had pictured the scenario a dozen times, the telegram, the fear and uncertainty, but not this leaden heaviness in her limbs.

She helped Mam out of the rocking chair and they went to the study. Last time they'd been in here together was to polish the floor and change the flowers. Now they had to compose telegrams.

Sitting at Tada's desk had an unreal quality, as she pulled open a drawer and found a sheet of paper, and took a pen from the stand. She carefully opened a bottle of ink, dipped in the nib and looked up, poised for Mam's instructions.

'Hannah first,' said Mam. 'Say, *Glyn reported missing*, then ask her to come in the morning as she won't get this in time to catch the evening train. To Huw, say Hannah is on her way and he should wait for further news. I'll write to him tomorrow.'

Mam leaned forward and picked up the photo of Glyn and brushed off imaginary dust with her sleeve. 'Such a beautiful boy. They both were.'

She must be thinking of Glyn's twin Tomos, thought Bronwyn.

Mam collected herself and said, 'Now you run straight down to the Post Office, and I'll make up a bed for Hannah.'

Bronwyn arrived at the station with time to spare and stood amongst the bustling crowd. There was a distant hoot and a porter shouted, *mind your backs*, and barrowed through. A mother snatched a child from the platform's edge at the sound of the approaching train. The advancing hulk and roar made everyone take a step back, except for the soldiers, oblivious to the noise. Some stood, others squatted on knapsacks, smoking and chatting.

Bronwyn saw Hannah waving at her frantically from a carriage window and she ran along to keep level, until the train wheezed and ground to a halt amidst a welter of steam and hot metal.

There was no porter in sight and together they wrestled Hannah's suitcase to the ground before any word passed between them.

'Dear Bron, how are you? You look worn out,' Hannah said at last, pulling her close in a hug.

'I'm so glad you're here,' Bronwyn said, feeling the weight of anxiety lift. Hannah gave her a wide reassuring smile, then waved for assistance. There was still no porter, but she attracted the attention of several officers and graciously accepted the attentions of a Colonel, who offered to carry her luggage to a cab with exaggerated English courtesy.

Mam was at the door to greet them. You could tell they were sisters even though Mam was a lot older; their voices were similar, both in the same amber tones.

'I've put you in the back room, dear,' Mam said, taking Hannah's coat. 'Bronwyn will help you up with your suitcase. Whatever have you got in there?'

It was a standing joke that Hannah never travelled light.

'Oh, you know, the usual, a couple of outfits and the odd hat.'

'My goodness, you'll be the smartest girl in town. Now let's get you settled and I'll tell you the little we know.'

Days passed with no further news. The worst of it was the uncertainty. Rumours ran like wildfire round Chapel and along queues in shops, and faces became graver as the names of the wounded, missing, and killed, began to circulate.

There wasn't a word about all this in the press, in fact quite the opposite. Bronwyn scoured the papers for clues as to what was going on and found nothing but positive reports:

On a front of twenty miles north and south of the Somme, we and our French allies have advanced and taken the German first line of trenches. We are attacking vigorously Fricourt, la Boiselle and Mametz. German prisoners are surrendering freely, and a good many have already fallen into our hands, and as far as can be ascertained our casualties have not been heavy.

She was sitting in the front garden shelling peas when the telegraph boy came up the path. He handed her the envelope deferentially and hurried away.

Bronwyn took it inside and caught the look that passed between Mam and Hannah, as Mam opened the envelope as fast as her shaking hands would allow. She lifted her glasses to her nose and scanned the page. Then she reached for the support of a chair.

'Come, sit down,' Hannah said, taking the slip of paper

from Mam.

'Fetch some water,' she said to Bronwyn, 'and the brandy.'

'He's gone,' Mam cried, 'they've killed my beautiful boy.' She doubled up, clutching herself.

Bronwyn brought the water and a tot of brandy. 'Here Mam, drink, it well help.' She moved mechanically, feeling nothing.

It wasn't until after they'd got Mam to bed that she read the telegram, with Hannah at her side.

Telegram: Post Office Telegraphs. Officers/War Office.

Deeply regret to inform you that your son Lt. G.C. Roberts was killed on July 3rd 1916. Lord Kitchener expresses his sympathy.

When Bronwyn looked up, Hannah's eyes filled with tears.

Bronwyn covered her mouth, wide-eyed and gasping as sobs rose. Hannah's arms held her, while her body convulsed.

'Here, mop up dearest,' Hannah said, as the crying subsided, holding out a large hanky, still sniffing herself.

'I can't believe it, Hannah. I feel he could walk in any minute and say, *Chin up Sis, it's not the end of the world*, or something equally silly. He's out there somewhere, I'm sure of it, he just *can't* be dead!'

The next morning a letter arrived from Glyn's superior officer, which crushed any hope.

'Read it, Bron,' Mam said, 'it's touching.'

Bronwyn took the letter and pulled a chair up to the kitchen table, part of her still refusing to believe this was happening.

Dear Mrs. Roberts,

I am sending you a letter that has come for your son, and should like to take this opportunity, if I may, of offering you my very deep sympathy with you in your loss.

I am afraid his death in action will have been a heavy blow to you, but I feel it may be some consolation to you to know he was shot quite dead and can have suffered no pain, also that he died while running to help a brother officer who had been wounded a moment before.

He had, as of course you know, been my Adjutant for some weeks now, and had been doing splendidly, and I had every reason to be more than satisfied with his work.

The previous day to his death he had crossed into the German line with me, and had taken a very active and leading part in our subsequent attack against the German position, and we were together when he fell.

His loss is deeply felt throughout the Battalion for he was beloved of all of us and respected by the men.

I miss him more than I can say.

Yours very sincerely,

R.A. Berners,

Lieut. Colonel.

9th Bn. Royal Welsh Fusiliers

Bronwyn turned to Mam and wept on her shoulder.

Mam cradled her head and said, 'Shush now child, enough. Glyn is at peace. We should be thankful for that. We are only crying for ourselves.'

'Was it my letter they sent back?'

'Yes, *Del*.' Mam handed it to her.

She'd written with such excitement about going to College, thanking him for the French exercise book with a jaunty tri-colour cover.

The randomness of death, the curt brutality, made her head spin.

So, this was war.

CHAPTER 8

August 1916

As she walked in, there it was on the morning room table, like an unexploded bomb. Square, tied neatly with string and covered with telltale military stamps, marked *URGENT* and *OHMS*. It was Mam's idea to open it together.

Bronwyn sat on the wicker chair in the corner, steeling herself. She wished the others would hurry. She knew in her heart this was the next step to accepting Glyn was dead. Questions still burned: was he really killed outright? Where was he buried? Who had he saved? There was nobody who could tell her.

Huw's usually unhurried footsteps came smartly from the study and Mam and Hannah arrived armed with scissors and knife.

Bronwyn watched as they snipped, sliced and unwrapped the brown paper parcel with utmost care. Her eyes were fixed on the box as it emerged. Hannah raised the lid. Mam slowly lifted out Glyn's 'flea-bag' as he called it. A dank musty smell filled the room as she unpacked its contents.

Mam lifted out a tin helmet first. 'Feel how heavy it is,' she said, handing it to Hannah. 'They must be dreadful to wear.' She looked enquiringly at Huw.

Huw cracked his knuckles and said, 'I've never worn one. We've only ever used soft hats in training.'

Next came a collection of frayed underwear. The garments lay limp and crumpled on the table, grey with ingrained dirt. Bronwyn was horrified, as Mam started folding vests and underpants, the schoolboy nametapes exposed. 'I'll have to burn them,' Mam said, setting the neat pile to one side.

Mam delved back into the corner of the bag. 'What's this?' she said, pulling out a sheaf of letters tied with string and a battered notebook, in Glyn's handwriting.

It was ceremonial, thought Bronwyn, this laying out of what remained of him, in the absence of a body. She watched as Mam handled every item with great delicacy, until the box was empty.

'You should both keep something of his. It's what Glyn would have wanted.'

Bronwyn surveyed the table of objects that he'd handled and used: his Sam Browne belt; a Welsh-English Bible; a family photo taken just before he left; a tin box of tobacco.

Huw tentatively picked up a silver cigarette case that Bronwyn hadn't seen before. It was finely engraved in ivy-leaf filigree. 'May I take this?' he asked.

'Of course,' Mam said.

Huw snapped it open and scrutinized the inside. 'From Gethin,' he said, 'it was a gift for Glyn's twenty first.'

Mam looked upset. 'I wonder if Gethin knows.'

Huw closed the case. 'I could find out. I ought to return it to him. They were close.'

Something clicked in Bronwyn's mind. 'Dietrich!' she exclaimed. 'Glyn asked me to write to his sister if anything happened. He gave me the address.'

They all turned to her in amazement, as it was the first time she'd spoken of it.

Huw smiled. 'Good for Glyn, I say. He wasn't going to let a war come between him and friendship.'

'He was full of surprises, even as a little one,' said Hannah. She turned to Bronwyn. 'I don't know how you send a letter to Germany these days, but I could ask my old friends at the Post Office.'

'Thanks, Hannah, that's kind,' said Bronwyn.

'Would you like this, Huw?' Mam asked, picking up Glyn's fountain pen.

'Well, yes, unless Bron would like it. She's the writer.'

Bronwyn reached for the notebook. 'I'd like this, if you don't mind. I'll pass it round once I've had a look.' She ached to know what Glyn had written. It would be like speaking to him again.

Retreating to her room, she ran her hand over the notebook backed in brown paper. There was a stain in one corner that smelled of hair-oil, and on the inside cover Glyn had written, *Jottings*.

She leafed through and saw there were poems and limericks interspersed with notes and crossings-out, as well as doodles and sketches. On the back page she found a drawing of a helmet that looked like a chamber pot, labelled, *Jerry!* Typical of Glyn's boyish sense of humour. Next to it was a diagram of a dugout complete with dimensions and labels specifying, *4 foot of sandbags* and *layer of corrugated iron sheet.*

Turning the pages, her eye fell on the title, *Good and Bad.* She read on:

The Colonel was a proper man,
The Adjutant a hero,
The Doctor was a charlatan,
The Major was a Nero.
The four of them together fell.
Shells can't distinguish very well.

She'd never heard him use such dark irony, though it was in similar vein to, *Sing me to sleep where bullets fall*, the lullaby he'd heard the men sing.

Next, were two verses, headed, *The Patrol.*

I called for volunteers
For the patrol.
'Three men,' I said, and out
Stepped three,
The best of my platoon.

A bomb it now appears
Got Henry Cole.
A sniper's shot hit Stout
And Lee.
I was alone quite soon.

The humorous form was a thin disguise for his pent-up anger, and she would surely have heard the scorn in his voice had he read it aloud.

Her attention drifted as she looked up from the desk, remembering when he'd more or less told her he was likely to be killed, that he was living on borrowed time; and she'd refused to listen, because it was too dreadful to imagine him not coming back.

She opened the centre pages and found a poem with two titles, one to protect the identity of the subject.

Lance-Corporal Davies
(or, The Night Before)

He was my runner: I was fond of him.
Not very tall but sound of wind and limb.
I always trusted him to find the way
From post to post. He never went astray
Until one night, when all his skill seemed gone.
In stilly silence we went on and on:
My thoughts were far away from No-Man's-Land,
When suddenly I stood stock still, my hand
Shot out to grip his shoulder. Not a sound
Broke the silence in the hostile gloom around,
And still we stood, as moveless as the dead.
I knew that we were lost before he said
'I'm sorry, sir,' in whisper hushed and low.
Then came a rifle shot, and in the glow

Of sudden flares we saw the German post:
Their bullets spat around us and a host
Of evil obstacles swarmed round our feet,
The wire caught us, barring our retreat:
The wire clutched us, like a fiend from hell,
An evil monster, whom we could not quell.
At every step it gripped and held us fast,
Until with bleeding hands we won at last
Our freedom from the brute, and found a gap
Through which to crawl out of the hideous trap.

That was the only time he went astray,
But, in the battle on the following day,
A bullet caught him, standing by my side:
'I'm sorry, sir,' he whispered, as he died.

Glyn's devotion to his runner and the raw misery of the poem took her unawares: she closed her eyes and rocked. He'd once spoken of brothers in arms, which she hadn't understood at the time. Here, he'd shown the no-man's land between life and death and the bond between two men facing extinction.

She put her head in her hands; tears came slowly at first, then hot and urgent like a wellspring, engulfing her in great drowning waves. It was like lancing a boil to purge the grief that returned at intervals.

The pale stone of University College glowed honey-yellow under the slanting afternoon sun. The 'College on the hill' was part of her everyday landscape, but today, as she stood waiting in the courtyard, she saw it with fresh eyes.

Huw had once taken her inside, and now she imagined herself in the brown-tiled corridors and green-tiled lecture rooms, as a fully-fledged student wearing her black undergraduate gown.

A sense of foreboding broke her reverie as she remembered why she was here: to visit Rhys with Maddy and Mrs Jones, in the Pritchard-Jones hall.

Maddy had warned her that Rhys was in a bad way. He'd been caught on the wire and lost both legs at the knee. When Maddy had said he was failing fast, Bronwyn blinked back tears and they ended up crying over their brothers' sufferings.

As she straightened her shoulders determined to be strong, Maddy and Mrs Jones appeared at her elbow.

'Hello, Bronwyn dear,' said Mrs Jones, giving her a peck on the cheek. 'I'm so glad you could come.'

'How was Rhys earlier?' Bronwyn asked, knowing she visited him three times a day.

'A little better, thank you. He took my hand. I'm afraid he can't say anything yet.'

Bronwyn took in the dark shadows, like tea-stains, under Mrs Jones' eyes. 'I understand,' she said, trying to hide her dismay, as they made their way slowly towards the building. Maddy's rueful look over her mother's head, confirmed that Rhys was still very poorly.

At the entrance, a soldier jumped ahead to usher them in; as he opened the door they were greeted by the clatter of trolleys on stone flags, and nurses, orderlies and soldiers buzzing like bees.

They stood aside waiting for a lull, until they were able to make their way to the double doors into the hall.

As they walked in Bronwyn smelled something sickly, akin to silage, overlaid with the sharp tang of carbolic soap. Her stomach heaved.

The black-clothed figure of Mrs Jones was already halfway down the hall, leading with her basket towards a bed surrounded by screens. The hall was lofty and beds lined the walls. Men lay at odd angles: some with legs or arms held by pulley-like contraptions; others with faces obliterated by bandages. The air was thick despite the open windows above the oak panelling.

Bronwyn caught Maddy's arm as they approached the screens round Rhys and looked away when a nurse emerged carrying a pail of blood-soaked dressings.

In her first glimpse he lay motionless, his bulky torso creating a mound under a thin sheet. Mrs Jones was dabbing his brow with a damp cloth. Bronwyn saw his face was puffy and grey and his breathing shallow.

'Bring out the barley water, *Del*,' said Mrs Jones.

Maddy took a bottle from the basket, and Bronwyn watched as she spooned droplets of liquid into his mouth through cracked lips as Rhys gurgled.

'Bronny's here to see you,' Maddy said.

Rhys groaned.

'Hello Rhys,' said Bronwyn, 'I'm so glad you're home. Mam and Huw send their love.'

An orderly, who looked like an old soldier, wheeled the screens away and the ward opened up around them.

Bronwyn watched as Mrs Jones bent double to take a pile of dirty laundry from the locker, then patted in a stack of fresh pyjama jackets.

'I don't think he'll take food today,' said Maddy, 'but he knows we're here.'

The anguish in her face was clear to see, and Bronwyn wished there was more she could do.

Looking across to the next bed, she saw a man with his head and eyes bandaged, twisting round and feeling towards a beaker on his locker.

'Can I pass you some water?' she asked.

'Thank you, nurse, if you would,' he said in flat English tones.

'I'm not a nurse, just a visitor. I'm a friend of Rhys, who's next to you.' She went over and filled the beaker.

'Here you are,' she said passing it, then realised she must guide his hand.

'His fiancée?' he enquired, taking the beaker with both hands.

'No, a family friend.' He wouldn't have asked if he could see her for the schoolgirl she was.

She stood by him as he brought the beaker to his lips and drank clumsily, water dribbling down his chin. There was still blood on his matted strawberry-blonde hair. 'Shall I take it now?' she offered.

'Thanks, Miss. What's your name, if you don't mind my asking?'

'Bronwyn, they call me Bron.'

'I'm George. Lieutenant Chisolm to be formal. I landed here because they've run out of space for Officers. Not that it matters when you're in my state.' He made as if to shake hands.

She took his hand for a second time. 'Pleased to meet you, Sir.'

'Please call me George. May I call you Bron?'

'Yes,' she said, to be kind. She was unlikely to see him again.

'Would you talk to me next time you visit your friend, Bron? My family lives in London, so I haven't got anyone up here.' He fell back on the pillow.

'I will,' she said, feeling herself blush. She touched his arm lightly. 'You should rest now.'

Mrs Jones was talking to the ward Sister who wore a starched cap, and Bronwyn could see it was serious. Mrs Jones leaned over Rhys, saying, 'I'll be back soon, dearest, wait for me.'

Maddy squeezed her brother's hand, welling tears.

Bronwyn put an arm round her friend and they left him.

She was sitting in her room when Glyn caught her eye from the dressing table, looking out from a photograph taken the day he left for war. There was something she had to face up to before the day was out. Glyn's room.

She went back along the landing, turned the handle and went in. Nothing had been disturbed since he was home: grey flannels and cardigan hung on the back of the chair as if he'd just changed out of them.

She walked over to the bookshelf filled with childhood treasure and picked up the painted box with a secret drawer that Hannah had given him for his tenth birthday.

There was a fine collection of tin soldiers that she'd saved up to buy him one Christmas; picking up the guard Glyn had painted black and red; she blew off the dust.

On the top shelf there was a fretsaw kit and a pile of jigsaw puzzles; he'd have these on the go for weeks, spread out over the floor. On the shelf below was an atlas, schoolbooks and piles of magazines: The Motorcyclist and The Light Car, he adored anything mechanical. And school photographs. There he was, the smallest of the football eleven before he'd shot up, unframed and propped behind a pewter cup that he'd won for the junior hurdles.

Her eye fell on a sheaf of music. She leafed through the songs and heard his clear tenor voice alongside Aubrey's baritone; they used to sing together on Sunday evenings and Mam would play the piano.

She put the music back and took one last look round. It brought back memories of childhood days when Rhys and Maddy came over to play and the boys let the girls join in French cricket; or when they all went swimming at Siliwen baths.

'Good bye happy times,' she said aloud, leaving the door ajar.

CHAPTER 9

August 1916

Bronwyn took Huw's arm as they walked along the pier, the black armband dissecting the sleeve of his light summer jacket. A stiff breeze took the edge off the burning sun and the sea lapped lazily under the wooden planks below. The kiosks were doing a brisk trade in sweets and iced drinks with soldiers and their wives or sweethearts. Dresses were bleached pale in the stark light and parasols bloomed like exotic flowers.

'You've been rather low recently,' Bronwyn remarked, hoping to draw Huw out of himself.

'I've been poor company, I'm afraid. It was the service that set me back. It's a shame Tada wasn't there to do Rhys justice.'

Rhys had died at dawn, the day after the visit. Maddy said it was a blessed release, but she was still wracked by grief. There'd been a private funeral followed by a memorial service, led by a visiting minister. His eulogy was all-purpose, capturing nothing of Rhys' large-heart and gentle nature.

'It was quite heartbreaking, seeing him in hospital,' said Bronwyn.

'I should have gone with you,' said Huw.

He'd wept at the memorial service, naked misery showing in his face. For days he'd been unreachable, and this afternoon was the first time she'd persuaded him to get some fresh air.

'The service brought home Glyn's loss for me too.' She searched his face.

He nodded, eyes glassy behind his spectacles.

'Mam says we'll have a memorial service once we're all home,' she continued. 'I'd like to lay flowers on baby Tomos' grave in the meantime. Glyn liked to visit St Tysilio's. We could go together.'

'It's the least I could do,' he said, shading his eyes. 'I think he'd like that.'

'I worry about Aubrey and how he's taking it. You know how he bottles things up.'

'You're right, Glyn's death will have hit him hard. In his last letter, Aubrey said I should do my best to stay out of it. Too late for that, worse luck.'

Bronwyn clasped his arm. 'Can't you stay a few more days? When do you have to go?'

'I can't postpone much longer. I was lucky to get leave for the funeral.'

No point in asking when he'd be going to France as she knew the drill by now. A boat and a train at short notice and a postcard home.

They were nearing the end of the pier and the wind came in gusts, puffing up skirts and tipping over wide-brimmed hats. Bronwyn didn't care that her hair was tangled with salt and her face nut brown, as it always was by the end of the summer.

Leaning against the promenade railings, Huw said, 'Tell me about your wounded soldier, Bron. I have a suspicion you have a soft spot for him, from the way you've talked.'

'George?' She felt her face flush. 'I'm befriending someone who's lonely and a long way from home. That's all.'

She'd visited him almost daily since he'd been transferred from the Pritchard Jones hall to an Officers' Ward at Bangor hospital.

They'd talked about her life at home and College plans. She knew all about his younger sister Amelia, firmly under her mother's thumb, and their grand home in London. She read him amusing snippets from the newspaper, and poetry, which he said kept his mind from dark places. Each time she visited, he smiled with delight when he heard her voice, and her heart soared.

'Is there any hope he'll get his sight back?' Huw asked.

'They're not sure about the left eye, but he's lost the right eye. He's asked me to be there when the bandages come off because his mother and sister can't make the journey. He wouldn't say why.'

Huw nodded sagely. 'Well, well. I think it's time I took a brotherly interest. What did he do before the war?'

'He worked in the family business. He wanted to be an architect, but his father needed a draughtsman, so he ended up designing cardboard boxes.'

'I see. Let's pop into the Wicklow and you can tell me more.'

She laughed. 'Don't be old fashioned, Huw. I'm not falling for him, honestly.'

Huw peered at her short-sightedly. 'Really? I don't believe you.'

She resisted making a sharp retort; Huw would say she'd proved him right. Her feelings were in turmoil.

The Wicklow, normally full of students, was quiet during the summer. They sat at an empty table, its surface stained with pale rings from spillage of tea and coffee served in earthenware mugs.

They had the place to themselves, except for two men in silent combat over a chessboard. A young waitress took their order, and Huw picked up an abandoned newspaper.

He chortled from behind its pages. 'Listen to this, Bron. They're showing, *Madame Coquette*, followed by, *Honeymoon for Three*. Whatever next?'

He folded the paper and pointed out an advertisement and grinned. It was for, *Lantern lectures on the history of Bangor*. 'What does that remind you of? Remember *The Rat Swallower?*'

'I do, it was terribly lurid. I used to love magic lantern shows.'

'Those were the days, when we marched behind the Band of Hope on wet Saturday afternoons.'

'It always rained, I do remember that. Singing *Happy on the Way*, which I definitely wasn't.'

They laughed, attracting disapproving looks from the chess players in the corner; they had to pull themselves together when the waitress arrived with a jug and glasses.

Huw drank two tumblers of lemonade, and looked her straight in the eye. 'I'm no expert on these matters, Bron, but I know that men can be selfish and inconsiderate when it comes to women.'

She felt her hands cool against the glass and sipped slowly. 'He's not like that, Huw, I'm sure of it.' She put the glass to her hot cheek. 'It will all blow over once he goes back to London, so there's nothing to get het up about.'

Huw smiled. 'I just don't want to see you hurt.'

'Thanks, Huw. How about you? Is there a lady in your life?'

'I get the message; I should mind my own business. But the answer is no, there's no girl on the horizon. I follow my old Prof's advice. He said, *admire the fair sex as the stars, from a distance.* The advice given by the army is rather less poetic, but I won't go into that.'

She laughed, glad to hear him joking, and her heart light after talking about George, who meant more to her than she'd cared to admit.

The telegraph boy tipped his cap as he cycled past, but didn't give his usual cheery smile. Bronwyn exchanged an anxious look with Huw.

As they went inside, Lizzie was standing in the hall, frozen to the spot with the envelope in one hand.

'There was no one in, I had to take it.' She sounded petrified.

'Give it to me, Lizzie,' said Huw. 'Make some tea and be sure to have a cup yourself. We'll be in the study.'

Bronwyn's mind was in ferment. Nothing has happened as long as we haven't actually opened the envelope, she reasoned. Don't let it be Tada, please, please don't let it be him; chaplains and doctors were supposed to be immune from danger.

'I think we should open it,' Huw said, pulling the door to.

'It's addressed to Mam,' Bronwyn said, playing for time.

'It doesn't matter; we should open it anyway.'

'Could it be Tada?' Her every pore filled with dread.

'More likely to be Aubrey.' Huw sounded grave. 'We should find out before Mam and Hannah get back.'

She watched as he took the letter knife to the envelope and slit it open as if gutting a fish. He pulled out the thin typed sheet.

She stood at his side and they read it together.

O.H.M.S. War Office London
Regret to inform you that Lt. A. P. Roberts, Welsh Fusiliers was
missing August 25th. This does not necessarily mean he is killed or
wounded. Will report any further news immediately on receipt.
Secretary War Office

'Oh no,' she said, shaking.

'He may be fine; we just don't know yet.'

'The telegram about Glyn was the same. It's too horrible.'

Her next thought was that Tada was safe. But then Aubrey could be wounded or a prisoner, so how could she be glad? She leaned against Huw's shoulder, holding back tears.

'There, there, don't cry, please don't cry,' he said, stroking her head.

She looked up and saw his eyes glisten like blue marbles behind his glasses.

They heard Mam and Hannah come through the front door.

'Anyone home?' Mam called out breezily.

'We're in the study,' Huw replied.

Bronwyn wiped away a tear as they walked in.

'What is it?' Mam asked.

'It's Aubrey, he's missing,' Huw said, handing her the telegram.

Mam's hand trembled as she read it, Hannah next to her.

'It may be all right this time, Mam.' Huw didn't sound convinced.

'Thank heavens you're here,' Mam said, letting the telegram fall to the floor. She flew over to Huw and clung to him, and he patted her shoulder.

It reminded Bronwyn of the way he'd comforted her in the Book Room, after reading Glyn's letters. That was the battle of Loos, before he was killed at the Somme. Now Aubrey had been taken prisoner, what more could happen? She prayed fervently for Tada and Huw to be spared.

Mam opened the official envelope a few days later.

'Shall I fetch your glasses?' Bronwyn offered, fighting her fears.

'No, dear, just read it to me.' Mam handed her the letter.

'He's alive, Mam! They say he's been taken prisoner, but probably not wounded. Shall I read it out?'

'Yes, dear, please get on with it.' Mam sank into the nearest chair.

Bronwyn read aloud:

Dear Mrs Roberts,
In case you have not already been informed, I am writing to say Aubrey is a prisoner in the hands of the enemy. I cannot enter into any details, but there is every reason to believe he is unwounded. I will write again in a few days and let you know as much as I can of the affair.

Meanwhile, let me say how sorry we all are to lose him and I hope and pray he is well and meeting with good treatment, and that you will hear from him before long.
Yours sincerely,
F.R.H. McLellan, Major

Bronwyn put her arms round Mam, kneeling at her side. 'At least he's safe.'

'What if he's wounded, will they care for him? I hope they don't treat him badly,' Mam said in a rush.

'Injured prisoners go to hospital on both sides,' Bronwyn said, remembering what she'd read.

'Will he be allowed to write? Can we send parcels? It must be cold out there. I'll let Tada know in case news hasn't reached him.' Mam's worry lines deepened.

Waiting for distant events to unfold was the order of the day. Mam baked and sewed and packed parcels. Bronwyn's own way of coping was to read the papers and write, to document the war. At least now she had George.

Huw stood in uniform ready to leave and Bronwyn's heart missed a beat.

'No need for you all to come to the station, it will be teeming,' Huw said. He bent to kiss Mam. 'I'm only in Ireland, remember.'

Mam took his hand and said, *ffarwel fy anwylaf*, goodbye my dearest, until he eventually pulled himself upright and she let him go.

'I'll come with you,' said Bronwyn, 'I don't want you leaving on your own.'

Huw kissed Hannah goodbye and heaved on his rucksack, while Bronwyn pulled on her coat. They set off, Huw turning at intervals to wave to Mam and Hannah.

Halfway down the road, he said, 'I'd like to give you something, Bron.' He reached inside his jacket and brought out a pen. 'It's a gift for College.'

'But Huw, it's Glyn's! Surely you want to keep it with you?'

'I'd like to think of you using it.'

'Are you're sure? I'm very touched, I really am.' She kissed the pen and put it in her bag. 'I will think of you both. You must promise to write, Huw, and you can say anything you want. I won't be weak kneed about it. I can take it now and besides, I need to know how you are, especially after Glyn.'

He took her arm. 'Thanks, Bron. As long as they don't start censoring Officers' letters, I'll let you know exactly what's going on.'

As they got to the station, Huw quickened his pace as if drawn towards the milling crowd. The noise was deafening. Bronwyn held onto his sleeve as they shuffled forwards surrounded by soldiers and their loved ones, inching their way towards the platform packed solid with uniformed men.

The train was already in the station, but nobody was in a hurry to board. Men sat on kitbags, joking and smoking; couples stood close, the women reaching up to touch a cheek or smooth a khaki lapel; a flower girl was selling bunches of violets to parting sweethearts.

'Please don't hang around,' Huw said, hitching his rucksack higher. A roar of steam rose up from the brooding engine and galvanized the crowd into action, and the cry of *all aboard* set doors cracking open.

'Goodbye, Huw, take care, I love you.' She kissed his cheek.

He gave her a stiff hug through the casing of his uniform, and his smile wobbled as he blew her a kiss before clambering up. She watched, as a man, already at the top of the steps, hauled him on board, and Huw pulled up the next man who looked as though he might topple backwards under his load.

Her heart contracted as the train moved off. When would she see him again? There were no flags waving now, just handkerchiefs, white against the maroon of the train. She couldn't be sure, but she thought she saw him amongst the bobbing heads and arms, through blinding tears.

She trudged home, looking back only once at the sound of the train's distant wail. Its steamy imprints marked the pencil-grey sky.

CHAPTER 10

September 1916

'Is that you, Bron?' George called out.

She found him sitting up in bed behind the screens, waiting for the doctor's visit.

'Yes, it's me, and I've got something for you.' She hoped the watch she was about to give him would take his mind off things. She greeted him with a squeeze of the hand, using touch instead of eye contact, as the nurses did.

'Are you going to read something to me? Or is it music? I bet it's a gramophone record.' He was still holding onto her hand.

'No, neither. Here it is.' She slipped it into his palm.

He put his head to one side and became still as his fingers worked their way round the plain metal disk. A smile crept across his lips as he pressed the crown and released the cover and opened it gingerly; he fingered the inside, rapt in concentration.

Bolt upright, he exclaimed, 'It's ten o'clock! Am I right?'

On cue, a distant church bell sounded through the open window, and they laughed.

'I'm glad you find it easy to use. Mr Wartski the jeweller, said he had just the thing, a Hunter with raised dots and special hands. He gave it a good clean and said it should work perfectly. I can always take it back if it doesn't suit you.'

'Bron, it's superb. When I can't sleep, I'll be able to count the hours till morning. It's worse at night when it's quiet and there are no sounds to keep track of time. I hate not knowing whether it's night or day.' He sank back onto the pillows. 'I appreciate your being here, Bron.' The lines round his mouth tensed. 'Any sign of the quack? I want to get this over with.'

She touched his hand and he took hers in a firm but gentle grasp.

'I know this can't be easy for you either.' He angled himself towards her as if looking into her eyes. 'What I mean is, no hard feelings if you don't come back after today. I will understand completely. You've been very good to me and you've become, well, dear to me. I couldn't bear your pity.'

Bronwyn wanted to say that nothing would change, whatever the doctor said, and it wasn't pity that brought her to his side. But the sounds of voices and a trolley intruded, and the doctor came in, followed by the ward sister.

Clean-shaven and smiling, the doctor approached the bedside, 'Good morning young man. I'm glad to see you have such agreeable company.'

'This is Miss Roberts, Sir. She's a friend. I'd like her to stay with me during the consultation if you don't mind.'

'Sounds like a good idea.' He had a kindly voice. 'Now let's have a look at this left eye of yours and see if there's anything we can do.' He sat on the edge of the bed and nodded to the ward sister, who obliged by carefully removing the bandages.

George winced as she pulled off the wadding covering his eyes.

'Thank you Sister,' said the doctor, 'that'll be all for now.'

George's face looked pale and naked without the bandages and his eyebrows were lighter than his thatch of strawberry blonde hair. Both lids looked red and sore.

The doctor took something from the trolley and leant forward. 'I'm just going to put a drop of cocaine in here. You won't feel a thing and I'll be able to have a good look.' He spoke casually, and opened the eye with his forefinger and thumb.

George's shoulders shot up as he pressed his hands to the bed.

Bronwyn forced herself to keep looking, despite the anguish on his face.

The doctor flashed a small torch inside the eye in every direction. He put the torch away and said, 'The good news is that there's very little scarring, so you'll look good as new once you've healed up. But I'm afraid that eye won't be any use to you.' The doctor paused, as if waiting for a reaction.

Bronwyn saw the muscles in George's cheek tighten.

'So that's it then, Sir, as I left the other one behind in France. No hope at all.'

'The optic nerve has died. With a bit of luck, we won't have to remove the eyeball. As for the right eye, it's time we put a shell in the socket so it doesn't shrink any further. Do you think you could put up with that now?'

'Yes, I think so, Sir. And thank you for being frank. I needed to know.' His voice was strained.

Bronwyn took his hand. 'Are you sure you want this, George?' She looked at the doctor. 'Maybe it can wait?'

'Best get it over with,' said George.

'Good man,' said the doctor.

The nurse swabbed George's right eye and handed the doctor a phial from the trolley.

The doctor prised open the lids and dropped in the cocaine; he inserted a piece of glass about the size of a marble. 'The tear ducts will start working and help lubrication,' he said, sitting back.

George moved his head around as if testing for new sensations, eyelids fluttering; then his chest heaved and he went into a fit of sneezing as though his body was in revolt against the foreign object. He fumbled for a handkerchief in his pyjama pocket and blew his nose.

'Sorry, old chap,' said the doctor, 'I know it's a bit of a shock.' He tapped George on the shoulder. 'I'll leave you in peace now, but I'd like to recommend you to Sir Arthur Pearson. He'll find you a place at St Dunstan's, where you'll learn the ropes. He was about your age when he went blind. I'll have you transferred to the London General first. I'll pop in before you go down South. Until then, I'm sure your charming friend will keep up your spirits.' He gave Bronwyn an encouraging smile.

'Thank you, Sir,' said George.

The doctor nodded to the ward sister who took charge of the trolley, and they left.

Bronwyn looked at George, grey with exhaustion, both eyes weeping, and wished desperately there was some way to comfort him.

'Here, use this,' she said giving him her hanky, 'it's clean.'

He dabbed at his eyes and wiped the tears from his cheeks.

'I'm so sorry, George dear,' she said holding his hand. She'd never dreamt it would be so final.

'It's funny, thinking back to what chaps used to say about being blind or deaf. Which would be worse.'

'What do you mean?'

'They're equally bad. It makes you feel cut off from the person you once were. The hardest thing is finding your way back. Sorry to ramble on.'

'Don't apologise. You're very brave.'

'I have this dream. I'm trying to light a bedside lamp. The match burns bright as I'm putting it to the lamp, but the match keeps blowing out. If only I could get the lamp to light, I'd be able to see. Then I wake up in the dark.'

'How horribly frightening.'

'I suppose St Dunstan's might help. I'll learn Braille and typing, that sort of thing.' His fists clenched. 'Whatever shall I do with myself, Bron? Father will put me out to grass.'

'I'm sure that's not true,' she said, trying to soothe him. 'Will your mother visit? Perhaps Amelia will travel back with you.'

'Amelia may come, but Mother can't tear herself away from her veterans' charity work. She's not much good with invalids.'

'What a shame. For you I mean.'

'She's not a bad old stick really. I'm quite glad she won't see me like this. By the way, do I look a terrible fright? I should probably wear dark glasses.'

'You look a bit tired, that's all. It's the first time I've been able to see your face properly.'

'Come closer.' He reached out and explored her chin and cheeks, her nose and mouth with his fingertips. 'I may never see your face, but to me, you'll always be the girl with the brown velvet voice.'

She could still feel his touch on her lips, when she said, 'About what you said earlier, George, I'm not going to run away.' She cared about him deeply and now knew he felt the same.

A nurse appeared round the screen with a trolley to give him his tablets and tend his eyes.

George sat there unmasked and vulnerable without the bandages and Bronwyn pored over whatever it was that had grown between them.

He was fascinated by the most ordinary details of her life, such as the way she rode freely about on her bike. She read him drafts of articles for the Magazine, and on the occasions she spoke to the orderly, he said it gave him a thrill to hear her speak Welsh.

'You're a schoolgirl,' he said once, 'how do you know so much?'

For his part, he led a simple life, enjoyed good food with friends—a man of the flesh with tender feelings.

He made her laugh, and wasn't ashamed to talk about his fears. Charming and vulnerable, she couldn't help herself.

When she'd told him about Glyn, he'd said, 'I'm so sorry. I was there, and it was unspeakable.'

She felt a special bond, as he became a living link, a survivor of the Somme.

The nurse had finished and steered the trolley away leaving a waft of witch-hazel. The intimacy of the screens was welcome, the sun hitting the canvas and bathing them in green light.

'How do you feel?' She could see the pain in his face and stroked his arm, feeling the wiry hair under her palm.

'It's the glass eye, it aches. Feels as if I've been kicked in the head. The strange thing is, I didn't feel a thing immediately after I was hit. I just knew I couldn't see. I remember being stretchered out, then nothing until after they'd operated. Then it hurt like billy-o.' He shuddered and looked drained.

'Shall I call the nurse? She could give you something.'

'No, I'm just having a gripe. A cigarette would do the trick. Would you light up? They're in the usual place.'

'You're turning me into a smoker,' she said lightly, opening the bedside locker. She reached into his jacket pocket for the now familiar silver case and lighter.

The first time, she'd choked trying to light up, but now blew out the smoke once the tip started smouldering. The tobacco still tasted bitter. 'Here you are,' she said placing the cigarette between the fingers of his outstretched hand. 'I don't know how you can breathe in the stuff.'

'Thanks, little Bron. What would I do without you? Beastly nurses won't light up for me.' He inhaled deeply and his whole body relaxed.

'I should hope not,' she said in mock disapproval. 'Here's the ashtray,' and she guided his hand.

After several puffs, he said, 'I'd like to take you out, Bron, once I'm feeling brighter. Would you like that?'

'I'd love it. We could walk into town or down to the pier.'

He frowned, between puffs. 'That's not quite what I meant. I'll order a picnic and we'll go off somewhere. On your birthday.'

'How exciting! I'd have to get permission from Mam.'

'Of course, I wasn't thinking, you're so grown up. Perhaps I should meet your mother first. I could invite her for tea, what do you think?'

'Good idea, she's always asking after you. You'd have her eating out of your hand.'

'If I won the hearts of mother and daughter I'd be a happy man,' George said.

'You're half way there already.' She hadn't meant to be so forward.

Mam had warned her against romance with a wounded soldier. 'We don't know his family; he could be anyone. Such a shame he's not from round here.'

'I'm only befriending him, Mam, but if you met you'd realise he's genuine. And be honest, you didn't know Tada's family; they lived in Barmouth.'

'That's different, he was a curate.'

She'd let it drop, realising her own horizons were far wider.

'I'll tidy the bed so you can get some rest,' she said briskly.

He sat up for her to smooth the pillows. 'It's about time I smartened up to appear in public. I don't want you to be ashamed of me.'

She'd only ever seen him in a dressing gown. 'Aubrey is tall and well built like you. You could borrow some slacks and a shirt, I'm sure he wouldn't mind.'

He smiled. 'Thank you dear one, but Amelia is sending a box of clobber from my wardrobe, it should arrive any day.' He stubbed out his cigarette.

'I didn't thank you properly for the watch. It's the best present I've had since my first cricket bat, and that's saying something.' With a boyish smile, he reached for her hand and brushed her fingers with his lips. 'Bless you for being here today, Bron.'

She thrilled at his touch.

CHAPTER 11

September 1916

Bronwyn watched as Mam turned the heel of a sock, sitting in the wicker seat under the window, her hands working from memory.

'I do hope you like him, Mam. He wants to take me out on my birthday, if you approve.'

'Approve of him, you mean?'

'Yes, if you put it like that. He wants to do things properly.'

'I'm glad. We don't want tongues wagging. I'd always imagined the boys would marry first.'

'I've told you, we're just good friends, and that's the way I want it.'

'I think you're being naïve, dear. How old is he?'

'Twenty-seven, the same age as Aubrey.'

'It's a good age for a man to marry. I wish Aubrey would find someone. I was your age when Tada first courted me.'

She'd heard the story many times, but this time her ears pricked up. 'How long was it before you got married, Mam?'

'We walked out for three years, long enough to know we'd be good for each other. Don't rush into married life, Bron; you have the chance of a degree and your whole life ahead of you.

'And believe me, there's no such thing as being *just friends* between a man and a woman. It doesn't stop there and it's the woman who suffers in the end. Except in certain circles, I'm told.'

Bronwyn picked up the newspaper to hide her irritation. 'What about David Lloyd George?' His indiscretions were common knowledge.

'Men who know greatness live in another universe,' Mam shook her head, 'his poor wife. I wouldn't want her life for a big clock.'

'Don't worry, I'm not about to be anyone's mistress.'

Mam shot her a look and the knitting came to a standstill. 'That'll do young lady, don't be cheeky.' She was soon knitting again. 'Shall I bring a flask of tea tomorrow?'

'No need, Mam, the cake will be ample. By the way, he's still nervous about his appearance.'

'He's no reason to be, not with me.' Mam took up her knitting again.

'You won't see his eyes, because he wears dark glasses in company. They'll replace the glass eye at St Dunstan's when he goes for rehabilitation.'

'It must be hard for a man to lose his independence.'

'He struggles at times. I once tried to help him do up his tie, but he wants to do everything himself. It's hard to stand by and watch. Yesterday, he burnt a hole in his jacket, said he missed the ashtray and the hot ash fell into his pocket. He smelt singeing wool and had to beat the jacket on the floor to put it out. He won't hear of me patching it up.' She sighed.

'His mother and sister should be there to help; I really can't understand why they haven't been.'

'I suppose they're not as close as we are.' It would be disloyal to say his mother was a cold fish.

'Well, I look forward to meeting him. Now play me some Schumann dear, before we draw the curtains.'

Bronwyn knew it by heart, *Scenes from Childhood* that Mam used to play in the evenings waiting for Tada to come home.

'I'll play my favourite; it always sounded like the saddest lullaby.' She went to the piano and ran her hands across the keys and played *Träumerei*, finding herself a child again. A wave of melancholy rose from nowhere, blurring her vision until she came to a halt.

'What is it, dear?'

'It's nothing, I'm being silly.' She blew her nose.

'Come over here.' Mam patted the cushion. 'You must be thinking of Glyn.' They'd been to St Tysilio's with flowers that morning, when the sky was bright and the Straits sparkled. She hadn't shed a tear then.

She sat next to Mam and picked up the ball of green wool, rolling it up tightly. 'It's the music, so full of longing. How terrible, to lose a baby. Were you playing for Tomas all those years ago?'

'Yes, *Del*,' Mam said without flinching. 'I used to think of him. And when you play, I think of Glyn and the promise of youth gone to waste.' Her eyes were deep pools in the fading light.

Bronwyn touched her hand. 'I'll gladly play Schumann another time, but not now. I'll light the lamp so you can finish those socks for Aubrey; we're bound to hear from him soon.'

She wore a plaid skirt that contrasted pleasingly with a fine lawn blouse and the lace collar that Glyn had given her.

Even if George couldn't see, she wanted to look her best. She found Mam in the hall ready to go out, holding the basket.

'You're looking lovely, Bron, I like your hair up.' Mam looked at her tenderly.

'It doesn't make me too tall? I'm such a beanpole.'

'You take after your grandmother Roberts, poppet. She carried her height with grace and had great presence. You're similar in temperament.'

'How so?'

'Mam gave a wry smile. 'She had a big heart, but it didn't do to get on the wrong side of her.'

'I see. You're saying I'm stubborn as well as lanky.'

'Don't be contrary,' Mam pinched her cheek. 'Like your father, you don't let obstacles stand in your way.'

'That's not so bad then,' said Bronwyn, putting on her velvet cape. 'Let me carry the basket.'

They walked along pavements strewn with leaves the colour of damp tobacco, and passed a straggle of whey-faced young men in dusty uniforms trudging up the hill, weighed by rucksacks.

Bronwyn noticed a wraith of a boy, and said, 'Look at that little lad; he can't be a day over fourteen. They'll take anyone these days.'

'I read a man aged seventy signed up,' said Mam, 'he'd served in the Boer war. And we thought Tada was too old.'

There was a group of women at the bus stop, hairnets showing under headscarves, who turned as one at the clanking of iron on stone when the bus rounded the corner, drawn by a steaming pair. The horses stopped neatly at the kerb and shook and snorted in the sharp air as everyone clambered on board.

'They must have been on the six o'clock shift,' said Bronwyn. 'How tired they look.'

'Lizzy wants to work there,' Mam said, frowning. 'I don't think she's got the stamina.'

'At the Vulcan factory? It pays well, but it's danger money.'

'I'm afraid she needs it, as the only breadwinner at home.'

'I suppose families rely on women's wages, now the men have gone. A private's pay won't go far.'

They got off at the hospital and Bronwyn's heart ran riot. Yesterday George had taken her hand and said she was beautiful.

Bronwyn took Mam's arm as they walked up the steps. 'He'll be in the conservatory, it's near the entrance.'

They walked into a glass-panelled room awash with sunshine and as warm as a summer's day.

'Here we are, George,' Bronwyn said brightly, seeing him in an alcove. He wore a blue suit that she hadn't seen before and he'd flattened his hair with oil.

'Mrs Roberts,' George stood up and stretched out his hands in greeting, 'how kind of you to come. I'm so glad to meet you.' He looked pale and his collar hung loose over the carefully knotted tie. He wore dark glasses.

Mam took his hands and said, 'Bronwyn has talked a great deal about you, George, if I may call you by that.'

'I'd be delighted. Please, do sit down.' He spoke with disarming ease and Bronwyn relaxed as she sensed it would go well.

'Mam has baked her famous fruit cake, George, full of cherries.'

He smiled engagingly. 'Thank you kindly, I shall enjoy every morsel.'

'What a pleasant room,' said Mam, 'it must be south facing. I see someone is growing tomatoes.'

'Yes, they smell wonderful, don't they? My mother grows them in a greenhouse at home. Not my thing, gardening, though perhaps I should take it up.'

'I understand you were in business, George, before the war. My eldest, Aubrey, was in banking.'

Bronwyn saw a twitch of anxiety in his cheek as he replied, 'Yes, box-making with my father. Ah, is that the tea trolley? I may not be able to see, but I have the hearing of a bloodhound these days.'

George's batman wheeled in the trolley.

'Meet Meredith,' said George.

'Madam,' he said to Mam, inclining his head.

Mam said, '*Prynhawn da*,' wishing him good afternoon as she would anyone.

He unloaded the tea tray with his gnarled hands, and Bronwyn set the table.

When he'd gone, George said, 'I landed with the Royal Welsh more or less by accident, you know. I soon learned the Welshman wants to know the reason for orders, before he follows you. I've never met a tougher and more reliable bunch of men.'

Bronwyn was taken aback to hear him speak of the Welsh as outsiders, and it wouldn't endear him to Mam. 'It comes from being overrun by the English,' she said hastily, 'that's why we have so many castles.

'We're a race of non-conformists; it's our nature. Shall I pour?'

The awkward moment passed and Bronwyn sighed with relief.

'Just half a cup for me, please Mrs Roberts. I tend to spill.'

He took the cup and saucer to his chest and sipped. 'Just the way I like it.' He put out a hand and felt for the table and put the cup and saucer down again.

'Do you know, things don't taste the same as they used to. It's all to do with appearances. Quite unconsciously, you look at your food and decide what it's meant to taste like, before eating it. Of course smell is important, but colour matters too. With wine, I find I need to know if it's a red or a white, to be sure of the difference.'

'Let's see if you can taste the special ingredients in Mam's scones,' Bronwyn teased, handing him one.

He nibbled, head to one side. 'Slightly spicy. Cinnamon and a hint of nutmeg. Am I right?'

Mam beamed with pleasure. 'Spot on, George. Nothing much wrong with your taste buds, I'd say.'

'I'd like to thank you for your daughter's company, Mrs Roberts,' he said, in serious tones. 'Bron is a tower of strength, a true friend and companion. I really don't know what I'd do without her. She even laughs at my jokes.'

Mam patted George's hand and said, 'She's only too pleased to help. It must be hard to be so far away from your family.'

'Indeed. I expect my sister to come fairly soon, to take me home. Before then, I'd like to show Bron my appreciation by taking her out for her birthday. If you'd allow it, that is.'

Mam held her cup mid-air. 'I don't see why not. Maybe Maddy could come with you, dear?'

Bronwyn's heart sank, but George stepped in.

'Bron is as precious to me as my own sister, Mrs Roberts. Rest assured I will return her safely into your hands.'

'Very well then,' Mam said, recovering her composure. 'Bronwyn deserves a day out. The last months haven't been easy.'

George nodded in silent acknowledgement of their loss. 'It's gone on far too long, this wretched war. Lloyd George is the man of the hour, to my mind. A man of vision. He'll sort out the munitions crisis if anyone can, and has the confidence of the coalition.'

'And the guile and charm to go with it,' Bronwyn chipped in.

Mam stiffened. 'Let's not talk politics when there's a birthday treat in the offing. You should take George on a ferry to Anglesey to get a breath of sea air. I'll make you a picnic basket.' Mam was getting into the spirit.

George chuckled. 'I'm not much of a sailor.'

'If you've crossed the English Channel, you'll make it to Anglesey,' Mam said mischievously. 'Will you have a slice of my cake?'

'I don't mind if I do.' He held out his plate.

'You must keep the rest and give some to Meredith. He seems a nice man.'

'Cake for Meredith? Goodness me, there's a thought. He'd be tickled pink; I'll tell him it was your idea.'

Bronwyn ignored Mam's raised eyebrow.

'I see there's a piano in here, George. Do you enjoy music?'

'Very much, in fact I'm a regular at concerts. Not much of a musician myself, but I'm a keen listener. And yourself?'

'Bron is the pianist these days. You must come to tea and she'll play for you.'

'George likes Chopin, so I'll have to brush up on my Waltzes,' Bronwyn said, feeling giddy. He'd already proposed teaching her to dance.

The conversation went pleasantly from music to the benefits of walking, and touched on George's favourite sports of cricket and tennis.

'Pity I've batted my last wicket,' he said with real sadness. 'Sorry, I didn't mean to be maudlin; I'm lucky to be alive. I hope I haven't caused offence.'

'You're mourning your life as it was,' said Mam, 'it's perfectly understandable.'

What a touching thing to say, thought Bronwyn, and resolved to be more patient next time Mam annoyed her.

When it was time to leave George reached for Mam's hand. 'It's been a delight and a privilege, Mrs Roberts. I hope we meet again soon.'

'I hope so too, George.'

'Bron?' he said.

She touched his sleeve and he caught her hand.

'Let me thank you for bringing your mother.' He kissed the back of her hand in a courtly gesture. 'As for the picnic, no basket required, I'll see to that.'

As they were leaving, Meredith arrived to clear the table.

When Bronwyn looked back and saw George, her heart ached. He'd have to wait for a nurse to take him to the ward; he would hope for some conversation, or perhaps ask someone to put on a record. He would have to regain independence and adapt to a life of physical hazards invisible to the sighted.

There was a letter on the mat when they got home.

'Mam, it's from Aubrey,' Bronwyn said turning over the envelope. 'Look, it's from Holland.'

'At last! I was beginning to wonder when we'd hear.' Mam looked perplexed. 'I didn't know he was in Holland.'

'He isn't. It's a neutral country and the route for sending mail.'

She slid a fingernail under the seal and pulled out the letter. There was a typed heading. 'He's in a prison camp in a place called Clausthal am Harz. I don't know where that is.'

'What does he say?' Mam said, twisting the buttons on her coat.

They stood in the hallway as Bronwyn read out Aubrey's small and careful handwriting.

Absender:
Name: P.A. Roberts
Dienstgrad: Lieut.
Regiment: Royal Welsh Fusiliers

Offizier-Gefangenenlager
Clausthal am Harz
Deutschland

September 1st 1916

My Dearest Mother,
It's been six weeks since I was captured and I suspect this letter is the first definite proof you have that I am fit (more or less) and well. Communications are quite chaotic out here. I have been extremely worried about you all. I received the terrible news about Glyn just before I was captured. I can't begin to say how sorry I am. I will always treasure the brief moments we had together when I could wangle a visit to see him. He was my little brother and always will be. I miss being able to write to him.

Is Huw still in training? I hope the show will be over before he's posted to France. How quiet it must be now, with just you and Bron at home.

Let me tell you a little about life over here. I'm living in rather cramped quarters with six other officers in a room 25 feet by 7 feet. We drew lots for our beds and I was lucky enough to end up in a corner near the window. We have just finished papering our room with sheets of brown paper fixed with drawing pins, and it looks quite good. We'll put up family photographs as well as some artistic pictures we've ordered from Leipzig and Munich. It should look almost homely by the time we've finished.

There are a number of things I need. I realise this will add considerably to your load, but maybe Bron could help out? I would be glad to receive a Welsh-English Bible. Also a cardigan and Wellington gum boots, both indispensable in winter. I'm in need of a pair of dark-grey flannel trousers with a red stripe (1/4 inch wide) down the side. The red stripe is compulsory here. Also a box of tooth powder as paste-tubes are not allowed. Don't ask me why.

Oh, and could you send me a cake as often as possible, especially when the colder weather starts? I should also be glad of self-raising flour and currants that I'll hand to the canteen to go towards communal puddings. A fairly liberal supply of cigarettes would be welcome as it will save me buying German ones, which are much more expensive than ours and not as good.

I'm sorry to send such a shopping list, but I hope to have more interesting news next time. Do tell Bron to write to me about her new life in College—not long now. I know she'll do well. I'm afraid I can't write to Tada for security reasons. Please send him and Bron my love and ditto Huw when you're next in touch. I've come to the end of my space now.
Heaps of love,
Aubrey

She turned to Mam. 'That's such a relief, isn't it? At least he's safe.'

'Poor dear,' Mam brushed away a tear. 'I hope he's not badly treated, one never knows. He'll need plenty of warm clothes; I hear they have fearful winters over there. If only we could send him some coal.'

'Coal?' Bronwyn gave her a hug. 'How funny you are!'

CHAPTER 12

September 1916

Birthdays and anniversaries were remembered with muted celebration. The children in Chapel still received a small gift, an illustrated bookmark or notebook, though some had suggested that was an unaffordable luxury. Bronwyn was glad when Mam won against the naysayers.

Sporadic shortages meant those at home went without, so that parcels to loved ones could be filled. The grocer ran out of flour, cooking pots disappeared from the ironmonger's shelves, then eggs were mysteriously in short supply. She'd read in the *Manchester Guardian* that these were more or less commandeered from farms, turned into edible powder for the troops, and the farmers were paid a handsome price.

However, today was going to be different, a special day, she told herself, as she brushed her hair in long strokes, making it crackle, and threw it back over her shoulders in one swift movement. She swirled it up into a knot, swung her hips a little, and laughed at herself in the mirror for being ridiculous. Even so, the young woman she saw was rather handsome, and she hoped George might imagine her so.

She took one last appraising look and declared, 'You *shall* go to the ball!'

When she arrived at the hospital, George was standing on the steps with Meredith, his batman.

'George!' She called out, running up to him, 'sorry I took so long.'

'Happy birthday, dear girl,' he said, catching her wrist and kissing her lightly on the cheek. 'We're all set, with a grand picnic courtesy of Meredith. He's rustled up the finest fare he could lay his hands on, isn't that right, Meredith?'

'I did what I could, Sir. I hope the young lady enjoys her birthday,' he said raising his cap.

'Thank you, Meredith, I can't wait. My mother sends her regards.'

'Just hand me the rucksack, would you, there's a good man, and we'll get a move on.'

She wished George would speak to him more kindly.

'I'll help you on with it, Sir,' said Meredith, lifting the rucksack onto George's back.

'Lead on to the ferry,' said George taking her arm. 'We'll have a little jaunt across the Straits, hopefully not too choppy. I'm so relieved your mother didn't change her mind.'

'You charmed her to bits,' Bronwyn said, though she'd called him a ladies' man, and told her to be careful.

He was broad shouldered under his great coat, and she admired the tallness of him, making her feel almost slight at his side. Today he wore his protective outdoor glasses, rather like goggles. He could be a dashing pilot.

'Are you looking at me?' he inquired.

'You're very handsome, George. We're going to have a wonderful day.' She felt light and carefree, even the sun had made an effort, hanging indolent in the sky with the promise of a final summer fling.

'The day is yours, dear girl. Is that the ferry? Will we make it?'

She laughed. 'Don't worry; they start hooting half way across the Straits. We've got plenty of time.'

'I can't wait to give you my present, even though it's a small thing.'

'Oh, George, you needn't have. Everyone's been so kind. The family clubbed together to give me money for College, and Hannah promised me a shopping trip to Liverpool. I can't wait, to go to College; I'm fed up with school.'

'You're the cleverest girl I know, and you'll make your mark, I've no doubt. I suppose sooner or later you'll meet someone who'll sweep you off your feet. Sometimes we meet the right person at the wrong time, don't you think?' His tone was light but his expression serious.

'If that happened, one would just have to wait,' she said, heart racing.

'Well, now Miss Roberts, what am I to make of that?' He laughed. 'Sorry, I shouldn't tease you, and of course you're far too young to contemplate life with a man my age.'

'You're hardly old!' she objected, thrilled at the notion of a future together, however distant.

'You mean a great deal to me, Bron, more than any woman I've known. I've never felt surer of my feelings. I'm not about to winkle you away from your studies, but there is one thing I would ask.'

She felt his arm round her waist.

'What is it, George?' she said, breathless.

'I'd like you to meet my family; visit me in London. What do you say?'

She moved closer to him, as they approached the waiting crowd. 'I'd love to, if I can get round Mam.'

'Excellent!' He nodded with an air of satisfaction. 'It'll be a while before I'm settled back home, but I'll hold you to it.'

She couldn't wait to tell Maddy, a trip to London was practically going abroad.

As they joined the queue, the ferry manoeuvred at the side of the jetty ready to dock. Ropes were lashed to capstans and George held onto her arm as they inched towards the gangway.

Once on board, she said, 'We'll sit port side, it's less exposed,' and guided him to a bench.

They huddled as the ferry got under way. 'I can taste salt,' said George.

'It's the spray blowing back from the sea,' she replied, taking a deep breath.

'I wasn't much looking forward to the boat trip,' he said. 'We had a rough crossing from France; like sardines. They packed in two trainloads and it took ten hours. The stench wasn't ordinary. Sorry, Bron, that was uncalled for.'

'You can't shock me, George, I've got three brothers.' As she spoke, she realised this was no longer true.

The breeze picked up as the ferry ploughed the clear water and George put a protective arm round her shoulder. 'Paint me a picture,' he said. 'What can you see out there?'

'Mountains, mostly, the peaks of Snowdon.'

'Go on.'

'Think of a horseshoe with Snowdon, the highest, embraced by four great peaks. Crib Goch and Garnedd Ugain rise up to one side, and on the other, the twin peaks of Y Lliwedd. They're often dark and brooding, but today all the mountains sparkle and the air is so clear you could see them from my aunt Marjorie's attic bedroom in Liverpool.'

He gave a full-throated laugh. 'I can see you standing tiptoe and nose pressed to the window, making out the shapes on the horizon. What magnificent names they have, like ancient gods that hold up the sky.'

'We have plenty of myths; Snowdon was home to Rhita Gawr, the giant who subdued the warring kings of Britain. He disgraced them by cutting off their beards, which he stitched to make a cloak for himself. In the end it was King Arthur who got the better of him.'

'That's a good way to knock heads together without killing people.'

'Oh, I expect he did away with a few of them.' She moved closer against the stiffening breeze, feeling the wind in her face.

'What wonderful images you paint, Bron. When you describe something, I see it in colour. In my mind's eye, the mountain is sheer, in shades of grey and emerald, against a stark blue sky. Am I right?'

'Yes, you have it exactly, though there are gentler slopes. We'll walk up there one day.'

He nodded as if reserving judgment. 'D'you know, the memories I have from last time I could see, are in murky shades of brown. They're not images I want to dwell on, I can tell you. They haunt my dreams.

'Last night something changed. I dreamt of a world of colourful shapes like pieces of stained glass. I could see gaps, but I knew it was within my power to fill them, like a jigsaw. With a supreme effort, I saw the entire picture blazing in the window. When I woke I felt enormously hopeful, as if something was restored even though it wasn't my sight.'

She squeezed his hand.

'The reason I'm telling you, is that it's largely down to you. I don't want to be sentimental, but you've helped keep a flame of hope alive. There's no way I could give in to misery and self-pity with your cheery self around.'

Bronwyn was silent for a while. 'I don't think I've had such an influence; you have great inner strength.' She meant it. He was mentally tough as well as physically strong.

He lifted his hat to scratch his head and let out a sigh. 'It's the truth, I assure you.' He frowned. 'It won't be easy going back home. I've had differences with my father, and Mother is tied up with charity work. Amelia will help, but I have to get back onto my own two feet.'

'Isn't that the point of St Dunstan's?'

'You're right, I should be more forward looking.'

The Anglesey side was approaching fast and people were collecting belongings and rounding up children.

'I can see the castle,' she said, to distract him. 'We'll be getting off in a minute.'

'Already? Now, don't lift that rucksack, it's far too heavy. I squirrelled away a bottle of champagne.'

They were soon walking arm in arm along the front at Beaumaris, which had a tired end-of-season look about it, despite the summery weather.

'I was last here with Glyn, we came out for a day's cycling. It was just before he went away.'

'I'm sorry I never met him.'

'Me too, you'd have got on well. He was huge fun and full of obscure and amusing facts.'

He gave her arm a squeeze.

'The castle's just here on the left, medieval, with whole sections intact. You can walk up the turrets and see chimneybreasts and great fireplaces. There's an inner chapel, which is remarkably well preserved.'

'No wonder it attracts visitors. How else do people make a living here?

'Fishing, I imagine.'

'Yes, the fishing boats are on the right, the other side of a grassy promenade. The tide's out and boats are at angles on the sand, anchor ropes lying slack. We could stay here or go to a secluded spot further along, if you prefer. It would mean negotiating a few boulders.'

'Is it far?'

'About half a day's march. No, I'm joking, we'll be there in no time. Let's trot.'

'Trot? You must be joking; the champagne will explode.'

She laughed. 'Goodness, I'd forgotten! What else is in the rucksack, George?'

'I don't want to spoil the surprise, but I think you'll enjoy it. Amelia sent a few items from *Fortnums*.'

'*Fortum and Mason?* Aubrey swears by them, he says they're the best grocers in the world.'

George grinned. 'He's right; I'll take you there one day. London, the bright lights, you've got it all to come. I know the city like the back of my hand, so I'll be your guide.'

'I don't want to think about you going back, George.'

He gave a flourish as if waving a magic wand. 'I hereby banish all unhappy thoughts. Are we nearly there?'

'Not quite. We'll take a narrow path, then I'll help you down to the beach.'

When they reached the end of the path, she said, 'Hold my hand, we have to scramble down.'

He was taking faltering steps as if afraid of losing his footing.

'There's a bit of a drop now, so sit down and I'll go first.' She leapt off the edge and called up, 'I'm over here. Lower the rucksack, that's it, I've got it. Now give me your hand and jump, it's not far.'

He followed her instructions. 'Gordon Bennett, what's this, an assault course?' he said, landing at her side.

'You'll be glad to know we don't have to go back the same way. We can walk to the next bay and take a gentler route.'

'Glad to hear it!'

They set up a makeshift camp in the lee of a rock and George unpacked the rucksack. Meredith had thought of everything, down to napkins, tablecloth and a tartan rug. There were blue and white enamel plates and mugs and a tin sandwich box with a faded picture of the old queen.

'Better get this into water and let it settle,' he said, handing her the champagne.

'There's a handy rock pool here,' she said, and submerged the aristocratic looking bottle under seaweed.

When it was all laid out, Bronwyn said, 'What a spread, George, a real feast.'

They sat on the rug, and George said, 'Time for your present, Bron,' and reached inside his jacket. 'Close your eyes and hold out your hand.' He pressed a small book into her palm. 'Sorry it isn't wrapped, but it's from the heart.'

Her eyes blinked open and she saw the red cover, embossed with a female figure. 'A poetry book, Christina Rossetti, how beautiful!' She breathed in the smell of new leather and ran her finger along the gold-tipped pages. 'George, thank you, it means so much to me.' She leaned over to kiss his cheek.

'My pleasure, or it will be when you read to me. I thought of buying you a fur collar or stole, but neither seemed right. I know you love books.'

'It's perfect,' she said, guiding his hand over the cover, 'can you feel the shape of the illustration?'

His fingertips explored the lines and curves. 'It's the figure of a woman, I hadn't realised!' He smiled.

'Your birthday's in May, isn't it?'

'Fancy you remembering that, my dear,' he said gently.

'I'll surprise you too.' She'd play the piano for him and perhaps they'd walk up Snowdon.

'Today's your birthday, so let's drink to it. Would you mind retrieving the bottle from its ice bucket? Try not to shake it.'

'Here it is,' she said, laughing nervously, 'I've never had it before.'

'Don't worry, it's very light.' He carefully removed the metal cage from the cork, covered the cork with his napkin and eased it out with a gentle pop. 'Ready?'

She brought each mug to the bottle as he poured, testing the depth with his finger.

'Hold steady, we don't want to waste it on the crabs,' he said, when her hand wobbled. 'Now wrap the bottle in a damp napkin, and it'll stay cool.'

She dipped a napkin in the rock pool, tied it round and secured the bottle with a heap of stones.

George raised his mug. 'To you, Bron, Many Happy Returns!'

'To you too, George, to both of us,' she said, clanking her mug against his.

The champagne bubbled deliciously in her face as she took her first sip. It was sharp, almost sour, and she decided it was an acquired taste.

'I'm getting peckish,' said George. 'Would you mind dishing out?'

There were olives, artichoke hearts and spiced eggs in aspic, as well as dainty sandwiches. She handed him a selection, 'Bon appétit.'

'This is tasty,' she said, biting into a sandwich. 'Is it salt fish?'

'Must be the egg and anchovy; some have pâté de foie gras and there should be smoked York ham.'

'Such luxury. Is this how you live in London? Bangor must seem so dull.'

'Not at all. I used to eat at a rather drab businessmen's club, so this is a treat for me.'

There was a twittering overhead and George tilted his head skyward, scanning for sound. 'Don't tell me, starlings! And he held out his hand as if one might land on his sleeve. 'It was in Givenchy; they were so tame they'd nest in the sandbags and we used to feed them. It was quite extraordinary, the way they stayed right through the shelling. When it was quiet, they sang.' He threw scraps of sandwich onto the stones and there was screeching above. 'Sounds as though the gulls got there first.'

The horizon wavered as her eyes flooded with tears, and she sniffed.

'Something the matter?'

'It's nothing, probably the champagne, I'm not used to it.'

'Bron?' He wasn't going to let it go.

'Oh you know, anniversaries, people gone, it's when you think of them. There's always sadness, even on good days.'

'You miss Glyn.' He put an arm round her.

'He went away full of hope, but I fear the war killed his spirit; he wrote such bitter lines of poetry.

'That time in Beaumaris, we talked about the future, and he asked if I could ever see myself settling. I wanted to study and travel, it was all so clear back then.'

'And now?'

'The same, I suppose, I want to study, but I also want to change the way people see the world.'

He pulled off his glasses and rubbed his temples. 'I hope you find happiness, Bron, whatever you do. This life is all we have.'

'Is that what you think?'

His unruly hair fell over his forehead; his eyes were well on the mend.

'I'm afraid I was never much of a churchgoer. I realise Chapel means a lot to you.' He put his glasses back on.

'I take it for granted; it's the way I've been brought up. When Glyn was younger he'd clash with Tada over religion, but I don't think he lost his faith.'

'And here you are with a godless reprobate. What would your father say?'

'He'd probably say you're still God's child whether you like it or not. I don't think he'd worry.'

'I like that. Eminently practical. I'm not a complete heathen; I used to attend services with the men. And I've met some remarkable padres. So, you don't mind?'

'About your beliefs? Not at all, it's a matter of conscience. I'm not going to sit in judgment.'

'Thank heavens for that,' he said, and chuckled.

'May I let down your hair, Bron?' he asked, already loosening combs before she had time to object.

She felt his fingers unwinding the thick coil, until it fell to her shoulders.

'There, I like it better like that.' He stroked her head.

'You'll be the undoing of me,' she said, her breath quickening.

'Time for dessert, then?' he said with a hint of mischief.

She passed him the dish of fruits.

'Can I tempt you?' he asked, and fed her a cherry.

There were greengages, figs and apricots preserved in syrup and they guzzled until their fingers dripped.

'I'd better rinse off,' she said, laughing.

'Here,' he said, taking her hand and licked her fingers one by one.

'George,' she said under her breath, 'stop, stop this,' and pulled gently from him.

There was a cool gust. 'You mustn't get cold, my dear, I should take you home. What's the tide doing?'

'Still coming in. We'll make it, if we get a move on.' She didn't want the day to end.

They got to their feet, rinsed the dishes in the pool, and packed.

'Rucksack's a lot lighter,' George said, allowing her to steady him across slithery rocks.

'George, I can see Angel's hair,' she said, catching sight of long strands of pale seaweed floating on the surface of a shallow pool. 'Here, bend down and feel it.'

He crouched low and let the slimy tendrils float across his fingers. 'Is it green?'

'No, more like damp straw.' She must remember to colour his world.

They continued hand in hand, squelching through sand, leaving temporary imprints as the advancing tide gained ground. They ducked under a rocky shelf hung with leathery bladderwrack before rounding the tip of the bay.

'We've made it!' she said, relieved. 'We'll be in time for the ferry,' there was a warning hoot. 'They run every hour.'

He turned to her with his boyish smile. 'Or we could find a cosy nook above the tide line and you can describe the view to me.' He kissed her hand.

There was a sheltered spot under the dunes and George laid the rug for them to sit. It was what she wanted, to let him kiss her.

He reached out and held her face with the tenderness of a large man cupping a butterfly and she closed her eyes as he gently found her mouth with his, brushing her lips with salt kisses. It was delicious, this mute getting to know each other.

Silence fell. A silence so long and intimate that the sun dipped red and the tide came and went without them.

CHAPTER 13

October 1916

When a place at St Dunstan's became available, the doctor declared George fit to go. George was keen to get started on rehabilitation and left within a few days.

It was such a wrench, saying goodbye to him. Amelia, who'd travelled with a maid, had tactfully walked away, but they still had to curtail any lingering kiss. George said he'd find someone to drop her a line when he arrived, and gave her a piece of paper with the address.

She'd hardly seen Maddy in recent weeks, every moment was spent with George, and today they met in the Wicklow Café. Bronwyn breathed in the aroma of Camp coffee, warming her hands on the earthenware mug.

'You've really fallen for him, haven't you?' Maddy said, as they sat in the window.

It was busy this morning, full of students returning before the start of term.

Bronwyn's mind drifted back to the passionate moments on the beach. They'd missed the last boat and walked all the way back to Menai Bridge.

'Sounds as if he practically proposed,' Maddy persisted.

'Not exactly. We talked about the future and finishing College. Three years is a long time and he said I could have second thoughts, which I won't.'

'He has oodles of charm, I'll give him that; and he's no callow youth. He struck me as a man used to getting his own way.'

'You didn't take to him, I saw that.' They'd met over tea, just before he left.

'That's not fair. I just hope you know what you're getting into, that's all.'

'At least I can rely on you to be honest, Mads. If you came with me to London, you might get a better impression.'

Maddy grinned. 'As a chaperone? That's hilarious, especially after what you got up to in Beaumaris.'

'Nothing I regret, I can assure you.' She took a gulp of coffee. 'It may turn out to be more of a long-distance relationship. We promised to write to each other.'

'At least I'll see more of you now. That's mean, I know, but you virtually disappeared over the summer.'

It was true; she'd neglected Maddy. 'I'm sorry, Mads, I'll make it up to you, I promise.

'We had so much to talk about; sometimes he'd tell me what he'd been through, he said it helped, and it made me feel less sad about Glyn.'

'I can see that; you're looking quite radiant these days.'

'Bronwyn felt herself colour. 'Enough about George. Do you fancy seeing a film? There's one called *Battle of the Sexes*, with Lillian Gish. Could be our sort of thing?'

Maddy gave a rippling laugh, 'Now you're talking, I've got my old friend back.'

'I expected to hear from him by now. Should I write first?'

'That didn't last long, not talking about him.' She tossed back her thick auburn hair. 'The problem is you're in love, silly goose, and your brains are scrambled. He'll be in touch soon enough.'

Maddy didn't mince words, but meant well.

They both turned, as a group of chattering girls burst in out of the rain, flapping their gowns like young crows trying out their wings.

'You're right, I'll bide my time.'

'Drink up, and we'll catch the matinée,' said Maddy, 'you need taking out of yourself.'

Bronwyn and Hannah sat face to face in an otherwise empty ladies' carriage, linked by a thread of brown wool. A skein lay stretched across Bronwyn's hands, flowing into a ball opposite. Hannah wound it up in a well-practised rhythm and a tinkling of her bangled wrist.

They were heading for Liverpool and for the first time, Bronwyn was curious to know what it was like for Hannah living away from home.

'Did you want to go to Liverpool, Hannah? Weren't you lonely?

'I just got on with it, dear, we did in those days. When Uncle Stanley found me the position at the Post Office, it meant one less mouth to feed. I stayed with your Aunt Marjorie and Uncle Stanley, so I was with family. It would be like you staying with Aubrey, if he had a wife. I didn't care for Liverpool one bit. It took a while to get used to nobody speaking Welsh.'

'And the Post Office, did you like working there?'

Hannah flashed a smile, showing even white teeth. 'I loved it, *Cariad*. You get to know people's lives. I remember a young lady who used *Poste Restante* for pamphlets she didn't want her mother to see.'

'Isn't that used when someone's travelling?'

'It is. It's also a useful cover if you don't want something posted to your home address. The lady in question was getting pamphlets from the Suffragettes. When her mother found out, she marched straight in and gave me a proper mouthful. I told her it was none of my business. And none of hers, for that matter, but I held my tongue. Sadly, the rather colourful packages stopped coming after that.'

'Go on, I could listen for hours.'

Hannah twinkled over her glasses. 'There was an unfortunately named Mr Handsome. He made out postal orders, regular as clockwork, to two Mrs Handsomes; we joked that he must be keeping two wives. One day we saw both women waiting in the queue and exchanging pleasantries, as people do to pass the time.'

'They didn't know each other?'

'I'm sure they didn't. It was the strangest thing to see them there, both with little boys who looked astonishingly alike.'

'No!'

'It was soon in the papers; he had nine children and had been married to both women for over ten years. They were only streets apart.'

'It's a wonder he got away with it for so long. Did he go to prison?'

'I'm afraid so. Both families suffered after that.'

'Surely, he deserved it?'

Hannah looked up from her wool. 'At least he'd supported them all. I doubt the judge took that into account.'

How full of surprises you are, thought Bronwyn.

The skein finally disappeared into a large khaki ball, which came to rest in Hannah's lap; she took a pair of needles from her bag and started deftly casting on. Fields of sheep slipped by and rain slid sideways across the glass as the needles fell into a gentle rhythm with the rocking of the train.

'How are things with George, *Del*? Your Mam tells me you're thick with him.'

'Did she? I may need your help, Hannah. George wants me to visit him in London and I'm not sure how to raise it with Mam.'

The click clacking stopped and she put her knitting to one side. 'Do be careful, Bron, dear. I fell in love once and lived to regret it. I was about your age.'

There was a loud bang as the door clattered open, which sucked in the air and noise from the corridor.

'Tickets please, ladies,' the guard bellowed above the racket. He pushed his cap to the back of his head as Hannah delved into her bag.

He examined the tickets closely, 'So, it's Liverpool you're off to?'

Bronwyn didn't like his familiar manner.

'Yes, we have family there,' Hannah said curtly.

He handed them back with a cursory nod and turned tail without tipping his cap. The train plunged into a tunnel, the door rattled and the air smelled of soot. As the train passed through, they were met briefly by their own reflections and Bronwyn wished she was pretty like Hannah.

'As I was saying,' Hannah spoke into the gloom, 'I was very young and like you, I fell in love.'

The train rushed out into the open air.

'Love is exciting and wonderful, but it can be dangerous. I'm not proud of what I'm about to tell you, but I hope it may help.'

Bronwyn watched as Hannah took an apple and a fruit knife from her bag and began paring, making a perfect spiral of russet peel that landed neatly on the handkerchief in her lap.

'We met at choir. He had a fine tenor voice, an older man and quite serious. He was married.' Hannah sliced the apple into quarters and shared it between them.

'Really? So you knew that from the start.'

'We were mere acquaintances. He asked if he could walk me home after practice, as we lived in the same direction. In fact, he suggested I ask my uncle and aunt first. Uncle Stanley didn't like the idea of me walking home alone, so he was pleased. He made enquiries at the Post Office and found out that my fellow singer and his wife lived at a respectable address.'

Bronwyn listened, alert.

'For months, we just talked each week and became good friends. It all happened very gradually, crept up on us almost. He often spoke of his wife, who was in delicate health; I would ask after her, and plucked up courage to ask what was wrong. He said she had women's problems, which made him very sad.'

'Did you ever meet her?'

'Yes, once or twice in the summer months, when he asked me in for tea. She was very sweet. She had spells in a nursing home, and it was then that it started.' Hannah spoke in staccato notes as if detaching herself from the account.

'What happened?' Bronwyn was already shocked.

'We snatched precious weekends together. He said I made him happier than he'd ever been. He made promises.'

'And you believed him?'

'I was in too deep. In the end he couldn't abandon her. He stopped coming to choir. Then he wrote to me,' Hannah's voice cracked, 'I'd never seen his handwriting before. He said he didn't ask forgiveness, but that I must remember he loved me. Soon afterwards they moved to Southport. I only saw him once after that.'

'Oh Hannah!' She crossed the carriage to sit beside her, as Hannah brushed away a tear.

'I almost went out of my mind. Your Aunt Marjorie helped me get back onto my feet. I would have gone to your Mam, but you were on the way at the time.'

Bronwyn's mind was in turmoil. She and George had exchanged several letters; his were warmly affectionate and written in Amelia's hand, so he couldn't possibly be engaged to someone else.

'Should I doubt George's sincerity? I'm quite sure there isn't another woman in his life.'

Hannah picked up her knitting. 'I'm sure you're right; what happened next was graver than that. It will have to wait for now.'

There was a sound of hooting and a long scream of brakes as the train slowed on its approach to Lime Street Station.

How hard it must be for Hannah, this journey back to the past, thought Bronwyn, looking at her aunt's mournful face.

The horse-drawn cab rattled along a crowded street and Bronwyn stared up at tall houses, three and four storeys high with brass nameplates on glossy doors, as they passed through the business end of the city.

At last they reached the outskirts where the roads became cobbled and the noise made talking impossible. Hannah, holding hard onto the leather strap, mouthed, *nearly there*, from under the grey half-veil arranged over her eyes. It wasn't long before they turned into a narrow street of soot-blackened terraced houses that Bronwyn remembered from childhood. She must have been twelve when she was last here with the boys.

Hannah tapped the cabby on the shoulder and he jerked his vehicle to a halt. Bronwyn saw a familiar figure coming down the street and before the cabby could get round, she'd opened the door and leapt out.

'Bronny, how you've grown, and so beautiful!' Aunt Marjorie gave her a huge hug. A little plumper and greyer perhaps, but warm and welcoming as ever.

The house seemed smaller and darker and memories flooded in at the scent of beeswax mixed with pipe tobacco.

Aunt Marjorie led the way up the narrow staircase. 'I've put you in your old room and emptied a couple of drawers. Come when you're ready. Hannah and I will put your Uncle's tea on the table, he eats early.'

Bronwyn looked round the room with its bare boards, iron bedstead and faded pink satin eiderdown. From the window she saw the patch of garden where a swing still dangled, the one Uncle Stanley had rigged up to the tree. How patient Alwyn had been, pushing her back and forth for hours, when he could have been out playing football with Huw and Glyn.

Sounds of clinking cups from the kitchen brought her back to the present and she started unpacking. She tried one of the drawers and found a layette wrapped in fine tissue paper; she ran her finger over an embroidered collar, before putting it hurriedly back. Could these have been meant for baby Tomas? The idea made her queasy.

The house shuddered as the front door banged shut, and Uncle Stanley shouted, 'I'm home.'

She really ought to go down.

Uncle Stanley was already at the table, his broad back to the room as he ate his tea. Aunt Marjorie hovered at his side with a gravy boat.

'Don't linger in the doorway, young Bronny,' he said, resting his knife and fork against the plate, 'come and sit down.'

'Hello, Uncle Stanley,' she gave him a peck on the cheek. 'Mam sends her love. It's been a long time.'

He looked at her. 'Well I never, you are grown up. How old are you now?'

'I'm eighteen, Uncle Stanley, and I'm about to go to College.' She sat next to Hannah.

'They're on a shopping spree for dress materials and the like,' said Aunt Marjorie, as she poured gravy over his dinner.

'Good girl, going to College. I always said you were the brainiest of the lot.' He returned to his plate, a signal that conversation was over until he'd finished his meal.

When he'd eaten, he said, 'I'll go to the parlour for a puff and let you girls have a natter.' He stood up stiffly, holding onto the table for support, and limped out.

'He's not his old self,' said Bronwyn, who hadn't seen him since the accident. A dog had mauled him on his rounds.

'He never will be,' said Aunt Marjorie. 'The pain makes him irritable. Things were bad between him and Alwyn, you know. They had terrible arguments. Stan would have gone to the war himself if it wasn't for his leg.'

'How is Alwyn?'

Aunt Marjorie dabbed her eyes with a corner of her apron. 'He doesn't say much in his letters. Stan said things he shouldn't have, and I told him, if the boy doesn't want to fight, you can't make him. It's what he believes.'

Bronwyn remembered what Glyn had said about stretcher-bearers. 'He's very courageous, Aunt Marjorie, we all think so.'

'When you lost your Glyn, Stan was so ashamed that his own flesh and blood wasn't fighting; but it would break his heart if Alwyn didn't come back.' She clasped her hands under her bosom.

'Sit down, Marjorie, I'll bring you a cuppa,' said Hannah, putting an arm round her. 'I'll give Stanley his tea.'

'Take no notice, I'm just feeling a bit sorry for myself. Let's go and keep the old devil company.' She wore a brave smile.

In the parlour, Bronwyn banked up the fire and Hannah poured. Marjorie brought the footstool over to Uncle Stanley; he put down his newspaper and levered up his bad leg with a groan.

Bronwyn passed round the cups of tea, before sinking into a leatherette armchair, ready to listen to Uncle Stanley.

'You don't know how lucky you are, Bron, going to the university. I started work in the post room at twelve. When all's said and done, my proudest achievement is improving conditions for the workingman. Not a bad life, all in all. Today, votes for women is the burning question. What do you think about that?'

'Perhaps women would bring fresh ideas and sweep away a few old cobwebs,' she said tentatively.

'I'd be one of them, I suppose!' He sounded jovial. 'So, what changes would you like to see?'

'As a country, we wouldn't be so quick to go to war, if women had the vote.'

'You think petticoat power would put an end to it? Then you've never seen a catfight. The point is that every man and woman should be enfranchised. Not just the landed gentry.'

'Bronny's right,' said Hannah. 'I think we'd do a much better job.'

'Any sugar in this tea?' said Uncle Stanley, after taking a sip. 'And why are we using these footling fancy cups? Are we expecting company?'

'You've got two sugars, Stan,' said Aunt Marjorie indulgently, and straightened the armrest cover, knitted in yellow and green.

Bronwyn noticed the green squares matched Uncle Stanley's jumper, and hoped Alwyn didn't have one in matching yellow.

She picked up a copy of *Women's Weekly* magazine, and started flicking through. 'This might give me ideas for a couple of outfits,' she said to no one in particular. She needed a day dress and something a bit smarter for visiting George.

A headline caught her eye, *The Girl I'd Hate to Marry*. 'I think you'd like this one, Uncle Stanley,' she said looking up.

'Ask your aunt, dear, I know nothing about clothes.'

'It's a letter to the editor from a man, listen to this.'

She read on. '*The homemade girl often marries before the Bond Street girl, as men admire her clever fingers. I hate this insane craze for independence and equal rights. Heaven preserve me from a girl like this. A woman's true happiness comes with a husband, a home, and children of her own.*'

'See what we've got to put up with? And this, in a Women's magazine.'

'Not all young men think like that; some prefer a woman with pluck,' he said, nodding vigorously.

'A woman can always steer things her way, if she wants to,' Aunt Marjorie said, nudging his foot on the shared footstool.

Hannah's eyes were fixed on the pages of a magazine and Bronwyn saw she wasn't joining in. Not having a family must be a great sadness, though she was still the dearest aunt anyone could wish for. Something ran deeper that Bronwyn couldn't yet fathom; she must find out what happened all those years ago.

'I say, give women a chance,' Uncle Stanley declared. 'So, good luck to you, Bronny, I have high hopes for you.'

Bronwyn smiled. 'Thank you, Uncle Stanley. I'll do my best.'

'Now, if you'll excuse me, I must get these old bones to bed. Ready Marjorie?' He heaved himself up on his stick.

Aunt Marjorie followed. 'I have to make sure he doesn't miss the stairs,' she said, over her shoulder.

CHAPTER 14

October 1916

Bronwyn was glad of Hannah's sure hand as they perused the bolts of fabric in George Henry Lee's.

'This one is soft enough for a full skirt,' said Hannah, fingering a plum coloured cloth, 'and the green plaid is a good weight for pleats.' She turned to Bronwyn, 'I think earthy reds and browns or even midnight blue would suit you. Definitely not yellow. It sallows the complexion.'

Bronwyn felt dazzled by the light bouncing off the sparkling counters and burnished brass fittings.

'Are you all right, Bron? You look distracted.'

'Actually, I'm famished. Is it too early for lunch?'

'Not at all, my dear, we'll go to the café.'

After several flights of stairs, they stopped on a half-landing as Hannah needed to catch her breath.

Bronwyn said, 'I remember the first time I came here. I must have been about ten. Aunt Marjorie brought me to spend my birthday money in the toy department.

'The minute we walked in I saw cherubs flying across the ceiling, it was like heaven, everything so bright and beautiful, just like in the hymn. Aunt Marjorie pointed to a cherub with a broken wing and said there was a legend that the plasterer had a daughter who died while he was making it, and he changed the design in her memory. It added to the fairy-tale magic of the place.'

'I never knew that, what a lovely story. I can see how it would appeal to a little girl.'

They made their way to the café and found a table, attended by a girl wearing a crisp cap and apron. They settled on lunch-of-the-day at a shilling each and ordered a pot of tea.

Bronwyn surveyed the décor and said, 'I'd better get used to all this splendour. When I visit George, he wants to take me to his favourite tea-house.'

'You must miss him.'

'I do.' She longed to visit, but knew it could be months.

'If he's chosen you, he must be a fine fellow, but you're still very young and it would be a mistake to limit your horizons, an intelligent fine looking girl.'

'There's no need to exaggerate, Hannah, I know I'm plain. I wish I took after you and Mam.'

'Goodness, what nonsense! You have a radiant smile and a graceful figure.'

The waitress appeared with the tea tray and they waited for her to serve.

'What I'm trying to say, Bron, is there are plenty of delightful young men in the world. You two were thrown together by chance.'

'Or good fortune. Does it matter, how we met? We get on so well and have heaps to talk about, and he makes me laugh. He tells me about plays he's seen, places he's visited, I've never known anyone like him before.'

Hannah nodded, 'So, he's a man of the world.'

'Exactly! He's really interesting and knowledgeable.'

'Well, he clearly adores you, and my guess is he'll want to marry you, however long he has to wait. Things have happened very fast for him, getting wounded, meeting you, and now facing up to civilian life. He surely knows that having a wife at his side would make a huge difference.' She paused, eyebrow raised.

'Don't tell me you think he'd marry me just because he's blind?'

'No, I don't. But I do think his need is greater than yours.'

The waitress came with two plates of mushrooms on toast, allowing Bronwyn a few moments to untangle her thoughts. Whichever way she looked at it, Hannah's stark balance sheet simply didn't add up for herself and George.

'I don't understand, after what you told me on the train; how you risked everything for love. Now you're telling me to be cautious. It doesn't make any sense.'

Hannah's eyes softened. 'You're right, Bron. Let's just say I don't want you to get hurt.'

'What happened after he left you, Hannah?'

Hannah adjusted her little grey hat and gazed into the middle distance.

'There was a child,' she said, eventually.

'A child?' Bronwyn's thoughts flew to the baby clothes in the bedroom drawer.

'Yes, a baby girl.'

'That's when Aunt Marjorie looked after you.'

'Yes, she was marvellous.' Hannah started eating her mushrooms on toast.

'And the baby?'

Hannah put down her knife and fork and said quietly, 'I gave her away; I had no choice. I had my reasons. Don't ask why. It's the biggest regret of my life.'

Bronwyn started to eat slowly. She felt winded. It dawned on her, the child must be her age, if Mam was expecting at the time.

'Couldn't Mam have helped?'

'I know what you're thinking, and believe me, I thought about it. So now you know. Don't make the same mistake, Bron.'

She didn't dare press any harder.

'Now what's the film you wanted to see?' Hannah asked.

Bronwyn pulled herself back into the moment. 'It's a documentary about The Battle of the Somme, at the Scala.'

Hannah frowned, 'Goodness, are you sure you want to see that? So soon after Glyn.'

'Yes, I want to know what it was like for him; unless you'd rather not.'

'Of course I'll come, if it means so much to you, *Del.*'

They bought cloth and dress patterns for two outfits and left George Henry Lee's, laden with shopping bags.

Bronwyn took Hannah's free arm and said, 'Thank you for everything, Hannah. Not just the shopping, for telling me about what happened to you.'

'You could do so much with your life, Bron, I don't want you to throw it all away.'

They rounded a corner and saw the Scala cinema, as grand and imposing as any theatre. They arrived in time for the start of the next showing and bought stalls tickets from a tiny lady perched on a stool, in a kiosk no bigger than a sentry box.

They joined the queue. On the other side of the doors, they could hear the orchestra rise to a crescendo with rolling drums and a volley of trumpets; the crowd shifted with impatience, filled with expectation.

The doors were finally thrown open and people spilled out into the foyer. When the usherette signalled with her flashlight the queue surged and Bronwyn took Hannah's arm in case they were separated. She felt the carpet soft underfoot, and looked at the Grecian style motifs on the walls and the ceiling glimmering gold.

They made their way along a row of plush red seats and sank into velvet, tucking the bags underneath.

'It's going to be a full house,' said Hannah. 'We should get a good view from here, if you can see over the feather hat.'

'Just about! How wonderful to have an orchestra. In Bangor there's only a piano.'

'S'cuse me love!' Three girls tried to barge past.

'Ouch,' said Bronwyn as one of them trampled over her foot.

The girl looked round and glared; she had coal eyes in a face the colour of parchment.

'Munitions girls,' Hannah whispered, once they were out of earshot. 'Makes their skin go yellow.'

There was no time to ask why, as the orchestra struck up a regimental march and the lights dimmed. The curtains drew slowly apart.

The atmosphere was electric, as the audience leaned forward to read the caption that filled the screen:

Platoons Of The Buffs, Bedfords, Suffolks And A Battalion Of The Royal Welsh Fusiliers Moving Up On The Evening Before The Attack

The Welsh Fusiliers! Bronwyn's heart jolted, it could be Glyn's battalion, she might catch a glimpse of him! Weary looking soldiers lined up along a narrow street and a young officer called the roll. Men quick marched two-abreast, flanked by officers on horseback; a column bearing slanted rifles made ragged progress along a cobbled street, then disappeared behind a covered wagon. It all looked so makeshift, like a shabby film.

The next caption read: *Men Refilling Limbers with Empty Cases; Munitions Dumps Receive Vast Supplies Of Shells, Thanks to Munitions Workers*, and the factory girls further down the row let out a whoop of delight and started clapping. Images skittered past; horses feeding from nosebags and a group of smiling men holding up a baby fox like a mascot. Heavily loaded wagons lumbered across fields, arriving at a vast and desolate place spiked with splintered trees.

So, this is the Front Line, like a vision of hell in a Dutch painting, too horrible to imagine, Bronwyn thought.

A drum roll accompanied, *Blowing Up Enemy Trenches By A Huge Mine*, and a rising column of mud engulfed the horizon followed by a vast plume of black smoke. The aftermath was a wasteland as far as the eye could see.

My God, no wonder they came back with their nerves in tatters.

The orchestra struck up a lilting tune and smiling men with billycans stood next to a steaming vat, *The Night Before The Great Advance*.

The same lads were eating round a campfire, utterly recognisable by any who knew them, and she wondered if any survived.

A group of gunners dismantled machinery parts and a boy wearing a spiked helmet, a *Pickelhaube*, grinned in the foreground. At some invisible signal the men looked up and started laughing and waving as if they could see the audience crouched in the dark; some people waved and shouted back.

The orchestra gathered pace as men attached bayonets to rifles before going into battle. A moment later they were scrambling up a steep bank in their hundreds like ants and she watched their silent progress in a black line along the horizon far, far away, out of reach and out of touch.

But what was happening in the foreground? A small shape slumped against a wire fence, then another and another, as the formation moved relentlessly on. This is real, she thought, men shot down over and over again until the line is taken. *The wire clutched us like a fiend from hell*, came to her from Glyn's poem.

Hannah patted her hand, and whispered, 'Shocking, isn't it?'

In *Toll Of The Battle Field* there was a man and his dog lying side by side in death, followed by men digging huge holes in the ground. It made her flesh creep, to think of Glyn's body cast into one of those holes.

'Not even a decent burial,' Hannah continued.

Bronwyn nodded and looked steadily ahead, not trusting herself to speak.

The audience around them fell silent.

In *Friend And Foe Help Each Other*, a man clung to another's neck for support, both filthy beyond recognition. Stretcher-bearers with Red Cross armbands wheeled the wounded on handcarts.

The orchestra lightened its tune for *The Walking Wounded*; men were huddled outside a field dressing-station, smoking. Nobody looked into the camera now.

The Devastating Effect Of Bombardment showed the shattered village of Mametz. Tada had been there after the battle looking for survivors, he'd said in a letter to Mam. She sighed, at the thought of him out there alone, picking his way through the rubble with a stick.

A lone figure climbed up the side of a crater as wide and deep as a quarry, and a horse stalked the edge on short rein, picking its way past a bicycle, a bathtub, the flotsam and jetsam of everyday life. An old woman stood next to the innards of a house, her vacant face framed by a stiff peasant bonnet.

The sombre mood was dispelled by a rendition of *Keep The Home Fires Burning*, as soldiers held aloft trophies from enemy trenches. The orchestra broke from a rising trot to a gallop with, *Till the Boys Come Marching Home*, and some people rose to their feet and cheered.

Bronwyn remained seated and said above the noise, 'Ghastly, isn't it? Shall we go?'

It was dark by the time they got outside.

'I'm sorry I suggested it,' Bronwyn said, 'I just wish I could do something to stop it.' Tears of anger sprang into her eyes.

Hannah took her arm. 'It's still very raw, losing Glyn; it was bound to be upsetting. Shall we sit on that bench over there?'

'Yes, I need to collect myself.'

They sat close, surrounded by shopping bags.

'I think a film like that stirs people up in the worst way, with its rousing music and captions.'

'You're right,' said Hannah. 'The munitions girls got quite carried away.'

'George still has disturbed nights. On bad days, before we met, he'd have gladly taken the place of his runner, who rescued him and was killed straight away by shrapnel. I can't help thinking of Glyn.'

An empty bottle rolled towards them and Bronwyn shivered.

'Come now, let's go,' said Hannah.

They linked arms and walked silently to the bus stop.

CHAPTER 15

October 1916

Bronwyn adored College, even the freezing lecture rooms with wooden benches and dry inkwells.

She'd already made two friends: Phoebe, whose parents had banished her from Oxford to Bangor because she was getting mixed up with suffragettes, and Rowena, whose mother was a suffragette and had so many children that the eldest brought up the little ones. Rowena said she loved her family dearly, but swore she'd never marry.

It was strange sitting in lectures with men, on the opposite side of the room. They often wore uniform, ready for Officers' Training Battalion drill on the terrace.

Professor Evans said it wouldn't last long, this sitting apart. 'The rot started with mixed tennis and you'll soon be supping from the same spoon,' drawing a laugh from the men.

Turning to the women he rocked back and forth on his heels. 'Those of the female sex are invariably among my best, and, it has to be said, my worst students.' He wheezed with smug satisfaction, his mortarboard at a rakish tilt.

He's trying to provoke us, thought Bronwyn, and refused to look away, while others around her shuffled uncomfortably.

The three friends usually met for lunch in the dining hall; Maddy joined them from the laboratory whenever she was able.

Today Bronwyn looked round for the girls and spotted Phoebe in animated conversation with a male student who'd crossed the invisible line to the women's side. Phoebe beckoned her from across the room to join them.

'This is Philip,' she said, 'he's agreed to be my seconder in the debate. Philip, this is Bronwyn. She's a pacifist but doesn't yet know it!'

Philip stood to give her a sturdy handshake and said he was a theology student and an objector, which was when she spotted the small badge on his lapel, issued to non-combatants.

Bronwyn sat and brought out her sandwiches, while Phoebe filled her in.

'Professor Reichel has agreed to be chair, which could be amusing, given his antiquated views on women, and Donald Fairchild is proposing the motion. I hear he's a smooth talker.'

'So, what's the proposition?' she asked.

'In a nutshell, that the nation will suffer if women go to work,' said Phoebe.

Bronwyn looked at Philip, round-faced and muffled up in a thick black jumper, and wondered what brought him to the debate.

'Before you ask,' he said, 'I've been on suffragette marches in Manchester with my sister. She's a bit on the militant side, but a great girl.' He rubbed his hands as if ready for the fray.

'I'm not actually a pacifist,' said Bronwyn, looking at Phoebe, 'but I do think the war is a dreadful mistake. On the other hand, it's opening up tremendous opportunities for women. Can something good really come of something bad?'

'No doubt about it,' said Phoebe. 'Women can't be denied the vote after all we've done for the war. Don't you agree, Philip?'

'I wouldn't count on it myself. I have to be careful what I say here,' he looked round as if checking for spies, 'but I think Lloyd George is more passionate about women making bombs than giving them the vote.'

'Sedition indeed,' Phoebe teased. 'I hope you won't say that from the platform.'

'Must be off, ladies, things to do,' and he got to his feet and grinned, tugging his forelock.

Phoebe leaned over. 'What do you think, Bron? Will he do?'

'For the debate? He'll be fine. Do you know what you're going to say?'

'I think so. I'll try and win them over with humour. With a topic like this there's a danger of being called strident or hysterical and then you've lost the argument.'

'I wish I had your confidence,' said Bronwyn. 'I'm not used to speaking in public.'

Phoebe had a physical presence that had nothing to do with conventional beauty, but made her a pole of attraction. She spoke and dressed like a teacher without seeming pretentious.

'With two academic parents I was weaned on argument, but I'm not relaxed with people the way you are. I'm too odd.' She gave a smile that softened her strong features.

'I'm used to getting on with all types, it's true. It comes of being a minister's daughter.'

Phoebe pushed her glasses up her nose and said, 'Tell me about George, Bron, is he the one for you? Rowena thinks so, but she loves a good rumour.'

It was the first time Phoebe had asked directly about him and Bronwyn felt herself blush. 'I miss him horribly; he's in London, at a rehabilitation centre.'

'Wounded?'

'Blind; learning to get around under his own steam.'

'I'd no idea. I'm so sorry.' She looked genuinely embarrassed.

'You mustn't be. He hates people to feel sorry for him.'

'So, you met here, in Bangor?'

'Yes, at the hospital. He's actually from London, but there was a mix up, and they didn't get him off the train in time. He came North with all the other Welsh Fusiliers.'

She could have mentioned Rhys in the next bed, but it was all too sad to think about now.

'Is he able to write to you?' Phoebe asked.

'Yes, he's learning to type and there are volunteers at St Dunstan's who read his letters to him. I'm quite desperate to visit, but I have to persuade Mam first.'

Phoebe reached over and squeezed her arm, 'Good luck with that, dear girl. I'm sure you'll find a way.' She gathered up her coat and briefcase. 'See you tomorrow, Bron. I'm off back to halls.'

Mam hadn't said she wasn't allowed to visit George, but there was always some reason why it was inconvenient: Lizzie had got a job at the Vulcan factory so there was more to do at home, or work was piling up at the Book Room. Would Mam ever let her go? Today, she must have an answer.

She found Mam making her own version of angel cake, with honey, as sugar was scarce. 'Can I give a hand?' she offered.

'Yes, dear, you could stiffen those for me.' There was a bowl of egg whites on the kitchen table.

She set to with the bent metal whisk. 'George has suggested some dates for a visit, Mam. Can we talk about it?'

'If we have to, but couldn't it wait until next term? You've only just started College.'

'I need to see him, Mam and it would only be for a week. Are you worried about the journey? Maddy and I will be quite safe together.' The egg whites remained obstinately translucent despite her efforts.

'It's hard for me, with Tada away; we would have talked about it.' Mam frowned, working a bowl of mixture with a wooden spoon. 'George may want you to move to London, you know; three years is a long time to wait.'

Bronwyn took a deep breath and beat her frustration into the bowl until the egg whites turned into starched peaks. 'I won't give up my degree, Mam, I promise you. We've talked about a future together, and he knows how much College means to me.'

Mam stopped stirring and gave her a level look. 'He may try to hurry things along.'

'Goodness, is that what you think? I wouldn't dream of it.' She laughed to cover her embarrassment.

'Don't be so sure of yourself. It's a fact of life that first babies arrive early.'

Bronwyn flashed her an incredulous look.

'It's no problem as long as you intend to marry.' Mam's wooden spoon hovered over the bowl. 'Once Aubrey was on the way, we made our wedding plans, there's no shame in it.'

Mam, normally shy in such matters, was sharing more than Bronwyn wanted to know. 'I want to finish College, so it just wouldn't happen, it's as simple as that.' She wasn't so sure about the last part.

Mam returned to her mixture. 'George is flesh and blood, the same as any man,' she said firmly. 'He's old enough to know what he wants, and I could see he wants you very much.'

'I trust him, Mam. George would never get me into trouble.' At least he'd know how to avoid it, she told herself.

Mam bent down to open the oven and pulled out a cake tin, tested the surface lightly with a finger and brought it to rest on the table. 'If he wants to marry you, he wouldn't find it a problem if you were having a baby; for him, it would be no more than a slight mishap, a happy accident.'

She tried to imagine it, falling pregnant, and remembered the baby clothes at Aunty Marjorie's. 'I know, Mam. Hannah had a word with me in Liverpool and I understand.' Even if Mam hadn't known about the baby, surely she knew now.

'Yes,' Mam said quietly. 'A man she loved took advantage of her, and I don't want the same happening to you.'

Bronwyn passed the bowl of egg whites across the table, ready for the last batch. 'Being a woman is so complicated; I don't want to have to choose between having children and a career.'

Mam looked up and smiled. 'You won't always think so. Once you carry a child you'll feel differently. Nature has ways of her own.'

She watched as Mam prepared the next cake, dropping spoonfuls of mixture into a tin. There was rhythm and ease in everything she did as if all the important questions in life had long since been settled.

As they were all growing up, Mam and Tada had sustained each other in barely perceptible ways. There had been the occasional glimpse, usually on the occasion of a birthday. She remembered the book of wild flowers, Mam's gift to Tada, prepared over months, in secret. Mam had pressed and labelled each flower between pages of blotting paper and finally presented the album to him at the breakfast table. And he'd wept.

Bronwyn remembered asking him why he was crying, she must have been about eight. He'd said it was because he knew how much Mam loved the flowers. It was a gift of love.

'I won't stop you going,' Mam said, slicing and turning the mixture over with a spoon, 'I just want you to realise what you're taking on. 'When I married your father, I knew the Parish would keep us apart, so the moments together were sweeter.

'You're making a more difficult choice; independence in marriage is an important ingredient and George will want you at his side more than most husbands.'

The chopping and stirring slowed as Bronwyn took this in. 'Because he's blind?' she said finally.

'Because the war has changed his life completely, poor man. In you, he has a loving companion full of youthful vim, which mustn't become a penance.'

'A penance?' Mam had lost her completely.

'It's occurred to me that saving George represents rescuing Glyn; I don't think it's far fetched.'

Bronwyn sat. 'I love George, Mam, isn't that enough? And yes, I miss Glyn dreadfully, but that's different. Sometimes I imagine he'll come back when the war is over, they all will. We won't really know they're gone until then.'

Mam dusted her hands on her apron. 'Go well, *Del*,' she said, stroking her hair, 'I won't hold you back. I'll write to Tada tomorrow to say you're going.'

Bronwyn sat next to Maddy and fifty or so other students in the library, and waiting for Professor Reichel; men and women sat on opposite sides, and the speakers at the top table underneath windows heavily draped with wartime blackouts.

There was a ripple of anticipation as the Professor, bald and spare with gold-rimmed spectacles, made his entrance. 'Ladies and gentlemen,' he said, standing before them, 'I am here to see fair play this evening as you pit your wits against one another.

'The motion before us is the following: *That in the opinion of the meeting, the large-scale introduction of female labour will have a deleterious effect on our nation.* Mr. Fairchild will speak for the motion.'

The Professor retreated into his high-backed oak chair and all eyes were on the dark-haired speaker to his right.

Bronwyn wondered how she hadn't noticed this man before, as he got to his feet with casual grace and surveyed his audience.

'I ask you this, ladies and gentlemen: for whose benefit is the gainful employment of women?' He spoke in a soft Scottish brogue, gathering them into his confidence. 'I speak not of ladies of leisure doing charitable work; nor of governesses or teachers who expect to marry before too long; nor even of those exceptional creatures, lady physicians, heaven fore-fend.'

A complicit chortle rumbled from the side of the men, and Bronwyn crossed and uncrossed her legs in irritation and exchanged a look with Maddy.

The speaker fingered his lapel. 'Is it for a husband's benefit, that his wife chooses to work outside the home? Surely not, when this must be at the expense of the warmth and security of a well-ordered household, which he longs for at the end of a working day.' He spoke fluently and without notes.

'Is it for the children's benefit that their mother labours outside the home and comes home exhausted, to her domestic tasks? Left to fend for themselves, greeted by a cold hearth and cold supper, they will, I contend, be the poorer.' He leaned in, warming to his theme, one balled fist on the table.

'Is it for the nation's benefit, that women work in industry? Yes, you may say, women are playing their part by filling the places of men who risk their lives for king and country. Desperate measures indeed, for desperate times, but what victory would it be for a soldier to return and find his place at the workbench taken by a *woman*?'

Bronwyn was drawn along by the cadence of his voice, and had to remind herself how much she disliked what he was saying.

'What about the interests of the woman? I hear you ask; surely she is entitled to the benefits of independence and the society of others, which accrue from paid work? I put it to you that if her husband and children suffer as a result, no one benefits, least of all the lady herself. For she is the heart, the soul and moral compass that guides the family through life's choppy waters. A family with a working mother is a family with its very heart ripped out!'

Professor Reichel fondled his pocket watch, weighed it in his palm and caught the speaker's eye.

'The future place of our womenfolk, my friends, is at home, and when their men return victorious, men and women will join together to rebuild our great nation.'

There was general applause and an effusive outburst from the men's side, quelled with a look from Professor Reichel.

You couldn't help but admire the performance.

Bronwyn caught Maddy's eye as Phoebe stood, the play of light emphasising her tall firm figure. She looked magnificent in a silk dress that glowed like mother of pearl, enlarging her dark eyes.

She adopted the intimate tone used by the proposer and her low voice came into its own. 'Ladies and gentlemen, far be it from me to advocate the abandonment of small children, or a heartless diet of cold suppers for toiling husbands.'

There was a murmur of approval from both sides.

'First, I wish to draw your attention to the so called *surplus women* in our society, as in numbers at least, we outstrip the men. This is due in part to emigration, and grievously, to war. What advice would you offer to a young woman with a modicum of education? Should she content herself with the pittance paid to a governess in the hope that one day a husband comes to her rescue? Or would you encourage her to develop her talents further and prepare, in short, for economic independence?'

She paused, holding the audience in suspense before elaborating her argument.

'Since, Sir, you speak lightly of women doctors,' she turned to her handsome opponent, 'I will draw your attention to Endell Street Military Hospital run entirely by women, from the most senior surgeon to the lowliest orderly. Womanliness and propriety are not in question under this feminine regime. So, let's have no more talk of battle between the sexes. How can we progress if half the human race is shackled by prejudice under the tyranny of men?'

The room was on the edge of its seat; even the Professor had stopped examining his nails.

'I exaggerate, of course. The point I make is that conditions are changing. Women today are healthier and live longer; we will have fewer children than our mothers. What would you have us do with our lives? I would rather share life's pleasures and responsibilities with a husband, than fester in an over-stuffed drawing room at a ladies' *"at home"*.'

Chairs scraped the wooden floor and there was a distinct shuffling of feet.

'You may fear that we will steal your jobs and drive down wages, as a woman's work is worth less than a man's. Yet you find us working on buses and trains, in banks and offices, as well as in factories and fields. Thus, we are putting our collective shoulder to the wheel and proving our worth.'

There were nods of agreement as the mood swung in her favour.

'History, ladies and gentlemen, is on the move and it is the labour of women that fuels the engine of change.

'Picture the domestic scene. The husband no longer yawns at tales of nanny and cook, but sits up and listens on hearing of his wife's day in court, or her work in the laboratory. In this modern world, clever machines have removed the drudgery of daily life and everyone has work to suit his or her talents, a world in which the labours and rewards of life are shared equally by men and women. If this is the world you aspire to, please join me in defeating this motion!'

There was a healthy round of applause as she sat, giving way to the seconder of the motion.

Miss Banks stood, a pretty blonde third year student whose hands shook as she held her notes. 'We don't want women to buckle under a double burden and we deplore mannish manners in our sex.'

Bronwyn's attention drifted to the fine panelled alcoves housing rows of books. A gust of wind buffeted branches against the windows and the sound of rain grew like waves, all but drowning out Miss Banks.

'Today it is not a slur, to be called *a woman of the world*,' she pitched her voice high against the elements. 'However the separate spheres must be kept intact, or all charm and attraction between the sexes will be lost. Women can no more go to war than men can bear children. We encroach on masculine occupations at our peril; let us not oppose nature!' She put her notes aside and there was polite applause.

Philip, the sturdy theology student whom Bronwyn had met in the dining hall, took the floor and peered from under deviant eyebrows. 'I'm perplexed by the proposition that women working on a large scale, poses a threat to the nation.' He sounded genuinely puzzled. 'I would like to ask the proposer, who laundered and pressed his fine suit? Who, I wonder, prepared his breakfast this morning? Who baked the loaf of bread in order to provide him with toast? If the answer to all or even some of these questions is *a woman*, perhaps, just perhaps these women who laundered, pressed, baked and even milked cows for a living, also have husbands and children and satisfactory households.'

There was an amiable chuckle from the men's side, and it no longer mattered that he was wearing a thick tweed jacket that he'd grown out of or borrowed, as he was well on the way to winning them round.

He ran his fingers through unruly hair and gave a bashful smile that said, I'm a plain man who knows his worth, and I know a thing or two about life. 'Any self-respecting man should be able to keep a wife, or so goes the argument. In my situation, this means waiting for years before I can hope to support a family. Who will want me then? At least now I have youth on my side.' He acknowledged the sympathetic laughter with a nod. 'But seriously, what has my plight to do with the interests of the nation? In marriage I seek a friend and companion, a partnership of equals, to take on the challenges of life. As a people we too face challenges, and once the war is over, we must continue to stand united. What better vision than a marriage of equals, where men and women play a full part in rebuilding our nation, both at home and in the workplace, each according to his or her capacities? I foresee a day when women are fully employed alongside men, not out of necessity, but from choice. As a nation we will be the stronger for it.'

He sat to clapping and some thigh slapping, until Professor Reichel signalled for Phoebe to sum up her argument, followed by the proposer, who by tradition must have the last word.

After lively and good-humoured contributions from the floor, Professor Reichel took a show of hands. A few diffident hands went up in favour and there was a whoop of approval from the floor as the motion was clearly defeated.

Chairs were pushed back as the men broke ranks and came over to mingle on the women's side and Bronwyn saw the captivating Mr Fairchild approach Phoebe.

'Miss Ballyn,' he said, 'please accept my congratulations. No hard feelings I hope.'

Phoebe smiled and held out her hand. 'Of course not; I'm Phoebe by the way.'

'I know,' he said, and kissed her hand, 'your reputation goes before you. Please call me Donald.'

It was the first time Bronwyn had seen Phoebe blush.

'Of course I don't believe a word I said, I'm entirely on your side. In fact my mother's a doctor,' he said.

Was he flirting with Phoebe? Bronwyn thought so, as the two stood close as turtle doves.

'He's taking it rather well,' said Maddy with a wry smile, 'losing the debate, I mean. And Phoebe is glowing, don't you think?'

'Yes,' said Bronwyn, 'and not only from success, if you ask me.'

Mam placed the letter next to her breakfast bowl and said, 'It must be from George; the postmark is Hampstead.'

'I'll read it later,' said Bronwyn. 'I've got to nip to the library this morning, if that's alright.' It was Saturday, and if she stayed, Mam would commandeer every second of her time.

'Of course, dear, the shopping can wait.'

She finished her porridge with indecent haste and was soon pedalling to College. She took the stairs two at a time up to the library, the letter burning a hole in her pocket.

She found a seat by the newspaper rack, and had the place to herself; other than a couple of students engrossed in newspapers.

She unsealed the envelope and pulled out George's letter, her heart beating so loudly it was a miracle her fellow readers didn't look up. Smoothing out the painstakingly typed pages she read on.

Pond House
Hampstead
October 28th 1916

My Darling Bronwyn,
This morning I'm the happiest man alive! God bless your mother for allowing you to come. Maddy is welcome, however Amelia would willingly act in her stead if your mother could be reassured on the point. Mother will write to confirm the invitation and dates etc, which I'd like to be tomorrow, 'the tooter the sweeter', as we used to say.

Please come for the whole week if at all possible. It's a long and tiring journey and I want you to rest while you're here. Father will meet you at the station and drive you home. He's asked me to hold the fort here, to which I've reluctantly agreed, so I'll be on the doorstep and will have to restrain myself from taking you into my arms. I miss you so much, your lovely presence and the sound of your voice. I can hear you describing the sky and the sea, though we'll have to make do with Hampstead Heath, I'm afraid.

Amelia says I don't know you very well if I can't tell her how long you wear your skirts, or your glove size. How do I know you? By your unhurried touch and sweet breath. I long to waltz you round the room till you're danced off your feet! Enough of this, I must be patient. Not my strong suit, as you know.

It's wonderful to hear what you're doing in College. I speak fluent trench French, so perhaps you'll teach me the posh variety. Your friend Phoebe sounds like a live wire, speaking for the women's cause, and good for her.

How am I doing? Pretty well, on the whole. Amelia has made me a cardboard plan of each room in the house with raised bits for furniture, a sort of Braille map. Mother reverts to type and treats me like a defective infant. She fusses, especially over dinner; I get irritable, she gets tearful, and I'm dreadfully ashamed. My worst fears have been realised on the fundraising front. I appear in full clobber at any number of Mother's worthy events, and am treated (for no good reason) like the returning hero. Father is, well, Father! He bangs on about the Boer war and asked me over a cigar the other night, if I regretted not being able to go back. I said my only regret was volunteering in the first place, but conscription would have caught up with me in the end. He went quiet after that.

The time spent at St Dunstan's served me well, rubbing shoulders with others in the same boat. I soon realised there's no point in feeling sorry for oneself, you just have to get on with it. I picked up plenty of practical tips, and now get about safely using a stick.

I'm back at work part-time, doing sales and purchasing, so lots of parlaying over the phone and visiting customers. I'll miss the technical side, but at least I know the packaging trade inside out. I'm a lot luckier than some poor blighters who will never work again.

I still get the breeze up at nights, but less and less so. It's as though part of my life is being lived out on the battlefield, in my absence. It makes no sense at all of course, as nearly all the men in my platoon are dead, but they turn up as ghosts and shadows and play havoc in my mind. Time and recreation are the cure, the quack says, but the dreams keep coming. It's the dark side of my life, in contrast with my feelings for you, dear heart.

Your letter has lifted my spirits, my darling, as only you know how. I long for your next letter, but most of all, I long to have you at my side.
Your most loving,
George

She looked up to see that the newspaper readers had already gone. Blinking, she felt tears prick her eyes.

His letter in hand, nothing could dent her joy at the prospect of seeing him, though Mam's warnings had unnerved her. If George had been a fellow student, would they have found each other, like Phoebe and Donald? George was lonely and vulnerable and might have fallen for the first girl who showed him kindness. If she were somehow atoning for Glyn's death, the relationship was on shifting sands.

Shaking off doubts, she got up to explore the shelves for a commentary on Racine's plays, in preparation for lectures next week. On the reading table, was a litter of papers and the headline, *Battle to secure Ancre Heights*, caught her eye.

Thank goodness Huw's battalion is resting in reserve, she thought. The first they knew of him being in France was a postcard: *In transit, safe and well, will write soon, love Huw*. There'd been a number of letters since, asking for kit and giving sketchy accounts of action he'd seen.

Her mind drifted and she was walking arm in arm with George along a tree-lined avenue in London to visit his favourite teahouse, her heart light as air.

CHAPTER 16

November 1916

It was Bronwyn's idea for the four of them to meet in the Women's Common Room on Friday afternoons when tea and toast was served as an end of week treat.

Today, Bronwyn got there early to bag a table and Phoebe and Maddy arrived soon afterwards.

'Sorry if there's a bit of a pong,' said Maddy, 'we've been making dreadful concoctions and the fume cabinet isn't working properly. I need to wash my hair before it turns a peculiar colour.'

Phoebe laughed. 'Sounds fun. I've just sat through the driest account of diachronic changes from Latin to French, it was diabolical.'

They sank into armchairs recently covered in pink and green chintz, courtesy of the Women's Common Room Committee. Bronwyn felt the money would have been better spent on new curtains to cover a chilly expanse of window.

Rowena wafted in wraith-like, dressed in black, emphasising her pale complexion and the redness of her hair. She fell into an armchair and said, 'I hope you haven't guzzled all the toast, you lot, I'm starving!'

'Don't worry, Tilly hasn't been round yet. Let's help ourselves to tea before the rush,' suggested Maddy.

They went over to the sideboard and filled earthenware mugs from a silver teapot dating from a more elegant era, then settled back round a low table.

'So what's the gossip?' Rowena turned to Phoebe, 'has Donald declared himself?'

'You make him sound like a character from an operetta, darling, which isn't his style at all. He's taking me to a concert, and wants me to meet his parents before he goes away. We're going to Edinburgh next weekend.'

'Gosh, Phoebe, that's rather sudden,' said Bronwyn.

'I suppose it is, but we don't know how long we've got together. He could be sent to France at any moment.'

'So, will you become his lover?' Rowena asked without flippancy. 'After all, why wouldn't you?'

'You're incorrigible,' said Bronwyn, though she was thinking the same herself.

'I'm not sure,' Phoebe replied calmly, 'we have talked about it.'

Rowena put a hand to her brow in a mock swoon. 'So romantic! I can see you in a rowing boat, cosying under a blanket, as the boatman takes you to Puffin Island; or gliding languidly on the Straits in the *Saucy Jane*, Donald manfully working the oars.'

'It's a trifle cold for that. Donald tells me there's snow in Edinburgh, so we'll be roasting in front of a log fire, more like.'

At this point, Tilly came in with a tray piled high with toast and there was a lull in conversation until Maddy came back with a plateful.

Bronwyn, warming her hands on her mug, said, 'I was buying buttons and thread at *Angharad's*, yesterday, and met a young Belgian woman.'

'You mean the quaint little haberdashery near the cinema?' Rowena asked.

'That's right. We got chatting; her name's Marte, and she arrived with her family from Malines. She makes lace and was delivering some to the shop. I tried out my French and she was really friendly.'

'There are so many refugees these days,' said Rowena, 'they usually keep themselves to themselves.'

'Marte isn't like that; she wants to meet local people. I'm sure there's something we could do.'

Maddy looked quite taken by the idea. 'Perhaps a coffee morning?'

'Yes, that sort of thing.'

Rowena leaned over to take a slice of toast, and said, 'Count me in, as long as it doesn't involve small people or games. I've done my share of that.'

'I forgot to say, she's married with three children and lives here with her parents. Her husband is at the Front.'

'Heavens, poor woman,' said Maddy.

'We could offer English conversation and ask Miss Hughes for a teaching room,' said Phoebe.

There was a general groan at the mention of Miss Hughes, the women's warden, whose job it was to prevent *skylarking*, College slang for fraternisation between the sexes.

'She's not a bad old stick,' Phoebe said defensively, 'we shouldn't be unkind.'

Rowena bristled. 'Didn't she have something to do with the couple sent down after they were seen holding hands on Anglesey? I know it was ages ago but we still have these stupid rules.'

'Walls have ears,' Bronwyn said under her breath, 'the woman in question came back, you know.'

'To College?' Rowena looked intrigued.

Bronwyn nodded. 'Not as a student, but as the Philosophy professor's wife.'

Rowena looked scandalised. 'He must be sixty if he's a day.'

'Well, they have two children, so it goes to show he's still capable!'

They burst into uncontrollable giggles, Phoebe recovering herself first.

'How on earth did we get onto this? A moment ago we were talking about Bron's Belgian friend.'

'You can't play the prude now, Phoebe,' Rowena teased, 'not after what you've told us about Donald. You'll be next, Bron, I'd put a bet on it.'

'Not me,' she said, and caught Phoebe's eye. 'It would be different if George were going back to the war.'

'I'm amazed your mother agreed to your visiting him in London,' said Rowena. 'A trifle risqué for a minister's daughter, *n'est ce pas?*'

'My good friend here is coming to protect my reputation, isn't that right, Mads?'

Maddy grinned from under her mop of auburn hair. 'More as an alibi, I'd say.'

Before Bronwyn had time to object, someone said *shush*, the chatter in the room subsided and all eyes swivelled towards the door.

Miss Hughes stood majestic, in her Oxford gown. 'Sorry to interrupt, ladies, but it's time to go to your rooms. I look forward to seeing resident students at dinner. Please be prompt.'

The train sped through a chequerboard of fields in browns and greens and cattle gathered under clumps of trees. Hedgerows and dry stonewalls parcelled out the terrain and every so often an outcrop of hayricks or farm buildings broke up the landscape, unrolling flat as a painting. Home, thought Bronwyn, was rugged and lush by comparison.

Telegraph wires criss-crossed the open spaces and human dwellings congregated at intervals round church spires. As the train sped southward, houses came thicker and faster until almost no green spaces were left, and eventually the skyline was lost to buildings.

Each time the train shot through a tunnel a blast of sooty air rattled the doors and windows as well as her nerves. It felt endless, this journey, sapping the excitement that had fuelled her until now.

At last the guard was passing along the corridor calling out, *London Euston, last stop Euston*, and she looked over at Maddy, who was on the edge of her seat ready to go. Not so the other ladies in the carriage who flapped round like wet hens packing away picnic baskets before the train pulled in.

'Here we are,' Bronwyn said, 'I hope they'll find us,' meaning George's father and Amelia.

She had no idea what to do if they missed each other at the station. She knew no one else in London and had precious little money if anything should go wrong.

'It will be fine,' Maddy reassured her, 'of course they'll find us. We can always go to the Station Master's office if there's a problem.'

Bronwyn stood to take their suitcases from the rack, and lifted down luggage for her fellow travellers as she was by far the tallest. The train drew to a standstill in an almighty hiss and rush of steam. Bronwyn led the way into the corridor carrying the suitcases and peered through murky windows. Maddy followed, wielding a basket of supplies sufficient to replenish a larder; Mam had insisted on sending provisions, including a dozen bantam eggs.

She half hoped to see George, but he'd stayed home to man the office; business before pleasure, he'd explained. Her skin prickled with anxiety as she scanned the pressing crowd.

There was no mistaking Mr Chisolm, as he strode towards the carriage with a fair-haired Amelia at his side. George had his father's thick blonde hair, turning grey in the older man.

The doors were open and Mr Chisolm stood ready to help people off with their luggage before porters arrived. Bronwyn waved and he raised his hat, a distinctive homburg. They moved slowly forward inside the train until it was their turn to get off.

His grip was firm as he handed them down. 'Delighted to meet you, ladies; welcome to London. Meet my daughter Amelia.' His manner was easy and he smiled with warmth.

'Hello again,' Amelia said shyly.

'I feel we almost know each other already,' said Bronwyn. 'George has told me so much about you. This is my good friend Maddy.'

Maddy said, 'I know we'll be friends. I've been so looking forward to meeting you all.'

Amelia gave a dimpled smile and linked arms, so they walked as a threesome.

'This way,' said Mr Chisolm, leading the way to a motorcar, not a cab as Bronwyn had supposed. At home, the doctor was the only person she knew who drove. Mr Chisolm opened the doors and helped them into the back seats, while a porter, who'd arrived ahead, put the luggage into the boot. Settling himself behind the steering wheel, he said, 'It's about half an hour's drive, ladies, so make yourselves comfortable. There's a blanket to pull over your knees if you're cold.'

As the car pulled away under the Euston Arch, Bronwyn was glad to be insulated from the baffling noise and bustle and to absorb her surroundings while Maddy and Amelia chatted. It was already late afternoon and a fine rain made the pavements shimmer as the gas-lamps came to life. They travelled along a wide busy street full of tall buildings, before turning right into an expanse of green.

'Regent's Park,' explained Amelia. 'It's where George stayed at St Dunstan's. I expect he'll take you there for a walk.'

'I'd like that very much,' said Bronwyn. 'He speaks highly of the people and all they've done for him, but you must be glad to have him home.'

'Oh, yes, he's made me his right-hand man, well not *man*, obviously,' and she laughed nervously.

'He told me you're helping him learn Braille and doing a fine job.'

'I like learning anything new. Sometimes I wish I could go to College, but I'm not nearly clever enough.' She must have forgotten she was being overheard.

'College isn't for everyone, Amelia,' said her father. 'Anyway, what would your mother do without you?'

Amelia said nothing, possibly used to his nonsense, Bronwyn thought, or maybe she'd grown to believe it.

'Not far now,' Mr Chisolm continued. 'That's Hampstead underground station ahead. One hundred and ninety feet below ground, deep as a mine, and if the lift breaks down, over three hundred steps to climb.'

Bronwyn smiled internally. George had inherited his father's love of numbers, but not his self-importance. She sensed his father wouldn't want to know about Nantgarw colliery, two thousand feet below sea level. It was one of those random facts she'd gathered along the way, probably from Glyn.

They were now in a district where the size of the houses could only be guessed at, set behind high walls and surrounded by trees. The car swung into a drive under low-hanging branches and the headlamps threw wild shadows in the twilight; the wheels crunched along gravel and finally came to a standstill in front of a pale double-fronted house, light flooding from the interior.

She saw him standing, holding up an umbrella and she panicked for a moment they'd be like strangers. He stepped forward towards the car, felt for the door handle and pulled open the door and said, 'Bron, is that you?'

'Dear George,' she said, taking his hand, 'here I am at last,' and felt an electrical charge pass between them. She stepped out of the car and he pulled her close, screened by the umbrella, and she felt the brush of his lips on hers. The sandalwood smell of his skin made her heart race.

'Hello, George, sorry to be a gooseberry,' said Maddy. 'Good to see you again.'

'Hello, Maddy, do join us under here and I'll take you inside. I expect you are best pals with Amelia by now, she was so excited to meet you both.'

Amelia, sheltering under her father's umbrella, said, 'George has been like a boy waiting for Santa, I've never seen him so happy.'

'It's true,' George laughed, as they walked into a blaze of electric light, bright as day.

Bronwyn held onto him tight and looked up at his face. He looks different, she thought; it isn't just the light. Well groomed as ever, but of course, his new eye. Nothing like the glassy globe the doctor had inserted in Bangor, and the same cornflower blue as his own sightless eye. This must be how he'd looked before, tall and handsome, like Aubrey's loping friends with loose athletic frames who played cricket like gods.

'You're looking well, George. Your eyes look wonderful.'

'Bit of a shock, eh? I hope you'll get used to the new me.'

George's mother appeared behind him, tall, in a well-tailored dress, with an angular face, a handsome woman, too large-boned to be beautiful. 'You must be Bronwyn; welcome to our home.' She hovered between offering a cheek and a handshake.

'I'm so pleased to meet you,' Bronwyn said, and gave her a peck. 'This is Maddy.'

'How do you do,' Maddy said, and inclined her head.

'Not too exhausted after your travels, I hope? There's time for a rest before dinner. Is there anything you need?'

'Nothing thank you,' said Bronwyn, though she was dying for a cup of tea. 'We've brought some gifts, a taste of Wales, Mam said; she hopes you'll visit us soon.'

'How kind. I'd love to, if only I had the stamina. Now, George, could you manage the ladies' luggage?'

'Of course, Ma.'

'Bronwyn will take your old room and Maddy, the guest room next door. The girls can share the pink bathroom.'

'And there's plenty of hot water,' said Mr Chisolm, 'I know what you girls are like.'

Bronwyn followed Amelia up the staircase, wide and sweeping with sinuous metal posts that grew into roses. Amelia stepped lightly, thick wavy hair flowing to her shoulders; she looked younger than her seventeen years.

'This is your room, Bron. There's a silk dressing-gown and a pair of slippers in the wardrobe.'

'How thoughtful,' Bronwyn said, thinking how out of place hers would look in this elegant room. Simply decorated in green and white, it had a wrought iron bedstead, and curtains patterned with a drift of pale hellebores.

George followed with the suitcases. 'Which one's yours, Bron?'

'The heavier one,' said Maddy.

'Brought books, have you dearest?' he teased.

'Hardly! I borrowed Tada's old pigskin case and it weighs a ton.'

'I'll take Maddy to her room,' Amelia said, as if suddenly conscious of them as a couple.

'We must leave these ladies to unpack and relax,' said George. 'No need to dress for dinner, by the way.'

It left her wondering which of her two outfits would be suitable if dressing for dinner were required.

Her clothes took up little space in the deep wardrobe. She splashed her face in warm water at the washbasin, fixed her hair, and too excited to rest, popped into Maddy's next door.

'This is pretty; matching curtains and bedspread, and so new looking.'

'There's a heated towel rail in the bathroom,' Maddy said, snapping closed her empty case, 'what luxury!'

'I like your blouse, Mads, dark green suits you.'

Maddy's mother had made her two blouses for College, this one in green paisley, and one in pale blue.

'Thanks, Bron; I hope I'll do. You look smart with your hair up like that.'

She smiled. 'Hannah sent me a box of coloured ribbons.' She'd secured her hair in a bun with pins and combs, tied with a black and white striped bow. 'Let's go down, I'm nervous already.'

They came onto the landing and saw Amelia posted at the foot of the stairs. 'I've been waiting for you; dinner will be much more fun now you're here.'

When they entered, George got to his feet and Mr Chisolm was carving at the sideboard.

'Come in dears,' said Mrs Chisolm from the end of the table. 'Bron, you sit with George and Maddy can sit here, next to Amelia.'

Bronwyn went to his side, dazzled by the display of cutlery and glass the length of the table.

'Have a seat,' said George, pulling out the high-backed chair next to him, finely inlaid, with a seat woven in cane. She squeezed his hand.

'Thank you, Jean, that will be all for now,' said Mrs Chisolm, to a woman of middle years who had brought out tureens of vegetables from a trolley.

'We've got a nice little joint of Welsh lamb for you, ladies, to make you feel at home,' said Mr Chisolm. 'You'll have to forgive my butchery; I'm getting used to carving again.'

George turned to Bronwyn. 'Pa means that I used to do it, but unless you want a slice of finger, it's not a good idea any more.'

His mother distracted attention with a cough and said, 'Tell us about your journey, ladies; I used to adore travelling.'

'It was quite an adventure, stopping at so many towns and seeing the landscape change as we travelled south,' Bronwyn replied, lightly.

Mr Chisolm, looking up from his carving. 'I suppose you're a bit cut off from things over the border.'

'It's our first visit to London,' she said, avoiding Maddy's eye.

'Have you always lived in the countryside?' asked Mrs Chisolm.

'We've moved a great deal following my father's ministry, but we've been in Bangor a few years.'

George cleared his throat. 'Bron's father is a padre in France; I believe I mentioned it.'

Amelia brought over the last plate of lamb and Mr Chisolm took his place at the head of the table.

'We don't say grace in this house, ladies, so, *bon appétit.*' He unfurled his napkin and tackled his plate with gusto.

'Shall I?' said Bronwyn, touching George's arm, offering to cut up his meat.

'Would you? Thanks.'

'How does your father find life over there?' Mr Chisolm asked, beckoning to Amelia for the gravy.

'He says it's pretty tough and the men are worn out; he's been collecting books and records for a mobile library, to help them unwind when they're off duty.'

'Not enough ammo, that's the problem,' Mr Chisolm declared. 'Lloyd George will change that. I'm not much for his politics, but he's the man for the job. Good for business too, eh, George?'

George looked uncomfortable. Knives and forks scraped on plates.

'This fine son of mine got us the contract, and all by talking to the right people on the telephone.'

George raised his head slightly, and said, 'We're going to package small items for the Ministry of Munitions, nuts and bolts so to speak. Pa exaggerates my part in it.'

'I'm glad business is going well,' said Bronwyn; she sensed how his father irked him.

Maddy looked up. 'Bron and I heard Lloyd George speak in Bangor; he said it's an engineers' war and we need more people in munitions. It means all the decent lecturers have been drafted, worse luck.'

'Maddy studies Chemistry,' George explained.

'That's an unusual subject for a young woman,' said Mr Chisolm. 'Don't you mind being with all those men?' His tone had shifted to something like interest.

'They're all perfectly pleasant; most of them spend more time in military training than in the lab.'

'Your parents must be proud of you, studying something useful for your country.'

Maddy smiled obligingly.

'Tell me about Bangor,' Amelia said, turning to Maddy. 'Are you by the sea?'

'We're on the Menai Straits, opposite the island of Anglesey, which is linked to the mainland by the Menai and Britannia bridges.'

Bronwyn said, 'It's very beautiful. We're surrounded by mountains and wake up to Dafydd and Llewllyn raising their tops to the sky.' This was for George's benefit.

'How romantic,' Mrs Chisolm remarked. 'I expect you're a great comfort to your mother, now the men have gone.'

'I do my best.' She didn't want to talk about Glyn.

Mrs Chisolm nodded sympathetically. 'I know both your families have suffered. I'm very sorry for it.' She looked earnestly at Bronwyn. 'George tells me you have a brother who's been taken prisoner. How hard for your mother, but I imagine a relief to know he's out of immediate danger.'

'He's getting by, thank you; we send him supplies and books, quite regularly.'

'So, you'd have me tucked up safely behind the wire, would you, Ma?' George said with a rusty laugh.

'Nonsense,' she replied, as if speaking to a child, 'you know what I mean.'

'How long was it before you knew what had happened?' she persisted.

Bronwyn wondered if they'd ever get off the topic. 'Over two months. We knew he was a POW, and finally he wrote to us. We got a letter from American Express soon afterwards to say he'd made a recent transaction. They went to the trouble in case we hadn't heard from him.'

'I didn't know they did that,' said George. 'It's remarkable.'

'Indeed,' said Mr Chisolm. 'So, what are your plans for the week, George? I expect these ladies would like to see the big city.'

'Yes, Pa, I thought a trip round the sights would be the thing.'

'Can we go by Underground?' Amelia pleaded. 'It's more fun than travelling by car.'

'No, it's too dirty and we'll see London better by cab. I suggest we arrive in time for the changing of the guard at Buckingham Palace, take a stroll along the Thames and see Big Ben, if that appeals?'

'Yes, please!' Bronwyn and Maddy said, almost in unison.

'That's settled then. We'll take it gently tomorrow and give you a chance to recover. Now, Ma, what's for dessert? One of Jean's famous apple pies, I hope.'

Mrs Chisolm tinkled a brass bell and Jean came in to clear away the dishes.

Bronwyn moved her chair back expecting to help, but George put his hand on her wrist; so different from home where everyone gave a hand, even when Lizzie was living in.

The pastry was nothing like Mam's, but the pie was full of sweet apples. Bronwyn noticed that Amelia played with her food and ate little. She'd become subdued, like a child among grown ups.

'I'm very excited to see London,' Bronwyn said, addressing Amelia. 'Do you get into town often?'

'Now and again, for birthdays or shopping. I haven't seen the sights since I was small. Shall we take your camera, George? Would you let me use it?'

'Goodness, there's a thought,' he said, dabbing his mouth with his napkin.

'It's such a heavy thing,' her mother objected, 'it would be dreadful if you broke it.'

Bronwyn regretted drawing Amelia into a conversation in danger of ending badly.

'I tell you what, you can all have a go,' George said, with forced jollity.

Bronwyn noticed a fine photograph of a bridge over sparkling water, hung by the door, and thought it must be one of his; another blank in his life since losing his sight.

'Join me for a cigar, George?' his father asked.

'Just a quick one, Pa, I'm ready to turn in.'

Mrs Chisolm got to her feet and led the way into the hall.

'I'll say good night to you, ladies,' said George. He kissed Bronwyn on the cheek, and to her astonishment, slipped her a piece of paper, which she hid in her pocket.

Upstairs, Bronwyn said, 'Thanks for being here, Mads; it means a lot to me.'

'Pleasure,' said Maddy. 'Good night, Bron; knock me up if you don't hear me in the morning.'

Closing her door, Bronwyn read the handwritten note, scribbled at an awkward angle, *With you soon, G.*

Is this what Mam had warned about? She breathed deeply and remembered the tender moments in Beaumaris, his tentative kiss, his diffidence. How could she doubt him? She tidied her hair in the glass and paced up and down with ears and nerves at full stretch.

The doorknob turned silently and her heart pounded.

He came in, finger over lips. She walked over and led him to the wicker seat under the window.

'I hope Maddy won't pop in,' he whispered.

'Don't worry, she goes straight off to sleep.'

He sat close, his arm round her waist. 'I won't stay long, Bron, but I had to say a proper goodnight. I'll fix it so Maddy and Amelia go off together and we can have some time alone.'

'I do hope so. I've missed you George; I hope this isn't all a dream.'

He pulled her towards him, 'No, it's not a dream, my darling,' and he held her in an urgent embrace, his mouth hot over hers and she pulled him closer. This was quite different from the slow exploration of each other in Anglesey. Now a current she had no will to resist was sucking her under.

'We mustn't, darling,' he said, and released her gently.

She longed for the sweet taste of his breath all over again.

'I must go now, my lovely, and you must get some sleep; these are powerful feelings and we can't allow them to run away with us. I'm sure you know what I mean. I will wait for you Bron, for as long as it takes,' and he kissed her forehead.

After he'd gone she lay on the bed. The quiet reasoning of her mind no longer prevailed. For the first time, she knew she had come close to throwing caution to the winds. She was grateful she could depend on George to keep his head.

CHAPTER 17

November 1916

Bronwyn sat at the dressing table brushing out her hair and Maddy sat on the bed.

'Isn't this beautiful?' she said to Maddy's reflection, pointing at the room with the hairbrush.

The dressing table was inlaid with flowing designs of seedpods and leaves, replicated in the frame of the oval mirror.

'It's like living in a magazine,' said Maddy, 'and so warm; radiators everywhere.'

'I wish Mam could see me here, living the high life.'

'Let's send postcards of Buckingham Palace, I know my mam would like one,' said Maddy.

'You and Amelia were having a good chat in the car yesterday. She seems very spoilt.'

'Overprotected, I'd say, and ready to fly the coop; I have a cunning plan.'

Bronwyn turned to face her. 'You want her to become a nurse!'

'Serving tea to the troops is what I had in mind, at a railway station.'

Bronwyn laughed. 'Heavens, she'd have to talk to all those rough men. What would her mama say to that?'

'My guess is that Pa wants to cut the apron strings and if Amelia were doing charity work, her mother couldn't object.'

'Clever!' said Bronwyn. 'We should mention it to George, I'm sure he'd approve.'

Maddy gave her a wry look.

'He has a way of getting round his mother, remember the camera business last night?'

'I noticed; let's hope it isn't the same with you.'

Bronwyn rolled her eyes and was about to say, *I've got a mind of my own, thank you,* when a bell rang from downstairs. 'That must be breakfast! We'd better hurry.'

*

Bronwyn, Maddy and Amelia stood hatted and coated in the hall. George had said it was a fine day for a walk, and they should set off at ten sharp.

'I should go and find him,' said Amelia. 'I expect he's lost track of the time.'

'I'll go,' said Bronwyn, and went to his study.

She heard the click clack of the typewriter and knocked at the door. 'It's me, George,' she said, and stepped inside.

He was at his desk while Jean worked her way silently round the room with a duster. 'Goodness, is that the time?' he said, running his fingers over the face of his watch. 'Sorry to keep you waiting, I shan't be a minute.' He stood, pulled a green hood over a shiny Remington typewriter, and made his way unerringly towards her.

'So now you see me in my natural habitat, what do you think? It suits me well enough.'

'It looks comfortable,' she said, helping him into his jacket from the back of a chair. 'And very tidy.' She thought of Tada's study with books and papers piled on every surface, as he was always preparing the next sermon. On George's desk there was a telephone, a small brass bell and a wooden box of paper next to the typewriter. If there'd ever been photographs or knickknacks the desk was clear of them. He faced the room and said, 'Thank you Jean, I'm sure everything's spick and span. You can take the day off now, as I'll be out for most of it.'

'Thank you, Mr George. I'll be back this evening if you need me.' Jean was plainly part of the household and had probably known George from a boy.

The four of them outside at last, Amelia and Maddy led the way down the tree-lined drive that had looked so eerie in twilight. The Heath was only a stone's throw away and once they'd crossed the road they walked straight onto open land. Amelia was laughing at something Maddy was telling her and the two looked like old chums.

Bronwyn, glad to have George to herself, said, 'It's thrilling that people allow a wilderness to flourish on the edge of a great city; it must never be boring here.'

'I love it and can't imagine living anywhere else. So, my dear, now you've met my family, is it as you expected?'

'They're very welcoming,' she said, treading carefully. 'Amelia is delightful.'

'I know Pa can be overbearing, but he's been a brick about having me back to work. We spoke about you last night. He said you're a mighty fine girl and I'd do well to hang onto you.' He squeezed her arm.

'I like him; he speaks his mind. Did he say anything about College?'

'As a matter of fact he did, but it's none of his business. He's got outdated views on certain things.'

'He was impressed by Maddy, studying Chemistry; more useful than French, I suppose.'

'That wasn't really his point; it was more about whether you needed to finish.'

She sighed. 'I'm sorry, I don't want to be the cause of tension between you.'

He shrugged, 'He needs time; he's set in his ways.'

His parents' views would be crucial, she realised; George was tied to the family business and they'd expect him to make a suitable match.

The trees opened up and a lake glimmered in the autumn sunlight. A man stopped to pick up a stick while his dog barked loudly, waiting to retrieve it. A young nanny pushing an enormous baby carriage overtook them.

'I realise we live very different lives, Bron. The last thing I want is to deprive you of your studies; I'm not only prepared to wait, I want to.'

She was awash with a rush of love as her body remembered last night's kiss, and said impulsively, 'Must we wait, George, when we love each other?' Mam's warnings seemed worlds away; they could take precautions, though she was light on details.

'Yes, my dear, we must wait; I don't want to spoil things. I suppose that's what engagements are for, to give people time to know their own minds.'

She thought of Mam and Tada, and the years they'd waited, but not until they were married. 'I know it's the proper thing to do, but not everyone does,' she said, cajoling.

They walked past the nanny, now sitting on a bench, lost in a letter and ignoring her charge, who whimpered in the giant pram.

'That's as may be, but I'm an old fashioned sort of chap.' He stroked her cheek as if to soothe her.

'Because you want me pure and virginal,' she said, half-joking. 'How about you, George?'

He adjusted his hat. 'Me? Well now, I see what you're getting at. I'll admit to the occasional fling, but nothing serious.'

'I should be grateful I'm not one of your flings, if that's how you treat them,' she said heatedly.

He shook his head in exasperation. 'Honestly Bron, don't be so childish. I'm no saint, but I want to keep what we have as special, if it's not too much to ask.'

She decided to let it drop. 'Listen, can you hear them?' She stopped in her tracks.

He looked puzzled. 'Hear what?'

'The swans. They're squabbling over bread.'

He smiled. 'Now, I can. They sound so bad tempered.'

She watched as two small boys, close in age, threw crusts into the chill grey lake, and the swans vied, snapping at the water.

'Two brothers are feeding them, by the looks of it. The younger boy is jumping up and down and he's too close to the edge. Goodness, he's about to throw himself in! His mother is almost there; now she's grabbing the collar of his sailor suit.'

George laughed. 'I remember being like that when I was small; a bit of a daredevil, apparently.'

They set off again at a gentle pace, he cradling her shoulder as she slipped an arm round his waist.

'One day I will ask you to marry me, my love, but not yet. It's far too soon and I don't want you to give it a second thought. Carry on with your studies and visit me whenever you can. What do you say to that, old girl, will it work? Do you think you could put up with me?'

A gust brought up a flurry of long-dead leaves and she leaned in closer. 'I don't know what to say, George.'

'About putting up with me?'

'No! It's too soon to think of settling down, but I can't imagine a future without you. I need to live in the world, get a job and travel, but how is that possible?' The two states were diametrically opposed, career and marriage were like oil and water. The only married career women she knew of had married late, which meant she and George had met too soon.

It took him some time to reply. 'I'm sure we'll find some happy compromise, my dear. Let's enjoy the present, *Carpe diem*, as they say.'

'We'll create a different way of life that fits us, not convention. I believe in us, George; together we can do anything.' She reached up to kiss him under the brim of his hat and thought herself the luckiest girl in the world.

At that moment, Maddy and Amelia turned round and beckoned vigorously.

'They're waving for us to catch up,' she said.

'Come on, let's sprint,' and he grasped her hand.

She resisted, worried he'd take a tumble.

'I won't break,' he said, pulling her along.

They caught up, breathless, and Amelia cried out, 'George, whatever are you doing?' Maddy was laughing. 'It's done wonders for your complexion, Bron, you're quite rosy.'

'We've had an idea, at least Maddy has,' Amelia said, animated, 'I can't wait to tell you, I don't know what Mama will think.'

'What's it about, Amelia? You haven't told us yet,' said George.

'Being a volunteer, serving tea to the troops at a railway station, I could easily do it, don't you think? I'd need you to put in a word for me George.'

'I would if I could get a word in edgeways!'

'It's a wonderful idea, you'd be perfect for it,' said Bronwyn.

Amelia clutched her arm, 'Do you really think so? Would you help me find out how to go about it?'

'Hold your horses, Amelia,' said George. 'Let's have a little chat with Ma first; we need to break the idea gently, don't you think?'

'I'm too impatient, I know,' she said, her wavy hair prettily framing her face. 'It's charitable work, which is what Mama says I should do, but I'd be doing it on my own account. And I'd enjoy it.'

'That's right, Sis, it would do you good.'

They ambled home chatting about this and that, until Amelia asked, 'How do you spend Christmas at home?'

'Quietly, on the whole,' said Maddy, 'but this year we're holding a party. It's for Belgian refugee children. Bron and I are involved.'

'We've got several Belgian girls at school. Last year they hardly spoke a word of English and now they're quite fluent. I'd love to speak another language.'

'I like your idea of a party, Maddy,' George said, joining in. 'If you need a hand with funds, I'm sure Pa and I could stump up from the Company.'

'That's very generous, isn't it Bron?' said Maddy.

Bronwyn agreed, and thought, how clever of you, to win Maddy round in this way.

Maddy and George were not on easy terms; to be fair, it was Maddy who was wary of George. She felt he always got his way, though Bronwyn assured Maddy she could stand her ground. The trouble started in Bangor when George was recuperating, and she went to the hospital almost every day. Maddy felt she was at his beck and call, but the truth was she'd fallen in love.

'Penny for your thoughts,' George said, breaking her reverie.

'Everything's changing, like when the sun rises over the mountain and the world is thrown into a new light. I'm excited and a little afraid.'

'You're a mystery to me, Bron. I think I need some lunch before I can take that in.'

She laughed. 'I'm not surprised! It's a mystery to me too.'

CHAPTER 18

November 1916

George had promised her lunch at the Ritz. Aubrey had once boasted of going to a ritzy banquet and Glyn had called him a show-off, so she guessed it must be swish.

This morning she'd dithered between her two outfits: the pencil-grey tweed suit with a lining of sprigged lilac, and the day dress in rayon jersey, the colour of bracken. It had a full skirt that showed off her figure, and a line of embroidery at the neckline in brown and cream silks. She decided on the dress as it was soft to the touch and made her feel feminine.

They were waiting for the cab at the front door and she looked up at George. He wore a beautifully cut suit, regimental tie and dark glasses. His coat was folded neatly over one arm. She thought he looked improbably handsome beside a plain girl like herself.

They hadn't been long in the cab when George took her hand and said, 'There's something I'd like to give you my dear, a pair of earrings; if you'll accept?'

She half expected him to produce them from his pocket, perhaps a pair his mother no longer wore.

'Thank you George, but I don't feel quite old enough for earrings. In any case, my ears aren't pierced and I hate needles.'

He looked crestfallen. 'I wanted to buy you something that you'd enjoy wearing, something pretty and discreet. A ring is too obvious, but earrings would be just the thing.'

'Oh dear, I'm not sure; perhaps a little broach?'

He squeezed her hand. 'Amelia wears studs. I was with her when she had her ears pierced and it was done in a jiffy. It's up to you, dearest, it's your decision.'

Wearing earrings came close to lipstick and perfume on Mam's list of poor taste, but they'd make her feel sophisticated and Hannah would approve. George was so set on it she hadn't the heart to refuse. 'I'd be delighted, thank you, George.'

'That's my girl.' He kissed her hand and called out, 'Mappin and Webb, King William Street,' and the cabbie lifted his cap in acknowledgement.

The cab was making slow progress along a bustling street, when the traffic came to a standstill alongside an oncoming bus.

Bronwyn looked up and caught sight of the driver. 'Fancy, there's a woman driving that bus, would you believe it?'

George laughed. 'Fancy that, indeed, and why not? Women are doing all sorts of things these days, as you often remind me. You could learn to drive yourself, Bron. How about it? It would be more fun than riding a bicycle.'

'Is that something else you've talked about to your mother? She asked if I'd thought about cutting short my studies; I had the impression she'd already spoken to you about it.'

'She mentioned you moving sooner to London, that's all. Ma spoke out of turn; I'm sorry.'

There was no time to pursue it as they were already pulling up outside a brilliantly-lit shop window. The cabbie jumped out to give them a hand and took his fare, leaving them abandoned on the pavement.

Bronwyn stood watching men in silk hats and bowlers hell-bent on some urgent business; George took her arm and waved his stick in the direction of the store.

The doorman strode across, immaculate in his gold-braided uniform, and took charge, guiding them past the human flow and into the building through heavy glass doors. These swung closed, dampening the noise of traffic and shutting out a grim November day.

A little bird of a man appeared from nowhere and said, 'Mr Chisolm, delighted to have you with us this morning. Do please follow me.' He spoke in falsetto and had a strangely smooth face devoid of eyebrows.

He led them through a palace of light past glittering jewellery, to a secluded corner and plush red chairs; he went behind the counter and unlocked a drawer.

'I hope the young lady likes these,' he said, taking out a roll of black velvet. With a practised flourish he unfurled the roll onto the glass surface, displaying a selection of earrings gleaming with gems.

'Take your time, Bron, and remember it's what you like that matters,' said George, as if warning against the salesman's blandishments.

'Allow me to show you this pair.' The jeweller leant forward and dropped a pair of studs into her palm. 'Single diamonds set in yellow gold; the quality speaks for itself.'

'What do you think, Bron?' George sounded anxious.

She was overwhelmed to be looking at jewellery that must be worth more than her allowance for the year. 'They're extremely beautiful,' she said, peering at the double starburst; she placed them in George's hand.

'They feel delicate,' he said, rolling them between thumb and forefinger.

It was too late to suggest something more modest, a bangle or even a locket. She took a deep breath and went on to admire rubies, sapphires and emeralds, holding each pair up to her ears.

'I imagine you'd look wonderful in rubies, with your dark hair,' said George. 'Are they a deep red?'

'I'd say Red-Admiral, sir, and quite exquisite against Madam's complexion, if I may say so.'

She held them against her cheek, then brought them to her ears and looked at her reflection. The rubies made her face glow. Too showy, she decided, and picked up the sapphires again. 'I prefer these, George, the sapphires.' She longed for him to see them, a pair of tiny bright-blue starlets that even Mam couldn't object to.

'Let me feel them,' he said and held out his hand. 'They're yours, my darling, they're made for you.'

She stroked his hand and said, 'Thank you George, I'll adore wearing them.'

Now the ear piercing was unavoidable. They went to a small backroom and the jeweller assured her it would be over in a trice. Like a good dentist he managed to conceal his weapon. He was swift and expert, but this didn't prevent her imagining a sewing machine hammering over each ear.

170

He handed her a mirror and she saw hot angry lobes pinned with gold studs under her dark hair. It made her ears look like a rare species of fleshy pink butterfly. This was the moment her brain connected with the pain and she squeezed George's hand until his knuckles cracked.

'I recommend a medicinal brandy,' said the jeweller and handed her a measure in a small glass.

'How are you feeling old girl?' George sounded concerned.

She downed the glassful and it was like swallowing liquid gold. It burned a trail down her throat and left her gasping. 'I'll be fine,' she spluttered, feeling the colour rush back into her cheeks. 'I could do with some air.' Her own voice sounded hollow.

George felt her pulse. 'Sit tight for five minutes. I don't think you should stand up yet, probably the effect of the brandy, you're not used to it.' His cool hand soothed her clammy forehead.

He was right, she needed to steady herself. When she did stand, George and the jeweller supported her on either side. The shop floor swam like a sickening hall of mirrors and light bounced off dazzling counters, as they made their way towards the safety of the outside world.

A blast of cold wind brought her to her senses. George wanted to call a cab, but she insisted on walking, saying she needed the fresh air and exercise.

'Sorry to make such a nuisance of myself.'

'Nonsense, I'm the one who should be sorry. It was meant to be a treat, not a torture.'

'I feel better outside, honestly. You'll need to give me directions because I haven't a clue where we're going.'

They set off at a steady pace as she read out street names and he said left, right or straight ahead. She looked about, wide-eyed as they passed cobbled streets, soot-blackened buildings and great churches.

They'd been walking a while when George fingered his watch, and said, 'Goodness, is that the time? I want to show you Regent's Park and St Dunstan's before lunch.'

'I'd like that,' said Bronwyn, as they approached the gates of St Pancras Church, and she noticed a bunch of ragamuffins. 'Stop, George, I want to give something to the children.' She poured her small change into the box on the pavement.

'Thank you Miss, much obliged,' said the oldest looking lad, and tipped his cap, revealing young eyes in an old face.

'It's shocking, children begging in such a rich city, don't you think so?'

'This is London, Bron. I suppose you're not used to it at home.'

'There's poverty in Bangor too: youngsters who don't go to school for want of a pair of shoes, but you rarely see them begging.'

'Sadly, I've become used to it. What really makes me angry is seeing their minders take the pickings at the end of the day. The police should crack down.'

'Surely not? Don't they have parents?'

'It's another world, Bron, I know you mean well, but certain things we can't change.'

She felt naïve and foolish in the face of this new and complex reality.

They eventually left the busy roads and walked along an avenue to the gates of a great park.

'We came past here from the station, George, it must be Regent's Park.'

'That's right; St Dunstan's is near the lake, it's not far. What can you see?'

The question was a thread that ran through their relationship, though these days he needed her less and less. In their first weeks he'd accepted her practical promptings to keep socks in shoes and gloves in hat, and allowed her to supervise the housekeeping of his pockets. It helped to limit the frustration of losing things. At St Dunstan's he'd learned new ways of keeping order that he'd turned into routine, an almost military discipline.

She saw a group of soldiers approaching, each on the arm of a volunteer nurse. One man wore glasses with wide-open painted eyes and a flesh-coloured plate to camouflage the side of his face, too disturbing to mention.

'I can see trees George, their branches black against the winter sky. And swans. Oh, the swans!'

He roared with delight, 'I see them clearly in my mind's eye! Come, I want to show you the lake.' Taking her hand, they walked briskly down the sloping path, his long legs out-stepping hers.

'Steady on,' she pleaded, as they gathered pace.

He laughed and slowed to a loose-limbed lope. 'I can smell water, there should be a bench over there.' He pointed to the lakeside.

They walked at a leisurely pace, he put an arm round her waist and they were like any courting couple enjoying the anonymity of a public park.

She led him to a wrought iron seat overlooking the jetty and they sat close.

'What are the swans up to?' He asked.

There was a swish of wings on water as a flock glided down.

'They're gathering like yachts at a regatta, dozens of them.' She looked over the lake at a grey-stone mansion topped with turrets. 'There's a grand house over there, behind a screen of trees. Is that St Dunstan's?'

He nodded. 'That's right. My alma mater. It's where I learned to be blind. Got my life back, you could say.' He turned towards her. 'I mean that only in a practical sense. It was you who opened my eyes to tenderness, Bron. No one else has done that.'

She kissed his cheek. The swans were describing arcs and circles on the surface of the lake and raindrops dimpled the water, though she couldn't feel the rain.

'I know I'm not the easiest person,' he continued, 'and I can't blame losing my sight for that. Be sure of one thing: I'll never tie you down. If nothing else, blindness has given me a certain insight. I understand you want your independence, I really do. So go if you must, discover the world, but come back to me, Bron.'

Her heart clenched at his sincerity. He'd said as much when they were in Anglesey. Now she felt certain of his love and knew he wouldn't ask her to forfeit her future.

'George,' she said, grasping his hand, 'you're the finest man alive.'

Unusually, he sat aloof, as if to underline the seriousness of his words. A light film gathered on the brim of his hat and on his shoulders, his back ramrod straight. She let go of his hand and sat quite still as the clock at St Dunstan's struck twelve.

'I love you, George,' she said, eyes filled with tears.

'I know, Bron. That's how you feel now; I won't hold it against you if one day you change your mind. Now let's find a cab, or you'll catch your death in the rain. I should have thought to bring an umbrella.'

Bronwyn gazed at the ceiling and the chandeliers blazed in daylight; the hotel was extremely grand. The commissionaire greeted George by name and took their coats.

No one was in a hurry; a smart couple walked arm in arm, and two young officers laughed. Uniformed staff stood to attention wherever one looked.

The headwaiter ushered them into the dining room, dotted with damask-clothed tables. Drapery hung in heavy folds and diners spoke in a low hum as if in a place of worship. They were shown to a table in an alcove and the waiter pulled out their seats and promised to return with the menu.

Bronwyn looked around. 'It's like a fairy castle in pink and gold; I've never seen anything like it, not even in paintings. The curtains are rose velvet, and the carpet, but of course, you've been here before.'

'Once or twice,' he conceded. 'Before you ask, not with a young lady.'

A waiter rustled in the background and George turned.

'Waiter! My fiancée will read the menu. Please bring us a bottle of your finest Champagne.'

Fiancée was more dignified than *young lady*, never mind if it wasn't quite true.

She leafed through pages of italic script and her heart sank. It wasn't the sort of French she'd learnt at College.

'Just turn to *menu du jour*, and if you read it out, I'll translate. No one teaches you this sort of thing in school.'

She read, 'Potage aux Huitres à la Crème, Poitrine de Boeuf à la Flamande, Sole au Gratin' and realised the menu was dressed up in language as elaborate as the surroundings.

'You say it beautifully; I'd love you to read to me in French one day. There was a nurse who read to me in hospital once,' his voice thickened, 'a local girl. She was very kind. Sorry, Bron, I shouldn't have brought it up, this isn't the moment.' He felt for his napkin, shook it out, and placed it carefully over his knees.

Bronwyn leaned in and said, 'An act of kindness can be transformed into love; perhaps that's what you experienced.'

She could see him swallowing hard. 'I remember it as a waking dream, nothing more. I was still in shock. Impossible to tell how I truly felt.'

She longed to ask the girl's name to make her flesh and blood, but could see it was too painful.

The wine waiter came with a silver bucket and served the Champagne with verve as they sat in silence; Bronwyn watched as it bubbled and frothed to the rim of the long-stemmed glasses.

'Here you are, sir,' said the waiter, handing George his glass. 'Are you ready to order?'

George named dishes from the set menu and the waiter stepped away discreetly.

George raised his glass and said, 'To you Bron, and everything you wish for.'

She clinked his glass and her whole being longed for him. 'To us, George; I love you more than I can say.' She took a sip and felt throbbing in her ears.

He reached over the table for her hand. 'If only I could see you now, dearest; your voice has the caress of velvet, and to hear you brings hairs up on the back of my neck. If you can do this to me now, imagine how it will be one day.'

The mix of champagne and seduction was going to her head; she knew he wanted her.

'I'm sorry if I sounded priggish the other day, Bron. If I were going back to the Front, I'd wed you and bed you tomorrow. There, I've said it. When the time comes, we'll savour our pleasure.' He gave a knowing smile.

A waiter arrived with fresh cutlery and brushed off imaginary crumbs. He backed away, with a discreet, *Monsieur, 'dame.*

'Until then, we'll grow closer in other ways,' George said, his voice intimate.

'You must come and stay, George, as often as you can.' She burned for him, and wished they were alone.

'If your mother will have me,' he said with mock humility.

'She's rather fond of you and finds you charming.'

'Really? What did she say?'

She would have flattered him further, but two waiters approached bearing silver salvers, followed by underlings pushing a trolley. The young waiters set hot plates on the table and stood back for their elders to perform.

Lids were removed to reveal chicken bathing in a creamy sauce with a rich aroma of herbs. The waiters used spoons castanet-style to serve the chicken and side dishes, each portion served with care, and *would Madame like a little more?* When the performance was over they gave a little bow.

'I was expecting a white rabbit to pop out at any minute,' Bronwyn said stifling a giggle. 'Glyn would have loved it.'

'Quite an art, isn't it? Adds to the sense of occasion, I find.'

'I just hope I'm using the right knife and fork. It's the first time I've been to a proper restaurant.'

'I don't think you need lessons in etiquette, my dear. *Bon appétit.*'

They ate for a while in silence until George said, 'you don't often mention Glyn. I'm sorry I never had the chance to meet him.'

'You'd have got on well. He had a great sense of humour.'

'Was he out there from the start?'

'Yes, though we all tried to talk him out of it. He told me he needed to prove himself, but I never really understood why. When he was last home, he said his nine lives had run out; he had a feeling he wouldn't survive the next battle. I suppose that happens after you've seen so many people killed.'

George nodded, his knife and fork idle on the plate. 'I remember a sergeant who led a charmed life. Everyone

176

wanted to be with him. He saw danger before it happened and looked out for those around him. It's a mixture of luck, skill and courage.'

Bronwyn took this in. 'Those of us at home don't hear much about what it's really like. What can we do to stop it happening again?'

'You mean beating swords into ploughshares and all that? Sorry, I shouldn't dampen your idealism. I'm afraid there will always be powerful countries jockeying for power and it will always end in tears.'

'Maybe so, as long as women are left out of the equation. Who knows what we can achieve once we have the vote?'

'The Pankhursts disagree with each other about the war, so what hope is there for women in general?'

She braced herself and said, 'Women can make a real difference, I'm sure of it.'

'Aha, now I understand. You're going to be a politician; I quite like the idea.'

'You're humouring me, George. Never mind, I'll surprise you one day.'

'I'm sure you will my dear,' he said, as if he meant it.

There was a time when George refused to eat in public, but after St Dunstan's he'd learned what to avoid. No soup, nothing with bones or a shell, and his motto was, *never apologise.* She admired the way he took charge when people were awkward and told them what he needed.

'More wine, sir?' The sommelier was at George's side and they talked about French vineyards. She was quite happy to listen while feasting her eyes on frescoes of plump cherubs frolicking among laden vines.

It was late afternoon by the time they got back. Amelia opened the front door and looked anxious. 'I'm afraid there's a telegram for you, Bron. I've put it on George's desk.'

Maddy was already at her side. 'Think about it, Bron, your Mam would have telephoned if it was Huw or your father.'

'Of course, Mads, but what could have happened?' Panic was in her voice.

George took her arm firmly. 'Let's go to the study.'

The envelope lay on the green typewriter cover and Maddy handed it to her. 'Open it, Bron.'

She ripped it open, read the stark message, and said, 'My God, it's cousin Alwyn. He's been killed.'

George put an arm round her shoulder. 'I'm so sorry. Come, you should sit down.' He led her to the couch under the window.

She burst into tears and said, 'Poor Alwyn, he didn't want to fight and now this; such a gentle boy,' and she sobbed into George's shoulder.

'It's the shock,' said Maddy. 'You need a drink.'

Bronwyn looked up with a start. 'I should be with Mam, we must go back; when's the next train?'

'Calm yourself,' said George. 'We'll get you onto a train first thing tomorrow and I'll telegraph your mother. Lie down here, I'll pull up the blanket.'

Maddy fetched a glass of warm milk and Amelia came in with a hot water bottle.

She closed her eyes and felt a bittersweet wave of relief that Tada and Huw were safe.

CHAPTER 19

November 1916

Bronwyn woke, startled out of a dream and unsure where she was. Lying still, she felt a cold draft above her head and knew it was from the window frame above the bed. She was definitely home.

Her mind drifted back to the dream in a train. Large blue butterflies flattened themselves against the carriage windows and George was sitting opposite, reading a newspaper. He lowered it and smiled, looking at her with blank blue eyes. Bright red spots burst from the newsprint, slowly spreading until the edges merged. She tried to warn him of the danger, but he said there was nothing to worry about. It made no sense and left her feeling uneasy.

Her tongue tasted garlicky, not the sweet-smelling wild garlic she knew from the woods, but heavy and cloying. Nausea gripped her guts and it all came back: the telegram, the hasty packing, the early morning start, Amelia insisting on coming in the cab so George wouldn't have to go back on his own.

It was awkward saying goodbye in public, but George still held her close in a final embrace until they were torn apart by the shriek of the guard's whistle. She'd clambered aboard and waved and waved, as George and Amelia got smaller until they disappeared into pinpricks. She kept on waving in case Amelia could see her and tell George she was still there, or must be, behind the tail of smoke billowing from the engine. When they'd finally vanished she felt sick and empty. Maddy said she looked ghastly and made her eat a meat-paste sandwich, which made her feel worse.

Sleep would surely return, if only the room weren't so icy. The hot-water bottle lay cold as a wet fish under her feet and she drew up her knees for warmth. She felt her ears throb in time with her pulse, and was glad Mam didn't mind about the earrings after all.

On the train home, she'd asked Maddy if she liked George any better. During the visit he'd spoken knowledgeably about the medical uses of radium and thanked her for befriending Amelia.

Maddy said, 'If I'm honest, I think you'll grow out of him. I say this as a friend.' The barb still stung. 'We're rubbing up against new ideas and changing, while George will stay the same.' She'd stopped short of calling George an old man, but that was her drift. There was no point saying that love changed everything, because Maddy wouldn't understand.

It was high time to get out of bed, Saturday and washday, as this was the only time Lizzie was free; it would be all hands on deck.

'It's a cracking day for drying,' said Lizzie, churning sheets with a dolly-peg in scalding water.

'And cold enough for chilblains.' Bronwyn's hands were red-raw from feeding sopping wet laundry through the mangle.

Mam looked at a pile in the tin bath. 'Let's get the next load on the line, girls.'

Bronwyn and Lizzy took the handles and Mam held open the back door. They had a system: with pegs in apron pockets, Bronwyn and Mam took a sheet at either end and secured it on the line, while Lizzie ran up and down, pegging the ballooning sails at intervals.

'That's it,' Bronwyn called to Mam, her voice carried away by a gust. The tub, used as a bath in the days before hot running water, was empty.

Lizzie pegged down the last sheet and they went inside.

Mam frowned, 'Those ears look sore, *Del*, I'll fetch the medicine chest,' and she bustled out.

A tentative touch told her they were on fire.

Mam returned with the familiar black metal box kept for small emergencies. Bronwyn sat at the kitchen table and pulled back her hair. The sweet smell of witch hazel brought memories of cuts and bruises Mam had nursed over the years. If a wound went septic she'd apply a hot poultice to draw it out, promising a special treat if you were brave. It was all right to cry as long as you kept still.

'Not too bad,' Mam said, examining her work. 'Was it George's idea, the earrings?'

'Yes, he took me to a fabulous jewellery shop.'

The night of the telegram, George had come to her room and given her the earrings, cushioned in a velvet box; he'd kissed her deeply.

'I hope you'll take good care of them, *Del*.'

'Don't worry, I'll save them for special occasions.' Mam was of the firm belief jewellery was more trouble than it was worth.

Lizzie came in carrying a family-sized teapot; she could never adjust to the fact that the boys had gone.

'Thanks, Lizzie,' said Mam, 'and we'll have the biscuit tin before you sit down.'

Bronwyn turned to Mam. 'So, Hannah's gone to Liverpool? I'm sorry I wasn't here when you got the telegram.'

'That's all right, dear; Hannah was happy to go, though I did offer.'

'They must be devastated. Aunt Marjorie was so upset when we visited; she said Alwyn and Stanley parted on bad terms.'

'Poor Stan; always at odds with the world and now this; Alwyn was such a lovely boy.' Mam's face softened as she spoke.

'He used to stand up for us you know, when the kids on the street made fun of our accents.'

'Just like his father; Stan couldn't abide injustice. Pity they didn't let Alwyn do his objecting on a farm instead of stretcher bearing. He'd still have been with us.'

Lizzie poured tea and Mam set out ginger biscuits on a plate.

'How's work, Lizzie?' asked Bronwyn.

'It's long hours, but we have a good laugh.'

'Better than pulling up turnips?'

Mam had tried to persuade Lizzie that farm work was safer, but she'd taken her chances in a factory.

'Not half. I've got something to show you, Bron, a picture book; I won't be a tick.'

She came back with a package wrapped in newspaper and tied with string. Inside was a large book with a glossy cover, which she laid on the table: *A Day in the Life of a Munitions Worker.*

Lizzie opened it and pointed to women in overalls working on cylindrical shaped objects. 'They're making eight pounders, and the girls are bronzing and soldering. We all wear special gloves for that job.' She paused. 'Lloyd visited the factory and said he's proud women can do a man's job. He's got his own copy.'

'Are you ever frightened?' Bronwyn asked.

'Sometimes. It's terrible on nights when the Zeppelins fly over. We'd go up with a terrible bang if they dropped a bomb anywhere near. The supervisor lets us sing to take our minds off it. I reckon it can't be as bad as sitting in a trench with bombs exploding all round you.'

'And what are the women doing in this picture?'

'They're working with TNT, a very dangerous chemical. You're supposed to keep it under glass because of breathing in dust, like in the picture, but it's not always like that. You see it in the faces of some girls, they go yellow as canaries. Mam says I'm leaving if I come home that colour.'

Bronwyn leafed through the rest of the album, showing women wielding tools and smiling at the camera; they looked incredibly young. She thought of the women at the cinema with complexions of yellow ochre, and hoped fervently Lizzie wouldn't end up the same. Handing it back, she said, 'Lizzie, I have an idea. I'd like to write something about your work for the Methodist Magazine. May I do that?'

Lizzie looked shy. 'I suppose so, if you don't put my name to it. We had to sign something about not talking to the papers.'

Bronwyn nodded, 'you're right, you can't be too careful. I'd write about life in the factory and the wages.'

'It's a good pay packet,' Lizzie said warmly.

Bronwyn knew women got half men's wages, despite facing the same dangers. 'What about when the war's over, can you see yourself working in a factory?'

Lizzie thoughtfully dipped a biscuit into her tea. 'I'd like it for the money; the foreman says they'll drop us women when the men get back. Maybe I'll have a fellow by then.'

'Can we finish tea and start folding?' Mam prompted, standing next to a basket of sheets, bone dry after only half an hour in the wind.

'Sorry Mam,' said Bronwyn and picked up the corners of a sheet and walked back while Mam held the other end.

'How's your Mr George, *pwtyn*?' Lizzie asked, hand on hips. The pet name, *little one*, was incongruous from someone so slight. 'Are you two planning to wed?'

'I expect so, one of these days. I want to finish College first. Would you mangle the next load for us, Lizzie?'

'Yes, Bron.' She gave a sulky look and dragged her feet to the scullery.

Bronwyn felt a tug at Mam's end of the folded sheet and tugged back, making it flat before walking forwards and folding it in half; they repeated the movement until the sheet was a manageable size. It was like a courtly dance, with time for a brief exchange with one's partner before proceeding to the next step.

'Do you plan to get engaged?' Mam asked, in a tone that expected, yes.

'We do, but it's too far ahead to fix a date.'

'I don't understand,' *sharp tug*, 'I presume he's proposed.' *Back, fold together.*

'We've talked about marriage and George understands about College. He's happy for me to finish my degree.'

'I'm glad of that, but it's a long time to make a man wait.'

'I know, Mam,' *fold together*, 'but he wants to, he said so.'

'Well, you could always move to London to finish your degree.'

Bronwyn stood mid-fold and said, 'I wouldn't do that, Mam, not while Tada's away.'

Mam continued folding. 'I don't see why not. Would you live with his parents once you're married?'

Bronwyn put the sheet on the pile. She and George hadn't talked about it; the practicalities seemed too remote.

'I love George dearly, but I'm not about to leave home,' she said, putting her arms round Mam.'

Mam pinched her cheek. 'He's lucky to have you, *Cariad.* I hope he's good to you.'

'He is, Mam, he's enormously kind and generous.'

'I really liked what I saw of him; we should invite him to stay, and his sister too, if she can. You seem fond of her.'

Lizzie came in from the scullery, forehead dripping with sweat. 'That's another pile mangled, Mrs Roberts. The last lot should be dry by now.'

They went out to gather in the sheets whip-cracking in the wind, already stiff as boards.

'You'd think they were starched,' said Lizzie, 'they'll be a terrible trial to iron.'

'I'll dampen them first,' said Bronwyn, wondering how she'd find the time, with masses of College work to catch up on. At least she had Phoebe's carbon copied notes and Rowena had promised to go over the prose translation with her.

CHAPTER 20

End November 1916

'What are you doing this morning, dear?' Mam asked from her writing desk.

'Hairdressing. Rowena is giving Maddy a bob. Do you think it will suit her?'

'I should think so, though I'd advise her to go to a hairdresser.'

Bronwyn noticed the 'busy shawl' on the back of Mam's chair. *Can't you see, I'm busy?* she'd say to them as children, wrapping the worn garment round her shoulders, and they knew to keep quiet until she'd finished her paperwork. Mam, who was queen of the household, never had a room she could call her own.

'Another letter from Aubrey?' The official stamps and postmark were familiar.

'Yes, the second one this week. He's bought a German violin and he's learning to play golf; it's good he keeps himself busy.'

'No requests for caviar?'

Mam smiled. 'Not this time.'

'I've heard from Hannah,' Mam said, becoming serious. 'She's staying on in Liverpool. Uncle Stanley's taken a turn for the worse since Alwyn died.'

'I'm sorry to hear that. I wish there was something I could do.'

'You already have, cutting your stay short for me.'

'I know, Mam,' and she kissed her lightly on the head. 'I'd like to write a piece in his memory for the Magazine; I'd have to explain he was an objector.'

'All in good time. You could drop a line to Stan and Marjorie with some photos of you and Maddy in London; they'd like that.'

'Good idea, I will. Must dash now Mam, see you later.'

'Don't let Rowena cut your hair short, it's much too lively for a bob. Tell her from me.'

'No fear, I wouldn't let her near it; George likes the feel of my hair as it is.' She could have bitten her tongue and hurried away, before having to explain herself.

Bronwyn and Maddy met in the quad and set off arm in arm to the Women's Halls. They passed along the arcade chatting about plans for the children's party, when a nurse came towards them pushing a patient in a wheelchair, which was not unusual as the Prichard Jones Hall was still occupied by war-wounded.

As they neared, Bronwyn saw how extremely young the man was, with a bright blue blanket covering what remained of his legs. The nurse was laughing at something he was saying, and the lad looked up at them and winked. 'Good morning ladies.' He gave a military salute accompanied by a wicked grin.

His infectious energy filled the air and Bronwyn said, 'He's bright and cheery,' then thought of Rhys who'd died so close by. 'Sorry, Maddy, that was crass of me.'

'Not a bit, he cheered me up too; Rhys had the same cheeky smile. I'm glad we've got the party to think about, aren't you? It's good to lose yourself in something useful.'

'You're right, it's what we all need.'

Maddy clung tighter to her bag as the wind picked up. 'I'm starting to get cold feet about having my hair chopped off. Does Rowena know what she's doing?'

'I'm sure it'll be fine,' she said without conviction.

'I want a short style, nothing fancy.'

They turned a corner and a sea-borne breeze puffed up their thin College gowns like parachutes, before they found shelter in University Hall, home to resident women students.

Rowena's room was steamy with jugs of hot water on the washstand. She wore a white apron over her customary black dress, and Phoebe was propping a mirror on top of a pile of books on the desk.

'Good morning,' Rowena greeted, 'we're all ready. I hope you haven't changed your mind, Maddy.'

'Not exactly, just a few qualms.' Maddy looked sheepish.

'Let's have a look at the magazines you've brought.'

Maddy took three copies of *Vogue* out of her bag; Amelia had given them to her. On each cover was an elegant drawing of a model set against a fantasy landscape. 'I need you to say truthfully what would suit me; it has to be practical. I can't afford to be a fire hazard near a Bunsen burner.'

'I can't imagine any of these creatures in a chemistry lab,' Bronwyn remarked.

Rowena was sizing up the task. 'Your hair is very wavy, Mads, so I can do a bob, but it will be more bouncy than silky. We'll wet your hair first, all hairdressers do that.'

'I don't mind bouncy; let's get on with it.' She removed pins and combs with a few swift movements, allowing her red-gold hair to flow down her back.

She looked more like a model in a Rossetti painting than a passionate chemist, Bronwyn thought. It seemed a shame to cut off such luxuriant hair.

Phoebe touched the thin bun at the nape of her neck and said, 'Are you sure you want to do this, Maddy? I would love hair like yours.'

'You wouldn't. It takes an age to wash and dry,' Maddy said firmly, apparently over her attack of nerves. She turned to the magazines. 'I quite like this style,' and she pointed to a model with short red hair under a pillbox hat, and sporting a brass-buttoned jacket in green.

'What about the girl in the spotted pink gown?' Rowena suggested. 'I hate the dress, but her hair is strong and wavy like yours; you could take a fringe with your high forehead.'

'What d'you think, Bron?' Maddy appealed.

'I prefer this one.' She pointed to a model hovering over shimmering grasses, amongst pastel butterflies. 'A sort of windswept look.'

'That's it,' said Maddy. 'Can you make me look like her, Rowena?'

'Close, maybe. Come here and we'll get you doused; we're definitely going to need both jugs of water with your mop.'

Maddy bent forward over the porcelain basin and Bronwyn poured warm water over her head as Rowena rubbed until the hair was evenly dampened.

'There, that's done. Towel, Phoebe?'

'Here it is, warm from the fire.'

Maddy settled into the chair, head in a towel topknot, her back to the mirror. 'Can I sit the other way round?'

'Definitely not,' Rowena replied. 'The others can tell you how I'm doing.' She placed a fresh towel on Maddy's shoulders and unwound the topknot. Maddy's hair fell reddish and springy round her face.

'It'll take half an hour, so we'll have to distract you. Tell us about plans for the Christmas party. Have you met the Belgian lady yet?'

'Yes, Madame Martens, we met this week. She doesn't speak much English. I need Bron or Phoebe to come next time.'

'I'd be glad to,' said Bronwyn.

'Thanks, I've arranged to see her on Saturday.' She looked at the hair piling up at her feet. 'I'm afraid she may not recognize me.'

Rowena had already lopped off great swathes that lay in damp clumps on the floor. 'This is the easy part. Once I've cut it to a reasonable length I can give it some shape. I used to cut my brother's hair before they sent him to the barber. You're going to love it, darling, I promise.' She snipped with confidence, stood back and frowned for a moment, then went back to work.

'It's looking good, Mads, honestly,' Bronwyn encouraged. 'Will Madame Martens come to the Refugee Committee meeting? It would make all the difference.'

Maddy swivelled her eyes, keeping her head still. 'I didn't get as far as that. Miss Hughes says she'll put a word in with a local Councillor, a friend of hers who serves on the committee. Hughesy says we'll have to argue our case; not everyone is head over heels with the Belgians.'

Phoebe sat on the bed, flicking through Maddy's magazines. 'It's the same in Oxford,' she remarked. 'When they first arrived, everyone wanted to adopt a family. Now they're treated like guests who've overstayed their welcome.'

She smiled over something in the magazine. 'This is hilarious, listen girls:

The time has come, designers say,
to talk of many things,
of shoes and furs and lingerie,
and if one flares or clings,
or where the waistline ought to be,
and whether hats have wings.

'The next lines are for you, Rowena.'

Some autumn frocks are moyen âge,
and some are directoire.'

Rowena curtsied. 'Fashion has finally caught up with me.'

They laughed, especially Maddy, who looked as though she'd forgotten what was happening to her crowning glory.

Bronwyn took in the transformation. Maddy looked like a choirboy with soft curls framing her face and the towel on her shoulders a surplice.

Rowena stood back to appraise her work. 'All done. I'll brush it out once it's dry, then you can look in the mirror.'

Maddy patted her head all over and a smile spread over her face. 'It feels so curly, like when I was little.'

'It's charming,' said Phoebe, getting up from the bed.

Bronwyn watched as Phoebe toweled Maddy's hair until it sprang into a coppery halo; Rowena took over with the hairbrush and tamed it into a respectable shape.

'Now you can look,' said Rowena. 'Ready?'

Maddy turned to the mirror and gasped, 'Rowena, you've worked a miracle.' She turned, patting and primping.

'What's the matter?' asked Bronwyn, as Maddy's eyes widened.

'I haven't told Mam yet.'

'Well, now she'll see for herself,' said Rowena, laughing. 'You look splendid. It came out even better than I'd hoped.'

Reading letters over breakfast had become a habit between them.

Bronwyn ate her porridge as she read. 'Huw says his new glasses have arrived, so he's back in the trenches.' He'd

189

smashed the old ones demonstrating the use of a bayonet. 'He wants an indelible pencil, and a cigarette lighter as matches go soggy.'

Mam looked over her reading glasses. 'I'm sorry he's back on the line.'

'I know; he shouldn't even be there with his eyesight. Any news from Tada?'

'He can't take leave before Christmas; he promises to come home at New Year, when he can stay longer.'

Mam must have seen the disappointment in her face. 'Don't take it to heart so, dear. Christmas is the worst time for the men, and Tada finds consolation in being with them, especially since Glyn died.'

'It's always been like that. He puts others first and expects us to do the same. It may be selfish, but sometimes I want him back so we don't have to share him with the rest of the world.'

Mam looked at her kindly. 'Aren't you off this morning to help the Belgians? You're alike in many ways.'

'Maddy's doing most of it.' She looked at the clock. 'Goodness, I'd better go. I'll try and get the pencil and lighter while I'm out.'

She grabbed her cloak and ran down the road, to find Maddy waiting for her at the corner. Maddy looked handsome with her hair under a little black hat, held in place with a pearl hatpin.

'Sorry, Mads, I lost track of time. You look great, by the way.'

Maddy smiled and they linked arms, setting off in the direction of the old railway cottages.

'What did your Mam say about the hairdo? Does she like it?'

'She thinks I look like a boy. My Da says it suits me, which is a surprise. I didn't think he'd notice.'

Bronwyn laughed, 'He'd have to be made of wood not to notice. You look very chic, quite French in fact.'

'Thanks, Bron. I saw Miss Hughes, and she practically walked past me. She tutted and said, 'What a shame, not very ladylike.'

'Poor Hughesy, she's such a stickler for convention.'

'Your turn next, Bron. What would George say?'

'I suspect he'd be old fashioned about it, though that wouldn't stop me.'

Maddy nudged her teasingly. 'Really?'

'Really!' she replied rather too quickly.

'Here we are' said Maddy, as they came to the cottage. She knocked on the newly painted door and it opened almost immediately.

A small woman stood beaming; *'Entrez, entrez Mesdemoiselles,'* and she beckoned them in.

Bronwyn shook hands and said, *'Bonjour Madame, je suis enchantée,'* and Madame Martens replied in a torrent of French expressing relief and gratitude.

She introduced her daughter Marte who was breast-feeding her baby in the corner. Marte's twin boys, Léon and Émile both with flax-white hair, sat close to their mother.

Madame Martens prepared coffee while Bronwyn and Maddy sat at the table, covered in a fine embroidered cloth. Bronwyn looked round at the whitewashed walls, and noticed a rag rug in rainbow colours on the stone floor. A large crucifix hung above the mantelpiece, but there were no ornaments or mementos on sills or surfaces; life had been pared down to bare essentials.

Bronwyn looked over at Madame Martens, whose grey-blonde hair was plaited and twisted into a chignon; she wore a large red apron tied round her waist. She busied herself at the range and the room filled with a heady aroma of coffee. Just breathing the air was like drinking it.

Coffee was served black in very small cups, with sugar. As Bronwyn took tiny sips, Maddy explained the reason for their visit.

'We need money for the Christmas party and we're going to ask the Refugee Committee to help. We'd very much like you to come with us, so they understand your situation.'

When Madame Martens look puzzled, Bronwyn translated, adding she could act as interpreter at the Committee meeting.

Madame Martens shook her head and said she'd be afraid to speak to such important people, but her husband would attend, as he understood these things. He'd been part of the team of men building the promenade.

Marte said something in Flemish from across the room and Madame Martens looked flustered.

'When did you arrive in England, Madame?' Bronwyn asked, to diffuse the situation.

Madame Martens answered in French. 'Two years ago. We come from Malines, a beautiful city near Antwerp. We ran our own *Mercerie Martens*, the best haberdashery in town, my husband and I together.' She fingered her lace collar in recollection. 'We were one of the last businesses to close down. When the church tower next door was blown up we knew it was too dangerous to stay a minute longer.'

Bronwyn nodded. 'And you escaped? All of you?' She regretted the second question as soon as she'd uttered it.

Madame Martens eyes filled with tears. 'My parents, they were sick and they refused to come with us. I pleaded and pleaded, but my father said they were too old to travel and he preferred to die at home. I still don't know what happened to them; I have no way of knowing. *Les Boches*,' she practically spat the word out, 'I hate them.'

Bronwyn summarised for Maddy, then said in French, 'It must have been hard to travel with small children.' She realised the baby had been born since.

'You cannot imagine how it was. Twelve kilometres were never so far. We threw all we could into a handcart. The minimum.' She looked bashful. 'I also took my embroidered table linen that was part of my trousseau. It's ridiculous, the things you cling to in a crisis. We were six, myself and my husband, Marte and the boys, and her husband Jacques. He was still with us then.'

Marte joined them at the table, now the baby was asleep in the cradle. The twins clung to her like limpets.

'It was hard,' Marte said, taking up the story in English. 'The journey was a *cauchemar*, how do you say, a nightmare. My father and Jacques pulled the cart and my mother and I carried the boys; they were babies. It was October and we thought we'd die of cold. For two days we walked, dragged ourselves, finding shelter at night in glass houses, you know, the ones for plants, though most of the windows were smashed. We survived on bread and cheese and milk for the children.'

'You must have been exhausted,' said Bronwyn. 'Did you have to wait long in Antwerp?'

'About a week. We were terrified we'd lose each other. There were so many people, thousands of us, pouring in all the time. We saw terrible things, messages scribbled on notice boards, asking have you seen my child, my aunt or uncle, with the names. We were the lucky ones. Thousands were left behind and now they're stranded in Holland. In camps, penned like cattle. My friend, she is there and we send parcels when we can.' She spoke in Flemish to her mother, who nodded sadly, as if confirming events.

Maddy turned to Marte. 'We wouldn't ask your mother to speak of such painful things to the Refugee Committee. Do you think she might talk about her life in Bangor, so people understand what it's like to start from scratch?'

Marte spoke to her mother again, and Madame Martens turned and said in English, 'I will speak. I tell everything, if you translate. I want to help.'

'Thank you, Madame,' Bronwyn said.

They stayed a while longer, and Bronwyn was shocked to hear how Jacques was beaten up at a bus stop in London, because he was overheard speaking Flemish; the man who broke his tooth thought he was German. Madame Martens was at pains to say, 'Most people are very kind. When we arrived at the station, the ladies from the Catholic Women's League met us, wearing white sashes. They were like angels from heaven after our long and difficult journey.'

On their way home, Maddy said, 'I think the Committee will be sympathetic, don't you? Once they've listened to Madame Martens.'

Bronwyn pulled up the hood of her cloak against slanting rain. 'They'd need hearts of steel to refuse, but we shouldn't take it for granted. Remember what Miss Hughes said, about not everyone liking refugees? We'll have to make a good case.'

CHAPTER 21

December 1916

After brief introductions, Councillor Mrs Forbes sat upright in her winged chair and said, 'don't be shy, ladies. We're quite informal. Tell us why you're here.'

The hats either side of her nodded encouragement.

Bronwyn sat between Maddy and Madame Martens in a musty committee room in the bowels of the Town Hall.

The eyes of the Committee fixed on them.

'We want to hold a Christmas party for Belgian as well as local children,' Maddy said. 'Madame Martens would like to speak to you about life as a refugee, and Bronwyn is able to interpret.'

The ladies of the Committee stared down at their papers, except for Mrs Forbes, who sat with her hands in a steeple as if waiting for someone to speak.

A lady with a sad puffy face and raisin eyes looked up. 'Perhaps we could hear from our visitor from Belgium. Have you been here long, Madame?'

Madame Martens looked dignified with her pale hair held in place with silver combs. Bronwyn saw her take a deep breath. 'Two years I am here with my family. The husband of my daughter is at the Front.'

A lady with a froth of lace at her throat, said, 'I hope you're comfortable in the accommodation our Committee arranged for new arrivals. Have you been able to find work?'

Madame Martens replied in French and Bronwyn said: 'Madame makes lace at home and her husband helped build the new promenade. They are grateful for the modest rent.'

Mrs Forbes asserted herself as chairman, 'in these difficult times, we do what we can to assist. I believe these young ladies have come in the spirit of mutual aid and friendship.'

The lady in lace persisted, 'that's all very well, but local families are struggling while their men folk are away. We don't want to be accused of favouritism.'

Madame Martens broke into a stream of French and Bronwyn did her best to keep up.

'Madame says, *I am very grateful for all you have done for our poor country*. She wants you to know she's not used to accepting charity... they owned... she and her husband... a haberdashery in Malines... a medieval town... they left because of the bombs... it was terrifying... now there will be nothing left.'

Madame Martens stopped to draw breath. 'Forgive me,' she continued, 'a party is good for grown-ups too. We left much behind. Our children are not sad like us, they do not know.'

A gaunt woman narrowed her eyes over half-moon spectacles. 'I approve if you invite local children too. Perhaps the Sunday schools could select deserving cases?'

Maddy sat up. 'Yes, that's what we had in mind; we'd be delighted if the Refugee Committee would join us at the party.'

'How kind,' said Mrs Forbes and looked along the table as if gauging the mood. 'What sort of help might we consider, ladies?'

The lady with the sad face said, 'I think it's grand, what you're doing. Perhaps we could provide a small gift for each child?'

'Gifts?' said the lace collar lady. 'Our funds are meant for hardship, not gifts. As a founding member of this Committee, I cannot agree.' She looked at the chairman.

Mrs Forbes clasped her hands. 'Thank you, Mrs Crane, for your advice on the matter. If we could agree to a donation in principle, I would refer the decision back to my Council colleagues. They are well versed in the rules governing the spending of public funds.'

'Of course we should agree,' said the bespectacled lady. 'It would be petty to quibble over how the money is spent. And why not spread a little joy?' She smiled at Madame Martens.

The sad lady looked suddenly brighter. 'I'm with you entirely, and I would certainly like to come.'

Mrs Forbes looked benign. 'That settles it then. It's been a pleasure to meet you ladies, and thank you, Madame, for speaking to us.'

'We're most grateful,' said Bronwyn. 'Any donation would be welcome, and we'd make sure it went on food.' They could raise money for gifts from a *bring and buy sale*, if necessary.

'Very well,' said the prickly Mrs Crane, with a nod and a quiver of her feathered hat.

It was dark by the time they reached the steps of the Town Hall and wild gusts from the Straits made for a chilly evening.

Madame Martens seemed electrified with excitement. '*Merci mes filles, mille fois merci, vous êtes merveilleuses*,' she exclaimed, and kissed them several times on both cheeks.

'We did it, and you melted their hearts, Madame. Even the ice lady thawed out in the end.' Maddy smiled.

Madame Martens looked baffled.

'You won over the lady in lace,' Bronwyn explained.

'Ah, *quel dommage*, such terrible French lace,' she said with a dimpled smile.

They agreed to meet up once Mrs Forbes confirmed the donation, and they went their separate ways.

Bronwyn braced herself against the wind and with each step a list of things to do formed in her mind. Open Aubrey's letter, Read Racine play, Help Lizzie with laundry, Finish Book Room accounts.

Ring George.

She didn't want to dwell on this; their last call had been awkward. After the initial burst of, *How are you, What are you up to*, they'd tripped over each other, and lost the thread of conversation. In his letters at least, she could hear his voice, and knew all was well between them. She longed to see him; if only he could visit in January and meet Tada, it would set a seal on their hopes for the future.

A billboard catapulted her into the present: *Explosion Kills Munitionettes*. Heart racing, she stumbled into the newsagent thinking of Lizzie, and bought the newspaper.

Turning the pages feverishly in the lamplight, she found the headline, *Sisters of Courage*, and scanned the column.

Twenty-six women killed… thirty wounded… explosion in a North of England factory on Tuesday night.

She breathed again.

Not Lizzie, nor any of the women who worked at the Vulcan factory down the road. Someone else's tragedy, at least this time.

She read more carefully: *These stalwart workers showed kinship with the men whose souls are unshaken in the trenches. We marvel at the courage and discipline which kept the other girls imperturbably at their work and who faced their fate hourly like thousands of others, probably with light heart and even jest.*

Walking on, she imagined it happening here in Bangor. Hundreds were employed at the factory; an explosion would hit dozens of families in the town.

The article gave no names, nothing about the families, the children left motherless. Where were the flesh and blood women who'd lost their lives? Mouthed platitudes wouldn't do them justice; they deserved better, every single one of them.

A sickening image of charred remains came to her as she remembered the identity discs Lizzie had mentioned; a metal tag with an embossed number worn by every worker, just in case.

Fuelled by indignation, she stormed home, and saw the house was in darkness. It must be Mam's quilting evening. She went inside and the air froze on her breath.

She set to work, putting coal on the range to get the kitchen warm. When she straightened up, Aubrey's letter reproached her from the mantelshelf. She picked it up and plumped herself down into Mam's rocking chair without bothering to take off her coat.

The thin sheets slipped out easily enough, which she unfolded slowly. Within were two cheques, written in a bolder hand than the letter, but still in Aubrey's distinctive crisp style. She made an effort to imagine him writing, sitting on the edge of a camp bed in a cramped hut.

Offizier-Gefangenenlager
Clausthal am Harz
Deutschland
December 1ˢᵗ 1916

Dear Bronny,
This time I'm writing to you rather than to Mam, so as not to burden her
with my list. In her letters she often says what a wonderful helper you are.

I'd be grateful if you could write to the Institute of Bankers and have
my magazine subscription sent here. I take a keen interest in foreign
banking as you know and I'm learning German again with this in mind.
Did you find my copy of *Crapper's Book-keeping and Accounts*, by the
way? I do hope so; I need it to stop getting rusty.

They've stopped our cigarettes for some reason so would you send me
tobacco and papers? A parcel once a month will do nicely. I should
mention that the onions arrived safely and were a great success. The same
parcel (no 34, I think) contained flour, jelly and trench boots. I'm well
provided with winter boots, but should like a pair of brogues. Has Mam
sent the breeches I asked for some time ago? A woollen scarf would also
be very useful here. I could do with a small mincing machine, like the one
at home, with three discs, handy for making curry from leftover scraps of
meat.

These days I'm able to keep abreast of events as I get a daily paper,
La Belgique, published in Brussels. Reading Lloyd George's speech made
me feel a lot less cut off from the world. Of course this kind of paper is
published under enemy scrutiny, but it's better than nothing.

I'm getting pretty homesick with the prospect of spending Christmas
here. We're rehearsing for a concert to liven things up and will play the
Teddie Foxtrot and Rubenstein's Melody in F. We're also singing a bit of
nonsense entitled, *'Je sais que vous êtes jolie!'* I wrote to Mam that I
bought a violin, from Zimmermann and Co. in Leipzig; it has a
beautiful tone. It came via the Red Cross who respond to all manner of
requests. We're learning some delightful Russian music at present. One
day we'll play some selections for violin and piano together and what a
pleasure that will be.

The barracks of the various nationalities are separate here, but we
bump into each other outside. In fact, the first friendly advance I
experienced was from a Russian, who offered me his deck chair to sit
outdoors. There's a wondrous babble of tongues, particularly amongst the

orderlies. I heard one of them backchat a guard with, '*Après la bloody Krieg!*' when ordered to move, which the guard chose to ignore. We all feel sorry for the Russians, who are by far the worst off as they rely entirely on camp rations. We, of course, manage quite well on the provisions we have sent in.

At present Cox & Co are sending me £5 a month per Rotterdam. I don't need all this, so will you please ask them to send me £5 every two months? This will leave more in the account for Mam. I enclose a cheque to cover the shopping list above; remember to cut it off at the dotted line and it will need a penny stamp.

One of the Welsh orderlies here wants to send some money home to his wife. The only way he can do this is through an officer, so I said I would help out. Will you send on the enclosed cheque for £5 to his wife, and explain to her how to get it cashed in case she does not know? Please tell her it is a gift from her husband. He has already paid me in German coin. I'm sorry to bother you like this, but an orderly's life is none too nice, and we are only too glad to do anything we can for them in little things of this kind.

I haven't asked about your new life at College or about George, so shame on me. I'm pleased to hear that you're not rushing into marriage. I reckon he must be a decent chap if he's happy to wait for you.

What news of Tada? Is he coming home for Christmas? He isn't mentioned in recent letters and I worry that he may be unwell. And Huw? I hope he isn't seeing too much action wherever he may be.

Thanks, little sister, you're a grand girl.

I have no more space, so must close.

Your loving brother,

Aubrey

She put the letter aside with sinking heart. Her poor brother was homesick. He was putting on a brave face, the way he always did. It must be a great strain to keep up one's spirits, especially at Christmas. She promised herself her next letter to him would be chattier. She'd tell him about Maddy's haircut, amuse him with an account of the Refugee Committee ladies, and tell him Tada was coming home for New Year.

He would be glad to know that Huw was in good spirits. Tada had written to say their paths had crossed and that Huw was going into battle armed with a volume of the classical poets; that would make Aubrey smile.

Tomorrow she'd make a start and draw money from the bank, pay a visit to the orderly's wife, buy a mincer at the ironmonger and search out the missing breeches.

Everyone got by as best they could these days. Maddy was right, the Christmas party was a godsend, something you could throw yourself into. This year no one was talking about the war being over by next Christmas. It had been said once too often.

CHAPTER 22

December 1916

A small girl with flaxen hair came forward with a bunch of winter violets and curtsied.

Bronwyn looked down and smiled, putting aside a box of Christmas crackers, as she stood in the women's dining hall.

'The flowers were meant for the Refugee Committee ladies,' Marte spoke over the child's head. 'Perhaps she can present them again later? I'm sorry we're so early.'

Behind her was a group of women with their children, staring wide-eyed at the golden Chinese lanterns and the paper chains strung across the ceiling.

'Welcome!' said Bronwyn, wishing she'd learned how to say this in Flemish.

'*Welkom!*' Marte said to the women behind her, who repeated it like a refrain, laughing at the similarity of sound.

The children remained serious and drew closer to their mothers and Bronwyn was at a loss as to how to break the ice. It was too soon to start games and the Sunday school children wouldn't arrive for a bit.

Maddy came in, thank the Lord. She must have heard them arriving. 'Hello everyone,' she said cheerily. 'We've got some lovely things for you to play with!' She pointed to a large toy chest surrounded by an inviting circle of plump cushions.

The children shifted from one foot to the other clearly reluctant to move, or clung to their mothers' coat sleeves.

'Who likes circus tricks?' Bronwyn ventured. A sea of faces lit up as if she were about to wave a magic wand. Instead, she beckoned over three students who'd volunteered as entertainers and were still in uniform from training that afternoon. She smiled at them. 'Could you show the children one of your tricks before tea, gentlemen? We need some jollying along.'

A slightly built lad stepped forward and produced three yellow balls from a deep military pocket and started throwing them effortlessly into the air. The children were attracted to him like bees and an excited buzz of chatter went up as they gazed at the juggling soldier.

The children stepped closer and with a wink he produced two more balls, red this time, his body flowing in rhythm as he made criss-cross patterns in the air; the children were on tiptoe with excitement. He slowed the pace, throwing the balls in ever-higher arcs and putting them back in his pocket one by one. He finished with a comic bow followed by applause from the adults as well as the children. The boys crowded round pleading to have a go.

Marte clapped her hands and they all went quiet, as she shepherded them uncomplaining to the cushion circle. Only a teacher could do that, thought Bronwyn, and realised it was the first time she'd seen Marte outside her role as a mother.

She imagined how Glyn would have charmed the children, making a polka dot handkerchief disappear up his sleeve or producing one from a hat. To see the children with the young soldier made her miss him all over again, and reminded her of his playfulness. He could always find a way to make her laugh. It was six months now since he'd died and the memory still had the capacity to knock her sideways, and at the most awkward moments.

Taking hold of herself, she saw the Sunday school children pouring through the door with a harassed looking young chaplain. Miss Hughes had arrived with the Refugee Committee ladies who were already arranging themselves along the top table. There was a general hush as the ladies settled into their seats and Bronwyn looked round in desperation. Maddy was to do the welcome speech but was nowhere to be seen.

Miss Hughes, dressed in green taffeta and an emerald brooch, caught her eye. There was nothing else for it; she'd have to improvise as best she could.

Stepping onto the platform, she stood tall, took a deep breath and looked round the hall, the way Tada used to before a sermon. 'Ladies and gentlemen, *children*, welcome! I believe St Nicholas visited Belgium a few weeks ago, and I'm pleased to say that he came last night and left a gift for each of you under the tree.' There was a ripple of excitement. 'So let's give a big thank-you to Miss Hughes for inviting him here.' She turned to the ladies behind her and everyone clapped for the lady in green, who smiled and looked gracious.

'Thanks too, to our guests who gave so generously. And a special thank-you to the mums who baked the cakes. A Happy Christmas to you all!' There was a burst of applause as she left the platform and relief washed over her, now the party was launched.

What followed, as she remembered it, was a whirligig of games, parcel wrappings on the floor and the juggler rattling out jingle-bells on the piano. Rowena was doing a good job entertaining the Committee ladies, judging from outbursts of hilarity from that direction. Merry on sherry from the senior Common Room, perhaps the ladies would overlook her riskier anecdotes.

At teatime, Marte called the children to order. They formed a crocodile and sat along benches, the local and Belgian children together, and waited obediently for the chaplain to say grace. This he did in short order, and the feasting began.

Bronwyn sat next to Madame Martens and the juggler, and opposite a frail looking girl she'd not met before.

'You saved the day with your juggling act,' Bronwyn said to the young man.

He grinned, and said, 'Thanks a lot,' before swallowing a sardine sandwich whole. 'It's something I picked up as a kid. My Da taught me.'

'What are you studying?' she asked before he downed the next sandwich.

'Electrical Engineering. My Da could never see the point of it. Now I'm a signaler he's happy enough.'

He saw her surprise and said, 'We're all quarrymen and bantam-weights like me. I was made for working underground, according to him.'

'And your mother, does she say something?' Madame Martens enquired.

He paused for a moment, the sandwich half way to his mouth. 'No, not much. Except she's not happy about me going to war. Not a bit happy about that.'

Madame Martens nodded, and said, 'I understand her very well. This war is cruel. It lasts too long. People are separated.' She patted the arm of the young woman next to her. 'This is Anna; we come from the same town.'

Anna fingered her wedding band; she looked too young to be married.

'How do you find the party, Anna?' Bronwyn asked. 'We hope the children feel at home.'

'They laugh and play wherever they are. It is the adults who are exiled.' She bit her lip.

'It must be hard for you. Do you have family here?'

'My parents, yes. I was separated from my fiancé in Antwerp when we were escaping. We found each other through the Red Cross.'

'When did you get married?' Bronwyn pressed, hoping her directness wouldn't make the young woman clam up.

'A year ago. We had three days together then he went back to Flanders. I haven't seen him since.' Her face was impassive as she delivered her account.

The young man next to her had been following Anna's every word. 'You're very brave, Miss.'

A smile lit up her face for the first time. 'I have my dear parents and also my husband's parents. They are in Elisabethville. His father works there in the arms factory.'

Bronwyn took this in. 'Where is that, exactly?'

'It's in the North of England, also called Birtley.'

Madame Martens explained. 'It is a new town built to provide arms for the war. We are not, how do you say, *feignants*, lazy, like some people believe; we are hard working people.'

'People are ignorant, Madame, they say things without thinking.' She was brimming with questions about the Belgian enclave.

'You are right. The workers in the Belgian factory are soldiers who are too badly wounded to fight.'

'Crikey!' It was the young man speaking. 'If I had my leg blown off, I wouldn't want to end up in a munitions factory. No disrespect, mind, I raise my hat to them.'

His disarming honesty made them all smile.

Phoebe was beckoning her, and Bronwyn knew she had to see Anna another time. 'I'm sorry to leave you,' she said, getting up, 'I'm on cake duty. I hope we may speak again, Anna. It's been a pleasure meeting you.'

She made her way past tables full of children wearing star-spangled paper crowns, now boisterous, as they'd devoured all the sandwiches and jellies.

Elisabethville. A place she'd never heard of until now; a whole town, presumably with shops, schools and churches as well as the factory. An idea for an article was already taking shape in her mind.

Maddy and Phoebe were waiting for her outside the dining hall.

'Come on,' said Maddy, 'we're lighting the candles.'

'Sorry, I got distracted; and where were you when I needed you?'

'Oops-a-daisy, the speech, I heard it from the kitchen; you did a great job.'

'Let's got on with this now,' said Phoebe handing her a lighted taper.

The cake sat on a trolley, and was a foot square, covered in white icing like rough snow; red and green candles covered the surface, with a tall gold candle at the centre.

'That's it,' Maddy, drew back for a moment to admire the blaze. 'Let's go, girls.'

Phoebe pushed open the doors and there was an, 'ah' followed by hushed silence as they progressed in the semi-dark, the trolley glowing with mellow light.

Bronwyn hummed a note to get them started on *Silent Night*. They sang in unison at first, then Phoebe's sweet soprano rang out above Maddy's alto, and Bronwyn wove a descant between the two.

The sound of their voices grew and Bronwyn heard with each refrain of *Sleep in heavenly peace*, others joining in. The children sang in high clear voices and by the third verse their mothers followed, making soft the sounds of Flemish in the well-known carol. Bronwyn imagined a world at peace. If only the spirit of Christmas could be rekindled and men would lay down their arms.

CHAPTER 23

January 1917

It had been a week since she'd written to George; creeping insecurity gnawed at her as their lives diverged; phone calls only amplified the distance. She missed the luxury of silence in his company and felt under pressure to say amusing things.

15ᵗʰ January 1917
Dearest George,
I miss you.

I find myself tearing up half-finished letters because the details of daily life are too paltry to relate. I sit in my room and imagine what you're doing. If it's morning, I see you talking on the telephone to important customers. In the evening you are in the green armchair, smoking a pipe and listening to a Chopin nocturne on the gramophone.

I have a confession. When you call, I have a written list of things to say, in case everything flies out of my head. Using the telephone doesn't come easily, though I love to hear your clear and steady voice. I need to read your face, catch a half smile or a frown when you're puzzling something out. Distance is wilting my spirit and I need you here to revive me.

Do come before Easter, please.

Meanwhile, I shall allow my imagination to run riot and whisk you to Bangor on a magic carpet, or in an aeroplane, if you must be prosaic. We'll skate on Treborth Lake, gliding hand in hand, and catch our breath on the frozen air. See if I don't dream you here, you'll be powerless to resist!

Maddy and I took Rowena skating the other day and she swanned round beautifully as we each held her hand. Did I tell you she's playing Tweeny, in the College production of J.M. Barrie's, 'The Admirable Crichton'? It's a wonderful romp.

Maddy is definitely going to Manchester next year as she's won the scholarship. I shall miss her terribly. Half the Chemistry department at Bangor has left for the Ministry of Munitions. In Manchester she'll have top-notch facilities as they're being trained to develop explosives. The alternative is to give up College and get a job, as her family can't support her. She's not happy about it, but hopes the experience will benefit her, if she pursues her interest in radium. I think she talked to you about this. It saddens me to see her sucked into the war machine to survive.

It's wonderful to have Tada home. He's a little stronger. The doctor diagnosed nervous exhaustion and prescribed a rest cure. Mam and I thought he was on the mend, until we had an incident last Thursday.

It's the day when the coal cart comes; you can hear it for miles clattering along the road. The coalman empties sacks into the bunker without knocking, and when the first load tumbled down into the cellar, Tada dropped to the floor and crawled under the table. When we helped him up he was ashen and shaking. He said it sounded like a bomb, and his mind didn't have time to realise he was safe.

To my shame, I burst into tears; I was so upset to see him in such a state. Mam and I are holding him back for as long as possible, but he's desperate to return to his men.

How are you managing now Amelia is working at Endell Street hospital? I'd be fascinated to know more; are suffragettes really running it? Note to Amelia: please write, as I'll never get the full story from your dear brother!

That is all for now, darling friend and companion, my husband to be.

Amelia, plead my case and bring him here soon. It's already been too long.

Your beloved,

Bronwyn

Sealing the letter, she wrote the address in firm strokes, and determined to take Tada for a stroll to the Post Office.

He looked bemused as he peered up from his desk. 'A letter, you say, do you need an envelope?'

'No thanks, Tada; I need to post it. Will you come with me?'

He roused himself slowly from the chair, an old man unknotting his joints. 'Good idea, I wanted a chat.'

He looked old, she thought, helping him into his heavy coat; it hung loose on him now. She handed him his brown felt hat. 'A chat about what?' she asked, before he lost his train of thought.

'Your future husband, my dear. George has written to ask for your hand in marriage.' He smiled benignly.

'He didn't tell me! About writing, I mean. I thought he'd wait until nearer the time.' She felt a thrill of pleasure to think of George writing to Tada.

'I want to be sure you know what you're doing, *Cariad*, before I put the poor man out of his misery.' They walked arm in arm, taking care to avoid ice as they went down hill.

'I love him, Tada. He's prepared to wait until I've graduated, though Mam thinks I should transfer to London. I wouldn't dream of leaving her while you're away.'

He nodded. 'Very loyal of you, dear. If you're committed to married life, you will have to reconsider your career plans. Have you thought about that?' Tada must be testing her resolve.

'George and I will have a modern marriage; I can still follow a career. It's harder with children of course, but that can wait.' She blushed in spite of herself.

They passed handsome redbrick villas, dwindling to humbler dwellings and shops.

'It's a remarkable man who allows his wife to work, unless she has to. He's dealt with blindness with courage and flexibility, so maybe he's the exception.'

An image of George lying helpless in the bed next to Rhys came unbidden. 'He's resilient, and hates any hint of pity. He needs a wife who's strong and independent, like Mam.'

A shadow crossed Tada's face. 'Your mother's a fine example, of course. She shares my burden in the Book Room and she's marvellous with parishioners; I couldn't do my job without her. Remember this, my dear, marriage is a garden to be tended and there are some things only a woman can do. You may have to temper you ambitions to make it a success.'

'Together we can make it work, I'm convinced of it. All we need is your blessing.'

'That goes without saying, my dear. By the way, you might start by wearing his ring.'

'He mentioned it?'

Tada nodded, pulling down his hat against the wind.

'He gave me earrings until we were properly engaged; I didn't know a ring meant so much to him.'

'You modern girls have some funny ideas.'

They'd declared themselves, which for her was enough, but George wanted the world to know. 'Being apart is hard for us both; I can see we should make it more public.' She looked into his care worn face. 'Will you marry us in Chapel?'

'God willing, child.'

'What do you mean?' A chill ran through her; Tada was frail, but he would surely come back.

His face creased with affection. 'I'll be the proudest of fathers, Bron. I've always been proud of you. I hope you know that.'

'Don't, you'll make me cry; and promise me you'll take care of yourself.'

'That at least, I can promise.' He looked more his old self again when he smiled.

Tada's words about married life had her thinking about the future; she saw children, a garden, George at his desk, but where was she? There was so much they needed to explore together before marriage was real to her. Feeling the shape of the envelope in her pocket, she willed it on its way.

'I must go back soon, Bron, you do understand?' Tada tightened his grip on her arm.

'I suppose I do,' she said, with a sigh.

'I'm worried about Mam; losing Glyn has taken its toll.'

'On you too.'

He shrugged. 'That's the way it is. Hannah is likely to stay in Liverpool with her brother, so I depend on you.'

'You can, Tada. But don't leave it so long next time. That's what's so difficult.'

He smiled without answering. 'Now then, let's talk about this career of yours. How's the writing?'

She swallowed hard. 'I'm trying to write about the war, but from a different perspective.'

He waited for her to continue.

'To show a truth that's overlooked by newspapers, a snapshot, if you like, of daily life.' A landscape of possibility opened up as she voiced her thoughts.

'Well, well, tell me more,' he said earnestly.

'I want to write proper articles for the Methodist Magazine; *A day in the life of a padre,* would be a good start, don't you think?'

He chuckled, 'I suppose so. I'm not sure I can help, mind.'

'You can, Tada, I'm sure you can.' Her eyes narrowed in concentration. 'Tell me about the service you hold for the men before they go into battle.'

He looked up at the steel-grey sky in recollection. 'Let me see now, where to begin? We make do with whatever space, usually the corner of a field; there are a dozen or so men. Some take communion.'

'Is there a table, an altar of some sort?'

'Not exactly, there's a groundsheet where the men kneel in front of me. As I bless them, we may hear voices in a nearby field, men returning from a game of football. Hanging in the air are observation balloons, like giant grey sausages.' His footsteps slowed as the story unfolded. 'And the men sing. It's always, *I need thee every hour,* gentle as a lullaby and in as many harmonies as there are men.' He hummed the melody to himself.

She saw Tada, wearing his collar and cassock over khaki, listening to young men's voices blending in the open air.

He cleared his throat and his step faltered. 'It's one of the hardest duties, even harder than ministry to the dying; the poignancy of slender hope, cuts to the quick.'

'I hope Glyn went into battle with such a blessing.'

He patted her hand. 'No doubt he did. The men bring out the father in us, and the nurses are mothers to them. I see untold acts of kindness each day, as well as tragedy.' A story hung in the air.

She looked up, intrigued, but he was silent. 'Tell me, Tada, what is it?'

'It's not pleasant, a case of weakness of the flesh and disease. Recently I visited a young officer at the hospital in Le Havre, who'd been affected.'

'George told me the French have licensed houses, called *maisons de tolérance.*'

'Did he now?' He sounded surprised.

'What happened to him? The young officer,' she persisted.

'Poor lad, desperate because his family had been told, his health and reputation in tatters; any words of mine came too late. He told me he'd rather die than face his fiancée. I told his commanding officer to keep an eye on him. The boy shot himself that night; he'd managed to smuggle in a pistol.'

'How shocking.'

'Indeed. A preventable disease that wrecks lives.' His brow furrowed in anger.

She'd expected Tada to comment on human frailty and morality, and was about to prompt him, when Old Tom with the twisted spine came round the corner. He advanced expertly with the aid of two sticks and came to a halt beside them.

Tada and Tom chatted as she retreated into her thoughts. George had said the men were warned against prostitutes, but many took no heed. Contracting disease in this way was more common than trench foot, and more fool anyone who got caught; the army wasn't in the business of supplying prophylactics, according to him.

Old Tom went on his way, and she tried to draw Tada out. 'What's the clergy's view on these matters?' she asked.

'What matters?' He looked up as if searching for an answer.

'The men who contract disease with prostitutes.' She might as well spell it out.

'Of course, yes, I was still thinking of Old Tom. I've given it a lot of thought, my dear, and come to my own conclusions. Practical compassion is my guide; to give comfort and not to judge.'

They arrived at the Post Office and it was packed, as usual, with a long queue at the parcels desk. For once, she could join the shorter queue to post her letter.

'I'll sit outside, Bron, I could do with a puff.' Tada slipped back out, to avoid small talk with parishioners and enjoy his pipe in peace, most probably.

The young woman in front was heavily pregnant, clutching a parcel to her breast. 'Bonjour,' said Bronwyn, thinking she must be Belgian from her pale hair and shy manner, and that she'd joined the wrong queue.

The woman smiled back, before going with her parcel to the grill.

The clerk spoke sharply in Welsh, pointing to the snake of people with parcels.

Bronwyn stepped forward. 'Excuse me, the lady must be new here, and she's in no condition to wait. Could you kindly help out?'

He raised his eyebrows with impatience and after a moment of suspense, nodded, and the young woman handed over her package.

'That's tuppence,' he said without looking up from the scales.

Looking confused, the young woman opened her purse and turned to Bronwyn.

'This is what you need,' Bronwyn said dipping in for the right coins.

The clerk stamped the parcel and frowned at the address, muttering lengthily about people who take advantage of a situation.

'*Merci beaucoup*,' the young woman said, turning to Bronwyn with forget-me-not blue eyes. 'I know next time.'

After dispatching the letter to George, she went to find Tada, sitting on a bench, nursing the bowl of his pipe.

'All done? Come and sit with me.' He was impervious to the cold.

She knew he wouldn't talk until the tobacco kindled and smouldered and a sweet pungency filled the air.

Biding her time, she said, 'You mentioned practical compassion; how does that work?'

'Good question. Let me tell you another story that may help. Soon after the suicide of the young man, I was kidnapped by a formidable lady called Miss Fortey.'

'Kidnapped? Surely not.' Tada wasn't given to dramatising.

'She arranged to have me driven to her establishment under false pretences; I thought I was going to a nursing home for soldiers, and instead saw young mothers with babes in arms, sitting in the garden of a villa on the edge of town. It was a mother and baby home.' He puffed while she took this in.

'A tiny figure came across the grass towards me, and apologised profusely for the subterfuge. She said if word got out, the place would be closed.'

'Why? Who would close it down?'

'The army. The children's fathers were all British soldiers. The home is supported by the Young Men's Christian Association, and YMCA activities have to be approved by the authorities. They no doubt turn a blind eye, but if they got wind officially, it would be a disaster. So, my dear, my job is to support the work of people like Miss Fortey. It's a tricky subject for a journalist to tackle and I advise you to proceed with caution.' He sucked on his pipe and exhaled a satisfying puff of white smoke.

'I understand. Why did Miss Forty send for you?'

'For a baptism: three infants! I'd forgotten the joy of holding a baby. I wet each head from a birdbath as we stood under a canopy of pines. The mothers wore plain white veils and I named the babes, Angélique, Honoré and Joseph.'

'Into the Catholic church?'

'Into the House of God.'

She closed her eyes for a moment to commit to memory what Tada had told her: holy communion before battle, the young man who shot himself, Miss Fortey and her mothers and babes; so she could record every detail as soon as she got to her desk.

CHAPTER 24

February 1917

The war is wearing us thin, literally.
The Front is consuming us all.

Bronwyn kept a notebook, a sort of scrapbook of musings to collect ideas and impressions and diary entries at the back.

Today, in a deserted corner of the College library, she spilled out her feelings:

I am devastated. Phoebe told us Donald is missing, presumed dead. I saw hope obliterated from her face by one short phrase. There's a gossamer thin chance his disappearance was misreported and he escaped unharmed. We hardly dared say so, for fear of redoubling her pain. She sobbed, we all did, Rowena, Maddy and I, and tried to persuade her to stay in Bangor until the advent of further news. One minute she was all for going straight to Edinburgh to be with Donald's mother, but no, that would be too much like accepting the worst; the next minute she was talking of heading for Oxford where she could retreat into her father's library.

Her life is empty of meaning without Donald, she said, and Bangor makes her feel emptier, in spite of having good friends. She looked utterly wretched, her eyes like ditch-water as if her spirit had been wrung out. We rubbed her hands to bring life back into her, but she still looked hopelessly forlorn.

She decided to go to Oxford in the end. We all walked to the station and made her promise to write. Rowena offered to visit and Maddy and I said we'd come too, which raised a wan smile.

As the train pulled away, she stood at the window and mimed scribbling with hand on heart, to show she would keep her word.

Putting down the pencil, she contemplated her loopy scrawl. How close the four of them had become. She and Maddy were the nucleus, so to speak; Phoebe and Rowena had gravitated towards them, lending a touch of class, or so she and Maddy had joked. They felt like Bangor dullards alongside Rowena's charm and Phoebe's intellect. In a heart to heart the four had revealed first impressions of each other, and Bronwyn saw herself reflected back. Phoebe first noticed her in Professor Evans' lecture, the only student to answer a question he'd probably meant as rhetorical. They'd laughed about that. Rowena had noticed her in the dining hall, moving round and chatting. That's my kind of woman, she'd thought.

Turning to the front of her notebook, she scanned what she'd written about Anna, Lizzie and Amelia, to find a theme she could plait. Start from experience, Tada had told her, write about what you know.

The house was lonely, each room a reminder of when he was home. Mam had started to close rooms to save heat, but more likely to lessen the feeling of emptiness.

A gull's shriek broke into her thoughts and she looked out of the window. Snowdon gleamed under recent snowfall and Bangor Mountain glowed lovely as a plain bride. The sea was sullen, outdone by comparison.

It came to her swiftly, the notion that women had earned the right to be heard, and as non-combatants, could speak more freely than men. She took a sharp pencil from her box:

Wind the clock back three years and we women wouldn't know ourselves.

Take Lizzie, former live-in maid, now working shifts in a munitions factory. The regime is exacting. Girls line up to be frisked each morning and anyone found with a cigarette is dismissed on the spot. Explosion is an ever-present risk. Does Lizzie like her new life? Yes, she likes the companionship and the money, despite the dangers. Her skin is still rosy and clear, not yet yellowed by cordite.

For Anna, war is torment. Her hometown was bombed beyond recognition and now she is a refugee in Bangor, living with her parents. She married her childhood sweetheart, Albert, who returned to the front the day after their wedding. She was just nineteen.

This is her story: 'We escaped from Malines with my parents and arrived in Antwerp, exhausted. Albert went to find bread and couldn't find his way back to us; it was so crowded. We had no choice but to get the boat and leave him behind. For weeks he tried to get aboard but they only took families. His parents had already escaped.

We wrote letters to the authorities for months and heard nothing. The Red Cross finally traced him through the railways; he was working at the station in Poperinghe. His parents now live in Birtley, a Belgian town in England, where we were married.'

Anna told me the town was built as a centre for the manufacture of heavy weapons. The locals call it Elisabethville, after the queen of Belgium. The munitions factory employs thousands of Belgian war wounded still capable of work. Albert's father is contremaître, a foreman and skilled engineer.

Amelia, by contrast, has escaped the clutches of her dear mama to volunteer in a military hospital run entirely by suffragettes. Now there's a young woman who's seen the frailty of flesh under fire.

Today women inhabit new spaces opened by war, providing opportunities to influence the long overdue peace. We have earned the right to vote and insist foreign policy be brought under democratic control. Men may be forced to take up arms, but women can cross borders of class and nation and raise their voice against war and its parasite, the arms industry.

It was pleasing to see her ideas fall into place on the page; she'd round it off, change the names and see if the College magazine would take it. Philip was editor these days, the theology student who'd seconded Phoebe at the College debate. He was deeply involved with the Fellowship of Reconciliation and its periodical, *Y Deyrnas*. Professor Rees, the pacifist so derided by Aubrey, was a staunch supporter. She leaned over for a copy left on the table and thumbed through.

With the love of Jesus, cooperation between nations was possible and would resolve the complicated problems of civilisation, the journal argued. Laudable to be sure, she thought, but lacks the practical appeal of the peace women of whom Madame Duchamp had spoken in school.

She took up her pencil to finish the article, and wrote about the fearless ladies who'd journeyed across Europe to reason and cajole, using influence wherever they could.

There, it was done and quite good, even if she said so herself.

George thought the Americans would come over and finish the job and be more effective than a bunch of well meaning women. She'd been shocked by this, and told him he sounded like his father. It was one of those sticky moments on the phone when he'd coughed and said sorry; war had made him cynical.

She felt an urgent need to speak to him. She would take potluck on his being home, the impulse was unstoppable. She packed her bag and pulled on her coat, ready to brave the cold.

Snow had whitened the Book Room door and the lock was frozen solid. She worked the key until the door finally creaked open. It felt colder inside. She made straight for the paraffin heater and hastily put a match to the wick. She smelled singeing and wound the wick down to soak up the paraffin. The match took this time, giving a bluish flame and she prayed it wouldn't expire.

Snatching up the phone, she gave the operator the number and waited through clicks and whirrings until she heard the familiar ringtone. George would answer after three or four rings if he were there. Her heart raced as she counted, one, two, three, click, and heard his distinctive baritone.

'George, it's me. I just wanted to talk. You're not too busy?'

'Bron, my dearest, I'm never too busy to speak to you. Splendid to hear from you. Is everything alright?'

'I was feeling miserable about Phoebe; remember I wrote to you about Donald? I tried writing to jolly myself out of it; it's easy to get sucked under and feel powerless to change anything.'

'Change what, exactly?' He sounded puzzled.

'Sorry, I sometimes expect you to read my mind; I mean this wretched war. Tell me you're coming soon, George, that's really why I phoned.'

He laughed, a deep reassuring chuckle. 'You're the mind reader; I was just writing to you. I can come early March, if that suits, and Amelia too.'

'I'm so happy, George, I can't tell you, I love you so much!' She didn't care if the operator was eavesdropping. 'We'll go to Anglesey, wrapped up warmly this time.'

'I go there often, and it's always a pleasure,' he said cryptically.

She caught her breath and whispered, 'me too.'

There was a thud down the line, as if the operator had dropped something and they both laughed.

Bronwyn sneezed, 'Sorry, it's a bit cold here.'

'You must be frozen in that Book Room; you should get home, sweetheart.'

'I'm wearing my hat and coat; I'll thaw later. It's been snowing hard, and I've seen children tobogganing on Siliwen slopes. It reminds me of sledging with Glyn and Huw when we were little and didn't feel the cold.'

An evil smell and spluttering came from the stove. 'Drat, I think the heater's packed in.'

'Go now, before you freeze to death. Call any time, Bron, it was such a delightful surprise.'

'I will, my love, not long now.'

'Goodbye, dearest, you'll have my letter by tomorrow.'

'*Au revoir* George, I can't wait.'

The receiver clicked and colour drained out of the afternoon. This time, at least, she could count the days until she was in his arms.

A letter from Huw was waiting for her when she got home. She scanned its contents to check that all was well before settling down to read it in full.

9th R.W.F
B.E.F.
France
February 10th 1917

Dearest Sis,

Thank you so much for the recent parcels, which don't always arrive in order of sending, but never mind. Last night we dined on Mam's Christmas pud doused with brandy, and glasses were raised in thanks.

I've seen Tada twice since his return and he looks remarkably well. I'm so glad you persuaded him to extend his leave. He seems much more his old self.

Things are quieter here now we're behind the line. After morning drill the men can play football, write letters or use the canteen. This is well stocked with bootlaces, metal polish, tobacco and pipe cleaners, and a mysterious surfeit of tinned pears.

About mid-afternoon we congregate in a barn for the daily service, where bales of straw serve as pews. Across the barn hangs a line of washing, mostly undergarments of every size and shape. We think nothing of it as we sing our hearts out to, 'Lead Kindly Light', for in this world the strange becomes normal.

On Fridays we have lantern lectures. I heard a brilliant debate on, 'Are We Progressing?' The atmosphere was electric and the standard as good as any university seminar. I find it transports the mind wonderfully from the joys of Shrapnel Street and Whiz-bang Corner.

I should have asked, how are you surviving this appalling winter? I hope the war hasn't guzzled all the coal supplies and the home fires really are burning.

I'm very impressed you're writing for the Methodist Magazine. Do send me a copy when your next piece is published. I hope to write myself one day. Probably something light and fanciful after this lot.

Cheerio and best love to Mam.

Your loving brother

Huw

She put the letter on the mantelpiece for Mam to read when she got back from her patchwork quilt ladies.

Tada was well and Huw was safe and in sanguine mood. George would be visiting soon. A surge of excitement took her unawares and she skipped upstairs to her room.

CHAPTER 25

March 1917

After arriving in Bangor George and Amelia stayed at the Regency Hotel.

Bronwyn looked up at Mam over her porridge, and said, 'I'll pop over this morning; I won't be long.'

'Don't rush; they'll sleep in, I shouldn't wonder, and be here by lunchtime. There are vegetables to peel and I need you to polish the glasses.'

'The wine glasses in Barbara's cupboard?' She'd called it this since her china doll took up residence there.

'Yes, do take care.' They were an unlikely wedding present for a Methodist Minister and rarely used.

Chores dispatched, Bronwyn sat at her dressing table and brushed her hair till it crackled. She imagined kissing George under a glittering chandelier. The clock struck ten; she couldn't wait.

As she walked into town, excitement heightened her senses: she saw bare trees sharply outlined with scalloped edges and daffodils a startling yellow against blackish bark.

The hotel lobby was dim and not at all grand, dominated by a mahogany desk the size of a battleship. A man in a neat suit stepped forward.

'May I help you, Miss?'

'I'm here to see Mr Chisolm; could you tell him Miss Roberts is here, please?'

'Of course, the gentleman is in the lounge. Follow me.'

The receptionist ushered her through a glass-panelled door and her heart took wing.

George was alone in the room and turned towards her; she flew into his arms.

'Bron dearest,' he said, 'I've waited so long for this.' He pulled her in and they kissed, wrapped in silence.

Now she was with him, she felt solid, defiant. *Be sure he's for you*, Mam had said, but how can anyone be sure? *If together you're greater than the sum of the parts, you'll feel it here*, Mam said, patting the bib of her apron.

Pulling gently away, Bronwyn said, 'I can be strong for you, George; we can be strong for each other. Isn't that how it works?'

'Yes, my love. Marry me, Bron; say you will. I want you with me always.' He kissed her hand.

She felt the warmth of his skin, and stroked his red-blonde hair. 'I will, George, as soon as I can, I promise.' She couldn't leave Mam on her own; he knew that.

He laughed, 'did you say *yes*? Are you sure? I shan't believe it until I hear it again!'

She was laughing too, and held his hands. 'Of course I'll marry you; we're meant for each other.' They'd talked about it before, but committing to a lifetime together made her dizzy.

He held her head and explored her face with his fingertips; it was delicate, more intimate than a gaze, his eyelids fluttering in concentration. 'You're the breath of life to me, Bron; you always will be.'

She felt his arm round her waist, and there was a rustle at the door.

Bronwyn turned. 'Amelia, dear, you've caught us; George has just proposed. You and I are going to be sisters!'

No longer the pale schoolgirl, Amelia wore her hair up and her face was radiant. She ran and kissed them both, and said, 'Thank heavens, I mean, congratulations, that's marvellous! I hope you won't make him wait too long.'

'Now, now,' George intercepted, 'one thing at a time. The poor girl hasn't even seen her ring yet. I hope you'll like it, it's one of Ma's, seed pearls and turquoises.'

'I'm longing to see it! I should go home and tell Mam; she'll be over the moon.'

'What time should we arrive for lunch? I so want to meet her.' Amelia clapped her hands in anticipation.

'About midday. Mam says we can open the drinks cabinet and have a drop of Aubrey's sherry; it's been a while.'

'It's an honour to be invited to your home, Bron,' George smiled.

'I'm so excited, my first wedding, will you have bridesmaids?' Amelia was bubbling over.

'Let's save that till later, shall we?' George said firmly.

'Sorry, I didn't mean to jump the gun.'

Bronwyn gave her a complicit wink and said, 'Must go and help Mam with the finishing touches, you know the sort of thing,' though Amelia probably didn't.

'See you soon, little one,' said George, blowing a kiss. 'There'll be rejoicing at home, I can tell you; I'm such a lucky fellow.'

'My dear child, so soon to be married,' Mam said, smiling and crying.

'Not so soon,' said Bronwyn weepily, 'I won't leave till Tada comes back.'

Mam looked serious. 'When Tada gave George his blessing, it was on the understanding you finish your studies; but you know that.' Mam reached up and kissed her forehead.

Mam never spoke about her own education, or lack of it; Tada said she was far cleverer than he, and entirely self-taught.

'Whatever happens, I'll finish my degree, Mam.'

'Good girl. Now turn your mind to setting the table while I see to lunch, and remember to use the best cutlery.'

There was a musty smell in the dining room, even after Mam had opened the windows. She spread a cloth on the table. It was fine Irish linen, embroidered with Mam's married initials, *S.R.* for Sarah Roberts. A needlewoman from the age of six, she'd stitched a once colourful alphabet sampler, now hanging in a dark corner on the landing. Aged twelve she made a christening robe for Hannah. It was the year Mam left school.

These things Bronwyn had known all her life, stories which became family fables, except now they showed themselves in a new light. As a young married woman, Mam was freed from the duties of elder sister and became an avid reader. Tada would find her asleep in the nursing chair with Aubrey at the breast, after she'd been reading by candlelight. It was years before she would allow herself to read by day.

'Ready?' Mam said, popping her head round the door, appraising the table.

'I think so.' The furniture looked heavy and old fashioned by comparison with George's home.

'They'll take us as they find us,' Mam said, answering her qualms. 'I see you're wearing the earrings; they go perfectly with the blue dress.'

'Thanks, Mam. Your grey silk looks well on you, too. I can't tell you how much they're looking forward to seeing you.'

'Quite an occasion, greeting my future son-in-law,' Mam said with a twinkle.

'Mrs Roberts,' said George, shaking Mam's hand, 'this is the happiest day of my life.'

Mam smiled. 'I'm delighted for you both. This must be Amelia, your sister.'

Amelia held out her hand. 'I'm glad to meet you at last, Mrs Roberts. My parents send their warm regards.'

Bronwyn took George's coat. 'I expect you feel the cold up here.'

'The air is so pure,' Amelia said, shedding a stole trimmed with fur.

'Do come into the sitting room,' Mam said, taking George's arm, 'I hope you'll have a sherry before lunch.'

'I'd enjoy that very much, Mrs Roberts. I feel at home already.'

Mam had set out four glasses and the bottle of sherry on a silver tray. Strong drink never passed her lips, but she would raise a glass of pink cordial on special occasions.

There being no man of the house present, Bronwyn took charge, pouring three small measures.

'A little drop for you, Amelia?'

'Thanks, Bron, I don't usually, but just this once.'

'This one's for you, George,' Bronwyn said, carrying the glass to his hand, 'and a cordial for Mam.'

She took a glass for herself and sat next to George.

'*Iechyd da,* as we say here,' Mam lifted her glass, 'and welcome.'

'Thank you kindly. Your good health,' George replied.

Amelia held her glass gingerly and took tiny sips.

'I remember the day your father proposed as if it were yesterday,' Mam said, mistily.

Bronwyn smiled; she knew the story.

'We'd been walking out for years, but we couldn't marry until he had a Parish of his own. He took me into the vestry, I thought we were to sort out hymnbooks, and sat me down. He was standing there nervously smoothing his hair, I didn't know what was going on, and next thing, he opened his mouth and sang. You know the sweet tenor he has. My tears came pouring; I knew what he wanted. He said the song was all he could offer at present, but soon there would be a ring, if I'd accept it, and he hoped I would.'

Bronwyn squeezed George's hand.

George took a sip from his glass. 'I know Bronwyn is remarkable, and now I understand why; not all parents are so open in their affections.'

'We're a close family, George, and I want you to feel part of it. Amelia too, of course. Drink up now, and Bronwyn will pour you another.'

Mam turned to Amelia. 'Bron tells me you're working in a hospital, my dear. I want to hear all about it.'

'I adore it; that sounds odd when people are suffering, but I believe we really make a difference. We befriend the men and help them recover.'

Mam nodded. 'It sounds almost homely.'

'Exactly! The caring aspect matters almost as much as the medical side. All the doctors are women; did I mention that? The men call it the flapper hospital.'

Bronwyn dreamt of working there in the holidays, if only Hannah could stay with Mam. Talk of Endell Street reminded her of Phoebe addressing the College debate in her low rolling tones. The last news from her was dismal, confirming Donald had been killed. If only Phoebe could be persuaded to work at Endell Street too, it might help her own recovery. She filed the idea for later.

'It's admirable, the way Amelia has thrown herself into it,' said George. 'I suggested she volunteer at St Dunstan's, but I suppose having me blundering about at home was quite enough.'

'You know it wasn't that, George, I just wanted to do something on my own initiative.'

'St Dunstan's more or less turned me round, you know, after Bron brought me back from the brink.' He patted her hand. 'Let's drink to the union of our families, and to the safe return of those fighting for their country.'

'Amen,' said Mam.

'And as soon as possible,' Bronwyn added. It brought a lump to her throat to think of Tada saying prayers with the men before battle, and she sent up a silent prayer of her own.

Conversation turned to food imports and German U-boats sinking thousands of tons every month. George asked after Huw and Aubrey, and Mam talked about the parcels they sent out each week, despite the shortages.

'Once the Americans join us, we'll soon finish the job off,' George said.

'The Russian side is on the verge of collapse and the country's in turmoil,' Bronwyn said, concerned.

'Your man Lloyd George will pull us through,' George said jovially. 'Father supports him, and he's no Liberal.'

Bronwyn saw Mam's lips tighten, and thought it time to change the subject. 'Shall we go for a walk after lunch? I'd like to show you the Belgian promenade.'

'I brought strong shoes,' said Amelia, looking down at her thin leather pumps.

Mam smiled, 'Sensible girl. I practically lived in boots as a young woman. I used to go with Tada to visit remote farms, and I certainly needed them. We could be out until the small hours.'

'I remember waking one night when Hannah was with us,' said Bronwyn, retrieving a hazy memory. 'She said, *Your mam will be back when the birds wake.*'

'Yes, you were very young; we lived out at Nefyn. Tada was called to a hill-farm on one particular occasion. There were four of them living in one room, including the old man's daughter and her husband; no mother, she'd died years ago. The son raised the alarm because the old man wouldn't leave his bed and the doctor couldn't go till morning. We took the pony and trap as far as we could, and had to scramble the last half-mile to get to the cottage.

'First thing we saw was the young woman curled up in pain; her time had come early from worry about her father. I attended her with the help of her husband, and after half an hour a baby girl was born, beautiful and healthy, she was. The old man soon came to himself and said he didn't need the prayer for the dead after all. A small miracle, you could say.'

The story still came fresh and Bronwyn glowed with pride.

George and Amelia were open-mouthed.

'Goodness, I hope I haven't shocked you,' Mam said, going pink.

'No, not at all,' said George. 'You've opened my mind to the lives of others; quite extraordinary.'

'Yes, you must be amazed at how we country folk live! Now, if you're ready, we'll go through for lunch. Bron, you wheel in the trolley, dear, and I'll show in our guests.'

'May I help?' Amelia offered.

'I'd be glad of it,' Bronwyn replied.

She could quiz Amelia about work at the hospital, and Mam would have George to herself.

CHAPTER 26

July 1917

Bronwyn sat cross-legged under the sycamore in the garden, trying one of its broad leaves for size against the palm of her hand. On impulse, she placed it inside the diary pages of her scrapbook. Below, she wrote the date, followed by: *This time last year, Glyn was alive and I hadn't met George. If I could flip an hourglass and go back in time, I would. I still miss Glyn with an aching sadness, as if part of me is torn away. My life falls into two halves and Glyn is the meridian.*

She put the pencil aside and stretched her legs under the gingham skirt Glyn had once found too short; no one would bat an eyelid these days, she thought.

The hospital in London, where Amelia worked, agreed to take her on as a volunteer over the summer. Mam was all for it, and Hannah would come and stay.

Phoebe had leapt at the suggestion of working at the hospital, and wrote: *T' is done, sweet Bron; it will be a relief to my parents when this grey shadow moves out of their house.*

The letter had given her joy, and they'd corresponded since, Bronwyn testing her ideas for the articles she was writing.

She'd reviewed the end of term play, *She Stoops to Conquer*, briefly under threat when the Principal complained of impropriety; the cast played to a full house after that, and as proceeds were for war wounded, there was no question of closing it down. Her piece, headed, *Women Aloud*, was a bit of a rant in first draft—she'd sent it to Phoebe for comment.

'Find a modern twist in the play,' she'd replied, 'show it's about a woman taking power into her own hands. Why bash authority when you can use the text to make your point?'

It made perfect sense, and the review found its way into the *North Wales Chronicle*, thanks to Philip, who regularly championed her writing. Dear Philip, Phoebe's valiant seconder at the College debate. He'd asked to be remembered to Phoebe, and confessed to a soft spot for the lady.

Bronwyn gathered her skirts and her scrapbook, reflecting on all the encouragement she'd received, especially from Tada.

After the engagement he'd written with such tenderness; she could recall every word.

My Dearest Daughter,
Forgive my silence; one is constantly kept at it here. I have three Casualty Clearing Stations under my charge until another chaplain arrives and we are abnormally busy. Yesterday I wrote 12 letters to bereaved families, which adds to one's labour considerably. Whilst I cannot tell you where we are, you will be pleased to know that I'm amongst the compatriots of your new friends at home.

The first time she read this, it took a moment to realise he must be on the Belgian Front.

My purpose in writing is to properly congratulate you on your engagement to George. I was very sorry to have missed the family gathering in Bangor, but I was with you all in spirit. Your Mam is quite delighted with the match and writes about George in glowing terms. She tells me he's kind and intelligent with a sharp mind and gentle manner and most importantly, he's clearly devoted to you.

It has been nothing but a pleasure to see you growing up. I will always carry you in my heart as the little girl in the photo taken all those years ago in Beaumaris. I see you as you were then, with a sweet face and tender wistful eyes looking at life with wonder. Your development has pleased me beyond measure.

Your Mamma and I pray your marriage will give you lifelong joy and succour, as has ours.

I am confident your hard work and success in your studies and your writing will continue. I always believed you would do well and go far. I know you will bring the precious qualities of compassion, usefulness and endurance to whatever you achieve.

May your marriage and its fruits be the crowning glory of your life, sweet child.
Your loving Tada

She remembered the seaweed crackling under her toes, the tang of salt, the tentative steps across slippery stones into the sea and up to her knees in water, holding Tada's hand; they waded out to the rowing boat and he lifted her in. *Hold tight*, he'd said.

It felt as if the boat would capsize as he hauled himself up, but she'd clung on. He rowed out to sea towards the lobster pots, his arms working steadily under rolled up sleeves. She must have been about nine.

On Friday afternoons, biscuits and lemonade—a rehydrated concoction—were served on the patch of grass behind the Women's Halls. It was the summer version of tea and toast in the Common Room.

Bronwyn propped her bike against a tree and found the girls sitting on a blanket, wearing straw hats.

'Take one,' said Rowena.

Bronwyn raised an eyebrow at the box of antiquated headgear. 'Not for me, thanks,' and sank down beside them.

'Miss Hughes says a girl should avoid freckles, it makes her look common,' said Maddy, grinning beneath a wide brim, nose brown and speckled as a hen's egg.

Rowena looked up from a lopsided black hat, pinned with a full-blown rose. 'So, when are you deserting us, Bron?'

'Oh, don't! I already feel guilty about Mam.'

'You'll be swanning about London while I'm looking after my pesky sisters in Manchester. I know which I'd prefer.'

Two first year students arrived with trays for the girls to help themselves. Maddy jumped up to fetch their share.

'Couldn't you get involved in voluntary work?' Bronwyn asked.

Rowena looked dejected. 'In theory, but Mother is rather chaotic and relies on me in the holidays. It'll be a come-down after the excitement of the play and that business with the Prinny.'

'You pushed him over the edge with your version of *Kate* as the saucy barmaid!' Bronwyn teased.

'I'd like to think so,' she smiled.

Maddy came back with grey lemonade and a plate of ginger nuts.

'Have I missed anything?' she set the tray on the blanket.

'I'm a bit miserable about going home, that's all,' said Rowena.

Maddy pulled off her hat and scratched her head. 'I'll be coming to Manchester soon and you could show me round. I need to find the Imperial College of Science, for a start.'

'Stay with us, if you can stand the mess,' Rowena offered.

'That's kind; I'll take digs out of town, but thanks. The bursary comes with a stipend, which I didn't expect.'

'That's wonderful, Mads,' said Bronwyn. It would be the first time Maddy had any money, thanks to the Suffrage Societies scholarship.

'How about you, Bron?' Maddy asked, handing round glasses. 'Will you see much of Phoebe?'

'We're hoping to share a room at the hospital. She's been offered work in the library and I'll be on one of the wards.'

Maddy looked up sharply. 'You're not staying with George?'

'We're not married yet.'

'Touchy subject?'

'Sorry. It's his mother; she's already arranged for Amelia and me to speak at some charitable event without even asking. You can just imagine; it'll be like the Refugee Committee only worse.'

'God, how ghastly. On the other hand, she's embraced you as one of the family. What does George think?' Maddy raised an eyebrow.

'He says I should do as I please. It's not up to him, anyway.' She went hot and felt her blouse stick to her skin.

'Did I say otherwise?' Maddy took on a wide-eyed expression.

'Now now, let's not fall out over men,' Rowena chided.

'You're right,' said Bronwyn. 'Let's plan a gathering before we go our separate ways.'

Maddy looked sheepish. 'I didn't mean it Bron, honestly.'

'I know, Mads,' she said, brushing it off. 'Now, who should we invite? I vote for Philip, he's a sweetie.'

'The conchie with a terrible taste in clothes?' Rowena looked affronted.

'You're a frightful snob,' Maddy mocked. 'How about Madame Martens and Marte? They'd bring great cakes.'

'Good idea,' said Bronwyn, 'and Madame Duchamp, my old French teacher; she supports suffrage and may have contacts at the hospital.'

'We're a bit short of men at this party. I know one or two at a loose end since the play finished.' Rowena peered from under her floppy hat.

'I'm not sure that's a recommendation, but let's have them anyway,' said Bronwyn, collecting the glasses.

'I know what!' Rowena exclaimed.

The other two groaned, but she carried on.

'A masked ball! We can all dress up and drink fruit punch and smoke black Russian cigarettes. I'll come as a debutante.'

Maddy leaned forward and snapped her fingers. 'You're getting carried away again, Rowena.'

'Let's go as *The Three Musketeers*,' Bronwyn chimed in, followed by gales of laughter at the idea of playing trouser roles and Miss Hughes' face if she saw them.

Hospital discipline suited Bronwyn and she enjoyed learning its routines.

It was late by the time she got back from the ward. She heard girls chatting and laughing as they got ready for bed behind khaki curtains, two girls to a cubicle.

She'd been lucky enough to share with Phoebe, as they were friends.

Phoebe came back from the washroom in pyjamas and parted the curtain.

'What is it Phoebs?'

Phoebe rarely cried and her eyes were red-rimmed and puffy.

'Missing Donald, that's all. A young Scot set me off. He said, *whit's yer name wifie?* and I filled up.'

Bronwyn put an arm round her shoulder. 'Poor dear; it's early days yet.'

Phoebe sniffed. 'Donald said if anything happened I should carry on with my life, but it's so hard, constantly awash with this ghastly misery; if anything it gets worse.'

'Come, let's get you to bed and I'll make a beef tea.'

Hannah had done the same for her when she was ambushed by grief after Glyn died.

They lay in bed whispering after the supervisor called, *lights out ladies,* and pondered the meaning of falling in love. Bronwyn said it was thrilling, like plunging from a rock and putting your trust in the sea. For Phoebe, it was a glorious flowering; Donald had shown her how to love and she'd discovered the life of the mind isn't all.

As soon as they'd turned over and said goodnight, Bronwyn felt herself sink heavily into sleep.

It might have been minutes or hours later, she couldn't tell, when clanging broke into her dream, waking her brusquely. All lights were blazing.

It was the bell in the square ringing out, the signal that a convoy had arrived.

They leapt out of bed and pulled on stiff uniforms over pyjamas.

Bronwyn felt a surge of energy and within minutes she and Phoebe were in the corridor with the others, joined by doctors and nurses, streaming from every corner of the building. An unstoppable army of women, thought Bronwyn, filing the phrase for later.

The drill was to work as fast as possible so the ambulances could rattle back empty and pick up the next load. The doctors operated a system of triage, sending each case to a named ward, based on the need for surgery. There were always one or two tragic cases that survived the gruelling journey, only to die within a few hours of arrival. It was something the girls talked about at night, the ones that hadn't made it. Bronwyn felt it as a failure if it was one of her patients.

Most ambulances held six stretchers, though some had been adapted from private vehicles and could hold more. The tricky part was manoeuvring the stretcher with the minimum of discomfort to the patient; you had to leap on board, hoist the handles at the far end, and inch forward, trusting your partner on the ground to keep the stretcher level.

Stretcher-bearers were teamed up in pairs to train the new girls, and Bronwyn was under Freda. The ambulances rumbled steadily into the square and Freda stepped forwards as one pulled up, and opened the heavy doors.

Sharp faced and slight, she'd served eighteen months as an ambulance driver in France and had been sent back for insubordination. 'Get up there, girl,' she bellowed.

Bronwyn scrambled aboard, holding her breath against the stench of unwashed bodies and human waste. No time to be squeamish, decide who to take first. Once her eyes had adjusted to the gloom, it was obvious; the body lying inert, head and left leg bound in heavily bloodied bandages, took priority over a groaning boy.

'This one,' she indicated, bending at the knee to heft the load.

'Got him,' Freda called back, skilfully handling the other end of the stretcher, compensating for Bron's fumbling.

Dr Louisa Garrett Anderson took one look and said, 'St Anne's Ward.'

'Move it,' Freda snapped, the stretcher now on a trolley. 'We don't want him popping his clogs before he gets there.'

They slid the trolley into the lift and Bronwyn took a proper look at the boy. He was still breathing, judging from the slight movement in his chest; he had a badly mangled leg, the boot hanging off at an odd angle. A straggle of dirty blonde hair emerged from the dressings that covered his head and most of his face.

'He'll scrub up alright,' said Freda. 'I've seen worse.'

The lift bumped to a halt and Freda threw the latch and hurled herself against the ironwork gate, forcing it to concertina open. They wheeled the lad onto the ward and Bronwyn sighed relief as they handed him to the team of waiting doctors.

And so the ambulances rolled, hour after hour until six in the morning when the next shift came on, when Bronwyn fell into bed, fully clothed.

Surfacing from sleep, she struggled to piece together the events of the night. At the end of the shift, Freda told her the lad, who was touch and go, had survived surgery.

Sunlight seeped through the grimy square of the basement window and she saw Phoebe's bed was empty. After an all-nighter you could take the day off, though most girls went back to work. Phoebe must have gone to the library.

The clock struck eleven, time to wash and eat before the afternoon shift. As she got out of bed, a half finished letter to Maddy reproached her from the bedside table. If she didn't finish it now, it would be hopelessly out of date. Pen in hand, she skimmed what she'd written so far.

Dear Maddy,

How are you? Any luck finding digs in Manchester? I'm glad Philip gave you an introduction to his sister; sounds like she's a live wire in the suffrage movement. He suggested I write a piece for 'The Common Cause,' about Endell Street, and I hope to find time.

When I first walked into the hospital, a converted workhouse, I saw the motto, 'Deeds Not Words,' over the entrance. It describes perfectly the ethos of practical compassion. More than that, it reflects the respect shown to everyone, from lowliest orderly to Chief Surgeon, Dr Garrett Anderson. It is she and Dr Flora Murray who set the tone.

Dr Murray's office is next to St Hildergard's ward, where I work, and we often see her arrive with her Scottie dogs. The wards are homely, with alternating red and blue blankets neatly tucked and cornered, and standard lamps placed here and there. A volunteer's job is to keep up the men's spirit. I bring books from the library, or take patients to the little theatre for entertainments, when they're able.

It's hard not to get upset when someone doesn't make it. A young man, Alf, liked me to read him Kipling's tales. He seemed to be on the mend, but died of an infection overnight. When the ward sister told me the following morning, I wept. She said, 'we can't take it all on ourselves, Bronwyn, we just do what we can.' It really is the only way to cope, as it happens quite often.

Miss Heston is the librarian and I was terribly flattered when she suggested I join the Women Writers Suffrage League. They refuse to pay tax on account of not having the vote. I pointed out that I've never received a fee for my writing; she said I was sure to one day.

*

The letter came to an abrupt halt, interrupted by the arrival of a convoy. She hadn't mentioned her role as an orderly, too raw to set down in words.

She added a few lines about Phoebe, and how they planned to visit the Welsh Chapel to remember Donald and Glyn and promised to say a prayer for Rhys; and for cousin Alwyn, she promised herself. Sealed and stamped, the letter was ready for the afternoon post.

Picking up her notebook, she wrote:

Here, I feel close to the battlefield as the wounded arrive directly from France, and some nights you can hear the distant booming of guns. When I asked Freda about the chances of another Zeppelin raid, she laughed, and said, 'You're more likely to be hit by a bus.'

The tiredness of physical exertion is far preferable to the creeping lethargy I felt at home, where one is at the mercy of events. It would be a fine thing to write about the hospital's work, if only I could find the time and energy.

CHAPTER 27

August 1917

Bronwyn pulled on her uniform; it felt like cardboard. Every inch of her body ached, even the backs of her eyes, and she hadn't had a proper wash for days.

Convoys arrived day and night; sleep was fitful, broken by the jarring bell. The occasional air raid added to the toll of exhaustion.

Freda passed her a grey facecloth and said, 'Put this on your eyes, it works wonders.'

She did as she was told. The cloth was warm and the scent of lavender permeated her skin, blotting out the world for blissful moments. She was grateful.

'Now let's get cracking, you little sap.' This was the closest Freda got to kindness.

They'd worked on an empty stomach for hours before grabbing a scratch breakfast, but the ambulances kept coming, so they were fed and watered on the hoof, orderlies arriving at intervals with trays of thick sandwiches that would have filled a shift of hungry miners.

When the handover volunteers finally arrived, Bronwyn said, 'Can I get off a few minutes early, Freda? I'm going away this weekend.'

'Aren't you going to the Doctor's talk? Freda asked.

'Yes of course; it went clean out of my mind. I'll catch a later train.' She'd been looking forward to the talk. If only she wasn't so tired.

'What is Dr Anderson's talk about?'

'The usual stuff about how women are as good as men.'

With Freda you could never tell if she was being straight or tongue in cheek.

'So, what do you think? Are we?'

Freda rolled her eyes. 'It's all very well for posh girls like you, but nothing really changes, war or no war.'

'The war has thrown us together, which would never have happened otherwise. I've learned a great deal from you, Freda, about sheer guts and endurance.'

Freda let out a harsh laugh instead of letting rip. 'Stir your stumps, Missy, or you'll be late for the talk.'

Bronwyn hesitated in the doorway. 'It's true, what I said. I've never met anyone like you.'

Dr Anderson's office was already crowded. Girls were sitting, squatting, sharing chairs, squeezed in wherever they could. Bronwyn stood in the doorway and Dr Anderson beckoned her to a bench where three girls budged to make space.

The Doctor sat behind her desk and gave a rare smile. She wore a khaki jacket and skirt, and a purple and green suffragette broach pinned discreetly onto her lapel.

'You are all very young.' She surveyed the room. 'You have given up your school or university holidays to work here and each of you will have her own particular reasons for doing so.' She spoke in a quiet, understated way.

'Many of you will have lost someone dear. Some of you have been inspired by the suffrage cause. Or you may simply want to play your part in the war effort. Through your work, each of you has proved her worth. Whatever your reasons for working with us at Endell Street, my message today applies to you all.' Her eyes swept the room like a searchlight and Bronwyn felt the intensity of her gaze.

'In working for the only military hospital run by women, you are part of an experiment. The experiment began in a hospital in France just three years ago. Since then, we have shown that women can take on a great enterprise requiring intelligence, courage and endurance. Furthermore, the medical procedures we have developed are now used in other hospitals. Tragically it has taken a war for this to come about. When the war ends these lessons must not be forgotten.

'My intention is simple. It is to prepare you for the responsibilities that will befall you once peace is restored.'

There was a slight shuffling and Dr Anderson waited with quiet insistence for the undivided attention of her audience.

'Out of necessity we have stepped into men's shoes. And we have made them our own.'

There was a collective intake of breath.

'This is not about the battle of the sexes. The work of women in this war has shown beyond doubt that we are more than able to work alongside men as equals, and we have brought down many of the old barriers to progress.

'I call on you to use whatever you have learned in your time with us here, to change the world in your own particular way.'

She rose to her feet and dismissed them all with the slightest inclination of her head. There was an almost tangible silence, as girls stood one by one and respectfully left the room, some turning to give a nod of acknowledgment, but Dr Anderson was arranging papers on her desk.

A shy and reflective woman, thought Bronwyn, driven by conviction, rather than pride. Yet she and Dr Murray must have battled authorities; it can't have been easy.

Her temple pulsated with questions that pressed for an answer; she could approach her now, seize the moment and ask for an interview.

The room had emptied and Dr Anderson looked up. 'Is there something you wanted to ask?' she said, helpfully.

'Actually there is, I hope you don't mind; would you allow me to interview you?'

Dr Anderson gave a dry smile. 'Who do you write for?'

'No one, I mean, a friend suggested *The Common Cause* might publish a piece about Endell Street.'

'You know the journal?' Dr Anderson sounded impressed.

'I'm afraid not, I should have read it first, I've bungled this, haven't I?' She felt weak with shame.

'Not at all, we need young writers like you. Ask Miss Heston, she'll give you a copy, and you'll find *Votes for Women* of interest as well. I'll arrange a time when we can have half an hour, in a couple of weeks, to give you time to prepare. What's your name?'

'Bronwyn Roberts, St Hildergard's ward. I can't thank you enough, Dr Anderson.'

The Doctor was already immersed in paperwork.

She could have danced for joy as she headed for the library, bursting to tell Phoebe.

Phoebe looked puzzled. 'Aren't you seeing George this weekend?'

She clapped a hand across her mouth. 'Goodness, yes, I'm horribly late. Dr Anderson said I can interview her and I wanted to tell you.'

Phoebe smiled. 'Well, that's a coup, Bron, well done you.'

'Actually, I made a real hash of it; I told her it was for the *Common Cause*, and she realised I hadn't even read it. I've come for a copy, as well as *Votes for Women*; may I borrow them?'

'Of course, jot your name in the book and I'll fetch some back issues. An interview with Dr Anderson would jolly it up no end.'

She leaned her head on George's shoulder as they walked arm in arm along Wigmore Street, and said, 'We'll be able to do this whenever we want, once we're married; hop on a bus and go to a concert.' He'd agreed to the bus to please her, but insisted on a cab home.

'Yes, darling, with our whole life ahead of us.'

This evening she wore a new azure dress and the skirt brushed her calves and made her feel like a princess. As they approached the concert hall, Bronwyn noticed a group of older women ahead, draped in unseasonable furs and speaking a language she didn't recognise.

'Russians,' said George. 'The concert is in aid of the Russian prisoners' bread fund.'

The women were so deep in conversation it didn't feel rude to stop and stare. They wore old-fashioned hats and chattered like girls. One laughed aloud and held her neighbour's shoulder as if recovering from a joke; another gesticulated to make her point, and they all spoke over one another, as the words flowed pell-mell in the foreign tongue.

She felt a tug on her arm. 'Haven't you seen a Russian before?' George sounded amused.

'Only half starved soldiers in hospital. Aubrey says they can barely survive on prison rations.'

'Well it's those poor fellows the concert is in aid of.'

They walked under a glass canopy and through heavy mahogany doors, into a panelled lobby. A lady selling programmes, asked, 'Programme Sir?' on seeing his dark glasses.

'Yes please,' George said, and handed over change from his pocket for the lady to take what she needed.

'The walls are marble,' said George as they walked into the concert hall.

They were pink and cream. She saw a cupola over the stage, painted with female figures in flowing garments around a male figure radiating streams of golden light. 'The painting is quite beautiful.'

'I thought you'd like it. It's the depiction of the soul of music. You'll see musical instruments if you look closely. I used to come here often.'

'This must be the first time you've been back.'

He cleared his throat and said, 'Yes, another first. It's good to know there's so much I can still do.'

She led him to their seats, plush, not worn and shiny like the theatre at home. The décor was muted and tasteful, not the gaudy reds and golds of the cinema.

'What are they playing?' He handed her the programme.

It had a dark red cover inscribed *Grand Russian Star Concert, in aid of Russian Prisoners of War in Germany.*

'Let's see. Tchaikovsky, Borodin and Mussorgsky and a recitation in Russian. The artists are performing without a fee.'

'Admirable,' said George.

Three artists came on stage and there was a hush. The pianist arranged himself at the keyboard and the singers stood expressionless, waiting for the first chords. It was a melancholic piece and reminded her of Tada and Aubrey singing together, Mam at the piano.

The audience clapped and cheered as the artists took a bow, the loudest cheering from young men at the front, some in wheelchairs.

A young woman in a black silk gown took the stage. 'Kreisler,' Bronwyn whispered in George's ear.

She drew soaring notes from her violin, transformed into dancelike figures and resolved in a plangent Russian melody.

She lowered her instrument as an outburst of applause and cries of *Bravo* rang round the hall.

George said, 'Superb, quite superb.'

Bronwyn clapped till her palms stung, as the young artist looked up between bows with a shy smile.

At the interval, they walked into the evening air among the concert crowd pouring onto the pavement. She felt uplifted by the buzz and a heady mix of perfume and cigar smoke in the air. 'I'm falling in love again, George; I simply adore this Russian music.'

'It's stirred your Celtic passions, my dear. I knew you'd enjoy it.'

As she steered them through the throng, she noticed heads turn and decided they must be a handsome couple. George looked particularly well, his skin had taken colour from the sun, and his thick hair bleached to a pale shade of gold.

'I'm proud to be with you, George. You're a fine looking man.'

He looked pleased and patted her hand. 'The music really has gone to your head.'

'At the hospital we hear all kinds of music on the gramophone, even jazz, which is raw and sad as well as exciting.'

'Call me a fuddy-duddy, but I don't care for it myself. Things going well at work?'

'It has its moments. I've got some good news, George. Dr Anderson has agreed to an interview.'

'In person?'

'That's right; isn't it marvellous?

'Very good. Where do you hope to have the piece published?'

'In a Suffrage journal. Actually, I've got one with me; it's really interesting. I could read it to you on the way home.'

'It'll be too dark in the cab, thank heavens,' he said jovially. 'I was rather hoping for a cuddle.'

'George,' she exclaimed, laughing, 'you're quite shameless!'

Bronwyn loved weekends at home with George, relishing luxury after the hospital regime. At breakfast there was fresh fruit and cream, as well as toast, porridge and a choice of tea, unheard of in Bangor.

'Did you enjoy the concert, dear?' Mrs Chisolm asked.

'Very much,' said Bronwyn. 'It was in aid of Russian prisoners of war.'

Mr Chisolm lowered his newspaper. 'The Russians, you say? If the Bolsheviks take over, the troops will pack up and go home. They're already deserting, according to this.' He jerked his head at the paper.

Bronwyn saw a look pass between Amelia and her mother; trouble was brewing.

'We had a to-do on the ward when one of the men came in tipsy,' Amelia said.

'You have to deal with drunken soldiers?' Mrs Chisolm looked horrified.

'No, Mama, Sister sorted him out. She said, *It's the Johnny Walker Ward for you, young man,* and we hauled him down to the basement. He was harmless enough.'

'How unpleasant for you, dear.'

George looked up from his plate. 'I'm sure Ma would like to hear about the Princess Royal's visit, Bron.'

'Not Princess Victoria?' Mrs Chisolm's eyes lit up.

Bronwyn nodded. 'She handed out gifts and had a quiet word with some of the men.'

'What sort of gifts?' Mr Chisolm ventured a glance over his reading glasses.

'Either an embroidered handkerchief or a walking stick. She sat with Bert, he's had his leg amputated, and she mopped his brow. He keeps the stick in bed with him in case someone steals it.'

Mrs Chisolm looked teary. 'Such a gracious lady, how touching. It's a shame you can't make time for my ladies' afternoon, Bronwyn. They'd love to hear your stories.'

'Bron's working, Ma, she doesn't have time,' said George.

'I'll arrange something when you've finished, dear, just a few friends, they'd love to meet you.'

'I look forward to it, Mrs Chisolm.' I could tell a tale or two to make their hair curl, she thought.

'We haven't heard the end of this Sassoon business,' said Mr Chisolm, from behind his paper. 'He's thrown his Military Cross into the River Mersey. What do you make of that, George?'

A muscle twitched in George's cheek. 'I think he's perfectly sane and I don't know why he's in a psychiatric hospital. Actually, I do. It's because he spoke the truth. I agree with him, it's high time the war was ended.'

Bronwyn put a hand on his. He was shaking.

Mr Chisolm lowered the paper and frowned. 'In my day he wouldn't have got away with it. Either it's a breach of discipline or he's mad. He can't have it both ways.'

George's foot tapped rapidly under the table.

'The patients I talk to want the politicians to make peace,' said Bronwyn, 'but they're still prepared to go back and fight.'

Popular headlines, such as, *Mad Jack sent to Dottyville*, which targeted Sassoon, were met with derision by the men on the ward.

'If it weren't for these,' George said, jabbing a forefinger at both eyes, 'I'd be back there too. Sassoon's *Declaration* is spot on; he's in touch with how men feel.

'Let's change the subject,' said Mrs Chisolm. 'It's bad manners to talk politics at breakfast, and plays havoc with my digestion.'

'It's complete tosh, if you ask me,' said Mr Chisolm, ignoring her plea. 'It caused uproar in Parliament, which is what the man intended, and now he's in a huff because the army won't court martial him. The man's having a fit of pique, not making a point.'

'I'm sorry, but I can't listen to this any longer. If you'll excuse me.' George shoved back his chair, pale with anger.

'I'll come with you,' Bronwyn said, getting to her feet.

She held his arm as they walked into the hall and through the front door, not bothering with coats.

'You must think me a complete fool, Bron. I fall into Pa's trap every time.'

'I don't think he meant to hurt your feelings; he just blunders about.'

George stiffened. 'So, it's my fault?'

'I didn't say that. When you left the table, he looked like a whipped dog.'

George stopped abruptly in the drive. 'I'm not fit to live with.' He rested his forehead on the crown of her head. 'I need you, Bron; stop me turning into a brute.'

'Nonsense.' She looked up and held his head in both hands and kissed him.

'This can't go on for much longer,' he whispered.

'The war or the waiting?'

'Neither.' He sounded unutterably weary.

CHAPTER 28

September 1917

Bronwyn wiped her palms on her rough tunic, knocked on the door and waited to be called.

'Good morning Miss Roberts,' Dr Anderson greeted her, getting up from her desk. 'I've been looking forward to this. Take a comfortable chair.'

'May I take notes?' Bronwyn pressed a satchel to her chest.

'Yes dear, of course.'

'I'm feeling a bit nervous,' she confessed, taking out notebook and pencil.

'No need, this isn't an exam. What is your theme?'

She took a deep breath. 'Women, war and our part in it; I'd like to know why you set up the Women's Hospital Corps.'

Dr Anderson sat in the armchair opposite, hands neatly folded in her lap. 'Necessity. We had to break down prejudice against female doctors before we could be of use.'

'I imagine your suffrage experience helped prepare you for this.'

'Indeed. For a start, we knew we'd meet stiff resistance in England, so we applied directly to the French. They handed over the Hôtel Claridge in Paris and we set up a hospital; that was in September '14. We were amazed when the Royal Army Medical Corps asked us to set up another in Wimereux.'

'Was that before patients were evacuated to England for treatment?' She met Dr Anderson's steady grey eyes.

'That's right; I see you've done your homework. We offered our services and it took off from there.'

'So, you came back to London?'

'We were summoned by Sir Alfred Keogh himself, the Director General. He gave us Endell Street, a shell at the time, with room for 500 beds. You can imagine our delight.'

'I suppose you met with obstacles,' said Bronwyn, wondering how to spell *Keogh*.

'Heavens, yes. Those ordered to assist were downright obstructive, until Sir Alfred intervened. One old colonel said he'd have nothing to do with *indelicate females*.

'There was a huge amount of work to be done, to turn an old workhouse into a hospital. We were up and running by May 15, with Doctor Murray as Doctor in Charge, and myself as Chief Surgeon.'

'How many doctors did you recruit at that stage?'

'Fifteen, all of them from the suffrage movement; we also had 36 nurses, any number of orderlies, cooks, cleaners, storekeepers, and of course our wonderful volunteers.' She smiled graciously.

'Would you say Endell Street differs from any other Army Hospital?'

Dr Anderson stared into space before replying. 'The care here is superior. It has to be. Dr Murray and I believe it isn't enough to be good; we have to be the best to be taken seriously. I'm particularly proud of our clinical research, resulting in better methods of treating infection. It means dressings don't have to be changed as frequently. We've led the way and our methods have been adopted by other hospitals.'

Bronwyn scribbled furiously, then looked up again. 'Do you believe your work has helped the cause of women? You use the suffrage motto, *Deeds not Words*.'

'Undoubtedly it has; we are educators as well as healers. In medicine, we've proved our ability in a great variety of surgical procedures, unknown to women doctors. As you may know, until now our experience was restricted to women and children.

'Our philosophy is to provide necessary treatment and large doses of care and understanding. The men thrive on it, don't you think?'

Bronwyn nodded, smiling. 'Are women essentially more peaceable, in your view? Would most women vote for an end to war?'

Dr Anderson frowned. 'We demand the vote, with no presumption as to how women should use it. You should talk to my journalist friend, Evelyn Sharp, if you want a more satisfactory answer. Do you incline towards pacifism, Miss Roberts?'

The question reminded her of the time when Phoebe introduced her to Philip as a pacifist who didn't yet know it.

'I think the politicians should negotiate peace,' she replied.

Dr Anderson laughed. 'In that case, we're all pacifists!'

'I'd like to take you back to before the war and your fight for suffrage. What is your opinion on the use of violence in pursuit of a cause?'

'I hope you're not too well brought-up to ask about my spell in Holloway prison!' She gave a wry smile. 'It was salutary, it taught me what we were up against. Whatever we did—protest, smash windows, go on hunger strike—the establishment hit back with greater force. It caused me to reconsider. A more effective way to achieve our ends was to demonstrate our abilities, in my case as a doctor, and to educate the next generation.

'Tell me, Miss Roberts, is there a particular memory you will carry away with you? I believe your stay with us comes to an end soon.'

Where to start? The young man, tossing and turning in pain, who'd asked for a book about a musician; she'd brought him *The Life of Chopin* and he'd smiled. That afternoon, the book still in his hands, he passed peacefully away.

No, it would make her cry if she mentioned it.

'I very much admire Miss Heston and the way she finds exactly the right book or magazine for each individual, from aeroplane manuals to texts on archaeology.

'Men's faces transformed by a brass band, a song or a conjuring trick, will stay with me. And the magic of the electrophone as men laugh out loud, listening to a London show through headphones. It makes them feel part of normal life. I know how important it is; my fiancé was blinded at the Somme.'

Dr Anderson nodded. 'You've made a fine start as a journalist, my dear. I'm sure Evelyn would be glad to offer guidance should you need it. I'll drop her a line.' She stood to return to her desk.

'I can't thank you enough, Doctor Anderson, it's been an honour to meet you,' she said, getting to her feet.

'Leave the door open,' she heard the Doctor say, as she left clutching her satchel, quite thrilled.

Her last shift finished at lunchtime and there was a surprise party on the ward. Freda had presented her with a card inscribed, *Don't forget me too quickly.*

The men had sung, *For she's a jolly good fellow*, and she'd cried.

After a chorus of, *speech, speech*, she'd managed to say a few words: 'When I lost my brother to the war, I lost my way in life. Working with the staff and patients at Endell Street has helped me find it again.' They'd all clapped and cheered making her shed more tears.

She longed to tell George. 'It's me,' she said, tapping on his door, and walked in. He was sitting at his desk.

'Bronny! Come here, my love,' and he drew her close.

His touch was delicate as he held her face and the kiss was tender. Longing welled up as she kissed him back.

'Now you're all mine,' he said, as they pulled apart.

She looked at his unseeing eyes and was stung by the cruelty. If he hadn't been blinded they'd never have met.

'At least you're mine after one last phone call. I won't be a tick.'

'Promise to be quick,' she said, with mock severity. 'I've got so much to tell you.'

She watched as he picked up the shiny receiver and asked for the War Office. He was explaining packaging density for heavy components and her attention drifted.

They would have a few days together and he'd take her dancing before she returned to Bangor. He'd waltzed her round the room a few times to a gramophone record and declared her a natural. It was exciting, describing circles to the music in his arms.

'Agreed,' she heard him say, 'delivery in two weeks.' He raised his eyebrows with impatience as the call came to a close, and replaced the receiver.

'Sorry, Bron, took longer than expected. Let's sit by the window. What's new? How was your leaving do?'

'Rather touching. There was cake, a few songs and they made me speak; I blubbed I'm afraid. I'll miss them, especially Freda. Doctor Anderson sent me a card. All the leavers get one, but she wrote a note saying I could contact her journalist friend for help with my writing.'

'That's nice,' he said flatly.

'It means a lot to me. She'll help me polish up articles and I could be published for a fee. I could be earning.'

He slumped back into the chair. 'That's wonderful, really. If I could see you, I'd say, you look so young—a fledgling writer about to take wing. Don't fly too far, Bron. Don't be seduced by those bluestocking women who would turn the world upside down. Amelia says some of them are positively anti-man.'

'Being single doesn't make them anti-man,' she said, leaning forward. 'But that's not what you're saying, is it? You feel if I get involved in something, I'll move away from you. Well, it's just not true.'

'I know, I know, I'm just fearful, that's all. I'm afraid there's something we need to talk about.' He reached for her hand. 'Ma is talking about a London wedding. How would you feel about that?'

'I want Tada to marry us, George, and it has to be in Bangor.' She pulled away her hand.

'We have to consider the expense; if we married here, Ma and Pa would pay for it.'

'It's not just about money, surely? What about Mam and Tada's feelings?'

He sighed. 'I know, it's difficult. I should have told you why Ma didn't visit me in Bangor; she has a phobia about being away from home. I can't see any way round it.'

'It's not fair, George. She could make an effort for her son's wedding. What do you want?'

'To be honest, I'd like a small wedding with as little fuss as possible. She'd make a meal of it in London.'

'That's it then. We'll tell her we want a quiet occasion, and I want it in Chapel. Can we do that?'

'It won't be easy.' He looked drained.

'No, but it has to be done. I love you, George. This is about us, remember; we have to stand up for ourselves or it will be harder later.'

'Come here, my darling,' he said pulling her onto his knee. His arms enveloped her and he held her tight for a long time.

She'd never felt gladder to be home.

'You look peaky, dear. I'll tuck a blanket round you.' Hannah fussed over the chill she'd caught on the train.

Warmth penetrated the morning room on a day of late autumn sunshine that burnished even the dullest surface with a pale gold sheen.

Bronwyn sneezed. 'Drat; six weeks working in hospital and not a sniffle, and now this.'

'You're worn out; and not much rest at George's from what I gather,' Hannah chided.

The days had passed in a social whirl with very little time to themselves, save for moments stolen on the heath. On the last evening, the question of the wedding came up and it was Mrs Chisolm who raised it. 'I wonder if you'd consider a London wedding,' she ventured. 'It's unconventional, I know, but there will be so many guests from our side, I don't see how we can all go to Wales.'

'We want to be married in Bronwyn's home town and for her father to marry us,' George said firmly. 'We could have a celebration here for those who couldn't attend.'

'Well you know my feelings about travelling, dear,' she said pointedly in George's direction.

'It would mean a great deal to me to be married in Chapel among people who've known me since childhood; we need both our families around us.' Bronwyn sounded braver than she felt.

Mrs Chisolm had answered with silence and her husband clipped a cigar.

She wanted to tell Hannah without sounding disloyal. 'To be honest, George's mother is rather controlling and it's getting me down. She's angling for a London wedding.'

'There must be a reason.'

'It's the journey; she has a phobia. I want Tada to marry us here, in Chapel. Surely that's not unreasonable?'

Hannah's bracelets tinkled as she flicked a wrist. 'You'll be married a long time, Bron; you and George have to find some sort of compromise. My advice is don't get off on the wrong foot. Sorry you asked?'

'I think I knew what you'd say. We just want to be together and seem beset by obstacles.'

'Better not upset Mam with this, my dear; you're not getting married just yet.'

Mam came in holding up a letter. 'It's Huw,' she said, handing over a buff coloured sheet. It wasn't hard to decipher the look on her face.

Bronwyn took the letter and Hannah leaned over her shoulder, as they read it together.

REGRET TO INFORM YOU LIEUTENANT H D ROBERTS 9TH RWF DANGEROUSLY ILL AT THIS HOSPITAL. IF YOU WISH TO VISIT HIM AND ARE UNABLE TO BEAR EXPENSE TAKE THIS TELEGRAM TO THE NEAREST POLICE STATION.

'Oh, God,' Bronwyn whispered.

Mam sank into a chair, covering her mouth with a handkerchief; Hannah went to her side.

'I'll go,' said Hannah, 'one of us needs to be with him.'

'Let me go, please,' said Bronwyn, wide-eyed. She had visions of Huw bleeding on a stretcher, like so many of the men she'd carried from the back of an ambulance. Conditions in France would be rudimentary and he'd have even less chance of survival.

'It could be weeks before he's fit to come home and you'd miss the start of term,' Hannah objected, stroking Mam's hand.

Mam looked up. 'You should both go; it would be safer.'

A shadow darkened Hannah's brow. 'And leave you by yourself? I wouldn't dream of it.'

'What would Tada say?' Bronwyn asked.

'I don't think he'd want either of you to travel alone,' Mam replied.

Bronwyn held up the letter. 'I'd be travelling with others, Mam. I'd see Tada as well as Huw; it would mean so much to me.'

Mam and Hannah exchanged a look and it was agreed.

'Very well, dear. I think we may qualify for free travel. You should go straight to the police station with Hannah while I make preparations. You must take calves foot jelly, it's a wonderful restorative.' Mam's face crumpled. 'What have they done to you, my poor boy?'

Maddy came to the station. 'Goodness, Bron, what's that you're carrying?'

'Glyn's rucksack. I wanted to travel light but it weighs a ton.' She shrugged it onto the floor and sank into a springless armchair. The waiting room smelled of damp coal.

Maddy crouched over a miserly fire. 'I hope he's all right, Bron. I wish I'd been able to do the same for Rhys.'

'You did everything you could, Mads. I just want to get there in time.'

'Seeing you will be a great tonic.'

Bronwyn shrugged, examining the holes burnt into the linoleum from hot cinders. 'He's very ill; I have to bring him home. I'm rather afraid of what I shall find. The men who'd made it as far as Endell Street needed specialist care, which isn't available out there. Very few field hospitals have X-ray equipment, for instance. It all depends on his injuries and we've no idea what they are.'

Maddy tilted her auburn head. 'Sounds like you picked up quite a bit at the hospital. Tell me, how's George? Everything going well?'

'We didn't have a lot of time together, thanks to his mother. She expected us to be at her beck and call.'

'Why doesn't he move out?'

Bronwyn sighed. 'He'd find it hard to manage on his own.'

Maddy rubbed her hands at the fire. 'I've found digs in Manchester, a room with a sink, only a tram-ride from the Institute. It's heaven.'

'They're a radical bunch over there; it should be interesting.'

The train whistled as it came through the tunnel.

'Already? Oh no, it's time to say goodbye, I can't bear it.' Maddy's eyes filled.

'Farewell, dearest friend,' said Bronwyn, with a hug. 'See you at Christmas.'

'Write to me, Bron. Let me know how things go.'

Bronwyn heaved on her rucksack and they left the fug of the waiting room.

It was hard to keep smiling as the train pulled away. With Phoebe down south and Maddy in Manchester, there would only be Rowena left when she got back from France.

CHAPTER 29

October 1917

The crossing to France was rough and she was one of the few relatives not to be sick, toughened by fishing trips in choppy waters with Tada and the boys.

They were met by volunteers and shepherded to billets. Bronwyn found herself with a mother and daughter from Cardiff, both exhausted by the unaccustomed travelling. They'd never been further than Swansea.

It was after midnight when they were dropped off outside a cottage. Bronwyn knocked several times before they heard movement. After the sound of approaching footsteps and keys rattling, the door opened and a small woman stood wrapped in a black shawl, holding a candle.

'*Entrez, entrez Mesdames, excusez-moi,*' she apologised, having dozed off in the chair. She led the way up narrow stairs to a room filled by an iron bedstead with a giant bolster. The old woman lit a candlestick on the wall and bid them goodnight.

Bronwyn ached all over and felt she'd been on the move for days. She longed to get out of her dusty clothes despite the cold. They took off their dresses, pulled nightdresses over underwear and within minutes were huddled under slightly damp covers. Bronwyn was glad of the human warmth as they settled three to a bed.

Next morning, they creaked downstairs lured by fresh coffee, and bread still warm from the oven.

'*Mes pauvres,*' Madame commiserated. She spoke of recent battles, '*terribles, vraiment terribles.*'

Bronwyn tasted fear as she thought about the reality of Huw's condition. 'We should pack and get ready to leave,' she told her companions.

They followed her lead and left breakfast on the table half eaten.

'We've got four or five hours on the road and it's going to be bumpy,' warned the young woman at the wheel.

Bronwyn hoisted herself under a canvas flap at the back of the lorry and helped her fellow travellers on board. There were already four women inside, all bound for the hospital in Rouen. They soon exchanged names and whether visiting husband, son or brother.

The horn blasted and the lorry jerked as the driver called out, 'Hold tight.'

Conversation became impossible and they clutched whatever they could to avoid being thrown to the ground as the vehicle careered along.

The lorry swerved violently and plunged. There were screams and a crunch of gears; Bronwyn steadied herself as they ground up a slope. The driver shouted, 'We've hit a crater, nothing to worry about.'

The woman next to Bronwyn let out a groan, doubled over and was copiously sick. It was going to be another long day.

The hospital was on a recent encampment thrown up in haste to meet the ever-growing needs of the war. Bronwyn saw rows of khaki tents and huts with corrugated iron roofs.

The lorry stopped near the huts and the women clambered down with suitcases; they picked their way across a track strewn with straw, towards a hut marked, *Hostel.* The rain was horizontal. Bronwyn was glad of the sou'wester Mam had insisted she take.

Inside the atmosphere was muggy; a volunteer led them along a central wooden causeway to cubicles at either side and told them to rest until called to visit their loved ones.

Bronwyn eased her rucksack onto the groundsheet. The cubicle was kitted out with camp bed, pillow, a pile of grey army blankets and bright knitted bedcover. A canvas washbasin and tin chamber pot completed the furnishings. She reached up and felt the rain's vibrations on the corrugated ceiling.

Be patient, the volunteer had said, but Bronwyn was desperate to see Huw. She paced back and forth, made up the bed, unlaced her boots and lay on the gaudy bedspread. She imagined the women who'd gathered to knit blanket squares in a village in England or France.

Her thoughts drifted to Huw as a boy, on the sidelines of rugby or cricket, but capable of running up mountains. Hardy as a goat, said an old woman at chapel as she pinched his cheek.

Someone was shaking her shoulder. '*Venez, Mademoiselle, venez avec moi.*'

Fumbling into boots, coat and headgear, she was ready. They headed out along the causeway, now slick with mud in drizzling rain.

'*Ce n'est pas loin,*' her guide reassured, only a minute to the tent where Huw lay. They went through a double set of flaps and the air was thick with the odour of disinfectant. The young woman explained this was a ward for officers who had been seriously wounded.

Bronwyn's spirits sank as she took in what was now familiar. The stilled bodies and grey faces, the quietness of those too weak to stir.

The American ward sister took over and explained briskly what to expect. 'When we sent for you he was on the morbidity ward, but since the transfusion the prognosis is quite good. We just need to keep any infection under control. If you could get him to drink it would help.'

She said nothing about his actual injuries. They walked through the tent and Bronwyn was sure she could see him in the far corner; her heart leapt.

The ward Sister continued in measured tones. 'The bullet wound to his back and shoulder was serious. It only just missed his heart and he lost a great deal of blood. Is he right or left handed?'

'Left handed.'

'Pity. He probably won't regain much use in that arm.'

Huw was asleep when they arrived at his bedside. He lay semi-prone, propped on pillows. His left side was strapped up so she couldn't see his arm. He looked peaceful, though flushed.

'I brought his spare glasses; he's very short sighted.' It was Mam's idea; it was an old prescription, but better than nothing.

'Well done, it will make all the difference. I'll leave you alone with him; it'll do him good to see you when he comes round. The operation was this morning.'

He always looked vulnerable without glasses and, asleep; he was just a boy. His thick hair was matted and dull and his nails still caked with mud. She held his good hand. As the ward continued its bustle she was struck by how young the staff looked: among the doctors, nurses and orderlies, there could be no one over twenty-five.

Huw stirred; she was still holding his hand. He'd be groggy from the anaesthetic, but would know her voice.

'Huw, it's me, Bron, you're not dreaming. I've come to look after you.'

She felt his hand tighten and his eyes opened. His mouth looked dry and she dampened her handkerchief in the beaker and moistened his lips.

'Would you like your glasses?'

He nodded.

She placed them gently on his face. 'That's better, can you see me now?'

He nodded again with the glimmer of a smile. She sat on the bed, hoping the nurses weren't too strict.

'Just rest, you don't need to talk.' He closed his eyes but she knew he was listening. 'Mam sends her love; and Hannah, she's staying with Mam.'

He nodded.

She brought a glass of water to his lips and he was able to sip, bringing poignant memories of early days with George.

Huw would only be able to cope with short bursts of attention at first. Each day she found snippets to amuse him, mentioning people he knew. How there'd been dissent in the quilting circle when Mrs King declared patchwork squares bearing officers' names shouldn't be joined with other ranks'. Separate quilts were proposed, until Mam had a word and the lady got off her high horse. *Only an Englishwoman could invent such a thing*, Mam said, which made Huw smile.

There were daily victories; he managed his beaker unaided and asked for pen and paper to practise writing wrong-handed, as he put it. After a week, he took his first faltering steps with Bronwyn and an orderly at either side.

The surgeon paid a visit. 'Beautiful handiwork,' he said, when the nurse gingerly pulled back the dressing. 'The X-ray shows we got it all out, so the rest is up to you, young man.'

Doctor Anderson would have praised the quality of nursing, Bronwyn thought.

One day she was helping Huw walk, when a familiar figure approached. Was it Tada? He looked so old; he smiled and she was sure.

Without a word, he took over and together they eased Huw into bed. Her heart felt light with Tada at her side.

Tada spoke in Welsh, saying, 'I'm pleased to see they've put you together again, Huw, dear. I heard it was touch and go.'

Huw's eyes magnified with tears behind his round glasses while Tada sat and stroked the back of his hand. 'I got a message through to Mam so she knows you're on the mend; she's heard from Aubrey and he hopes to be released to Holland soon.'

He turned to Bronwyn in mock seriousness. 'How about you, young lady? I see you've taken to studying abroad.'

Impossible to hold back tears, seeing them together like this. She sat next to Tada and laid her head on his shoulder, feeling the rough cloth under her cheek as he put an arm round her.

Huw was finally able to speak. 'How did you know I was here?'

Tapping the side of his nose, Tada said, 'Padres' telegraph; word soon gets round. I've arranged to stay a few days to help out with the American boys.

'How are you getting along with that arm? Reckon there's any life in it?'

The bandages were much lighter, leaving his hand free. Screwing up his face, Huw wriggled two fingers. 'It's improving. Still pretty numb, but I can write moderately well with the other hand.' He reached for his notebook to show Tada.

'Not at all bad. So what's this you're working on?'

Huw looked sheepish. 'Nothing much; jottings for stories, that sort of thing. The odd poem.'

'Good lad, keep it up. I must leave you for a while; don't run away now.'

Bronwyn went for lunch in the canteen, always a hub of news and gossip. Today she sat near the volunteer who'd met her on arrival.

'I'm afraid your compatriots left this morning, Miss Roberts.' The young woman touched her arm.

It could only mean one thing. Afternoon bugle calls were a regular reminder. She'd seen none of the women from the lorry and thanked God for sparing Huw.

Sipping a mug of Camp coffee, she watched a flock of black-cloaked Voluntary Aid Detachment girls loosen velvet bows on their straw bonnets and settle for a chat before duty. You had to be twenty-three to be a VAD abroad, but they looked more like schoolgirls.

There were romances of course, away from matron's eagle eye. Although fraternising was frowned upon it happened all the time.

A scurrilous rumour circulated about a couple of girls renting a room at the Hotel de la Poste in the afternoons. They were merely treating themselves to a hot bath, as it turned out. A little anecdote for her piece, *A Sister's Visit*.

In the evenings she caught up on letters. To George, she wrote:

Time is oddly sped up here; you could wake one morning and find ten years have passed. You learn the line between life and death is infinitesimally fine, each of us a breath away from extinction.

She wrote daily to Mam chronicling Huw's progress and improving spirits, and promised to bring him home once the doctor signed him off.

She wrote to Maddy: *Endell Street article accepted by Miss Sharp, editor of Votes For Women and veteran suffrage campaigner. I'm so excited! Does it make me a proper writer?!*

Time to go back to the ward. Huw was impatient to go home and Tada said he'd come when the Medical Officer came on his rounds. There was a hospital train due out in a few days and Huw's heart was set on it.

As she ducked under the tent flaps, there was a tremendous commotion. A man was screaming, two orderlies were restraining a writhing body and Sister stood by with a syringe. Tada sat next to Huw shielding him from the worst, but Huw still looked rattled. She skirted round to Huw's bed.

He nodded towards the knot of people attending the afflicted man. 'Been like it the last few nights; it's the first time he's gone off in the day.'

At Endell Street, shellshock cases were moved to private cubicles, for the patient's dignity as well as to protect others. Once medically fit, they were transferred to one of the neurasthenic centres.

The screaming continued, then silence.

The doctor who injected the sedative walked unhurriedly to Huw's bedside. 'So, you're pining to go home, I hear.'

Huw talked about the mobility he'd gained and the doctor observed him closely. A lesser physician would have listened with half an ear, but he gave Huw his full attention. 'Will your sister be travelling with you?' He turned to Bronwyn.

'Yes, I will Doctor.'

'That's good enough for me. Fit to travel in seven days.' He looked down at Huw. 'That's next Monday at the earliest.' He signed the form with a brief flourish and was already on the move.

CHAPTER 30

October 1917

Bronwyn and Tada walked in step, as they made the circuit of the camp. It was once a racecourse, the grass long since churned to mud.

She felt the air like a scalpel to her skin, and tightened her headscarf. 'Before we leave, there's something Huw needs to know. He's asking about his men and if any of them came through. Would your contacts help?'

Tada looked doubtful. 'His battalion almost certainly no longer exists; it would be hard to trace individuals once dispersed. There were terrible losses at Cambrai.'

She knew this from the press. Lloyd George decided to divert divisions to Italy, and the line was brutally pushed back.

Tada plunged his hands deeper into his pockets against the cold. 'I think Huw's still suffering from shock. You must have seen it at the London hospital.'

'You're right, he's not himself; he seems restless and lethargic by turns. It takes people in different ways. George had nightmares for months.'

Tada nodded. 'How is George?'

She could feel his gaze and looked ahead. 'He's well, thank you; though I have to admit, his mother is quite demanding. She rather upset me.'

'Reading between the lines, she's frightened of losing him. You ought to make a friend of her; have you written to her since you've been out here?'

She swallowed a mouthful of icy air. 'Not yet.' She'd sent formal thanks, but nothing to dispel the *froid* over the wedding.

'Marriage brings new ties, a mixed blessing on occasion. You're fond of Amelia, I believe?'

She took his arm. 'Yes, very. What would I do without you, Tada? You've given me a well deserved nudge and I'm grateful.'

They'd reached the perimeter of the course and turned, the wind at their backs, joining a metalled road pitted with potholes.

'I have to go tonight, beloved daughter, *merch annwyl.*' He smiled wearily. 'I'll be relieved to know when you've arrived in England. Hospital trains can be targets; the red-cross flag doesn't count for much these days.'

'Tada, we'll get home safely, I promise.'

'Good girl. I hope to follow you soon. Very soon.'

Dear George,
Forgive the long silence; once you've read this you will understand.

The hospital in Rouen was bombed two days ago, so we took the first train out. We've been on board twenty-four hours. Progress is slow as we're shunted from one siding to another to make way for troops, supplies and munitions trains.

I was sitting with Huw when they bombed the camp. We heard engines humming overhead and hurried outside to see a plane in the glare of searchlights, before all hell let loose. Anti-aircraft guns pummelled and flashed as flares descended from the night sky. A shell exploded and hit three tents, we later found out. It was chaotic, people scrambling and running for cover in all directions, ambulances wailing. We went back inside the tent and I persuaded Huw to lie down while I made myself useful.

The American Sister in charge looked deathly under the candle-lantern; within minutes she'd enlisted anyone capable. Temporary beds, trolleys, buckets, primus stoves and all available emergency supplies were brought into service. I felt the earth vibrate under my feet as anti-aircraft guns raged against the sky and sirens grew louder. It was only afterwards I felt frightened; there wasn't time under fire.

The shell hit medical staff, orderlies and patients alike. The twice wounded came off worst, taken directly to be X-rayed and treated. Others were brought into wards outside the bombed area. Doctors, nurses and any number of orderlies were wheeled into our tent, many crying out in agony before nurses reached them with doses of morphine.

I can never forgive those who did this! To attack a hospital is utterly despicable.

You find me now in the Staff Carriage mess-room. As Huw's sister, I've been given the honorary title of VAD. From the window I see snow giving a light dusting to the blackened land, turning the charred remains of trees into whitened bones.

I'm afraid the last few weeks have left me bleak of spirit, dear George, and I long to be home. However, it has confirmed that my mission is to write about the cruelty of war and why we must never let it happen again.

I've written to thank your mother for accepting me into the family and apologised for leaving on a sour note. Seeing life in the raw has given me a sense of proportion.

I miss the kindness in your voice and your gentle touch, most dear, and patient man.

Your ever loving,

Bron

Since the bombing she'd staggered from one day to the next, head filled with horrific visions of Huw being killed. She must keep busy.

The kettle was whistling, balanced on the primus stove. The train jerked forward and she steadied herself, holding the edge of the bunk as the train made a series of jolts. It was late afternoon and time to take the men tea.

She poured boiling water onto tea leaves in a giant's teapot, followed by condensed milk and stirred the brew with a wooden spoon; the tea was sweet and thick as treacle, the way the men loved it. A teacloth protected her hands from the metal handles as she carried the pot to the first carriage. Huw was further along with the *sitting-ups* in need of less attention.

Patients lay stacked in three tiers on bunk beds. It wasn't designed for feeding or nursing patients, especially on the top bunks. She'd watched nurses adjust splints, change dressings and charge carrel tubes, nimble as acrobats. The train was fully loaded with over four hundred sick and wounded. Crawling towards Abbeville and only halfway to Boulogne, the promise of home kept the men cheerful and they laughed off any discomfort after the trenches.

The moment she walked into the carriage, anti-aircraft guns sprang into action. She saw the look of alarm on the men's faces as explosions punctured the air and fear coursed through the carriage.

'Put down the teapot, Miss, before we're all christened,' said a voice from a lower bunk.

She dumped it under a bench and crouched on the floor. The seam of electric ceiling lights faded to yellow and died, leaving a greyish darkness.

I should be scared, she thought, but I'm not.

There was a battering on the roof, like a downpour, followed by the sound of shattering glass. The carriage rocked violently and she felt her head hit the floor; her throat burned with cordite. The train surged forward in a violent spasm and there were thuds and shouts as men fell from their cots onto the central aisle.

She heard Sister Mahoney's clear bright voice. 'Do be quiet, boys, till I get this wretched little lamp to burn.' There was the sound of a striking match and a light appeared at the other end of the carriage. 'There now, we'll have you all in bed in no time. Anyone who is able, come and give me a hand.'

The moaning subsided, the men reassured by her presence.

Bronwyn scrambled to her feet and nurses came in from other carriages. Cuts and bruises were the only visible injuries as they helped men back into bed. An orderly dished out tea and something like calm was restored.

'Did we take a hit?' one man asked, when the lights went back on.

'Not directly,' said Sister Mahoney. 'I'm told we're fit to travel.'

Bronwyn remembered Tada's fears for hospital trains. 'Have other carriages been affected?'

'I don't know, Miss Roberts, but visit your brother if you must.'

'Thank you, Sister; I'll be back directly.'

Hurrying along corridors she imagined him helpless, good arm broken, glasses smashed on the floor.

She opened the door of the compartment and saw him reading alongside men playing cards. Everything looked strangely normal.

Huw looked concerned. 'What happened to you, Bron? That's a nasty bump you've got. Come and sit down.'

'It was you I was worried about.' She felt the swelling on her temple and shivered.

'You got a hammering further down?' asked one of the card players.

'Drink this.' Someone handed her a beaker, which she clutched as the scene flashed across her mind. 'There was a dreadful noise and men were thrown from their bunks. Sister Mahoney took charge and we soon sorted everyone out, more or less.'

The train inched forward. 'About time,' said Huw. 'How about a drop of brandy to settle your nerves?'

Before she could answer, one of the card players took a flask from under the seat. 'This'll sort you out,' he said, pouring a tot into her beaker.

The tea tasted like fruit punch and made her dizzy.

'I'll fetch something for that bruise,' said another man. 'It's going to be a shiner.'

'Lean on my shoulder,' said Huw.

She obeyed and allowed her eyes to close for a moment.

'Take this,' said Huw, handing her a folded wet flannel. 'It will ease the swelling.'

She applied it gingerly to the bulging bruise and the men in the carriage, variously bandaged, smiled in sympathy.

'That's a nice little *blighty* you've got, Miss,' a young officer teased.

She gulped down the medicinal tea, head thumping.

'May I?' Huw took the mug and sipped. 'Good Lord, that's strong.'

The young officer grinned. 'It's a fine sister you have, coming all this way to take you home.'

'It was a close shave yesterday,' said Huw, as they stretched their legs in the corridor. 'I believe your carriage was closest to the blast.'

'Really? It did sound like a ton of earth raining down.'

'That's pretty much what happened; it must have been terrifying.'

'I remember thinking, I'm not frightened. It all happened so quickly, I just did what I had to.'

He looked out at the forlorn countryside. 'God, I'll be glad to leave this place. At least they can't send me back.' He worked his fingers inside the sling.

'What will you do, Huw?'

'A backroom job, or training new recruits in Litherland; good experience for the schoolroom.'

She turned in surprise. 'You want to teach in school? I thought you'd do something more academic.'

'I want to write stories for children; I doubt I could make a living out of it.'

She could see him, war veteran and schoolmaster, the gentler type who kept order with his wits. He'd still be the one with the gammy arm.

They stood, rocking with the rhythm of the train.

'Being out here has made me think a lot about Glyn,' said Bronwyn. 'They called him, *The Babe*, you know. Tada told me. He was the youngest officer in the battalion. His last note to Mam was bright and hopeful. I wish we knew more about what happened in the end. They said he died running to save a brother officer.'

Huw winced as he eased his left shoulder. 'I've written similar letters to bereaved families. You write about what you know of the man, not actual events. Glyn would have given his life to save a man.'

'No grave, nothing to mark Glyn's passing?'

She felt his arm round her shoulder. 'There are thousands of unmarked graves, and thousands more with no grave at all; no point in glossing it over.'

The deadly horizon drained her of feeling and the sky was leaden.

Huw went quiet, as if allowing her to absorb what he already knew: there would never be any trace of Glyn.

'How's the writing, Bron? Plenty of material out here, I reckon.'

She looked into his owlish eyes. 'I'm writing about coming to France and taking you home.'

He looked bashful. 'I'm a very lucky chap.'

'What do you think of my Endell Street piece?'

'It's good the way you subvert the notion of petticoat power by showing women working in their own right. I like your tantalising snippets about the patients, leaving the reader hungry. I've said before, you've the makings of a journalist. You should get on with it.'

'Meaning?'

'Move to London; I can look after Mam.'

She nodded, encouraging him to continue.

'There's a college called Birkbeck where you could study part-time and still write. I dare say they even take married women.'

'Do you realise what you're saying?' She felt mounting excitement.

'Where there's a will. You could get married and move to London over the summer; the war may be over by then.'

She rose on tiptoe and kissed his cheek. A couple of rooms would be ample; they'd live simply.

'What is it, Bron?'

The wave of joy collapsed as she viewed the scarred landscape through the tobacco stained window. 'Being here changed me; it's hard to explain. I just know I have to return after the war, to write about people rebuilding their lives. It's going to be hard on George.'

Huw pushed his glasses up his nose. 'I can see it's complicated.'

She felt the train lose speed. 'Are we stopping?'

'Signal. Boulogne by tonight, with any luck.'

They ground to a halt in the middle of a field crossed by a line of telegraph poles, wires dangling. The rich brown soil made her think of Glyn immured in a trench or entombed in No Man's land.

She sprang to the door, wrenched it open and descended the metal steps before her courage deserted.

'Bron,' Huw yelled, 'in heavens name!'

It wasn't far to jump. Heart racing, she scooped a handful of earth and crammed it into her jacket pocket.

The train breathed noisily.

Huw stood horrified at the gaping door as the train gathered steam.

She looked aghast at the distance between track and bottom step.

'Jump, Bron, grab hold, *now*!'

The train inched forward. She leapt, felt the iron-rung slice her hand and clung on. A man was dragging her by collar and sleeve, enough to wrench her arm from its socket.

She fell facedown on the floor.

'No harm done, I hope?' It was one of Huw's carriage chums.

'Sorry, sorry, I didn't mean to be a nuisance.'

Huw helped her to her feet, speechless.

'I don't know what came over me.' She felt badly bruised in body and pride.

Huw shook his head in confusion. 'All for a handful of mud?'

'A piece of French soil, for Glyn. It's not much, but it's something.'

A smile crept across his face. 'You silly chump. If only Glyn could see you now! *The Wreck of the Hesperus* springs to mind; let's get you cleaned up.'

The train slid silently into Boulogne in the early hours, the hospital ship looming in dock.

The walking wounded boarded first.

'Let me take your kitbag,' she said, as Huw struggled under its weight.

'It's alright, Sis,' he said lowering it from his right shoulder, 'I must learn to adapt.'

They settled on a bench below deck and watched the bearers carry on stretchers. It was daybreak before the ship rolled out.

When they arrived, they were greeted by a gloriously crisp English morning. They took a train to London, still under military escort, and a lorry to Euston Station; rail passes covered the last lap to Bangor.

London without George felt alien—so near yet so far. The prospect of returning to France had entered worm-like into her mind. Her whole happiness was at stake.

'That's it, Bron, we're on our own now.' Sweat beaded Huw's brow, his face grey with fatigue.

'And you're out of it, thank God. Mam will be overjoyed to have you home.'

He flashed one of his rare smiles and she felt the warmth of his affection.

'Me too, *pwtyn*, thanks to you.'

CHAPTER 31

December 1918

Bronwyn reached for her diary next to the bed and wrote:

How long before my dream-mind accepts the war is over? Done, finished, I can't say won, because there's too much to grieve about.

I try to exorcise bad dreams by remembering Armistice Day, in the hope of making peace stick.

The Bursar, never seen outside his office, ran along the corridor, opening doors and calling, 'The war's over, it's official, the war's over.'

Impossible to work after that. Everyone rushed outside, clapping and laughing. I saw Huw and we hugged and wept with relief.

Professor Reichel passed a group of girls making a joyful racket. He turned and says, 'Quiet ladies please; the occasion is too solemn and sad for laughter.'

At College there's no longer an invisible line between men and women. Miss Hughes has retired and the old rules are swept aside as men in high revel, throw themselves into student life. Scores of them swarm the corridors and the air resonates with the sheer volume of masculine sound. Poor old Macadam, the porter, has lost control of his domain.

Putting the diary aside, she slid under the covers in the hope of sleep.

A loud purring announced a visit from Tiger; he took an elegant leap, landed noiselessly on the quilt and coiled himself in the crook of her arm. A warm paw pressed against her cheek and she obliged by stroking his marmalade head, mulling over what had happened.

It was the question of where they would live; they'd spoken about it yesterday. George called almost daily, now they had the telephone. It was Aubrey's idea to install this modern necessity, and it sat in the hall. Calls weren't private, but more personal than Amelia reading letters to George.

Was she being unreasonable?

'There's a grand little house by the Heath come up; I could move straightaway and get used to the geography of the place,' he'd said, brimming with enthusiasm.

If she closed her eyes, she could see him in the green leather chair and smell the woody smoke of his favourite tobacco.

'Can't I see it first?' she'd asked.

'It may be gone by next month. Come for Christmas and we can go together!'

'I'd love to, but it'll be the first since the war; I really couldn't.'

'That's a shame. So when can you see the house? I'd hate to lose it for the sake of a few weeks. You know how impatient I am.'

She'd suggested he send descriptions of suitable places so they could talk it through, including the one he and his mother visited and liked.

It wasn't the first time they'd had a difference of opinion. After France, she'd offered to move to London and study part-time, but there'd been too many obstacles. For a start, George wasn't keen on her going to College in a rough part of London, though, as she'd pointed out, Endell Street wasn't very different. His parents took the view that marriage was a career in itself, particularly in George's situation. He didn't agree, naturally, but downplayed her writing. So they set the wedding for the summer, after finals.

With all the talk about houses, she'd forgotten to tell him she'd been shortlisted for the Young Journalists' Award for her essay, *A Sister's Visit*. The prize was £50 travel bursary to report on post-war Europe. If ever she won, she'd have to break it to him gently.

Aubrey was having a hard time adapting to civilian life and doing his utmost to get a foreign posting. Bronwyn felt sorry for him, but lost patience when he treated her like a batman and expected her to run errands, oblivious to the fact she was studying for finals.

He rarely mentioned his years in prison camp. She noticed he regaled Huw with incidents from the trenches as if it were yesterday, and wondered if he felt ashamed of coming back without a mark.

Aubrey burst in cursing the newspaper, as she polished the dining table.

'Women have got the vote, what more do they want?' His solid frame blocked the light as he stood brandishing the pages.

'We want the vote at the same age as men,' she said, rubbing furiously.

He gave an avuncular smile. 'Come come, we've just been through a war; if women voted at twenty-one, men would be outnumbered.'

She hated the way he talked down to her. 'Women have been through it too, Aubrey, *and* given their lives. We deserve to have a say.'

'Granted, we couldn't have done it without nurses and VADs, but war is a man's game and so is politics, if you ask me.' He rocked on his feet complacently.

A dozen ripostes came to mind, but Mam had warned her not to upset him.

'We'll have to agree to differ. Could you help set the table, please?'

'Surely. I forget there's no Lizzie these days.'

She shook out a crisp white cloth the length of the table while he counted out the cutlery: knives, forks and spoons, lined up meticulously.

He caught her eye. 'Everything in its place, shipshape; it's how we managed.'

'In the camp?'

'Boredom was the enemy. Barbed wire disease, we called it. Flaming hell, I can tell you.' He laid the table, placing cutlery in perfect symmetry.

'We'd hear rumours of defeats,' he continued, 'revolution in Russia; we hadn't a clue what was going on really. A transfer to Holland was the best one could hope for.'

'I don't know how you coped.' She touched his arm and he recoiled.

'Sorry, I'm a bit jumpy. Letters from home kept me going when I was mouldy.' He chuckled and glanced up. 'It wasn't all doom and gloom. We had laughs, mostly at the Germans' expense. They thought we were quite mad.'

'Was there talk of escape?'

'I didn't get involved. Didn't fancy getting shot. We had to bury the men who didn't make it.'

'Some scars remain hidden,' she said, trying to reach inside his shell.

'Better than being dead; I suppose.'

'I'm so glad you're home, Aubrey. Truly, I am.'

He rubbed the back of his neck. 'I'm off again soon. A job with the bank in Valparaiso. It'll be a fresh start.'

'Oh, Aubrey, why so far?'

He adjusted his tie. 'I'll get furlough every two years, and a branch of my own within ten. So they say.'

'I don't blame you, brother dear, but I'm very sad. The war is still tearing us apart.'

George would agree; he said the war was pulling her back to France and he was afraid of losing her.

Tada called her into the study. 'Let's sit by the fire,' he said, leaving his desk. 'I have something to tell you.'

She knew from his tone it wasn't good, but better to hear him out before sharing her own news.

'I'm going back to serve with the army of occupation.'

Winter sun drained from the walls and the room darkened.

'Why, Tada? We need you here.' She bit back humiliating tears.

His tired eyes met hers. 'It won't be for long, my dear. You're a young woman with your own life to lead; I'm sure you can spare me a few months longer.'

She nodded, ashamed of being selfish.

'The army is using German prisoners to rebuild France. There will be reprisals, abuse, and I've been called to attend to spiritual matters.'

'Called by the army?'

He examined his shoes. 'No. But I can't rest until peace is secured. Allied terms will be harsh; I want to see justice done on the ground.'

She'd read something of it in the papers. 'I gather fishing in the North Sea is forbidden. It's not a good sign.'

Tada shook his head. 'Germany is in a frightful state, and Russia. Starvation everywhere. The Quakers have teams of volunteers setting up feeding stations. Quite remarkable people.'

'I've had good news, Tada. It means I may be able to report these things myself.'

He looked up with his kindliest smile.

'I've won! The letter came this morning, first prize for *The Young Journalists' Award*. I can hardly believe it.'

Tada took her hand. 'I'm proud of you, Bronwyn.'

'There's just one problem,' she said, trying to stay calm. 'It's a travel bursary and I can't bring myself to tell George.'

'Why not, my dear?'

'I'm afraid he won't want me to go away for long periods, and perhaps it would be unfair after we're married. On the other hand, we'd always agreed I would write for a career.'

George could agree a thing in principle, she'd noticed, but didn't always accept the reality.

'If you're having doubts, you must talk to him. Most couples go through a period of questioning, it's quite normal,' Tada reassured her.

'I love him deeply and don't want to hurt him.' She felt a lump in her throat.

'If George accepts you must travel, well and good, but prepare to meet him half way. Perhaps he could come with you on longer trips. If he wants you to stay at home, you will have to think very carefully about your future. It sounds as though winning the Award has brought to light problems which would emerge sooner or later.' He glanced at the embers.

'Writing means everything to me, Tada, to show the world why this war must be the last. If we're not alive to its dangers, entire societies will be destroyed.'

'You're driven by a passion for justice, little one. Perhaps you're too much like me for your own good.' He got up to add wood to the fire and stood back for the warmth to reach her.

CHAPTER 32

January 1919, London

The cab set off down the drive. 'I'm so glad it's just us, George.'

'Me too. I can't wait for you to see the house. All it needs is a lick of paint and few feminine touches to make it home.'

They'd kissed in the study in a gentle exploratory way after so many months apart. It was a private space, but one had to keep half an ear open for a tap at the door in case some new wedding arrangement had occurred to his mother.

She'd spoken to George about winning the award, said how uneasy it made her feel. He'd been quiet at first, but managed to say she'd done well and they'd work things out somehow. It irked her that they hadn't talked it through.

'There's something we haven't discussed, George,' she said now.

'Can't it wait? Let's visit the house, my darling; I don't want to spoil the day.'

The cabbie dropped them outside a row of red brick houses at the top of a narrow street.

'Holly House,' said George, handing over the key.

'The one with the pretty fanlight?'

'I knew you'd like it.' He held up the umbrella as she opened the door.

It was bare downstairs save for a couple of chairs and a Toby jug left on the mantelpiece, and the kitchen had a modern electric oven; all pleasingly simple. 'It's lovely, George, there's even a little garden,' she said, looking out of the window.

'Ma says she'll send Jean over if we want,' he said casually.

'To keep tabs on us, you mean? No thanks.'

'We'll see. Come upstairs with me,' he reached for her hand. 'There are three bedrooms and you could have one for your study.'

She was touched.

'Is that the main bedroom ahead?' he asked as they reached the landing.

'I think so.' She guided him in.

'There's a wonderful view of the heath,' she exclaimed, looking through a rain-streaked windowpane.

He slipped an arm round her waist and said, 'I like to save the best till last,' and kissed her deeply.

She drew back, breathless. 'George, I love it, we could be happy here, but things have become complicated. We need to talk.'

His shoulders drooped. 'If we must.'

'Come, there's a window seat.'

'I hope you're not thinking of leaving me,' he said, half jokingly.

She smoothed his forehead. 'No, George, I'm not. I want to be a good wife to you and I want to be a writer. It's not something I can always do from home.'

'It's this war stuff you're still obsessed with, isn't it? Some of us are glad to turn our backs on it, you know. I don't see the point in dredging it up.'

'I have to, George, I feel compelled to write about it. We need to find a way to make this work for both of us.'

'Something changed after you came back from France, Bron, and I still don't understand it.' He stood, hands buried in his pockets.

'My feelings for you haven't changed, George. Seeing the devastation in France sharpened my focus, that's all. The war isn't over; it never can be. It's still a struggle, a struggle each day for you and thousands of others, in as many different ways.'

She was thinking of the Martens family getting back onto their feet in Malines; and Huw, coming to terms with his wounded arm, and even Aubrey, who couldn't settle after his experiences in the camp.

He threw his hands in the air, 'Am I complaining? All I ask is a quiet life with the woman I love.'

'Oh George!' She went to put her arms round him, but he pulled away.

'Let's be clear about this. You'll only marry me if you can travel abroad for weeks at a time, in the interests of your career, needless to say.' His anger bounced off the walls. 'You're a clever woman, Bron,' his tone had softened, 'you could turn your hand to any kind of writing. It's what I'd rather hoped for after we married.'

Now her blood was up. 'What did you have in mind? Writing *Handy Hints* for a woman's magazine? That's not me, George, you should know me better.'

Standing, he felt for the wall, balled his fist and pounded. 'I need you to be my wife.' He turned to face her. 'My wife, do you hear?'

She froze and looked over the rooftops. 'I see. You'd have me boxed in, day in day out, under your mother's watchful eye.'

'Don't pretend this is about Ma, Bron.' His voice was dangerously low.

'Your mother *is* part of the problem, George. She bosses you about and expects us both to fall into line. I'd like to see you put your foot down occasionally.'

'That's a damn cheek, coming from you. Ma's around all day and knows my every need.'

She stood up and took him by the lapels. 'That's unfair. We could have been married by now, if you'd agreed to it. But, no, you didn't want me mixing with dubious student types, or was that your mother talking?' She let him go.

'Good God, am I not man enough for you? I may be blind, but I can still speak for myself.'

'So speak! You once said, *go explore the world but come back to me*. We sat on a bench in Regent's Park, remember?'

'Only too well. I hadn't meant it so literally. Or else I'm a little older. We've both changed since then.' His hands hung limp, the anger drained out of him.

Still aggrieved, she said, 'I feel you don't take me seriously as a writer. I wonder if you ever believed in me.'

'Not many men would be as patient as I've been, Bron. I want to marry and have a family; meanwhile you seem to be heading in the opposite direction. What sort of a husband let's his wife do that?'

Tada's counsel of compromise was no use now. 'I feel tricked into coming here, George. However much I love you, I won't give up my dreams.'

'Turn your back on me now, Bron, and walk away forever. Perhaps you're one of those women who gets on better without a husband.'

'How could you?' she spluttered, tears down her face. He'd never spoken to her like this before.

She blew her nose and gazed blankly at the curtain of rain outside. 'It's strange; we've waited all this time for one another and imagined a life together; getting married was supposed to be easy. It turns out that joining our lives, actually making the pieces fit, is impossible.'

'If that's the way you want it,' he said, his voice cracking.

'Of course it isn't. I thought we were different. I'd hoped we could rise above convention and make a marriage to suit us.'

She felt him shutting her out, as he stood stiff and unreachable.

He fingered the face of his watch. 'The cab will be here shortly,' he said curtly.

She tried to make sense of the cataclysm. It felt as though they'd crossed a line.

'I'm so sorry, George,' she said, wary of approaching him, 'I never dreamt it would come to this.'

'Nor me,' he said, hands behind his back.

'Don't do this, George, I can't bear it, don't cut me out.' She flung herself round his neck, weeping for their bruised and battered love.

He stroked her hair gently, as one might comfort a child.

June 1919, Bangor

Bronwyn sat at her desk surrounded by books, alive to the delicious unrest of the sycamore from the open window. She shook and stared at her notes; a light breeze caught the loose sheets and made them flutter like butterflies' wings and the marks on the pages swam. Finals loomed, she ought to be revising, but her mind had other ideas.

After they'd split up, there was no question of contact; the rupture was complete. She'd remained friends with Amelia, who wrote occasionally about her social work, and gave brief news of her brother.

George had moved out of his parents' house, and had a German shepherd dog he was training to become tolerably useful. He'd also volunteered at St Dunstan's to help blind ex-servicemen, which he found therapeutic.

Bronwyn grieved for him, and in a feeble moment confided in Evelyn Sharp, her mentor since winning the writing prize. Miss Sharp offered small comfort.

To be candid, I'm no guide in such matters as my heart belongs to a married man. Life has taught me we must learn to live with our decisions.

She'd kept her promise to Glyn and written to his penfriend Dietrich, to say her brother had been killed. Thomas Cook and company dealt with it, forwarding her letter in a Cook's Packet via Holland.

She'd often wondered if it had arrived and whether Dietrich had survived to read it.

He replied briefly, saying how sad he was to hear about Glyn. He'd spent the war in North Africa as a horse and camel vet.

They'd corresponded regularly since, and she asked about life in Germany. His latest letter grieved her.

We live in poor conditions and it is hard to see how it will end. The family shoe factory is closed because there is no leather and even with leather nobody would work because there is nothing to buy.

English Quakers bring food and clothes. Last week two lady Quakers came to our house with a letter from my brother; he is obliged to stay in France and rebuild roads. The ladies brought a photograph of him. You cannot imagine our joy to see his picture after all these years. My mother wept and brought out a tin of sardines.

I tell you our difficulties not to complain but to say, never again. We must assure peace for all time, for the sake of our children.

I must show Tada, she thought, he'd like to know about the Quakers' work.

She couldn't find him in the study so went to the kitchen. He was sitting in Mam's rocking chair while Mam baked and there was an aroma of bread and beef tea in the air.

'It's a letter from Dietrich,' she said, handing it to him. 'He writes about the Quakers.'

Mam looked over her glasses, frowning; she tried to shield Tada from anything to do with the war.

He read the letter. 'It's true; we're starving the German people. They eat nothing but turnips, in soup, in stew, even jam. The children all have rickets.'

He passed her the newspaper and jabbed a finger at the column headed, *Peace Treaty*. It read, '*140,000 milch cows confiscated by the Allies.*'

'Poor innocents,' Tada murmured, querulous. Cruelty to children could bring him to tears.

'See what you've started, upsetting Tada like that,' Mam reproached her.

'We've made a mess of it, an unholy mess, I tell you,' said Tada. 'We need the likes of you, Bron, wayward young women who shout, *enough is enough*.' He looked thin and frail as he touched her hand. 'You'll make a fine job of it.'

Mam said, 'I'll cut some warm bread,' and Bronwyn knew she was forgiven.

It had been hard telling them the engagement was over. Mam embraced her, 'I'm sorry, so sorry,' as if someone had died. Tada said it was a brave decision.

'We heard from Aubrey today,' Mam said, handing her a buttered slice. 'He's in good spirits and mentions a young lady.'

'I'm glad,' said Bronwyn.

He'd sailed from Southampton without fanfare; he didn't want any fuss. Six weeks later there was a letter with exotic stamps to say he'd arrived safely and would send money soon.

How sad he'd had to travel so far to find happiness.

Wicklow's café offered a special price for pie and mash on Saturday evenings and Bronwyn had booked a table. She wanted to surprise Maddy, who'd been offered a post after College, at the Radium Institute in Paris—her dream.

'I'll bring Maddy and pretend we're just meeting for coffee,' said Rowena. 'Is your brother invited now he and Phoebe are inseparable?'

Bronwyn laughed, 'Indeed he is.'

'Sorry, I can't hang about, Edward awaits; see you tomorrow, darling.'

'Bring him along, why not?'

Rowena made a moue and flung a shell pink scarf over her shoulders. 'I'd rather leave him to pine for me.' She'd abandoned her taste for black and preferred diaphanous pastels.

Wicklow's buzzed as Bronwyn stepped inside and recognised most of the faces from the library this morning, bent over notes in an orgy of last minute revision.

The air in the café was humid and a tang of sweat mixed with coffee and tobacco filled her nostrils as she spotted Phoebe and Huw in the corner. Too absorbed in each other to notice her, she was caught off guard by a longing for George.

She would have told him about Maddy going to Paris and the little celebration this evening; they would have talked about preparations for the wedding, now only weeks away, if they hadn't ended their engagement. Returning the ring was horribly final. Trust, a very fragile thing, was broken after their stormy argument and she'd agonised over it since; perhaps there could have been a way. She still loved him.

'Hello Sis, we got here early,' Huw said, somewhat unnecessarily. Sporting an open-neck shirt, he was more relaxed than she'd ever seen him.

'How's the revision?' Phoebe asked, with a sympathetic smile. She looked handsome in a sprigged blue dress and hair tied with matching ribbon.

'It's hard to concentrate in this heat; I can't wait to get finals over.'

A bell tinkled when the café door opened and they looked up to see Rowena and Maddy.

'Ready?' said Bronwyn, and started with, *for she's a jolly good fellow*, and soon everyone in the café got into the swing of it.

There was a round of applause as the two sat and Maddy blushed.

'What's going on?' She looked round the table.

'We're treating you to dinner,' said Bronwyn.

Maddy looked bemused.

'To celebrate your new job in Paris, remember? I'm green with envy, by the way.'

'You kept this quiet; I hadn't a clue!' Maddy sparkled with pleasure.

'To think, you'll be working with Madame Curie,' said Phoebe.

'With her daughter, anyway; she's a scientist too.'

'Didn't she travel with her mother in an X-ray van?' Rowena asked.

'They were called, *Little Curies;* the vans, I mean.' Huw chuckled.

'Amazing what they did,' said Maddy.

An article about the *dames Curies* was already forming in Bronwyn's mind; how fascinating it would be to interview them.

Huw poured coffee. 'What are your plans, Rowena, once exams are over?'

Her eyes fluttered. 'I'm going on holiday with the gorgeous Edward; he wants to whisk me off in his Pa's Rolls Royce. Exotic, *n'est ce pas?*

'I imagine that's part of the attraction,' said Bronwyn. 'What else do you like about him apart from his looks and his father's car?'

Rowena smiled.

'He must be special,' said Phoebe, leaning on Huw's shoulder.

'You will visit me on your travels, Bron?' said Maddy, fondly.

'Yes dear, of course; I'm going to Belgium first to see Marte. She tells me her mother located the grandparents after all these years; a small miracle.'

'Madame Martens found her parents? How extraordinary. Any news of Anna?'

'She's expecting a baby and living in temporary housing. It seems there's tension between the townspeople who stayed behind and those who escaped; trust as well as buildings have to be repaired.'

Phoebe blew on her coffee. 'If neighbours can't agree, how can trust be restored between nations?'

'It takes time and patience,' said Huw. 'I believe your writing will make a difference, Bron, showing how ordinary folk find their feet. Bringing the human dimension into the equation is a powerful way to break down prejudices.'

'Thanks, Huw.' Her cheeks burned.

'Meanwhile, some of us have another year to do.' Huw looked at Phoebe, who'd missed a year of study while working at Endell Street, and he'd lost a year in the war.

'Still want to be a teacher, Huw?' Bronwyn asked, recovering her composure.

'I'd like to, if I can.' He looked down at his gammy arm.

'Not to mention your writing,' said Phoebe, stroking his hand, 'the adventures of *Heron, Cat and Rabbit*.'

'Phoebe's hoping to do a Master's degree, so we'll both be staying in Bangor,' he said, eyes limpid with love.

The waitress arrived and strong-armed a large tray of pie and mash onto the table.

Passing round plates, Bronwyn said, 'I propose we make this a habit and meet for pie and mash in a year's time. It promises to be nothing if not eventful.'

CHAPTER 33

July 1919

There was something familiar about his face and the knit of his body as he stood on the doorstep. He was holding a helmet under one arm and kitted out for a motorbike.

'It's Gethin,' he said apologetically, 'forgive the intrusion, but I wondered, you must be Bronwyn, sorry, Miss Roberts.' He gave a little bow from the waist.

'Call me, Bronwyn, please,' she said flustered. 'Of course, I remember, the photo. I suppose you know.'

'Yes, yes, I just wanted to pay my respects.'

It was a visit she'd half expected, but less as time went by.

'Do come in, please. I'm sorry everyone's out; just me I'm afraid.'

The charm of him lit up his face as he stepped inside and there was an awkward moment when they might have shaken hands. He looked so earnest as he stood pressing the helmet against his chest.

'I was just making lunch. Would you join me in the kitchen? Glyn spoke so warmly of you. I feel as though we know each other.'

He eased his shoulders and handed over his helmet. 'I left the bike outside.'

'Oh good,' she said, making him laugh.

The photo hadn't prepared her for the intense blue of his eyes.

'He was my friend and a dear one,' he said.

Her heart lurched at his sincerity and sensed this was the first time he'd been able to talk about Glyn.

'Yes, we miss him a great deal. I'm always glad of a chance to speak of him.'

He followed her into the kitchen.

Gethin was Glyn's senior by a year, but looked a lot older, until she realised her memory of Glyn was sealed in time.

'Can I make myself useful?' He opened his palms to show willingness.

'Yes, you can make tea while I rustle up sandwiches.' She turned and smiled. How glad Glyn would be if he could see them now.

'I should have written before turning up. But then I might have bottled it, and that would have been awful. So I just jumped on the bike and motored north; I'm rather nervous.'

'Don't be.' She held his gaze. 'I'm so pleased you came. Huw heard you'd made it through the war, and I've often wondered if you'd be in touch. You must know he was killed in July '16.'

He would be hungry for information, any scrap she could offer.

'Yes, the Somme. I found out after I was released.' He went towards the kettle.

'You were a POW?'

'Captured in August '16. I spent the rest of the war in Holzminden. Beastly place.'

He put the kettle on the hob and she watched as he moved easily about the kitchen, finding the tea caddy and milk and taking cups and saucers from the dresser, as if he belonged.

'That must have been tough,' she said, assembling ham and lettuce on slices of bread. 'Aubrey was in Clausthal. He's older, so you won't have known him at school.'

'No, but I remember Huw. Studious chap, not much for the sports field and very bright. He came through in one piece?'

'More or less. Shrapnel wound to the shoulder.'

'Clausthal, eh?' He filled the teapot. 'There's a thing. The Niemeyer twins ran Holzminden and Clausthal . We called them the Brothers Grimm. Commandant Niemeyer treated his dogs better than us. He turned the showers into kennels, except Tuesdays and Fridays, which were officers' bath days. The floors were unspeakable, so we froze under the outdoor pump.' His face closed down.

'Grim indeed,' she said, in an attempt to bring him back. 'Ready for lunch?'

'Sorry, I shouldn't get sucked back in.' He sat and poured tea.

'Tell me about College; you must have finished finals by now. Exams went well?'

'Pretty well.' She didn't care to admit to a First, it would be boastful.

'Glyn was so proud of you. He used to say, *Bron can do anything she sets her mind to.*'

She welled up at hearing Glyn's words. 'I want to be a journalist,' she said eventually.

'He told me. Your letters meant a lot to him.'

It was strange to think he would know this, and possibly other things about her.

'What drives you, Bronwyn?' He leaned in towards her.

She put down her sandwich. 'The legacy of war, largely. The moment we forget, war will seep through the cracks and threaten peace. I want to broadcast the effects of the war by reporting on the work of the Quakers, and show how people are piecing their lives together again.'

'You're so like Glyn, with a passion to change the world.' His eyes were blue as a mountain tarn. 'My happiest moments are on my motorbike now the war's over.'

'I never really understood why he volunteered,' said Bronwyn. 'He said it was to prove himself as a man. I just hope he knew happiness before the end.'

Gethin looked into the middle distance. 'He made me very happy.'

He looked at her intently. 'I loved him, Bronwyn. We loved each other. Not just as brothers. Do you understand?'

Frowning, she tried to take in what he was saying. 'You and Glyn?'

He nodded and reached across the table to offer his hand.

She didn't take it.

'He loved you so much, Bronwyn.'

She covered her mouth and looked away.

'We did know happiness,' Gethin persisted, 'even joy, brief moments of joy. We loved each other and death can't take that away. If he had to prove himself, it had nothing to do with shame about his nature. Like you, he wanted to make his mark on the world; he just never got the chance.'

She swallowed hard and looked at him; this man whom Glyn had loved, just as she loved George. A forbidden love she'd failed to notice.

He was delving inside his breast pocket. 'I want to show you something. We had an arrangement with the College porter; quite a few did at the time. We left a letter just in case.' He handed her a folded sheet. 'Don't feel you have to. It's rather personal.'

She saw Glyn's handwriting and couldn't help herself.

My Dearest Gethin,

> *I am filled with grief at leaving you*
> *For that bleeding selvedge*
> *We call the Front.*
> *Someday trippers will come*
> *And marvel at moonscapes,*
> *Wonder at earthworks beneath their feet,*
> *Trample unmarked burial mounds*
> *And weep.*
> *Our tattered flags long gone,*
> *Nature will heal the ravaged land to*
> *Make glorious banners of everything.*
>
> *Sweet friend and brother, my other half,*
> *If you survive me, don't dwell on this but*
> *Live joyously that I may live through you.*

Your ever loving,
Glyn

Her tears blurred the page. 'I had no idea.'

'I wasn't sure if you knew.'

'No,' she sniffed, 'but now things make more sense.'

'We planned to travel to Rome and Athens when it was all over; take off on the bike and go far away where we could be ourselves.' His voice faltered, 'Oh, Bronwyn, I miss him more than I can say.'

She reached out and touched his sleeve and waited long moments as a wave of loss engulfed him.

'Forgive me.' He blew his nose and looked up with a crooked smile.

'I wish he'd been able to tell me,' she said. 'He must have felt terribly alone with his secret.'

'You were very young, perhaps too young to understand.'

Bronwyn heard Mam's footsteps in the hallway.

Gethin looked panic stricken.

'Don't worry,' she reassured him, before Mam walked in.

'Mam, this is Gethin, Glyn's good friend.'

He stood up, arms dangling.

'Gethin dear, I'm so pleased to meet you after all this time.' Mam went over and took his hand. 'Glyn spoke so fondly of you.'

'Thank you, Mrs Roberts, and forgive me for arriving unannounced. Please accept my condolences. Such a huge loss.'

'Yes, we feel it still. Sometimes we forget others loved him too. I hope you'll stay until my husband returns; he's out fishing this afternoon.'

Gethin smiled. 'I've already taken up enough of Bronwyn's time. I'm staying overnight at the station hotel. If it's not too much trouble, I could come back tomorrow.'

'That's settled,' said Mam, flushing with pleasure. 'Come for lunch, and you'll see Huw as well.'

'I can't tell you how much this means to me, Mrs Roberts.'

At the door, Bronwyn kissed the man who'd made Glyn happy.

Chapter 34

July 1919

Tada was still not back for tea and Mam was fretting.

'It's been a good day for fishing and he'll be sorting out the catch, I shouldn't wonder,' Huw reassured her.

'I'll cycle down to the boathouse,' said Bronwyn, a bad feeling in her bones.

'No, we'll go together.' Huw spoke with unusual firmness.

They hurried to the shore and found the boatman. 'Is my father back?' Huw asked, breathless.

The old man said, 'I'm glad you're here; I haven't seen him or the boat. Here, take the field glasses; I've been looking this past half hour. She's red and white.'

Huw took the binoculars and scanned the Straits. 'I can't see anything. Here, take a look, Bron.'

She scoured the waters, trying to keep panic at bay. There were various small boats, but no red and white fishing boat. 'I can't see him, Huw. What do we do now?'

'Alert the Coast Guard,' said the boatman. 'I'll come with you myself.'

They stepped over rope and tackle on the narrow beach and headed for the road.

'Bron, you'd better go and tell Mam,' said Huw.

'I will, but hurry back.' She set off, vowing to keep calm.

Bronwyn saw Mam standing by the gate, still in her apron.

'No sign of Tada yet; Huw's gone with the boatman to get help from the Coast Guard.' As she spoke, her worst fears took shape.

'If only I hadn't let him go,' Mam said, wringing her hands. 'I could see he wasn't well.'

'Don't, Mam, please. Come inside. Huw will bring news.' *Dear God, don't let this happen*, she prayed.

Huw got back an hour later looking drawn. 'They've got three lifeboats out and there's still a bit of light,' he said, unconvincingly.

Bronwyn hugged herself and felt sick to the stomach, the same as when the telegram about Glyn arrived.

'Come, I can't wait indoors any longer,' Mam said, hurrying into the hall for her hat and coat.

They walked down to the Straits and onto the Menai Bridge, and fell into single file along its narrow pavement.

Bronwyn felt a chill as the last of the sun withdrew, turning the water to lead. The wind whipped up angry little waves and the lifeboats bobbed and swayed on the rising tide, each one marked out by hurricane lamps glowing in the gathering twilight.

'I should have gone with him,' said Huw.

'I tried to stop him,' Mam lamented, 'but he wouldn't hear of it.'

'No one could have stopped him, Mam, not even you. It was a perfect day for fishing and it's what he loves best.'

'I'm sure he won't have ventured too far out,' Bronwyn said out of desperation.

'That's right, he's an excellent boatman,' Huw seconded.

We're none of us saying anything about the treacherous Swellies, she thought, because we know Tada would be helpless if the boat drifted into their turbulence.

They linked arms at the Belgian Promenade, and walked along its broad avenue; interpreting the pattern of lifeboats was a welcome distraction, providing fleeting glimmers of hope. At St Tysilio's the promenade came to an end; there was nothing for it but to turn about and go home. Bronwyn felt fear tighten its grip as they faced into the wind under the hard bright sky.

'He was only wearing a cotton jacket,' said Mam.

'Fishing boats carry an emergency blanket under the seat, Mam; he'll wrap up,' Huw reassured her.

As they crossed back over the bridge, Bronwyn searched the inky waters for splashes of yellow, marking the progress of lifeboats criss-crossing the Straits.

On Bangor side, Huw said, 'I'll go up to the Coast Guard and wait for news. You both go home and rest.' He stood wraithlike under the lamplight, all colour drained from his face. Kissing them both, he turned his weary back.

'Bron *bach*,' Mam said, taking her arm. 'My strength is ebbing, your poor father is going, I'm sure of it.'

'Mam, please don't say that. There's still hope. At daybreak they'll find him, he'll hold out till then.'

Mam nodded. 'They'll find him, yes, but he was in no fit state to spend a night at sea. *Mae e'n sâl ar y gallon*; he's suffering a sickness of the spirit. He's speaking to me; I can hear him now. *I'm waiting for you, Sarah, we all have our time*, is what he's saying.'

It's the effect of shock, Bronwyn decided; Mam never spoke this way.

'Come, I'll fetch blankets and you can put your feet up in the sitting-room.'

'You're a good daughter to me, Bron,' Mam said, stroking her cheek.

Once Mam was settled, Bronwyn sat in the kitchen rocking chair and waited for Huw to return.

He slipped in the back door looking deathly.

She was on her feet. 'Have they found him?'

'The Coast Guard picked up a boat at Menai Bridge. A red and white dinghy. A fishing line, walking stick and pipe were in the bottom of the boat.' Tears welled behind his glasses.

She grasped his hand to stop the horror. 'And Tada?'

He took a shuddering breath. 'He was found tangled in fishing nets near Ty Calch; they saw him as the tide went out.' He couldn't go on.

Flinging her arms round his shoulders she sobbed, 'No, no, it's can't be, it can't.'

Huw patted her back.

They stood apart and Huw struggled to take off his glasses with his good hand.

'Here, let me do it,' she said, and wiped the lenses before blowing her nose.

'His watch stopped at ten past one,' said Huw.

'What?' she asked, unable to comprehend.

'It was the time he went under; we'll never know why. Heart, probably, struggling to pull up the anchor. The tide swept him away.'

'We have to tell Mam,' she said, leaning her head on his.

'My poor dear children,' said Mam, surveying them from the doorway.

The next days were mired in grief.

Hannah arrived and daily life was reduced to simple tasks between outbursts of weeping, or in Huw's case, withdrawal. He still felt guilty about leaving Tada to go fishing alone.

'You couldn't have done anything with your bad arm; we could have lost both of you,' Bronwyn said.

'That doesn't make me feel any better,' he said miserably.

'I'm sorry, Huw.' He wouldn't be comforted.

They had to write dozens of letters to inform people, but the first note she penned was to Gethin, to cancel his visit the day after Tada drowned. She read it back to herself in disbelief. Only yesterday they'd been talking about Glyn, in some other world.

Together, they drafted a telegram to Aubrey. After several attempts, they settled on,

Deeply sorry to send sad news. Tada died 11 July in tragic accident while out fishing. Mam bearing up. She sends her love, as do we. Huw and Bronwyn.

How awful to be so far from home when he receives it, she thought.

In her diary, she noted her own feelings.

My nights are shipwrecked by nightmares. Tada heaves at the anchor, the dinghy lists, he clings to the rope and the dinghy overturns. Tada goes under. He surfaces, normally a strong swimmer, but something's wrong. He sinks again and comes up gasping, and down one last time. The water closes over him. No Swellies to blame, just a fisherman's net, and the sea calm as a millpond.

I wake fighting for breath, throwing off bedclothes and cry out for help, still trapped in the dream. Daytime, the images cling to my skin; at night the demons return.

Mam appeared almost serene as she picked over Tada's clothes for something to bury him in.

'These are far too large, he lost so much weight,' she said, holding up a pair of trousers.

Bronwyn's heart contracted; one day she'd be doing the same for Mam. Tada had already secured a plot in Glanadda cemetery for himself and Mam, as well as space for Glyn's memorial stone.

The Coroner's Inquiry was swift and the Clerk came directly from the Chapel Schoolroom to report the verdict. The sight of his black gown brought Bronwyn to her feet and left her weak.

'Sit, please do, I don't want to be overly formal.' He remained standing.

Bronwyn sat next to Mam and Hannah and Huw stood to one side. Perhaps they should have heard it in the study, she thought; the sitting room was too domestic for such a momentous occasion.

'It is my sad duty to report the verdict on the death of your dearly loved husband and father, the Reverend Peter Jones Roberts. The Coroner found a verdict of accidental death by drowning.'

The Clerk paused.

Bronwyn burst into tears. She hadn't meant to. Breathing deeply, she pulled herself together.

'There was a vote of sympathy for you, Mrs Roberts, and for his family,' he continued. 'May I add my personal condolences, as I knew your husband well. His death is a loss to us all.'

'Thank you,' said Mam. 'You have been a comfort.'

Huw shook the Clerk's hand and Bronwyn listened in a daze as he and Mam talked about arrangements for Tada's body.

Hannah took her hand. 'We've been here before, *Del*, haven't we? At least this time there will be a decent burial.'

CHAPTER 35

August 1919

Bronwyn sat with Mam in the hall receiving condolences. The banisters and grandfather clock were draped in crepe and curtains closed. Mam wore a dress of old fashioned bombazine with hat and veil. Her own dress was high-necked and plain, the one she'd worn to Rhys' memorial.

Women she'd known since childhood touched her arm and offered words of comfort. This was going to be a very public leave-taking and she dreaded it.

'Be strong, dear, he's with us in spirit,' Mam said, from behind her veil.

'I promise, Mam, at least I'll do my best.'

She was glad to see Maddy, who pulled up a footstool beside her, while Mam was occupied with a neighbour.

'How are you, Bron?' Maddy asked. So much had happened since Tada drowned, they'd hardly seen each other.

'Hellish, to be honest.'

'Bad nights?'

Maddy must have seen the circles under eyes. 'Frightful dreams. I go over and over what happened as if somehow I could bring him back.'

'This will all be over soon.' Maddy kissed her. 'I'm so sorry.'

Huw led the way with Mam on his arm and Bronwyn held onto Hannah. The Reverend Williams, dark robes and surplice, bowed with two young chaplains.

The four sat on mourning chairs as the room stood in silence.

Bronwyn saw people squeezed into every corner, women mostly, and old men too infirm to follow the cortege.

She heard the hearse draw up and the singing began outside; she pictured the men gathered round the coffin as they sang, *O Jesus, I have promised,* in swelling harmonies.

With quiet dignity, Reverend Williams placed notes on the music stand and surveyed the room.

'When the Great War broke out in 1914, it worried the mind of our friend to its utmost depth. He believed it was everyone's duty to help win the war and within two weeks of the beginning he said to me he would like to see all his sons join the Army. He saw this happen rather soon.

'He also felt it was his own duty to join. Some of us tried to persuade him to give up the idea and resign himself to staying at home, but he had no peace of mind. He committed himself to the Army as chaplain and received his commission. He sought to serve the Welsh contingents in France and was appointed Chaplain of a hospital and of a casualty clearing station.'

Bronwyn remembered all too well the campaign he'd waged, despite his age, and Mam's stoic resignation.

'There followed anxious years for him and his family. His second son, Glyn, fell in the battle of the Somme in 1916. Soon afterwards, hearing that Aubrey, his eldest, was missing, he lived through weeks of uncertainty before learning he was a prisoner in Germany. His youngest son, Huw, was wounded and for some time they feared for his life. Mercifully he is with us today.'

She daren't look at Huw for fear of breaking down.

'Mr Roberts was a man with a gentle and kindly spirit and the boys thought the world of him. He clung to the belief that civilisation and humanity must triumph and he won the undying love and respect of all the men.

'He told me personally that he believed he fulfilled the most important work of his life as a Chaplain with the soldiers.

'On his return, the mental and physical strain had taken its toll. When he felt able, he would hire a boat and go out for a few hours fishing, a pastime he always enjoyed. On the last occasion, he didn't come back. When the news became known that the Reverend Peter Jones Roberts had drowned, Bangor town was dazed and a deep sadness spread across the country. It is a tragedy and a loss that touches every one of us.'

The Reverend paused.

Bronwyn sobbed, and saw the whole room was in tears, even the two chaplains. Mam wept under her veil.

The Reverend closed his eyes; *May the wing of the Most High be over his widow and children.* Bronwyn closed hers, and felt him touch her head as he said, 'Bless you, you are in my prayers.'

She looked up to see Huw following the Reverend and chaplains and she put an arm round Mam's shoulders. It was over, for the women at least, as only the men could go to Chapel and the graveside. For this at least, she was grateful.

Huw was pacing the study and smoking when she walked in.

'I need your advice, Bron. I've had a letter asking permission to publish an incident in the war concerning Tada. Take a look at this, and tell me what you think.' He handed her several typed sheets.

Glencairn
Neston,
Cheshire
20ᵗʰ August 1919

Dear Mr Roberts,
Please forgive me for intruding on your grief and allow me to offer my most sincere condolences for the loss of your father, the Reverend Peter Jones Roberts, for whom I had the utmost liking and respect. I would be grateful if you would convey my condolences to your mother.

I knew your father whilst serving in France, and a better man never lived. He was of the greatest sincerity in small things and great, and I am convinced this was the secret of his tremendous influence. By this I mean, and I hope you will not misunderstand, he made no attempt whatever to imitate the conventional padres in their heartiness and 'I am one of you, damn it all, pass the whisky' sort of pose.

He was a 'gweinidog' or Minister in khaki, convinced his mission in all the madness was to stand for better things, unashamedly reminding us by his very presence that those things that had influenced us for good in our childhood were still valid and authentic and everlastingly 'there'. I now see that his non-acquiescence in the prevailing mood of fatalism was in itself an inspiration. He didn't shout, but he was a signpost. A great man, great in his simplicity and his gentle kindness, and it is good to remember such men in the glory of their achievements.

I am writing a memoir of my wartime experiences and would very much like to include a particular event, concerning your father and your brother Glyn.

In this, I record a conversation between the Brigade Signalling Officer and myself, who told me of an encounter with your father. The Officer said he'd seen him at daybreak, wandering about and talking to himself in North Wales Welsh. The Officer asked him why he was up so early, and your father said he hadn't been to bed. He'd been to Fricourt looking for a grave. Someone you knew? the Signalling chap asked. Yes, he replied. My own boy's grave.

The Officer's verbatim account speaks for itself:

'He walked till he could walk no more, got a cup of tea from some gunners, and had a rest, and then walked back here. And now he's out again. Going to bury other people's boys, he said, since he couldn't find his own boy's grave to pray over. My Welsh isn't very good, as you know, but I managed to say to him, "I'm not a soldier now, padre; I'm taking off my hat to you." And so I did, I took off my tin helmet. You couldn't talk English to a Welshman who had lost his boy.'

'But there's a man for you, Gruff, off to bury other men's boys at five in the morning, and maybe his own son not buried yet, a couple of miles away. There was some shrapnel overhead, but I saw him going up the slope as if he were alone in the world. If I come through this bloody business, I'd like to go to that man's church. The only thing he said that I could make out was that bit of a Welsh hymn, you'll know it, the one they sing at funerals to the tune that curdles your blood worse than the Dead March.'

I hope to do justice to the memory of father and son in my memoir, under the title "Up to Mametz".

Please forgive me if my request is premature, coming so soon after your bereavement.

Yours sincerely,
Ll. Wyn Griffith

She scanned it again, head reeling. 'Tada keeps surprising us, doesn't he?'

Huw raked his hair. 'I know, it's very affecting. What should we do?'

'We must tell Mam.'

At that moment, Mam popped her head round the door. 'What are you two up to?'

'I've had a letter from a Mr Wyn Griffith, Mam. He talks about Tada and Glyn and asks to include them in his memoir.' Huw held up the letter.

Mam didn't have her reading glasses, so Huw read it, glancing up when he got to the description of certain Padres; Mam didn't flinch.

When he'd finished, Bronwyn asked, 'Did you know about this, Mam?'

'Not in detail; Mr Griffith expresses it well.' She dabbed her eyes. 'Your father was the dearest man in the world.

'Please tell Mr Griffith I'm happy with what he's written. I'd like to meet him one day.' She swept back a mesh of silver hair.

Mam would never again hear Tada call her, *my dear badger*, Bronwyn realised.

She exchanged a look of concern with Huw; they both felt Mam wasn't at all herself, and hadn't been since the funeral.

Turning to Mam, she said, 'When I was in France and saw farms destroyed, I couldn't imagine the land going back to normal. It would be a desecration to go ploughing while the earth still held Glyn and thousands unburied.

'But it must be so. The earth does its work and the farmers follow, though God knows, they must still find remains. Now Tada has found Glyn, we can think of them together, at peace.'

Mam smiled. 'Thank you dear. You're like your father in so many ways.'

There was one last thing she must do before leaving. It was time to say goodbye to Tada.

She'd visited Glanadda cemetery with Mam and Huw and they'd taken anemones in glorious colours to place at the foot of the Celtic cross that bore his name.

Today, she approached the spot holding a small cardboard box and stood before the granite cross. The inscription was simple:

IN MEMORY Of
THE REV
P. JONES ROBERTS C.F.

Chaplain to the Forces, his life's work. A *gweinidog*, indeed, minister and pastor to all who needed him.

'Goodbye Tada; I'm taking over the baton now. It's time to rest. You will be with me always.'

No flowers today, just a handful of French soil she'd brought back in memory of Glyn. The plot behind Tada's grave was for him, waiting for the new stone.

She stepped onto rough ground, took the dusty red earth from its box and scattered it to the winds.

Transfixed by the mountains, she felt their darkness pulling her back, their ancient shapes reminding her where she belonged. Could she really leave home?

A train sliced the landscape, its hooter calling in a rising major third, giving her permission to go.

She would anchor her life to no one, but trust in providence and let her dreams be her guide. Of one thing she was certain, she would honour Tada and Glyn.

Book Club Questions

Characters
- Which characters do you particularly admire or dislike? Why?
- Bronwyn loves her parents in different ways. Does she tend to idealise her father?
  Is she unfairly critical of her mother?
- If Bronwyn and George had met in peacetime, do you think they would have fallen for each other?
- Bronwyn says she's not a pacifist. Is this true by the end of the novel?

Plot
- Does the story engage you?
- The novel is set a hundred years ago. Do the characters' stories make the period come to life?
- Are there particular twists and turns in the plot that hold your attention?
- What do you feel about the conflicts faced by Bronwyn? Does she make the right choices?
- Is the ending satisfying?

General

- Is it a good title?
- Did anything surprise you about the lives of those left behind?
- The family was real. The deaths happened. Does this mean it's not a novel? What do you suspect the author made up?
- Did the First World War change women's lives for the better?
- Are the issues presented relevant to the world today?
- If you could ask the author a question, what would you ask?